Foolish for Piper

Christine Young

ISBN: 978-1-62420-522-4

Credits
Cover Artist: Designs by Ms G
Editor: Christie L. Kraemer

Chapter One

1820

Strolling through Vauxhall Garden Brett MacLachlan concentrated on the little brown and white dog with the curly tail that terrorized the visitors of the gardens. No one was immune to his quick feet and even faster nose. In less than a second the dog was able to pick a handkerchief or a small purse from its intended victim's pocket before darting away to safety.

The quick-footed animal snatched something from a young man then scurried into a secluded corner of the park before the victim realized what had been done. Brett laughed at the animal's antics. He'd been watching now for the better part of ten minutes and was sure he knew precisely where the animal disappeared.

The slight pressure to his hip caught his attention. "Bloody Hell! Scoundrel. Demon dog." He sprinted after the animal, having a good idea the direction the dog would take. Dodging through the people, the dog made substantial speed. The small animal was agile and quick on his feet. Brett swore again then watched the mongrel duck down an untraveled and unlighted path.

His frustration kept him from rational thought as he followed the dog into the shifting light of the darkened footpath. A slight scuffling noise to his right brought him to an abrupt halt as he reached for the knife he kept in his boot.

Poising on the balls of his feet, he waited; patience in battle, a strong suit. Silence seemed to encompass him, shadows painting an eerie picture in the waning light. All his senses tuned into the tiny area he knew was inhabited by the dog and the boy. What exactly he would do when he trapped them, he wasn't at all sure.

He ran after the unlikely pair because he wanted his purse back, but now he craved something more, an answer to his curiosity perhaps. At the moment he wasn't sure what that was, but he meant to figure it out once he had the young man by the scruff of his tiny neck.

A small noise in the bushes sent his body on edge, muscles tense, all instincts honed, but it seemed to be nothing more than lovers looking for some privacy in the darkness. A male groan then a slight mew told him he was right to refocus the direction of his task.

Slowly moving forward, he meticulously studied the dancing shadows and listened for any sound. Breathing was hard to conceal. One had to take in air and let it out, after all. He supposed the boy could hold his breath, but the dog wouldn't. The couple most likely had experience in hiding and adapted to task. Indeed, to succeed in this game they played and not end up in Newgate prison, he had to win the game and never lose.

"Show yourself and it will go better for you. If you give me back my purse, I'll give you a reward." The command, he knew, would not be obeyed. In this case the boy stayed alive by outsmarting the opponent, and showing himself would not work to his advantage. He had to try though and perhaps his words would give him some advantage. Didn't know what that might be yet, but he was willing to try.

The slight breeze shifted the air before the wind stilled. Sultry and hot, it seemed stagnant this deep into the forested area, as did the shadows. Attuned to every movement, he froze, ready for whatever the boy would try. If he were the cornered prey, a mad dash might seem the best course, but from experience he knew sitting still would serve the lad well. If he tried to scurry away, he knew he could catch him.

No way in hell, though, would he abandon this quest. Since the boy single handedly put a damper on the evening with his mistress he had planned, the lesson he intended teaching changed dramatically.

"I mean you no harm," he said, hoping his words were believable. Once more he watched for the wild rush to freedom he assumed would eventually materialize. "Come out and we'll talk."

Then...the dog dashed in one direction and the lad in the opposite. He wasn't swayed in his purpose. The animal could go anywhere it pleased. Two strides put him next to the boy. He grabbed him by the collar of his shirt. The lad turned, swinging at him and kicking, connecting more times than Brett wanted to count.

"Oy, governor, le' me go! Bloody eyes but yer hurtin' me." For a second the lad broke free.

"No, don't think I mean to let you go anytime soon. You stole my purse. I could hand you over to the magistrate if it pleased me, but fortunate for you it doesn't."

Brett grabbed him by the neck before he could get away, gripping him tightly. "Whether you're agreeable to my plan or not, it's your lucky day. I found you and I do believe I'm going to enjoy taking you off the streets."

"Not lucky in my mind." The lad squirmed, trying to escape his hold.

"I'm going to give you a chance to improve your lot in life. I'm sure you'll find my home more amenable than what you can find in St. Giles." Brett felt a bit smug at his thought, but he didn't know why he had this sudden feeling of charity. Improving this lad's life would not be an easy feat, especially if the lad fought him every step of the way.

"Like it just the way it is," the lad bit out, taking another swing at his benefactor and connecting.

Brett let out a slight grunt. "Perhaps boxing lessons should be one of your first lessons. That was pretty weak even for a boy of your age. Would think you had a bit more muscle to put into that punch."

"Don't want no boxin' lessons." But he stopped as Brett's fingers tightened around the lad's neck as did the grip on the boy's arm.

"You have a name, lad?" Brett asked, wondering if the boy would give him any information.

"None that I'd tell you."

"That's what I thought." By now they had reached one of the better lit and traveled pathways in the park. "I'd like to call you something besides boy or lad.

For some reason the lad stopped fighting him, yet Brett didn't let up, tightening his hold and waiting for an attack from some unknown angle, perhaps the dog. No one appeared to defend the boy or help him from this predicament.

Keeping a watchful eye, Brett looked to other attackers, a friend of the boy, someone who might care what happened to him. For all anyone knew, he was on his way to find a constable.

No one came to the lad's defense.

Brett hailed a cab, keeping his grip tight on the boy's neck and looking over his shoulder for the dog to materialize.

Nothing.

"Get inside," he directed the boy, staying close but obviously having to loosen his hold and expecting the lad to duck out the other side. Instead, the boy sat on the middle of the seat, his hands between his legs and his head down, appearing contrite and amenable, something Brett didn't think the boy was capable of pulling off.

"What you plannin' on doin' with me?" he asked without looking up, his defiance seeming to vanish.

"Not too sure at this moment. Depends on how you decide to act." Rubbing his chin, Brett wondered at the lad's sudden inquiry. He could have asked any number of questions. He had ideas, but that's all they were—ideas.

"Don't want to go to Newgate." The boy looked at him, his deep blue eyes shimmering with what Brett could only define as fear.

Brett leaned forward, his arms resting on his legs as he studied the boy. "Don't plan on sending you there. But if you give me any problems..." He didn't want to delude the boy. If he had to, he'd call in the law.

"Not going to give you any problems, governor, but I can't vouch for Jocko and his crew. They'll come lookin' for me and they're mean devils."

"Who's Jocko?" This was something new to consider. Jocko was probably his handler, the man who received all the stolen bounty. Bounty he'd forgotten about in his quest to catch this thief. The purse was inconsequential, having only a few coins in it. He never carried anything of value when he visited Vauxhall.

"None of your business. What you don't know won't hurt you more." He squirmed in his seat, looking uncomfortable.

"Perhaps I need to know in order to keep you safe from this man. You say he's going to come after you. Why?" Brett asked, studying the lad whose features seemed too delicate for a boy. And yet... If this boy were unimportant, no one would look for him.

The incessant barking behind and around the carriage brought him to the most immediate present. "What the devil, is that your dog?"

"He won't stop until you let him inside. Rogue, for some reason, wants to protect me. He's loyal to me."

"Rogue, you say. Is that his name?" Brett asked, trying for as much information as possible. He didn't want to take a dog into his home along with this unpredictable lad, yet he saw no other way.

He tapped on the roof and the carriage rolled to a stop. When he opened the door, the dog leapt inside and with a growl before he settled beside the boy. His obvious protective nature gave Brett a reason to smile.

Brett sat back, crossing his arms over his chest, waiting to reach home and not feeling as if anything could be gained from further conversation. Every instinct he possessed told him there was something wrong with this scenario, but he couldn't figure anything out. He didn't dare close his eyes and try to think.

The townhouse he just purchased was his destination, and he decided the first order of business when they arrived would be a bath for both boy and dog. Maybe it would take two dunks in the tub for the lad to really be clean. He didn't dare tell the boy. It might cause him to bolt, and Brett didn't have any desire to chase him again.

"You takin' my dog too?" the boy asked belligerently, hands on his hips.

"If that's what you want," Brett said, hoping to learn more about the boy who now didn't seem to want to leave. "You know you have to give over the handkerchiefs and the purses you and Rouge stole. They will go back to their rightful owners if the constables can locate them."

The boy shrugged and his shoulders pressed against the fabric of his shirt seemed too slender for a boy his age. Perhaps he'd not been fed or perhaps this was part of what didn't quite seem right.

"Doesn't make no difference to me. I would've had to give everything to Jocko anyway. He only lets me keep a coin or two."

Curious about this man, "What does this Jocko give to you in exchange for all the risks you take," he paused, "besides a coin or two? There must be more for you to keep going back to him."

"Protection," he said quickly, perhaps too quickly. "And food. Gives me clothes, too, when these wear out." He plucked at his shirt. "He's training me for when I'm older, too old to pick pockets."

"So," he paused in thought, "you take all the chances and he gives you food, none of the money these things merit. Not even half? What is it he's training you for?"

"Not my place to question what he does and doesn't do. He gives me a safe place to sleep and something to eat. Don't have to look over my shoulder just to stay alive. Know I'm not going to be attacked in the middle of the night."

"I suppose some place to sleep at night is important as well as food." Brett rubbed his chin thoughtfully, understanding there was a lot more to this story, and he was going to discover every intricate nuance.

"Then there's the scarred man, even Jocko's afraid of him. He says I've got to be careful of that man and try not to do anything to get on his bad side. Says he knows something about me that could hurt me. He also said if I discovered the truth, he'd kill me. Seems he's keeping me alive only because I'm ignorant."

"The scarred man...why are you telling me all of this when you won't even tell me your name?" This tale grew more interesting with every passing sentence.

"You haven't asked me my name since I've not been scared of you anymore. When you stopped to get my dog, I knew you were nice, and I didn't have any reason to think you'd do something bad."

"What's your name then?" He smiled, wondering if he would continue to give him information.

"Piper. What's yours?" he shot back to him.

"Brett MacLachlan. Do you have a last name?"

"Not that I know of, but Jocko knows, at least I think he does. He once told me that I'd never know what it is because the scarred man would make sure I didn't. If I asked too many questions about my name, I wouldn't live to see another day.

Hearing those words, a shiver shot down Brett's spine. This lad's truths caught every instinct he possessed and stretched them thin. For some reason, he wanted to solve the growing mystery surrounding Piper.

"We're here," Brett said, wondering how difficult it would be to get this boy into a bath. Confined in the tight quarters of the carriage, his stench was overwhelming.

"This yer home? It's quite the thing. Never been inside one of these." He peered out the window, nose poking outside as if he tried to see everything. "Only been in little houses, ones with a room or two.

"Yes, and now it's yours." He tried to figure out what he was going to do with the boy. Supposed he could be a stable hand if he wasn't afraid of horses.

"Why aren't we goin' in the front door?" the boy asked, watching him with wide eyes. "Isn't that what civilized folks do?"

"Well..." Brett didn't know how to answer his questions without giving his intentions away.

"Get on with it. Bloody eyes, just tell me the truth. Not used to hearin' lies except from my enemies and I'm hoping you're not my enemy."

Brett wanted to get him in the house before he confronted the lad, Piper, with a bath, figuring the boy might not even know what a bath was. Then there was the dubious thought the lad would work for him and in what capacity exactly.

They stepped inside, Rogue following. "Mrs. Pickery, this is Piper. He's going to work here, and he needs a bath, the dog too."

Rogue settled down in a corner, his head resting on his paws, seeming to watch the scene enfolding.

"Oy, governor. Don't want or need no bath. What you tryin' to do? Torture me?" Piper asked slowly, moving backward, arms stretched out in front of him as if he could stop Brett.

"No torture intended. Have you ever had a bath?" Brett asked and while they spoke, he watched Mrs. Pickery begin to heat the water. "There's a large tub in the scullery, Mrs. Pickery. We'll use that one."

"Not that I can remember. Never had a bath. Not goin' to take one now."

"Then you've years of dirt to wash off." Brett grinned, watching the delightful and at times horrific play of emotions sweeping across the lad's face.

Piper stood in one corner, pale faced, while he watched the tub as it was brought into the kitchen then the hot water dumped into the large vat. Brett didn't understand the sudden terror in the boy's eyes. Piper seemed resolved to what was going on here, even pleased that he would no longer live on the streets, until the bathtub appeared.

"Don't want to wash any dirt off," he mumbled then pushed against the wall as if he wanted to become one with it. "Like me just the way I am. I do."

"You won't know how great a tub of hot water feels until you try it. I'll stay in here with you and Mrs. Pickery will find something to do in another part of the house. You don't need to be shy."

His eyes grew wide and his gaze focused on the door as if he longed to dash through it.

Mrs. Pickery nodded, slipping from the scullery. "I'll leave the two of you and I'll put out the word that we need some britches and shirts. Those clothes can't be salvaged."

"There it is. Take your clothes off and get into the tub." Brett watched as Piper started shaking, his face pale as a ghost, his eyes wide.

"If you leave," Piper asked the impossible, yet seeming adamant in his request. "Not taking my clothes off with you in the same room. Can't do that, no siree. Jocko told me never to do anything like that. He'd have my hide if he ever found out as well as the man who saw me."

"You'd rather have Mrs. Pickery stay in here with you?" Brett tossed that out as an afterthought, but when Piper nodded, his misgivings escalated. "Bloody hell, what the devil are you thinking?" He stepped forward, believing he needed to shake a bit of sense into the lad.

When the boy darted across the room, picking up a butcher knife and waving it in front of him, Brett backed up a step. This wasn't something he expected.

"Bloody eyes, governor, don't test me or I'll skewer you through. Don't you ever doubt my intentions. I'll use this sticker. I will." He backed away, the weapon held in front of him, his hands shaking.

"Put it down, Piper. You don't want to hurt anyone." He searched his mind for the reasons behind this bazaar behavior. "Just hand it over to me and if it's Mrs. Pickery you want, then I'll get her. Problem is, it might make her very uncomfortable to see a young man naked. Do you want to make her uncomfortable?"

"No..." Piper's voice wavered. "No, no I don't but..."

For a moment and another time, he looked to the door as if he meant to run. Brett lunged, grabbing his wrist. The knife fell to the floor before he kicked it aside. "I'm not playing anymore games with you. The bath is getting cold while we waste time with this nonsense." He ripped the shirt. "Mrs. Pickery is looking for new clothing as we speak."

The boy seemed to freeze, his arms wrapped around himself. "Now that you got your way." His voice weakened, sounded as if he suddenly gave up. His narrow delicate shoulders were shaking so hard, his breath seemed to catch in his throat before turning to sobbing gasps.

With the shirt off, without stopping to reflect, Brett reached for the knife and slit the bindings that were wrapped around his chest from top to bottom. Frustrated and irritated with the boy, he didn't stop to think about the bindings and what they might mean. "Britches off now." He understood the force of his voice and wished he wasn't letting his annoyance get the best of him.

With his back turned to him, the boy stepped from his pants.

The air Brett was holding in his lungs rushed out painfully. It seemed he finally saw the entire picture.

Brett suddenly realized the bindings around the boy's chest and the baggy pants were hiding a girl. Her slender waist and wide hips without the fabric covering her curves was obvious. "Mrs. Pickery."

"Mrs. Pickery!"

Good God, but he couldn't take his gaze from her perfectly formed figure. Her tight butt was nothing like the women he bedded, his mistresses. In a flash, his body hardened with a desire he couldn't control. "Mrs. Pickery!"

"Yes, sir." His cook poked her head in the door. "What is it?"

"He's a she."

"What did you say?"

"Get her in the bath. If you need anything, ring for me and I'll be here even though she's naked. Don't let her leave." Well, that was stupid. He really didn't think she'd run out the back door stark naked.

His gut rolled. He'd never forcefully disrobed a girl, ripped her shirt. He rubbed his face then roughed his hands through his hair. Trying to make excuses, and attempting to convince himself, he truly believed Piper was a boy. He inhaled a long deep breath, wishing he could take the last few minutes back and do them over.

"It's alright, sir. You didn't know. None of us knew. I'll take care of her now." Mrs. Pickery touched him on the back. "Don't you worry about her."

"That's just it. I should have known. Every instinct I possess was telling me there was something wrong, but I didn't listen to my gut." He berated himself then before he strode through the kitchen door. "Don't give Mrs. Pickery any grief. You'll rue the day you were born if you do."

"I've already done that too many times to count," she told him, looking over her shoulder, her breasts visible to him.

His hands fisted tight, he strode through the house and out the front door. For a few seconds he thought to get his horse. A good ride might ease the tension radiating across his shoulders and throughout the rest of his damn body. The site of her naked evoked a powerful sensation through him.

He stopped himself when he rounded the corner of the house and saw the back door, the entrance to the scullery, reminding him of the girl soaking in his tub. A young lady who'd had one hell of a life. He decided to find out more about her.

Swiveling on a heel, he walked back to the house, entering through the front door. Brandy seemed to call his name. At the sideboard, he poured a full glass and thought to sit down and wait for the outcome of the bath. He didn't hear anything emanating from that direction and decided that was a good thing.

"Ah." He swirled the amber liquid in the crystal, mesmerized by the changing colors or thoughts of Piper, he wasn't too sure. What was he going to do with the lass? And what about Jocko and the scarred man? If anything, she said held a hint of truth, her life might be in danger now that she was out of their fold.

The alcohol burned an enjoyable path down his throat. She would need clothing, everything a woman likes as well as a position in the house.

The downstairs maid perhaps.

He didn't need one but she would have to have some means of employment. The last thing he wanted or needed was gossip surrounding him. She would have to live in his home. There were small servant quarters on the third floor.

Perhaps Mrs. Pickery could help with the clothing. She did have a daughter who he thought was about Piper's age. That was another thing. How old was Piper? Dressed as a boy he guessed her to be about thirteen. Now as a girl, he paused in thought. She could be any age. However, he supposed her handler would hand her over to a pimp as soon as possible.

That didn't make sense. Fourteen-year-old girls were sold to whore houses and pimps. By the short glimpse he caught of Piper's curves, she was well past fourteen. He'd guess at least eighteen. If he'd looked closely, he would have seen her hips and even the curve of her breasts beneath the bindings. He'd been intent on one thing, catching her, so he'd lost his concentration.

He snatched a side view of her when she looked over her shoulder to give her parting shot. She rued the day she was born too many times to count. He decided he'd be the man to change that.

Smiling to himself, he sipped again closing his eyes and trying to image her naked, all of her, from tips of her toes to the top of her short cut hair. He bolted upright, reminding himself he had no right to do that. Well, something about Piper intrigued and fascinated him more than he wanted to admit.

There was something regal about her.

He reached over and rang the bell signaling Molly, his scullery maid. A few minutes passed before she appeared.

"Sir." Molly curtsied before stepping back to wait for his order.

"Can you poke your head into the scullery and let me know how it's going in there? If Mrs. Pickery needs any help," he asked, downing the last bit of brandy, wishing he dared look instead.

"Yes, sir." She turned to do his bidding.

Waiting didn't suit him. He stood again, pacing the room, needing to occupy himself. He turned in the direction of the scullery.

"Sir," Angus, his valet, stood in front of him. "I set out clothes for you, for tonight. Are you wanting a bath first?"

"What? Oh, I forgot." Muira, his current mistress, would be waiting for him. He'd agreed to take her to the opera tonight. A boring night for him, but she begged. Now the little interest he had in the opera as well as Muira vanished. His only concern now was Piper and what would happen next. He was captivated and excited to discover more about Miss Piper.

"Sir," It seemed Angus was losing patience with him.

"Send a message to Muira with my apologies, but I've pressing business to attend to tonight. Don't want a bath or a change of clothes."

"Yes, sir."

Brett chuckled slightly, hearing the censure in the man's voice. Angus usually berated him for seeing Muira, a mistress, and now it seemed she was the preferable entertainment.

"Master Brett." Mrs. Pickery stood in front of him. "You should come see Piper. Except for one thing, I think you'll be pleased."

~ * ~

Piper hugged her arms around herself. She couldn't remember the last time she'd been stark naked and humiliated in front of anyone let alone a man. Brett saw her with nothing on, naked. Even when she took a quick swim in the lake, she wore her clothes. Now she stood in the scullery, naked, with a man staring at her backside, a man she barely knew. Her long-kept secret was secret no longer.

When she decided to stay with the man, she never thought her identity would be uncovered, never expected a bath, of all the nerve. Over the years she'd taken huge steps to keep people from knowing she was a girl. Jocko helped but it was only because he had something in mind for her, something he said that would make them both rich. Said they'd live a life of luxury. Jocko told her he would train her to be a rich man's mistress and—

"Come on now, get in the water, dear. Let's not be wastin' anytime. Master Brett is going to want to see you when we're all done here, and I want him to be proud. Need to check for lice and make sure you're squeaky clean. After that, we'll give your dog a bath." Mrs. Pickery seemed to chatter nonstop.

Slowly, she turned and feeling as if she walked to her execution, she approached the vat of steaming water. She looked at Mrs. Pickery before accepting her fate. Heaving a huge breath of air, she stepped into the water.

"Ouch!"

"Now, Miss Piper, the water is not too hot. Cold water will not soak off the layers of grime covering you. God knows what some of it is, but no one else wants to know. Would you like me to wash you or can you do it yourself?" Mrs. Pickery held out a soapy sponge, eyeing her as if she was a little child.

Catching her bottom lip between her teeth, she started to shake her head. The last thing she wanted was someone else doing something to her. "Want to do it myself, but not really sure what to do. Never had a bath," she mumbled, swirling the water around with her hand.

"That's easy, dear. Just rub this," she held out the sponge, "with the soap on it all over your body. Don't miss any spot or I'll have to do it myself. While you're doing that, I'm going to wash your hair and make sure there's no little nits in it."

Minutes later the water was a cesspool of filth. Looking down, Piper couldn't see her body for the dirt. Inwardly cringing, "How am I going to get clean when the water is so dirty?"

"Good question lass, that's why I've got more water heating for a second bath in another tub. Angus brought one from upstairs a few minutes ago. Seems Master Brett had the same idea." She nodded toward the kitchen stove and the pails of steaming liquid. "Now let me pour this bucket over your head and rinse out the soap."

To Piper, it seemed an eternity before Mrs. Pickery was finally finished and handing her a towel. "Wrap it around you then we'll get you dressed. Sent Molly out lookin' for a dress that might fit. We'll see how she did."

After the second bath, mindless and confused, Piper followed the cook's directions. She cloaked herself in the towel and waited for what would come next. Mrs. Pickery vanished for a moment then reappeared holding a dress in front of her and what appeared to be underthings.

"You want me to wear that? What is it and how does it work?" She pointed to the garments. "Don't believe I've ever worn one of those things. How does one..." she paused, "put it on?"

"Don't you worry your pretty little self about that. Molly and I will help you then when you're ready, we'll take you to Master Brett."

"Molly?" She thought it had just been the two of them.

"Molly, there you are," Mrs. Pickery said.

"Master Brett wanted me to check on you. Let me just tell him you'll be ready soon and I'll be back." She curtsied and disappeared only to return in a few seconds.

Piper felt pushed and pulled in every direction possible while the maid and the cook laughed and chatted. Finally, she was laced into a contraption she had no idea how she would get out of and clothed in a dress that left her breasts revealed for anyone to see.

She pulled at the top of the bodice, trying to cover herself then looked at Mrs. Pickery, hoping she would have the answer to her problem. "I don't think this is supposed to be this low."

"Oh dear," Mrs. Pickery said, rubbing her hands together, clearly distraught. "Her bubbies are too big for the dress." She wiped her hands on her apron. "Can't show her to Master Brett like this."

Molly whispered, "They're more like kettle drums."

"Hush now, Master Brett not's going to like this on her, but it's the best we have right now. Maybe he'll have a solution."

"We can't present her to him like this," Molly moaned softly, shaking her head as if that would give her some clue as to how to fix this. "Can't, just can't. He's a refined gentleman."

"You'll never convince me he's never seen a woman's breasts before," Mrs. Pickery said indignantly.

"No, of course not but it might put wayward thoughts into his head," Molly said with a slight moan of despair.

"I've no doubt he'll make this right. The sooner we show her to him, the sooner we can get back to our regular work. He's not going to ravish her just because he can almost see her nipples. I've not started anything for dinner and as you well know, he's had a change in plans. He's not visiting his mistress tonight. Come along, Miss Piper. Let's show you off."

Mrs. Pickery held open the door and waited.

Piper inhaled a long breath of air before starting forward. Being talked about and around had not been enjoyable. "Why do you have to show me to him?" she asked but her experience with men in her short life told her they always wanted to have all the information so they could be in charge.

When she stepped in front of him, she closed her eyes. She didn't know what she expected, not complete silence, but that seemed to be what was happening. Jocko was never silent. She always knew what to anticipate and what he was thinking simply because he told her.

"Mrs. Pickery?" His voice held a tinge of irritation.

"Yes, sir." She stepped forward, her hands clasped in front of her. "The dress, it's all we could find on such short notice, sir. Didn't expect her to be so..." She looked to Piper then back to Brett.

"So well endowed?" he asked pleasantly, one eyebrow tilted upward. "Can you find her a small shawl, something to cover herself, privacy you understand? And something to pin it with?"

"Yes, sir, I'll be back soon, sir, but you might not get your dinner until later." She started to leave.

"Forget about dinner. We'll be going on an errand soon. Sit down, Piper. Would you like something to drink?" His smile seemed pleasant enough.

Piper sat down next to him where he patted the seat. "You don't like the way I look?" she asked, not sure if she felt meek or was acting strangely. She wanted to please him simply because she needed him to like her. If he kicked her out, she no longer had her disguise, so she'd be sold to a pimp or a whorehouse. His opinion meant everything to her, meant her life.

"You clean up very nicely. The dress is wonderful on you but shows a bit too much you. I think we can rectify the situation."

He handed her a drink. "Sip it slowly."

His words came too late. She coughed and droplets of brandy splattered in front of her. She covered her mouth with a hand. "So sorry. I didn't know..." Jocko warned her about spirits and the consequence they might have for her. Told her never to drink anything stronger than tea.

"It burns a little, but you can get used to it if you like." He smiled. "Mrs. Pickery could bring you tea if you would rather have that."

The look in his dark brown eyes melted her heart. "I've never had spirits. Jocko says they're the root of all evil, but this is fine."

"Jocko never drinks? For some reason I've trouble believing that. Maybe you should tell me more about this man you've spent a lot of time with."

"Oh, he drinks. It's just what he tells me. Says my mind shouldn't ever be impaired." Yet she sipped again, this time more slowly. "I think I like it. What is it?"

"Brandy." He took the half empty glass from her hand. "Perhaps Jocko has a point."

"I've known Jocko ever since I can remember," she said, recalling the times he played with her on the floor of his apartment.

"How long is that?"

"I might have been two, but I've never known anyone else. He's always taken care of me. He's sort of like a father. What are we going to do now?" She smoothed her skirts and when she did, it seemed the bodice slipped farther down.

He was staring at her and when she looked where his gaze was riveted, she saw the circles that surrounded her nipples. Quickly, she tugged her dress upward. His eyes shimmered with something she'd never seen before. Jocko never looked at her like that.

"Here you go, sir," Mrs. Pickery hurried into the room, holding out a small lace shawl, one that would just cover her bodice.

"Thank you, Mrs. Pickery. You may go home for the night. Piper and I will be at the dress shop. I'm hoping Madame Chantal will have something appropriate for Piper to wear. She can't run around popping out of her dress."

Popping out of my dress. "A dress shop? A place where you buy clothes?" Hands shaking, she picked up her glass of brandy and downed it all before Brett could take it away from her.

"Where else would you get clothes?" He smiled at her, one eyebrow cocked upward. "I hope you don't regret downing your drink. If your head starts feeling a bit hazy, let me know. Don't want you to faint."

She wondered how he did that, lift one eyebrow and not the other. She scrunched her face, trying to do the same thing but to no avail. "Never got any clothes in a dress shop."

"Of course dress shops are where you get clothes. Where do you get your clothes?" he asked, seeming to watch her intensely.

Unable to help herself, she smoothed her skirts. When his eyes darkened farther, she moved uncomfortably. Jocko warned her about men and the way they looked at women, but she never believed him. Now she understood but she didn't feel dirty, not like Jocko said she would. She liked the way he looked at her.

"Piper?"

"Oh, I was just thinking about your eyes." His gorgeous dark brown eyes that seemed to change color according to his mood.

"You were—my eyes?"

She started to smooth her skirt again then stopped herself. Instead, she moistened her lips before sucking the lower one into her mouth. "You had that look Jocko told me about. The one where men stare at you and make you feel dirty, but I didn't feel that way, dirty."

"Oh," he sat back, his arms across the back of the sofa, grinning. "I love your honesty. It's refreshing. How did my looking at you make you feel?"

"Hot."

He ran a finger around his collar before clearing his throat and laughing. "We should leave now. There's Angus. The carriage is ready. You can tell me more about yourself on our ride through town."

"Two rides in a carriage in one day." She stood, feeling as if she was in a brand new world. "Before this day I've never set foot in one, a carriage."

"Wait." He stopped her and wrapped the shawl around her shoulders, his finger brushing the tops of her breasts when he fastened it.

Then he held out his arm for her, his gaze touching hers, her heart pounding out of control.

She wasn't positive what he wanted her to do, but she placed her hand on his arm and walked with him. It must have been the right thing because he made no comment.

Inside the carriage, she watched him settle back on the seat, his arms spread wide on both sides. "Tell me about yourself."

"Only if you tell me about you," she countered, watching his brows draw together and shrugging her shoulders. "It's only fair."

"Very well, you're right, I suppose it's only fair. In fact, I'll start. I grew up in Scotland. Ran wild and did pretty much what I wanted until I turned fifteen." He stretched his legs, crossing them.

She leaned forward, fascinated by the size of the man, not so much by what he didn't tell her but by the width of his shoulders and the muscles that seemed to stretch his jacket to its limits. "What brought you to London?"

"My turn." He picked up her hand and studied it, tracing tiny circles in the palm, sending shivers of heat through her. "They even got your fingernails clean. What's the first thing you remember?"

Feeling sensations she didn't understand begin to spiral and surge through her in the strangest manner, she pulled her hand from his. "I must have been about two, I think. No one knows how old I am or where I came from. No one but the scarred man and maybe Jocko knows."

"What is it you remember?" He prodded.

"Just Jocko playing with me. I had this little doll. I've always had it until now. I suppose they'll throw it away now that I'm not living with them." She wasn't sure how she felt about that. The doll was her only connection to her past.

"A doll, it might lead us to your mother or father."

"Don't know why you'd want to do that. If there was any family who wanted me, I wouldn't have ended up in the orphanage. Mother and father must be dead, dead for a long time." She heard the bitterness in her voice well up inside her.

"Not sure I understand. If Jocko and the scarred man were taking care of you, why would they put you in the orphanage?"

She was shaking her head, unable to stop the barrage of memories. "I was in the orphanage to learn how to pick pockets, nothing more. I rarely stayed there at night. Jocko started my education for after my pickpocket days last year. He told me I wasn't going to get away with pretending I'm a boy much longer."

He leaned forward, his forearms resting on his thighs. "And what would that be? What are his plans for you?"

"Jocko was training me to be a mistress to some rich gent," she blurted, not really sure of the difference between a whore and a mistress, but Jocko reassured her many times that it was infinitely better to be a mistress than a whore.

"We're here and I hope to continue this conversation when you're finished." He walked her into the dress shop.

"Blimey, never seen anything like this. What do I do now?" she whispered, clutching Brett's arm as if he could protect her from the woman descending on them. Her breath seemed to catch in her throat, and she could barely breathe.

Brett cleared his throat, smiling. "Chantal, how nice to see you. I need some everyday clothing for this young lady. She's going to be my downstairs maid and she has nothing to wear. I'd also like one walking dress."

"I see," Chantal said as if she truly could see through the miniscule scarf Brett wrapped around her for modesty sake. "You have a large problem. Where did you get this dress?"

"My cook's daughter was happy to lend this to Piper. They are approximately the same size except for the bust." Brett said, grinning while he kept his gaze averted from her bosom.

Piper didn't understand anything that was going on or why the size of her breasts was the topic of conversation.

"This will take some time but let me get her measurements while you choose some fabrics," Chantal said, picking up the tape. "We should go into a fitting room."

"I'll need one dress finished by tomorrow morning and delivered to my house as well. I don't mind paying the extra fee to make sure that happens. She does need something decent to wear," Brett called out as they disappeared into the room.

"Now, let's take the shawl off so I can measure you. No reason to take all your clothing off. I can get everything I need without doing that. I'm assuming you're not wearing a corset and don't want one."

"I..." Piper swallowed hard before clearing her throat. "Never wore one," she managed to mumble. Wasn't too sure what the dressmaker was talking about.

"Never? My dear, where have you been?"

Piper didn't really think the lady should know anything about her, so she chose not to answer. And she didn't appreciate the dressmaker's tone of voice. She stood still for her while she moved the tape from place to place then wrote something on a piece of paper.

"Done, shall we see what Monsieur MacLachlan has picked out for you? She smiled, opening the door for her.

They stepped outside the room. Brett was immersed in the fabrics and fashion plates as if this was a second home to him. The two spoke while she fiddled with the shawl and the pin, unsure of what she should do with them.

When they were finished, "Come here, Piper." Brett reached for the shawl and adeptly fastened the scrap of material. "There you go," he whispered as the backs of his fingers floated across her skin.

She felt the touch to the tips of her toes, saw the look of disapproval on the dressmaker's face. "Can we get out of here? Please?"

"Of course, are you hungry? There are food carts. We can walk if you like since the sun is out and it's not too cold. We could find a pub and get something to eat there."

"I suppose I'd like that, but I don't have any money. You took the purse I stole from you." She shouldn't have said that, somehow knowing Brett wouldn't like to be reminded of this afternoon.

He cleared his throat, seeming to ignore her statement. "Mademoiselle Chantal will have one dress ready for you tomorrow morning as well as underclothes. I've arranged for them to be sent to my home."

"Underclothes? Except for the bindings, I've never worn anything under my clothes. Why would you want to do that?"

Brett roughed his hands through his hair before letting out a bellow of laughter. "Don't know exactly," he frowned. "We just do. I don't think I could get much done if I knew you didn't have anything on under your dresses."

"Do I have to?" she queried, wondering at the ridiculous waste of time of putting on more clothing than what was essential as well as trying to figure out what he just said about getting things done. "Why would it make a difference to you if I wore underthings or not?"

"You should wear them." He laughed softly and the look in his eyes told Piper he was thinking of something pleasant.

"Why?" she persisted.

"It's not important. Let's go inside here," The pub sat on a corner. "This is a nice quiet place to eat and have a pint."

"A pint?" It seemed she didn't know about anything he talked about. She guessed from some of the conversations she'd overheard Jocko and his friends it was something to drink.

"You'll like it. At least I hope so." Brett took her hand, leading her into the tavern and finding a spot in the corner of the room where one could see everyone. "Had no idea just how innocent you were. Didn't expect a street lad to be naïve."

"Promise? Will it be like the brandy you gave me?" She laughed, enjoying herself even as she heard her stomach rumbling noisily. "Don't really care about the pint, but I am hungry. Haven't eaten since yesterday morning."

He ordered and it was only a few minutes before they each had a pint of ale in front of them and a basket of bread on the table; cheese followed.

She watched him, so in his element and here she was, unsure and hesitant. Sipping the ale, she wasn't all that positive she liked it, but with most of the glass gone, she was beginning to feel a bit lightheaded.

"As to your duties, you'll start tomorrow, and I expect you to dust everything every day and sweep the floors."

"Is that all?" she asked. "It's not going to take very long to sweep and dust. What will I do the rest of the time?"

"For now, that's all and you can do anything you want the rest of the day," he told her, leaning forward. "Tell me more about Jocko and this mistress training."

She sighed, letting out a long breath of air. "Shouldn't have told you about his intentions. Doesn't make any difference now that I've a job and a place to live."

"Of course you should. If I'm going to protect you from this man, I need to know everything about the people you used to live with and how they treated you. You did live on the wrong side of the law."

"I didn't really live with anyone. Jocko gave me a room to use, that's all. I never shared it with anyone because he didn't want the fact I was a girl to get out. He told me he couldn't protect me if it did."

Brett's brows drew together as if he was muddling over what she said. "Why would he want to protect you? What makes you different than every other pickpocket in London?"

"Not really sure. Think it must have had something to do with Scarface. Jocko's afraid of the man, and I think he knows something about me he won't share."

"Think I'll find out everything I can about Scarface," Brett mumbled.

"Wouldn't do that if I were you. Jocko says Scarface would murder his own brother if he could turn a profit." Suddenly, she didn't feel all that well. "Brett..." she began then closing her eyes, she rested her head on the table.

"What is it?" He reached out, touching her.

She moaned, looking up and licking her lips, which had turned suddenly very dry. "I don't feel well. Can we go home?"

Without answering, he left coin on the table then sweeping her into his arms, he carried her outside. She clung to him, finding comfort in the warmth emanating from his muscled body. Letting her head fall against his shoulder, she let down her guard for the first time since she could remember.

He hailed a cab and set her inside. She leaned back, her head against the back of the coach. "I think it was the drink."

"On no food," he added. "We'll be home in a few minutes, and I'll put you to bed. No, you should eat first. I'll have to see what cook left for us. Then I'll put you to bed," he repeated.

Drowsily, she mumbled. "Never slept on a bed before. How does one put someone else to bed? Seems like something a person can do by themselves."

He laughed. "Only if you know where your bed is. Do you?" He picked up her hands, warming them.

"No, do you?" she countered.

~ * ~

"What happened to Piper?" Jocko paced the two-room apartment in St. Giles he called home. The only place Piper had ever lived. "She can't just vanish. Someone has to have seen something."

"Saw her get into a cab with some gent, an aristocrat if my guess is right. He stopped the carriage for the dog too," Bobby told him.

"Saw him too," Billy said, rubbing his jaw as if thinking. "What's goin' to happen' to him? The gent didn't seem to be takin' him to the constables. Looked like he was headed in the wrong direction for that."

"The two of you are going to find out where he took Piper and bring the lad back to us," Jocko stared out the one window, his grip on the sill tightening. "Needs to be done before something happens to the boy."

"How we gonna do that?" Bobby asked, cleaning his nails with a knife. "We ain't got no way of finding out who the bloke was."

"You two just sit tight while I put out some feelers. I'll find out the details and get back to you. The two of you can break into his house in the middle of the night, take Piper back and pick up a few valuables in addition." Jocko tried to hide the trepidation he felt. Scarface might just kill him if he didn't get the girl back.

Except for Scarface and the man's anger, Jocko thought the plan a fine one, but he had to find out where she was for starters. A trip to see Scarface was in order. The thought of confessing he lost Piper sent a shiver down his spine. Perhaps it would be best to wait until he got the girl back.

"Not real good at waitin'." Billy said, "Need to be out and about.

Don't mind the idea of robbin' the place but don't know if Piper will come with us. If he's got a nice place to settle down, he won't want to come back here."

"Fine then, get out on the streets and see what you can find out. Go to Vauxhall, maybe someone saw him there and knows who took him."

Jocko watched the boys leave before picking up his jacket and setting out to find Scarface. The man would be angry he contacted him, but under the circumstances Jocko didn't see another choice. He'd be angrier if he didn't tell him.

With the sun setting, Jocko stood at the back entrance to the townhouse of Viscount Avery Bainbridge. Stepping inside, he waited for someone to realize they had a visitor.

On his way across town, Jocko took every precaution to make sure he wasn't followed. Now he hoped Avery would appreciate the effort and not skewer him through for doing the unthinkable, visiting him at his home.

"Bloody hell, what are you doing here?" Avery stepped through the door from the kitchen into the scullery. "My butler told me I had a visitor. Didn't expect the likes of you. Did anyone see you?"

"Couldn't wait for our next meeting," Jocko said, running a finger around his collar. "Important information. Something that you have to know now."

"It better be." Avery stood back, feet apart, his arms crossed over his chest. "As you know, I've no patience for failure or surprises."

"Piper's gone," Jocko blurted waiting for the explosion of wrath that was sure to follow the words. What he didn't expect was the calmness of Avery.

"Just where has she gone? A lass or lad, with no means to her name can't go very far. Find her."

"Got a couple of lads workin' on it."

"She's important to my plans, plans that were going to be put in motion in the next year. I don't want any problems."

"You never told me about any special plans." Jocko suddenly felt the world he planned falling apart. If Avery wanted her as his mistress, there would be no extra funds coming his way. He remembered the day Avery brought the baby to him. The viscount told him to keep the child alive but nothing else.

"You didn't need to know. Your instructions were to make sure her virginity remained intact. I assume you've done that." His calm seemed to escalate to anger.

"She's still a virgin, but I can't guarantee anything now that she's lost to me. A gent took her and if he knows he's a she, then..." He'd seen her naked, helped her from time to time with her bindings, knew any man would love to get a hold of her tits. They were very pretty and large. He'd been hard pressed to keep his hands to himself for the last several years.

"Make sure you get her back before something happens. It won't go well for you if you don't."

Avery's subtle threat didn't go unnoticed by Jocko. "Have her back in my lair tomorrow. The boys will find her. They're out doin' their jobs right now."

"I'll check in with you tomorrow night. Whatever you do, don't come here again. I'll let you know where to meet me."

Chapter Two

A couple weeks later, Brett sat in his office watching Piper dust the books and the decorations. It was the third time she had dusted the room. He managed to avoid her for the most part. Piper set emotions swirling in his brain that would be considered inappropriate to most of the ton. Everything about her fascinated him, tantalized, leaving a mercuric primal heat simmering inside.

When he closed his eyes, he could see her breasts peeking out from the bodice of her gown. Then he would recall her beautifully shaped derrière when he saw her naked before her bath. Every rule about servants was clear; you don't seduce or mistreat your female servants. Yet that was exactly the thoughts prominent in his mind every time he looked at her.

"There can't be any dust in this room." He rose, striding quickly to her and taking the duster from her hands unable to watch her any longer.

She let out a tiny cry of surprise. "I have to stay busy. Can't seem to find enough chores around here. Asked Mrs. Pickery if she'd teach me a how to cook, but all she did was sigh and shake her head."

"You want to cook? You don't need to learn. Take some time to relax," he said, setting the duster on a nearby table. "Do you know how to do that, relax?" He smiled at her, wishing he could take her into his arms and kiss her, a slow deep kiss, one that reached all the way to the tips of her toes, his too. He'd wanted to do that for the last two weeks, since he first saw her as a woman and not a boy.

"No, sir, but I can try."

He laughed, "You're so stiff. I'm sure you don't know the first thing about enjoying yourself. Have you ever just done nothing?" The obvious answer to his question was *of course not. When would I do that?*

"Not allowed except when it's time to sleep." She fiddled with the buttons on her bodice as if when her fingers were moving she would be all right. "Had to find another mark, steal a purse or a handkerchief, anything to prove I was working. Take them to Jocko so he can sell them to the lady."

"What lady?" Brett pursued the information she gave him.

"Not sure, heard Jocko talking about someone named Mrs. Fields. She keeps a shop that has a cockloft through a trap door where she keeps an immense number of silk handkerchiefs. Jocko said she gets away with it because she takes out the initials of the marks."

"I see." And it seemed he understood more about her life each day. An urgent need to hit Jocko came over him. He wanted to meet the man in a dark alley and show no mercy. Piper had been working for pennies since she was a child, and the man intended to sell her to someone as mistress.

"Sit down and rest. Take a nap if you'd like." He needed to put distance between them before he gave into his desire to kiss her. Striding to his desk he sat down and stared at the papers in front of him. A few moments later he looked up. She was sitting in the same place, her hands folded tightly in her lap.

"If you don't mind, I'm not tired. Can I look at one of your books?" She stood, walking to the rows of books before gazing upward.

"Of course," he said, pretty sure she didn't know how to read but if she wanted to look there would be no harm. "Pick out anything you like."

He tapped his pen on the table a few times, unable to look back to her. For a few seconds he held his breath then, "Piper?"

"Yes?" She looked up from the page she'd been staring at him with her huge deep blue eyes.

"What are you reading?" he asked, as he watched her brows draw together as if concentrating.

She shrugged her too thin and very delicate shoulders, a strange expression on her lovely face. "I don't know. Just thought if I studied the page long enough, I'd figure it out, but nothing seems to make sense.

There aren't even any pictures. I might be able to make sense of this if there were pictures."

He didn't want to laugh at her but what she said did spark a bit of humor. On a more serious note, "Would you like to learn how to read, sweet imp? Everyone should be able to read."

"Yes. Jocko told me he'd teach me one day but there was never any time. Then there was this nice lady at the orphanage where Jocko took me to learn my trade who offered to help the young ones learn their letters and numbers. I think her name was Ella, but I had to work so I didn't qualify for lessons."

"You know Ella Hepburn?" he asked. The lady had been the subject of a great deal of gossip over the summer. Not only did she run off with Drake Montgomerie, but they just returned a few weeks ago. Talk was they were going to get married because he compromised her and got her pregnant.

"No, saw her one day when she was visiting. She found out what happened to the girls once they turned of age and the uproar that followed was huge. I think she wanted to protect the girls but of course she thought I was a lad."

"I'll see what I can do. Might be able to find some readers. If anything, I could ask around." He'd sent a message to Montgomerie about Scarface and hoped to hear from Drake soon.

"I'd like that." She smiled at him.

"Let me see what you're reading." Still sitting at his desk, and understanding he was treading on dangerous ground if he sat by Piper, he procrastinated and poured himself a drink then one for Piper.

With brandy in hand, he sat down beside her, his leg brushing hers. He handed her one of the glasses.

"Not sure I should drink this. Drinking didn't work out so well last time." It seemed she remembered the day a few weeks ago when he gave her a brandy, followed by a pint of ale all on an empty stomach.

"Have you eaten today?" Truly, he didn't want her drunk just relaxed and able to enjoy life.

She nodded. "This morning."

"And it's almost dinner time. Perhaps we should find something in the pantry." He thought to ring for Molly but wasn't sure Piper would eat anything if Molly did bring food.

"No, really, I'm fine." She sipped. "See. Nothing wrong. It was a big breakfast. Mrs. Pickery doesn't think I eat enough. So, she stands over me until I eat everything she's dished up."

"You probably don't." His fingers rested on the book as he gazed at the page in question then, "This is difficult even for someone who can read."

For the longest time they stared at each other. Her lips were moist and inviting. One hand fiddled with another button and it seemed every time she did, one came undone. He could see the valley between her breasts, but right now he needed to kiss her, taste her lips.

Slowly, he leaned forward, her eyes huge as she licked her lips again then sucked the bottom one between her teeth. He was a breath away from her, could feel the whisper of her breath against his mouth. This was heaven, a magical moment between them and one he needed to savor.

"Sir." Molly called from outside the door. "I've something for the two of you. Can I come in?"

Piper gasped, moving away, her voice shaking.

The mood was broken but not at an end. "What is it, Molly?" he asked in an attempt at patience.

"Mrs. Pickery thought you might like a bite to eat seein' dinner will be a little late tonight. I've a tray here. She told me Piper hasn't eaten since dinner last night."

"Set it on the table." He looked away from Piper to nod toward the nearby table. He was sure he heard her stomach rumble in hunger. She lied to him and that didn't sit well. If he asked her a question, he wanted the truth.

"Anything else?" she asked.

"That's fine and I expect your silence about what you almost saw here. From now on, I want you to knock and wait for an answer before you enter a room." It would not do if she interrupted them in something more familiar than a kiss that had not taken place yet. He fully intended for their relationship to grow to encompass something more intimate. "Do you understand what I'm asking, Molly?"

"I understand, sir." She fled the room, her skirts swishing wildly around her feet.

"Now, where were we? Hmm..." He touched her chin and turned her so he could see her face as well as her eyes. "Ah, I believe I was about to kiss you, wasn't I? Would you like that Piper? A small afternoon kiss?" *And maybe something more when you've grown used to my kisses.*

"Never been kissed so I can't say for sure." Yet she touched him, her hand resting on his chest before she realized what she did and quickly pulled away. "Maybe I'd like to try."

"After this afternoon, if you like, you won't be able to say those words. Hmm... Never been kissed." Picking up a slice of plum, he held it to her lips, smoothing the fruit along their fullness. "Do you like these? I do. Take a bite. They're almost as sweet as you. I'll know better after I kiss you."

She did open to accept the slice and her teeth brushed gently against his fingers, the sensation mercuric and raw, his body responding. He watched the tiny shiver race through her, pleased she was affected as much as he was. "They're good," she said. "I've never had a plum before."

Most likely Piper's experiences with food as well as other things were limited to what could be found in St. Giles Parish; Buckeridge Street and Church Lane. Thoughts of her living her entire life in those dens of iniquity gave him reason to cringe. She was lucky to still be alive. Perhaps there was something to thank Jocko for. Even if it was for devious reasons that he protected her.

"What else haven't you eaten?" He searched the tray for more delicacies, found some blueberries. "Try these." Once again he fed them to her, this time tracing her lips with the berry before placing the food on her tongue.

"I...I don't know what to say. So hot." Waving a hand in front of her face, she undid another button on her dress.

He smiled, pleased with the few moments of seduction, his intent far from finished. Bending close, he lightly touched her lips with his. "Hot is good." *Undo another button on your dress and I'll have to change my plans for today.*

"But..."

His hand wove through her short but appealing hair, reveling in the silken locks while pulling her to him. He watched her eyes, the changing hues with her growing passion. "I'm going to kiss you now. Is that all right?"

He smiled as he watched the tip of her tongue sweep across her lips and the tiny nod of agreement. "I think I'd like to try."

Almost touching, he hesitated. Her eyes were closed and he wanted to see her reaction. "Open your eyes, sweet imp."

Her eyes were darker now than he'd ever seen them. His mouth closed over her lips, while he touched and explored. Sucking her lower lip into him, biting gently then repeating with the top. Tentatively she explored him, touching, discovering him. She didn't hesitate or even pretend shyness.

The tiny noises coming from the back of her throat delighted him, and with this unspoken permission he continued. Kissing, withdrawing to watch her then almost as if he tried to inhale her into himself, he molded his lips to hers, again and again. He gently tweaked and pinched her mouth with his teeth, enjoying the wet softness.

His attentions changed then. Nipping, licking and touching her neck, he followed a path to her throbbing pulse, sucking for a few seconds, enjoying the racing of blood. He found an ear, discovering the tiny shell, his breath whispering against her. Shivers wracked her body as she brought her hands to his shoulders and squeezed.

"What are you doing to me?" Her whisper was so thin it was barely audible. "I've never felt anything like this before."

"Do you like my lips on yours?" he queried, praying for a yes answer. "We can continue if you want."

"I can't think." Her fingers wove into his hair while she pulled him toward her. "You have to get closer."

He smiled, "Why?"

"I want to kiss you."

He paused, close to her, allowing her to do what she said. Her movements were hesitant but evocative in their own way, in her innocence. She copied his movements, enclosing his lips with her mouth, her sweet tongue dueling now with his.

His seduction would never remain controlled if he allowed her to take the lead. Again catching a lip with his teeth, he bit and laved, and pulling back delighted at what he wrought. They were kiss swollen and told the tale of her willingness to explore and be explored.

"Some brandy?" he asked as he slowed the pace, allowing his hand to rest on her waist, his gaze drawn to her heaving breasts and the gap of material that allowed him to see the swell of her breasts. "More food?"

"I can't think and I don't know if I've any bones left in my body," she said but accepted the glass he handed her.

"Drink up." He smiled at her, wishing he dared continue this to the next stage. He needed her to crave him as much as he craved her before that could happen.

"Bloody hell," he growled, hearing the knock on the door. Truly he didn't want to share her with anyone right now. "Who is it?"

"Drake Montgomerie is here at your request. He came as soon as he got the message. Seems this is important to him also," Molly said from behind the closed doors.

Brett closed his eyes, knowing this was for the best, but the sight of her sweetly curved breasts so close to unveiling left his body hard and in need of relief. Quickly, he buttoned her dress. Good God but she appeared as if he ravaged her, kiss swollen lips, eyes darkened with passion as well as beautifully flushed skin. Recriminations were not what he needed.

"I've asked Montgomerie for information about Scarface. You can stay here if you want. You might be able to give us some details that will help us understand what he plans for you."

"I will if that's what you suggest."

One look at Piper and Montgomerie would know what they were doing. There was nothing he could do that would change that fact. "Come in," he said.

"That took long enough..."

It seemed he saw Piper and as Brett assumed, he knew exactly what they'd been doing. "Sorry, couldn't be helped. I guessed you'd want this meeting as soon as possible."

Drake roared with laughter. It seemed he studied the couple. "I've been caught in that same predicament with my Ella. All you can do is keep the embarrassment at a minimum, but by my way of thinking there is nothing to be embarrassed or concerned about."

"Brandy?" Brett asked. "I assume you're here because you've some information concerning this Scarface or Jocko."

Drake accepted the glass before sitting down. "I do. Scarface is Viscount Avery Bainbridge, at least I'm assuming that is who he is. The man has a scar from his forehead across his nose ending at his chin."

Both men looked to Piper who was fiddling with her buttons again. He hoped they didn't start popping free. Her shoulders lifted slightly while she ran her tongue across her lips. "Never saw him. Jocko never described him. Didn't seem necessary to portray the man."

"He's seen occasionally near St. Giles Parish. Never seems to stay long but I'm still looking for connections to your young lady," Drake said. "At the moment none of the information I've uncovered points to any associations with Piper."

"I appreciate all you can do. Seems her life might be in danger." Brett downed his brandy before offering the plate of snacks Molly brought into the library earlier.

"From what little I've learned, and if what I was seeing when I walked into the room is even half true, you should consider marrying the girl. It's the only way you can really protect her."

Brett had never thought of marrying but everyone did at some time or other. An heir was always nice and he liked her, no was mesmerized by her. He turned his attention to Piper and she seemed shocked by what Drake said, but she sat nearly still, giving no indication she heard the proposal.

Drake cleared his throat and continued. "One of my men has linked Scarface with several scandals involving second sons and attempts to steal the inheritance of the first son by murder."

"You were already looking into this? Why?" Brett poured himself another brandy then refilled both Piper's and Drake's glasses.

"It's no secret. My younger brother covets my inheritance to the point I don't trust him with my life or Ella's. The girls, cousins, remember a case in Scotland where the first son suffered a strange accident and died. The wife just before the accident bore a baby, don't recall if the child was a boy or a girl then she committed suicide. The child disappeared, vanished without a trace. None of her friends believe the mother would have killed herself."

"Avery Bainbridge is not to be trusted, in any case," Brett said.

"Jocko never trusted him, but Scarface seemed to hold something over Jocko's head. They had secrets. I was always sent to another room when he showed up. Several times I heard them whispering and seemingly in a heated argument," Piper added.

"And some of them had to do with you," Drake guessed.

"I'm not sure but I think so. Jocko was always protective but even he admitted that he couldn't keep my identity hidden much longer," Piper said. "He was hoping he'd find a wealthy aristocrat to keep me."

"Your identity," Drake probed. "As a boy, I assume."

Brett recognized the very real fear in Piper's eyes. "Is there anything else?" he asked Drake.

"For now no, but I'll keep you informed on any new information available to me." Drake rose to leave. "Brett, Miss Piper. You don't need to see me out. I'm sure the door is in the same place as it was when I entered."

When the door closed, Brett let out a long deep breath. Then, turning his attention to Piper whose once flushed face turned a ghostly shade of white while Drake was here, "Are you alright?"

"No." She downed the glass of brandy. "Don't think I'll ever be fine or alright ever again."

He sat down beside her, picking up her hand. "Perhaps Drake has a good idea. What do you think about marriage?"

"Don't know what you're talking about." She turned away from him, her small frame shaking.

"Would you marry me?" he asked, unsure why her answer was so important to him.

"No."

"Why not?" He didn't understand why she wouldn't want to be wed to him. After all it was more than one step up in status. He'd been called a good catch by many doting mamas.

"We don't love each other." Her voice whisper thin, she looked as if she wanted to vanish into the walls.

"True," he mused. "But we do well together. I enjoy your company and your kisses." He almost laughed at the sudden return of color to her face. "Should I prove it to you again, my lips pressed against yours? My tongue deep inside you."

She plucked at her skirts, keeping her gaze averted. He didn't want that, needed to see into her expressive eyes. "I'm not someone you can marry." As if she read his mind she looked up.

Shocked by her comment. "I'll marry whoever I damn well please if they return the sentiment."

"I'm a guttersnipe from St. Giles parish. It's not fitting, an aristocrat wed to a pickpocket, a hoyden. That would never do. What would your family say?"

"Perhaps you do need convincing." He should kiss her until she agreed to marriage. He muttered, realizing the hour was getting late and dinner would be served soon.

"No, it's you who need convincing. I'm not meant to be anything but a whore or a man's mistress."

Her words angered and frustrated him. "Just because you were born poor doesn't mean you're not fit for anything but whoring."

She plucked at her buttons, a few bursting free. He didn't think she was aware of what she was doing but to him it was delightful.

When she set her hands in her lap, "Jocko was training me to be a whore or a mistress if he could get me cleaned up real nice."

"Like you are now?"

"If I were your mistress would that help you protect me?" she asked, her gaze riveted on her feet.

"No."

"You didn't even think about it," she complained, her words resigned though. "He used to take me to whore houses, you understand. We would go into a small room where we could watch the whores and the johns in their intimacy. He wanted me to understand what I can expect. I'm not really innocent or naïve, not what you think I am."

He didn't know what to say, having heard of the practice. Appalled once again that she'd been subjected to something like that, he remained silent, searching for the right words.

"I'm sure I could show you some of the things I learned. Jocko told me I was a fast learner. Before he found a rich man who would keep me, he was going to have me so I wouldn't be a virgin."

Her lower lip sucked into her mouth, she paused. "I know several different ways to have sex. You wouldn't want that in a wife, no one would. I can relieve you with my mouth, if that's something you'd like. Do you want me show you? I can tell you're in need of respite." Tears started falling from her eyes. She didn't wipe them away just let them fall down her cheeks.

He wanted to pull her into his arms, keep all the demons at bay for the rest of her life, but he didn't think she'd be receptive to that. She was wrong though. None of what she told him mattered, at least not to him. Somehow over the last few weeks, she found a way into his heart no woman ever possessed before.

His glib reply, he held back, something else she wouldn't be receptive to hearing. He could always make love to her until she was pregnant with his child, perhaps then he could convince her to wed him.

Or perhaps not.

He didn't like that idea at all.

"Sir, dinner is served. Will Piper be joining you?" Molly said from outside the door, her hesitant knock following.

"Yes, she will. We have unfinished business to discuss," he said as he watched Piper's reaction.

She was shaking her head, "I'm sure it's not appropriate."

"Don't give a damn what's appropriate and what isn't."

~ * ~

Despite Piper's reluctance to eat dinner with Brett and listen to more of his persuasive words to marry him, it was true. She was unsuitable. Sitting in front of the mirror in her room, she brushed her hair. Until she lived under his roof, she'd never owned a brush or anything for that matter.

All she ever owned were the clothes she wore and Rogue, who seemed to love his new home. He slept and ate then slept some more. Mrs. Pickery gave him huge bones and let him sleep in the scullery next to the fireplace. He seemed to love that. Now he was curled up on her bed. She always slept with him beside her. He gave her comfort and warmth and now, she knew, a false sense of security.

Still Brett seemed hell bent on something that wasn't right. Really, he couldn't possibly want to marry her, a street thief from Gin Alley. If she admitted anything, marrying Brett would be her dream, Piper's dream, but she wouldn't dwell on something that would never happen. That would be foolish.

In her shift, she pulled the covers back before plumping the pillow. Until she came to live with Brett, she never slept in a bed or had a bath. Now she treated herself to a bath anytime she wanted. Rogue was even on his second bath but he didn't like them. Mrs. Pickery insisted, didn't want a filthy dog in her kitchen. He seemed to understand if he wanted to keep his place by the fire, he'd have to abide by the cook's wishes.

Brett wouldn't allow her to wander outside in the gardens. Sometimes she felt as if the walls were closing in on her. From her window she could see the roses and other flowers, sometimes the gardener as he puttered around the yard. Maybe when all this trouble surrounding her settled down, she could ask him if she could help the gardener. Goodness knows she finished the dusting and sweeping by ten each morning and nothing really needed to be dusted everyday. She had more than enough time to do anything else he needed done.

She set her forehead on the windowpane, cool now that the sun had set. The room was too hot most days and she left the window open except at night. Now she closed it. Her days in St. Giles taught her not to take chances. Even though she was on the third floor, she needed to take heed. Trees could be climbed. Carelessness could get a body murdered.

The bed was almost too soft. She pushed at Rogue who seemed to want the entire bed for himself then plumped the pillow again. She must have dozed because the small bedside candle burned itself out, wax melting on the base. The crash sent her bolting upright.

Jocko.

She knew he'd look for her, wouldn't let his dreams of the wealth she would bring him vanish. Brett told her the house was secure, but was it really? Billy and Bobby were real good at finding their way into homes of the wealthy aristocrats. That's how they made their living, not picking pockets but robbing homes in the middle of the night, and they knew how to back slang it, get out the back way before anyone noticed.

What she did know was that she wasn't going to leave Brett's home willingly, not without putting up a fight. Brett would protect her, but she knew first hand that she had to protect herself if she was going to survive. Without thinking further, she rushed down the steps to his room and without knocking she ducked inside.

The room was dark, curtains closed keeping out the moonlight. With her back to the door, she stood for a few seconds, trying to let her eyes adjust but to no avail, listening to her heart pound double-time. Now that she was in his room, she didn't know what to do. For a few seconds she froze.

"Piper? Is that you?" Brett's voice thundered in her ears but now she knew where the bed was or at least Brett's location.

"Yes." Her heart in her throat she moved slowly toward the sound of his voice, wishing she could see him.

"What the devil are you doing here?" he asked, his voice sounding hoarse. "You decided you wanted me enough to marry me?"

He lit a candle then sat up.

"Oh! Oh my. Are you naked? You sleep without clothes?"

"And you're semi dressed? But that isn't important right now. What are you doing here?" It seemed he demanded an answer. "Piper, you know what I told you earlier."

"I, well, I heard a noise and I was sure it was Jocko coming for me or at least his minions, Billy and Bobby. He would never come himself." She sat down next to him, mesmerized by him and the play of muscles across his chest. Reaching out she touched him, trailed a finger down his chest to the sheet then back. "I just need you to check out the noise."

He cleared his throat, "What kind of noise."

"A bang and shuffling. Thought I heard someone talking, but I was sure it was Billy and Bobby."

"I need to see for myself. Turn around." His hand settled on the sheet as he poised to rise from the bed.

"Why? Not like I haven't seen a naked man before, but so far what I'm seeing of you is far better than anyone else I've laid my eyes on." She understood provoking him sexually would only lead to her discomfort not his.

"If that's what you want, I can oblige." He rose then finding a pair of buckskins, slipped them on. "Still like what you see? I'm liking what I'm seeing of you."

In her rush to find Brett, she didn't put on her dress and the sheer shift must be akin to nakedness. Yet she didn't feel embarrassed or uncomfortable. She wanted him to make her his mistress, to have sex with her.

"If you keep looking at me like that, I'm not going to find out about the noise downstairs." His voice was whiskey smooth and she found herself wanting him even more than a few seconds ago. Perhaps he forgot his refusal to see to her pleasure until they married.

Pushing her thoughts aside, "We have to find out if anyone broke into your house. They are after me and I won't go back to the life I used to live." She wrapped her arms around herself, now, wishing she'd thought to take the time to dress.

"Not we, me." He picked up a pistol resting by the side of his bed. "You're staying here. Lock yourself in when I leave."

"I'm going with you." She stood behind him at the door, determined not to be left behind.

"Stay here," he repeated harshly. "I don't want to have to worry about you or keep looking over my shoulder so I know where you are."

"I can take care of myself, probably better than you." She'd done so ever since she remembered. Even as a child she had to protect her possessions and at times by force.

"Very well, stay close and don't get in the way." He paused then, "Wrap a sheet or something around you." Wait." He tossed her one of his shirts. "Put it on."

Quickly and smiling, she slipped his shirt over her shoulders and buttoned it, and when they left the room, she did stay close. Her heart thundering, she watched the shadows flit across the walls. There had been times when she had to sneak home, stay in the shadows so no one would see her, too many close calls. Shadows could be friend or foe.

"There, by the ivory figurine. Bobby's put it in his sack right now. I see them. They've come for me, but they're going to treat themselves to a few of your things too."

"Hold it right there." Brett's voice resounded in the small room, his pistol poised to shoot.

"Blimey," Billy spoke from behind them, rushing toward them as if to tackle Brett and send the gun to the floor.

Piper stuck her foot out, tripping the young man and watching him fall. "Leave now and I won't tell Scarface how you let this fop get the better of you. It won't go well if he learns of this."

"Well now he hasn't got the better of us yet." Billy spoke from his spot on the floor, staring at her.

"No," she paused, laughing, "I did take you down and that will make him even unhappier, taken down by a pickpocket. Best you take what you already stuck in the sack and hightail it out of here. Tell him the information wasn't right. Tell him we left town because I knew Jocko was after me. Tell him I'm not going back to St. Giles Parish, ever. Tell him whatever makes you look better."

"Everything Piper is saying is true. Thinking of finishing up my business and heading home to Scotland. There's a bit more peace and quiet in Scotland, and no one will be breaking into my house." He waved the pistol in the air. "Get going while you're still alive. Seems the law gives me permission to shoot an intruder."

She watched the two young men who guarded her back more days than she wanted to count, flee Brett's home. Without asking she poured herself a Brandy. "Do you want one?" Betrayal loomed large in her mind. A few weeks had passed and all she expected as well as her loyalties had changed.

He grinned shamelessly while she realized she didn't ask permission. "Something a wife would do," he told her. "Pour me one and we can talk about this break in, as well as our future."

She curled up on the sofa, Brett sitting beside her. "They will come back. Don't know if there is a way to secure the doors and windows well enough to keep them out." The warmth of the brandy slid down her throat, something she was getting used to. She closed her eyes, enjoying the benefits of her new life.

"They saw you in next to nothing and me wearing just my unfastened buckskins. They're going to assume we were sleeping together," he told her, accepting the glass she handed him then sat beside her.

"They did. They would assume I'm your mistress, nothing more. Of course before today they didn't know that I'm a girl and not a boy."

"They didn't seem too surprised. Are you sure they didn't know? And, we are in the same house. They'll assume and report back that you're my whore. In that case I have very few means to keep you safe. You're fair game for any man." His voice was ruff and harsh. "Neither one of us wants that."

She shivered at his words. "I'm neither and I'll tell anyone who asks." Yet she understood the more she denied the more her obvious circumstances would be believed.

"For the moment you're right. Who knows what tomorrow will bring? When I see you, touch you..." He ran a finger along the length of her leg. "Don't know what I'll do. No, suppose I'll do just about anything you'll let me. What are your limits where I'm concerned? When will you say no?"

She inhaled sharply, realizing she'd let him do anything. Since the kiss this afternoon she wanted so much more from him, craved his touch with every thought. Thinking about him doing some of the things she witnessed in the whorehouse made her pulse race, a small inferno burning within. When she closed her eyes, she imagined so many ways he could touch her.

"We should go to bed."

"I'd like that. Are you propositioning me?" His feral smile sent another charge of emotions spiraling inside her and centering deep inside.

She swallowed hard, wishing she had more skills to counter back his words. "I don't want to go back to my room. It's too hot and too far away from you. I want to sleep in your bed, with you."

"Will you marry me, Piper? I'd like that. Then we can talk about sleeping in the same bed." His finger swept a path along her thigh to her hip then back.

"You would regret the marriage. I'm sure of it." She had to remain stubborn. It would be so easy to give into him. Lord knows she wanted to marry him.

"And you'd be wrong." He repeated his exploration up her leg and back so close to parts of her she'd never thought would ache so sweetly before she met Brett. "I'll never regret anything I do with you as long as you respond with the same passion as you are right now."

"Just because I won't marry you doesn't mean I don't want to know what it would be like to have sex with you. I've seen too much yet I've experienced nothing."

"How much do you want me?" he asked, tempting her even more when he found her veiled breasts with his questing lips.

She couldn't help herself, reaching out to touch him. "More than I've ever wanted anything." She didn't like the smile he slanted her, was sure he held the winning card but didn't know yet what that was. It seemed he kept his thoughts as well as his intentions close to his heart.

"You'll have to marry me if you want me." He withdrew his hand, his gaze resting on her breasts.

"You don't play fair," she told him, understanding the blackmail. Still she meant to lobby for mistress status. She couldn't allow him to demean his position by marrying a guttersnipe. She knew who she was and it seemed he didn't.

"I play to win," he told her smoothly, rising and extending his hand. "I don't like losing, never have. Are you ready to go back to bed?"

"Now you want to go to bed with me?" She was clearly confused but if they were in bed together, she had a better chance of getting what she wanted.

"Always." His hand still held out for her to take.

She touched his hand and he enclosed hers within his. He helped her to her feet then swept her into his arms. "Is the house guarded? Billy and Bobby might try to get back in. I'm sure Jocko has threatened them with their lives if they failed."

"They won't come back tonight because the sun is almost ready to shine. Mrs. Pickery will be in soon as will Molly. Angus is up, puttering around ready to pass judgment when he finds you in my bed with me."

She found herself caught off guard by his statement about Angus. Sleeping with him was one thing, but someone finding her in bed with him violated her thoughts of privacy. "Why would Angus find us in bed?"

Giving her a quick kiss on her lips, "Because he always comes into my room in the morning and sets out what he thinks I'd like to wear. He also makes sure my bath is ready for me. We could bathe together. Would you like that? I know I would. I could wash your back and your..."

This was a provocation she wasn't sure she could endure. She didn't want anyone to see her in bed with Brett or imagine her in a bath with him. It seemed wrong and a violation of decency. "I'd like all of the above if Angus wasn't involved. I don't want him to see me without clothes or even beneath the sheets in your bed."

"If we were wed, I'd make sure he stayed away until you were dressed or I would go into another room, but a mistress as well as a whore are not treated to such niceties. Their wishes are never considered." He stopped, his kiss deepening then slowly withdrawing, tantalizing and giving a promise of so much more. Starting up the steps again, "I like to see the pleasure on your face, can only imagine right now when I give you a woman's pleasure how your eyes will darken with emotion and desire."

Perhaps she could change this, seduce him, a man and prove she couldn't be toyed with. "A mistress could give you all that and more. I could give you things that aren't acceptable for a wife. I could suck your rod inside my mouth until you spill your seed."

He let his head fall back and roared with laughter. "Behind closed doors and with me anything a wife wants to do is more acceptable than a mistress. I want my wife to be honest in every way, including sex with me. When we're wed, I'll let you have your wicked way with me anytime you like."

"Under the circumstances, laughing at me is not very nice. You told me you wouldn't make me do anything I didn't want. Are you a liar?"

"Never. In time you will want to marry me. And if you tell me no, I'll always stop."

"You think your blackmail will influence me to change my mind?" She knew it would but she wasn't going to give in without a fight. Truth be told she craved him more than she'd ever craved anything even when she had no food for a week.

He pushed the door to his room open with his foot before closing it in the same manner. "When we're husband and wife, your dog will have to sleep somewhere else."

"Rogue always sleeps with me. He protects me." She knew what he'd say.

"I won't share my bed with a dog." He laughed again. "Only my beautiful and slightly reluctant bride to be and from what I've seen, you don't need protection from me or your dog, but it doesn't mean my manly protective instincts won't kick in."

He set her on the bed before pulling a chair up to the bed. His knees rested between her legs, spreading them. "What are you doing?" she asked, unsure of this new approach at seduction.

"Giving you a small taste of what you will enjoy when you're my wife." He unbuttoned the shirt he loaned her before slipping it off her shoulders. "Very pretty. Your shift barely covers you. Do you mind?" he asked as he cupped one breast in his hand, flicking the peak and watching her as she felt her eyes widen with desire for this man who didn't know how to accept her wishes over his.

Before his eyes she felt her body melting, giving over to him and the escalating sensations he so easily created. He would torment her, give her almost what she craved then he'd withdraw. She would have to stay strong.

"Do you mind?" he repeated the question, running his hands up the inside of her leg, stopping just shy of...the intimacy she'd seen in the whorehouse. Yet she moved her legs farther, parting them, giving him easier access.

"Should you do that?" she asked, unable to remember anyone she watched, running their hands along the woman's legs. This was just something she never imagined, something she'd never seen.

"If you'd like, raise your arms so I can cool you off a tad bit." She did and he swept the shift up her arms. Naked in front of him, she knew no embarrassment or discomfort.

"Can I see you?" she asked, craving more of him than she saw when he rose from the bed naked.

"When you're my wife and not a second before. I am a bit shy in front of women."

She couldn't stop the small groan, embarrassed when he slanted an amused smile her way. Yet she reached out and touched his chest, raked a nail across his tiny nipple. With his groan she smiled back. "I won't cave into your marriage proposal no matter how well planned this seduction is. And I don't believe for one second you're shy."

"You will crave my seduction." It seemed his confidence exuded from him and with each tiny flick of his fingers, the subtle play of his lips on her flesh, he was rewarded with her compliance.

"I..." She closed her eyes and let her head fall back, unintentionally giving him permission for his erotic play to continue. She was so far out of her element, but she could not give in to his proposal.

"Speechless?" he asked touching and kissing everywhere but where she thought she wanted him the most. He toyed with her, played with her body while he sought to blackmail her into becoming his wife.

"There's nothing left to say." Unable to stop them, tiny mewling sounds emanated from her, proving inadvertently to him just how skilled he was and how much she desired him.

"Flabbergasted, amazed, perhaps even dumbstruck," he murmured close to her ear before swirling his tongue inside then pulling away to look at her.

"None of the above," she murmured, attempting once more to make herself indifferent to his attentions, yet she couldn't.

With his knees he pushed her legs wider, staring at her more intimately than anyone ever looked at her before. "Look at yourself, sweet little imp. You are the most beautiful woman I've ever seen."

"No," she said, shaking her head unable to understand what he was trying to do. No one in the whorehouse or on the streets ever asked such a thing.

"Very well, I'll look at you and tell you what I see."

She watched as he looked at her. "You're ready for me to come inside you. Of course I won't do that until you agree to my proposal. Ah, but I've said that before. If you were to look at yourself, you'd see just how ready you are for me."

Piper jumped when she felt something inside her. "Oh!" she looked at herself. One of his fingers was pushing inside. When she looked back at him, he grinned, that devilish grin she was beginning to understand was his victory smile yet it was part of him she was falling in love with. She loved him and how could that be?

"My finger is buried within but that's not the same as my rod. You're going to have to wait for that." His voice was low and gruff, seductive and oh so enticing. Every part of her wanted to give in to him, tell him yes, she'd become his wife but she knew he'd regret the decision.

Her hips moved and she arched as if trying to draw him farther inside. Unexpectedly, he withdrew. "Don't stop." Her breath came in short pants, desperate for something she didn't understand.

"You like this? I thought you would. I touched the tiny barrier inside you. You didn't lie to me, not that I ever thought you did. You are a virgin, my sweet little imp, and on the marriage market very valuable. I suppose you should know that before you agree to marry me. Perhaps you could hold out for a duke or someone with a better title, like viscount Avery."

"Brett, please..." She didn't want to beg but she needed something she somehow believed only he could give her.

"When we're wed, you can beg and I'll give you your release, your woman's pleasure. Something I know you'll love and want every day and night."

"You're stopping then," she said, understanding for the first time the power he wielded over her. Her body felt ripe and swollen, sensations so intense and unfulfilled she wanted to scream. As he told her, ready for him, for his rod, his control be damned. She'd have to rethink this.

He pulled her shift over her head, covering her. "Go to sleep. See, the sun is up. I don't want to see you dusting or anything else until at least noon."

"Where are you going?" She thought he would lie down next to her. Sleep with her at least. Obviously, he would do what he wanted.

"Sir!" Angus stood in the doorway, a shocked expression on his face before he backed out, closing the door behind him.

"One minute," he told her, stepping outside to confront Angus she supposed.

She wasn't the least bit sleepy. No, she was aroused. There was no other way to explain what she was feeling. Running her hands down her body, touching herself, she realized how sensitized she was. Hot and wet, she was indeed ready for his penetration. She touched the folds in her most private area then groaned softly, her body arching even with her attentions. "So sensitive. He did this to me and created this haunting need within me."

"I see your discovering the pleasure you can give yourself. Perhaps I'm teaching you too well." He leaned against the door watching her. "Really don't want to do that."

"But..." She swallowed hard moistening her lips. "I'm still so hot and..."

"You still need me. I'll finish this..."

"Never." She closed her eyes, swinging her legs onto the bed before hugging a pillow close to her chest.

"Little imp, I'm truly sorry it's come to this. I don't like leaving you this way but you've forced my hand. I've no other choice. Until you agree," he reminded her.

She groaned again, moving on the bed as if that would make her more comfortable. "Choices, there are always choices."

He walked to her, and bending over, he kissed her cheek. Then he watched her for a few more seconds before pulling a cover over her. "I talked to Angus and while he didn't like the fact you are in my bed and will be there whenever it suits you, he agreed to ask permission before he walks inside."

"That was nice of you. While I've no inhibitions where you're concerned, I don't want anyone else seeing me without any clothes on." She felt a sob well up inside but refused to give Brett the satisfaction. Yet a part of her understood Brett would not find happiness in her discomfort. Perhaps he was just as uncomfortable as she was. She could only hope.

"Don't go into the bathing room unless you want to see me naked," he grinned.

~ * ~

Angus stood in the kitchen shaking his head at what he saw in the Lord's bedroom. His shock had been apparent to Master Brett. "I say, Mrs. Pickery, it's just not right the way Master Brett is treating Miss Piper. He has some explaining to do. Problem is there's no one to call him out."

"Never seen him act that way either. You say you interrupted them this morning in his chambers," Mrs. Pickery said. "Known him since he was a small tyke. His mother and father would never condone this course of action."

"Yes. It's a damn shame too." Angus continued. "If he's going to bed her, he should marry her."

"I saw them kissing in the library," Molly said while she heaped a tray of food to take to the master chamber for the couple. "He told me I have to knock. Don't want to walk in on something I shouldn't. Never had to knock before," she said indignantly hands on her hips. "What's this world coming to?"

"What I do know is that we shouldn't be gossiping about the master and what he's doin' with the lass. It's none our business," Mrs. Pickery said, finishing the scrambled eggs and heaping the tray with slices of bacon.

"There's enough food here to feed an army," Molly said.

"Maybe she likes eggs. She doesn't eat half enough," Mrs. Pickery said, waving with her hands. "Go on, take this up and make sure you knock as he told you. Who knows what he's got planned for Miss Piper."

"The way I see this situation is we're obligated to protect her innocence," Angus said, stealing a piece of bacon from the tray. "Even though she grew up on the wrong side of the law, doesn't mean she's not deserving to be happy."

"Pshaw," Mrs. Pickery told them. "If she spent the night in his bed, she's no longer a virgin and has nothing left for us to protect. Don't know what we should do now that we let him have his way with her."

Angus cleared his throat. "She was on his bed, half dressed but not in it when I interrupted them. My guess is I stopped what Master Brett intended so there's still time."

"Well then it's up to us to keep an eye on the two of them," Mrs. Pickery said. "We can't let him get away with deflowering her."

"How is that possible?" Molly asked as she backed out of the room with the breakfast tray.

"Just like we're doing now. We keep bringing them something or interrupting them with whatever we can think of," Angus said. "Seriously though, Master Brett has lots of resources. If he wants too, he'll find a way to seduce her. We can't follow them from the house and we can't interrupt constantly at night."

"Master Brett told me yesterday he wanted to take her on a picnic somewhere," Mrs. Pickery said while she poured a cup of tea. She sat at the table, sipping the hot drink. "He wanted me to pack a basket. At the time I thought it was a great idea and happily agreed."

Angus heaved a huge sigh before joining the cook. "The poor lass, jumped from one fire into another."

"What did I do?" Piper stood in the doorway, her hands clasped in front of her.

"How much did you hear?" Mrs. Pickery asked.

"Enough to know the lot of you think Brett took advantage of my innocence. What you should all know is that I'm far from innocent and he did ask me to marry him several times last night," Piper said with a sigh. "I said no."

"Why would you do that?" Angus asked.

"I'd make a very unsuitable wife for him," Piper said. "What do I know about the kind of life he leads?"

"Why on earth would you say that to him. You're a lovely girl."

"For starters, I grew up in St. Giles parish," she said. "I've seen and done things."

"That's not a good enough reason," Angus said. "Can't you do better than that?"

"If I gave you more reasons, I'd embarrass the lot of you. I've seen and done things that would make you blush."

Angus studied her closely. "Hard to make me blush, lass," he told her. "You can't shock an old man who's seen and done more than you could have possibly experienced in your short life. But if you don't love Master Brett or at least care for him then you should tell him no."

"I'm glad you agree. What's for breakfast?"

"Sent yours upstairs. Thought you'd be eating in the Master chamber," Mrs. Pickery said.

"And playing in his bed. Not that you all need to know but he's made it perfectly clear that he won't take my virginity until I say yes to his proposal."

"Thought you said you weren't innocent," Mrs. Pickery said.

Angus laughed, "So you've managed to wrap him around your little finger. I like that. He's never been challenged before. Stand your ground, lass, until you understand what it is you really want."

Piper pulled off a chunk of bread. "I want to be his mistress. Until then, I think I should get to work."

"No, you don't. Not until you explain yourself, little lady," Mrs. Pickery said. "I won't stand for that. You need a husband and a family not someone who will keep you until they are tired of you then toss you away."

"Never believed I'd have a husband or a family. Thought I'd end up in a whorehouse so I'm just setting my sights on what makes sense. He wants to have sex with me, that's apparent. So, if I become his mistress, we can both have what we want with no regrets."

Chapter Three

Brett pushed his horse hard trying to rid his mind of Piper's resounding no. His body ached from the restraint he prided himself with and showed her last night. He wasn't going to force her hand so he had to figure out how to make her understand she was worthy of becoming his wife. After last night he didn't think he could live without her, and he prayed she felt the same. It was strange to him how easily and quickly she became such an important part of his world.

Slowing his horse to a walk, he absorbed the sun on his skin, let the warming powers heal his ragged nerves. Billy and Bobby would be back, he didn't doubt it. There were reasons beyond his imagination that Scarface wanted Piper. Nefarious reasons he assumed. Getting to the bottom of it would not prove easy, but with Drake Montgomerie on his side they would uncover the man's reasons.

A message had been sent to Drake Montgomerie informing him that he was uprooting his household and returning to Scotland. He felt safer there and knew it would be easier to protect Piper with his clan surrounding him. In any case he wouldn't have to sleep with one eye open expecting B&B to turn up unannounced.

With the sun nearing its zenith he headed back to town. Before he left for Scotland, he was going to find a few readers. Teaching Piper how to read, write as well as her numbers, could keep his mind occupied on the long trip home.

Several stops later, including a few quick minutes at the dressmakers to buy a few more dresses for Piper, he left his horse with the stable boy and headed into the house only to find the servants in an uproar. Piper was nowhere to be seen and Angus was waving his pistol at a man he assumed was Jocko.

"Bout time you got home, sir," Angus said, rubbing the back of his neck, a sheen of sweat beading on his forehead. "This man wants to take Piper away from us. Says he has her best interest in mind, but we both know he doesn't. Want's to keep her on the streets making money for him. In any case, Piper said no she won't go and that's good enough for me."

Brett stepped into the hallway, giving the man a harsh look. "Jocko, I assume. Brandy?" Brett proceeded into the parlor, expecting the man to follow.

"Suppose your polite hospitality means you're amendable to me taking Piper with me." Jocko sat, a grin on his face.

"Not at all. Just want you to understand the consequences if she disappears." Brett handed the man his drink. Then, "Mrs. Pickery, can you send Molly in with some of your berry tarts."

"Consequences? She's like my flesh and blood to me. Made sure she grew up without a scratch on her and also made sure she didn't end up in a whorehouse," Jocko defended himself.

"Didn't stop you from taking her to whorehouse though and making her watch people in the most intimate acts. No lady should have to watch something like that." Brett leaned back in the chair behind his desk, studying the man who knew more about Piper than he did.

Jocko stiffened at Brett's knowledge. "She's no lady. Just did it to protect Piper. She needed to learn what goes on there."

"Piper doesn't need that type of protection, no lady does," With this short conversation Brett confirmed everything Piper told him. Jocko wouldn't give up easily. "Why is she so important to Scarface?"

The man's face drained of color. "Scarface wants her that's all I know. He gave her to me when she was just a few months old. A beautiful little baby, she was. Told me to keep her safe until she was eighteen and I'd be rewarded. She turned eighteen a few months ago, and now I want my reward. I've earned it."

"You've earned everything from Piper you're going to get. From what I've heard about Scarface, the only person he rewards is himself." Brett smiled watching as Jocko squirmed in his seat, turning a bit pale.

"Now that's not true. He's given me money to feed and clothe her when times were hard. We haven't had it easy, you know."

"Well, at least for Miss Piper, times are no longer hard. She's never going to end up in a whorehouse or as anyone's mistress and you, Jocko, are never going to have her beneath you. Do I make myself clear?"

The man nodded and stood, shifting from one foot to the other. "I'll leave now." He drained the glass before sticking the crystal in his pocket, a childish act of defiance but Brett chose to ignore it. B&B had taken more valuable things from the house the other night than that single glass.

For a few minutes after the door shut behind Jocko, Brett held his breath then, "Mrs. Pickery, Angus, Molly!"

They must have been listening at the door and that didn't surprise Brett. "Sir?" They practically fell over themselves getting into the room.

"How much of that conversation did you hear?" he asked, knowing they didn't miss a word of the discussion. "Molly, please retrieve Piper. She needs to hear this also."

"Yes, sir." She left, skirts flying around her feet.

"Take a seat all of you. We'll wait until everyone is here. I intend to say this once and I expect all of you to listen carefully." Brett tapped his glass on the desk impatiently, his gut churning, fully understanding Piper's fear of this man but in his case the emotion was fury.

When Molly returned a few seconds later, "Sir, I can't find her. Looked in her room and yours. She's no place."

His heart caught in his throat, ready to track down Jocko and ring his scrawny neck then he thought, "Did you try the library. Piper loves the library. It would be the perfect place for her to escape seeing Jocko." He couldn't help but hold his breath for a few seconds.

"No, sir, I'll be right back."

He breathed in long breath of relief when he heard the girls talking outside the parlor. The fear swirling in his stomach evaporated for the moment. He didn't doubt it would return from time to time though.

Molly stepped through the door first then Piper who was covered in what appeared to be flour. "Found her in the kitchen, not the library. She had flour spread all across the counter and floor as well as herself."

Piper smiled, "Thought Mrs. Pickery could use some help with the bread. I think I did everything right."

"Oh, my." The cook rose, panic on her face.

"Sit all of you. Whatever mess Piper made will not go away. The flour can be cleaned up later. This dialogue is more important than a loaf of bread."

"No, you're right, Master Brett. You're right. The mess and the bread will be there until someone cleans it up."

"I'll be happy to clean up the spilled flour when we're finished here." Piper sat down, her hands folded innocently in front of her.

"You just leave it to me," Mrs. Pickery said. "Don't want an even bigger mess when you're finally done trying to clean everything up. What did you do with the bread?" she asked almost as an after thought.

"Put the loaf in the oven. Doesn't it have to bake before we can eat it?" Piper asked, the unknowing expression on her face was priceless.

Brett held back the laugh rumbling in his chest and nodded for Mrs. Pickery to rescue the loaf of bread. "Go on, make sure it's not going to burn the house down."

"Thank you." Mrs. Pickery rushed to the kitchen.

"I suppose we should all have a drink. Molly, will you pour the brandy while we wait for Mrs. Pickery?" He wondered if life with Piper would always be this unpredictable and interesting. He was thoroughly enjoying himself.

An eerie silence permeated the room after the cook left in a whirl of petticoats. It seemed no one dared speak. In the interim Brett decided he and Piper would leave the following morning instead of waiting for the rest of the household. She didn't have much to carry with her, and Angus could bring his possessions later. He'd pack what he needed in a small valise. He suddenly found himself eager to be on the road with Piper and see the highlands again.

"Everything's fine," Mrs. Pickery was back. "The bread wasn't burnt. Indeed, I pulled it out and it was baked to perfection. Good thing Piper told us she put it in the oven."

"Then," Brett began, "I've made arrangements for all of us to travel home. Piper and I will leave tomorrow morning and the rest of you by the end of the week."

"For lands sake," Mrs. Pickery let out what sounded like a frustrated sigh. "Seems we just got here. Now you want to uproot us again? My, my, what's this world coming to?"

"It's best for Piper that we leave London and go somewhere I don't have to constantly look over my shoulder to make sure she hasn't been kidnapped. We had a break in last night, the two men were sent to bring Piper back to St. Giles. At home our clan will surround us. Besides I feel the need to breathe clean fresh air and see the heather on the hills. London is not where I want to live."

Piper stood, her face a blank slate, her delicate hands fisted at her sides. "You didn't ask me how I felt about this sudden move?"

It never occurred to him to ask her. This was the most logical and realistic solution to her problem. He wasn't used to anyone questioning him. "Do you want to stay here? I can personally take you to Scarface or I could give you to B&B if that's your preference. Maybe they would get some reward for handing you over to the man you're trying to stay away from."

His sarcasm and anger were more than evident in the tone of his voice, but he didn't regret a moment. She needed to understand the depth as well as the danger Scarface presented. Until they discovered why the man coveted her, he would have a devilishly hard time protecting her.

She paled perceptibly, seeming to understand the reality of his statement. "It still would have been nice if you asked or gave me some hint of what you intended." Her back stiffened even more. "I suppose I'm not too used to anyone telling me what I'm going to do."

"Now child," Mrs. Pickery patted her on the back in what seemed to be an attempt to reassure. "This is for the best and as a woman you best get used to Master Brett telling you what to do. You'll see. Despite my earlier dismay at leaving, I concur with Master Brett. I'm more than eager to return to Scotland where the air is clean and you're not in danger of being swept away from us."

"Well, I'm terrified. All of this is just too new and different for me. All I know is St. Giles and this home and now you want me to settle in somewhere else." Piper left the room without a glance back. Rogue followed, barking at her heels.

Brett decided to give her a moment before going after her. He nodded to Angus. "Make sure she stays in the house. Whatever you do, don't let her go outside."

"Don't know if I can do that, sir, not if she sets her mind to walkin' outside. The lass will do what she wants when she wants. You've got to realize she's not used to takin' orders from anyone let alone me."

He'd seen men outside the townhouse and he hoped all along they were Montgomerie's men lending assistance and not people Scarface or Jocko set to watching the place. There had been no messages. Brett assumed then there was no new information. The reasons for Scarface's interest in Piper were still obscure.

Turning his attention to Molly then, "Do you want to go home or would you like to stay here?"

"Do I have a choice?" she asked, wringing her hands nervously. "If so, I'd like to stay."

"Do you have a job here if we leave?" He was immediately concerned for his maid. Her family had always worked for his.

"No, but I've a proposal. I love him, sir, and I think I can find one, a job. Will you write me a recommendation?" Her shaky voice gave Brett reason for concern, but the look on her face was determined.

"Of course, Molly, and if you ever want to come home, you'll have a job. All you have to do is send me a message and I'll arrange for your transportation." Brett roughed his hands through his hair, hoping to get word from Angus that Piper was fine and taking refuge inside the house. Bloody hell, but he couldn't concentrate on anything.

"So, are we all in agreement? Angus will be in charge starting tomorrow morning. Mrs. Pickery, Piper and I will have dinner downstairs in the dining room in an hour. Please serve the bread Piper attempted to bake whether it's edible or not. I've put men on both the doors and changed up the locks in hopes it will keep the two ruffians who invaded our home last night out and anyone else who is not welcome inside my home. Not planning on any midnight visitors tonight." He would have to insist Piper stay with him this evening and he wasn't sure right now her frame of mind.

The servants dispersed while Brett mulled over his decisions. He wanted to discover the truth about Piper and he was beginning to think there was much more to her story than was originally thought. Jocko didn't know more than he told him this afternoon. That left the truth in the hands of Avery Bainbridge, Scarface, and he wondered if Montgomerie had enough power to uncover that truth.

At home he had more men at his disposal, and he had a few guesses about what might have happened when she was a babe. Drake's story of his younger brother sparked some ideas but they all seemed too farfetched to be true. Even if they proved to be factual there was no proof.

He strode to window, staring at the gardens, dismayed to see Angus rushing after Piper, waving his hands. The man was too old to deal with someone like Piper. "Bloody hell." So much for discretion but the last place Piper should be was outside with only an elderly man to guard her.

Pulling out his desk drawer, he grabbed his pistol and stuffed it into his britches behind him. Then, with another curse he strode forcefully from the house then into the gardens. When he caught up with her, she was bending over a rose and seeming to inhale its fragrance.

"You take chances you shouldn't. Do you want to be whisked away to a whorehouse or to Scarface?" He looked at Angus, "I'll take over now. Go on inside and start the preparations for Piper's and my journey tomorrow. We don't need much. Piper has two more dresses in her room upstairs. I'd like you to pack those and there is also a valise for her to use for her things."

"Thank you, sir. I'm sorry I let her go outside. I'll pack a few things for you. I'll tell Molly and she will pack up for Miss Piper." His words were very nearly breathless and it seemed he practically ran back to the house.

Brett chuckled softly, watching his long-time valet, "Don't think I've ever seen him run quite so fast."

"Angus is a sweet man. I appreciate the fact he wanted to protect me, and I know I shouldn't go outside but..." she turned to look at him. "I'm also sorry if I caused you concern for my health. I've been feeling so confined I have this burning need to scream."

He pulled her into his arms, her back against his chest, his arms settling beneath her breasts. "You're going to love Scotland and the rolling hills. Near my home there's a huge loch. We can go swimming, but the water is almost always cold. Can you swim?" he asked as an afterthought.

"Not very well." She leaned into his chest, relaxing the softness of her body against him.

He was reminded of last night and all the unfulfilled promises between them. "Something else I will look forward to teaching you, my sweet little imp."

"Are you going to torment me again tonight?"

"I don't know. Will you say yes to my proposal?" If she said yes, he'd be pleasantly pleased but shocked. If she said yes, he'd make love to her or at least make sure she discovered the pleasure of lovemaking.

She turned in his arms then and he tried to keep the contact platonic, but it was devilishly hard when he was gazing at the swell of her breasts beneath her half open dress. She had this penchant for fumbling with her buttons until she was half undressed. When they were wed, he'd have less to do to get her naked and beneath him.

She sucked her bottom lip between her teeth, "If you were a commoner and had no money, no status as a Lord, I would say yes without question. But that's not the situation here. I'm a thief, a pickpocket and just not a suitable wife for a man such as you. There is no way around the facts."

"I've heard that argument too many times, Piper. It doesn't matter to me who you were and what circumstances molded you. You have a sweetness about you that is undeniable, and I've found I want to be with you, see you and taste that sweetness every day for the rest of my life. You belong with me through all our good times and bad as well."

"Does that mean you like me." Her laugh was awkward. "I like you too. I also like the way you kiss me and all the places..." She breathed in deeply, seeming loath to finish the sentence.

He didn't know why he felt this way, never felt it with another woman, but he wanted to kiss her until he kicked up his toes. Needed to hold her in his arms every night and know she would always be by his side. "Like is always a good emotion to feel about a person you intend to share a bed with."

It seemed she ignored his statement. "Will you teach me how to shoot? I want to be able to protect myself." She paused and with what could only be considered a flirtatious smile. "Only when you're not around to protect me, of course. I think I'm beginning to understand your manly needs."

Manly needs? I suppose she saw through him and all he'd been taught. "I will teach you anything you like." He could think of a few things he wanted to teach her right now, but he just told her he wasn't going to torment her tonight. Would stealing one kiss be torment? It would be for him because she would give him everything he expected and craved then that would lead to other things.

"Good then, there is reading, shooting, swimming and my numbers for now. I've always had a need to learn but had no one to teach me. Now I have you. Can we start on our way to Scotland? I assume there will be little to do during the carriage ride. Never travelled anywhere before either."

"I did pick up some readers this morning as well as a few more dresses for you. You'll need them. You are no longer my servant."

"How will I...Brett, that's not fair. I need a job and as you well know I can't pay for the dresses." She was breathing heavily, her body shaking.

"I thought you wanted to be my mistress. Was I wrong?" he said trying to maintain a blank look.

"And I believed you wanted a wife, me. Is that why you're not going to torment me tonight? You're actually going to have sex with me because I'm now officially your mistress?" she questioned him and he thought perhaps he found a better way to get her to agree.

"Haven't really thought about any of that. Not sure if we'll have sex even if you're my mistress," he smiled, hoping he was gaining an upper hand as well as a better understanding of his future wife. He was beginning to believe he couldn't force her to his way but could lead her there. If he could figure out how marriage would be her idea.

"You're talking in riddles," she persisted. "I don't like it when you say things and I don't understand what you mean."

"I don't intend to confirm or deny what you're asking simply because I don't have a response. Perhaps we'll have sex or I might make love to you. Then, if things are wrong, I won't touch you and maybe if they're right, I won't either."

Enveloped in his arms, she plucked at his shirt then looked at him, moistening her lips with that tiny sweet tongue he needed to taste. He held back though, unwilling to give in to her obvious ploy.

She pushed away, "We should eat dinner. I don't remember the last time I ate. Mrs. Pickery wants me to eat more. She torments me every day with food. Didn't she say dinner would be in the dining room? I don't think she wants us to spend time in your bedroom."

Brett laughed outright at her antics. "Let's eat and perhaps I've a bottle of wine or two. It's not as strong as the brandy you've been drinking but it's enjoyable."

Seeming to forget the questions at hand, arm in arm they walked to the house and into the dining room. The table was filled with trays of food. "She expects the two of us to eat all this?"

"I suppose she does. We can give it a try. The food might not be very plentiful in the next couple of weeks. Life in a carriage can be uncomfortable. We'll stop often since we're not in a hurry."

"Couple of weeks? It's going to take that long?" She sat down and watched him pour a generous glass of wine.

"More if the weather turns bad." He lifted his glass. "To a safe and speedy trip. And finding a way to convince you to wed me."

"To a trip filled with learning. I want to be able to read when we reach your home." She sipped the wine, smiling at him when she set the glass down. "Don't think we'll be able to swim."

"I don't want to burst your expectations. While you should be able to read very basic texts, that book you were staring at the other day will still elude you." He didn't like the fact he caused her smile to change to a frown.

"I'm determined. I understand it won't be easy, but I'm going to try so hard you'll be proud of me." She drank again, her eyes closing slowly then opening. "This is very good. I like the way it tastes. Unlike the brandy the wine doesn't burn going down."

"I'm always proud of you. You've overcome so much. I think you had your dog pick my pocket because you wanted me to catch you."

The shock on her face seemed calculated. "That's not true," she protested too quickly.

"Maybe. Maybe not." He smiled, dishing up her plate. "You need to eat tonight. I watch you pick at your food and wonder why you don't eat. You have to be hungry."

"Honestly?" she asked, her fork pushing items from side to side.

"Yes."

"I don't know what most of this is. I've always eaten bread and sometimes when things were really good, cheese and a meat pie here and there. Once in a great while an apple if I found an apple tree."

"You liked the plums I gave you the other day. If you trust me, I assure you everything except maybe the Brussels sprouts are tasty. I dare you to take one bite of each thing on your plate." He issued a challenge expecting her to accept the test.

She grimaced, scrunching her features together. "Alright, I'll take that dare and when I think of something appropriate, you will take the challenge I dole out to you."

"I accept." He set his fork on his plate and watched as she separated each item and took the smallest bite possible.

"I liked everything." She set her fork down, grinning.

"Even the Brussels sprouts?" he questioned, watching her expressive face.

"I must because I don't know what here are Brussels sprouts." She began to eat again, then waving her fork at him. "You need to eat too. Enough tests for this evening. Let's just enjoy ourselves."

"I love watching you too much." Another button on her dress slipped free and he wondered just when that happened. Wondered too if it was calculated then dismissed his own question. Was she trying to seduce him? Even after last night?

"I like watching you, more so when your shirt is off." She bit into a piece of salmon she separated earlier.

"I'd like to see you with your dress completely unbuttoned." He smiled watching her eyes darken. The little imp was calculating and hinting at kisses.

He poured her a third glass of wine trying not to show emotion. "Should we take our wine to my room?" he asked rising and pulling out her chair. He grabbed the bottle of wine and offered his arm.

"I'd like that a lot. Do you think Angus started a fire in the fireplace?" She leaned into him, pressing against him.

In the art of seduction his little imp was indeed a fast learner. "If not, I'll make sure we've a fire."

In his chamber a fire crackled merrily, inviting a seduction that wasn't going to happen, at least not tonight. "Do you think anyone will try to break in tonight?"

"If so, they'll meet more resistance. I made sure B&B know if they're caught, they will end up in prison. I don't think they'll come. Scarface could send other men."

She sat on the bed, crossing her legs, watching him over the rim of the crystal glass she held. "Are you going to let me sleep here tonight?"

He swirled the wine in his glass, wishing she would say yes and at the moment he had no wish to repeat last night. "You can sleep anywhere you like, but Rogue is not going to join us on the bed. Actually, I do prefer you stay in this room."

She plucked at her skirts, looking at him, moistening her lips and seeming uncomfortable as hell. "I can't stop thinking about the way you touched me and kissed me the other evening."

"I can't either. Like to do it again but I'm going to wait." He leaned against the bedpost.

With a heavy sigh she closed her eyes. "Scotland..." she paused. "What's it like?"

Good. She was curious and perhaps resigned to her new home. "Where I live in the summers the sun stays out longer than here. Sometimes it's light until almost midnight and in the winters the sun sets too early. The days are short."

"And the weather?" she queried. "I don't much like the snow. I'm always so cold when it snows here. Don't have warm clothes or a fireplace to warm my hands."

He pushed away, walking to stare out the window, wondering how long it would take to make her his. "You won't be left outside where it's cold. I'll make sure you stay warm and my home has a fireplace in almost every room. You'll also have a warm coat to wear if you go outside."

"You can't promise something like that," she said, finishing the wine before pouring herself a bit more. She looked at the liquid in the glass for a few seconds. "I've heard my share of promises and none have ever been kept."

"I can." He sat down beside her, lightly touching her face. He needed to kiss her again but he would wait a little longer. "You'll have warm clothes, everything you'll need, unlike the way you used to live in St. Giles."

"That sounds nice" She rested her hand on his chest. "I have to find a way to pay for everything you give me. If I've suddenly become your mistress, I should start tonight."

At that small contact, he sucked in a breath of air. "You shouldn't play with fire," he told her. "And, you'll never be my mistress."

"Is that what I'm doing? Playing with fire?" she asked even while she daringly flirted with him.

"You know it is, but I've got things to do if we're going to leave early tomorrow morning. I'll either leave you here or walk you to your quarters." He watched her reaction unable to tell what she was thinking.

She rose, glass still in hand but looking expectantly at him. "Can I help with whatever you have to do? Don't want to stay here alone."

"You can't. It would only take more time and neither of us will find sleep." He didn't like seeing the disappointment in her eyes but there was nothing for it. "You can lock the door behind me. I've a key to get back inside."

"You go. I'll finish the bottle of wine." She tilted her head slightly. "When you come back, who knows what you'll find."

"You'll wait up for me then." He loved the passion in her eyes and the slight movement of her breasts. He could see the curves, needed to see more.

"I'll warm the bed." She moved closer to him, placing her hand on his chest, toying with the fastenings of his shirt.

Little imp, single handedly and in one night he created a sex monster. She didn't care if he left her needing something more. All this cemented the notion that he had to discover a different tact if he wanted her agree to the proposal.

"That would be nice. Hmm...a warm bed. I'll look forward to it. Just make sure Rogue isn't part of this bargain. I shouldn't be gone for much more than an hour," he said, holding her hand in his then kissing the palm.

"What are you going to do?"

"Make sure everything is ready for our departure. Nothing you need worry about."

~ * ~

The hours sitting in the carriage rolled on endlessly. The nights were even longer while he slept next to her without touching her, barely speaking to her at times. The only consolation was that she was learning to read. The task was harder than anything she'd tried in the past. He was right though in his assessment; she wouldn't be able to read everything that was set in front of her for a long time.

It seemed she did better with numbers than letters though. She could add and subtract big numbers in her head and she was learning to multiply and divide. He always looked so amazed when she got the right answers to the problems he tossed her way.

"Are we stopping so early?" she asked, brushing hair from her eyes. It had grown but it still wasn't long enough to secure away from her face and out of her eyes. She'd wanted to cut it because it just got in her way and tickled her nose when breezes blew, but he encouraged her to let it grow, telling her he wanted to see it long.

He smiled helping her down then giving orders to the driver. "It's the last inn before home. We should be there early tomorrow morning, unless you want to sleep in of course. We have some decisions that need to be made."

"You look awfully pleased with yourself." She loved seeing him so light hearted. When they were in London it seemed he always sported crease lines between his eyes. Of course, she felt different too. She couldn't remember the last time she looked over her shoulder to see if Jocko stalked her.

"Breathe in the fresh air." He turned, inhaling a long deep breath. "Didn't realize how much I missed this place. What would you like to do? A walk maybe? This is my family's land. I grew up running across these hills."

She looked around, except for the land the inn sat on and the road, trees reached to the sky. "A walk but where would we go?"

He pointed. "There's a loch just beyond this building. You could have your first swimming lesson. I could strip you naked and..."

"Let's just settle for a walk today." She wasn't sure she was ready for a lesson in the cold water. She also wasn't sure what he'd expect her to wear. He wouldn't strip her naked when there were people everywhere.

"Is my sweet little imp a coward or a bricky lass?"

Her back stiffened at the word coward. Yet she vowed to herself early on this trip she would be honest with him. "Don't know if I'm a coward, but I am afraid of what I don't know. Since I've been with you, everything has been new and so different. Now we're a day away from your home in a place... It's not anything like London. There are no carriages and buggies whizzing by, no vendors on the streets, no stench..."

"No, thank God." He grinned, holding her hand in his. "Let's walk to the loch and we'll decide there. Perhaps another day I can teach you to swim."

"Is this some kind of trick?" Since they'd been traveling Brett didn't mention marriage nor did he touch her intimately and there had been no kisses shared between them. She wanted him to kiss her again, craved his touches. At night in bed together, he held her but that was all. Confusion and annoyance at her insecurities assailed her. While she needed to please him, she also needed to please herself.

"Trick? I don't understand. It's just a walk, nothing more." Wrapping an arm around her, he pulled her close. "I might steal a kiss or two."

"I don't trust you. Well, that came out all wrong. I do trust you but..." Her thoughts were all in a jumble. "Never mind anything I just said. I trust you with my life and I know a lot of what I said and did in London was," she paused, "I don't know what it was. I acted as if certain things didn't matter... Never mind," she said again, thoroughly frustrated with herself and what she was trying to tell him.

"Piper, relax we both know that speaking your mind is something you do very well, but since we left London it's been different for you hasn't it?" As if to give reassurance, he squeezed her shoulder.

"I still think you're up to something. I don't know what it could possibly be, but I mean to find out sooner than later."

"Like what?" He laughed. "You're suspicious today. Why?"

She needed to ignore his question as well as the statement. On a narrow trail, they walked beneath the trees, listened to the animals as they chattered to each other. As he told her, the loch was in front of them, sunlight shimmering off the water, leaving a breathtaking silver hue. It was beautiful and she'd never seen a lake so large.

Well, for that matter, she'd never seen a lake.

"You didn't answer me," he told her, stopping then and turning her. Slowly his lips descended to meet hers, hovering so close as to nearly touch. "I've wanted to do this since that last time when we almost had sex. May I?"

She sucked in a deep breath of air, knowing how much she craved the same thing. She couldn't deny him. In any case, she didn't want to deny him anything. That thought shook her to her core. She'd been doing just that by refusing to marry him. "Yes," she whispered. "Kiss me, please."

"It's about time you said yes to something I asked. Maybe you'll agree to other things too." His finger under her chin, he slowly lifted it. She could see into his eyes, his were such a dark shade of brown. She closed her eyes when he lowered his mouth to her lips. His were soft, pressed against hers and he touched her lightly then ran his tongue across them.

"You taste sweet, just like I remembered. Will you open for me?" His hands rested on the small of her back. She moved in closer needing to feel the warmth and comfort he offered even though there was a chasm between what he needed and she wanted.

Piper didn't have a reply for him, but she gave him access to her, would do anything for him. He explored her, the inside of her mouth and she reciprocated, feeling the nirvana he created inside. She moaned softly as he deepened the kiss.

Moving closer to him, her hands resting on his shoulders, she ran her fingers through his hair. The leather thong he bound his hair with fell to the ground. He taught her well and she'd forgotten nothing. She became the aggressor, afraid he might stop with just the kiss. She needed to prolong this as long as possible, craving him and so afraid she'd lose him with the truth.

She ran her tongue across his teeth then into his mouth. He growled low and from the back of his throat. Their lips met again and again, tiny sounds emanating from her.

She didn't want to let him go but he pulled away. His features were shuttered and she didn't know what to make of his expression or lack. He paused, watching her so intensely she shuddered, "You didn't really want to go swimming."

"No, I wanted to kiss you and let you know I've decided to give you what you want." He ran a fingertip along her cheek. "I'll give you everything you want. All you have to do is ask and it's yours."

"How do you know what I want when I don't even know that?" She pushed away from him and headed for the water's edge, unsatisfied and annoyed, perhaps a little bit confused.

He caught up with her, held her arm for a moment to stop her. "Have you changed your mind?" His gaze bore into her and challenged her in so many ways, too many ways to count.

"About what? I think I've changed my mind about everything." She began walking again, gazing at the water, counting the ripples as they reached the shoreline.

"You haven't told me how you're feeling. I need for you to do that."

"And you haven't asked me," she countered, breaking away from him now nearly running along the water's edge, distraught. Needing the distance to figure out what to say to this man who turned her world upside down. He meant everything to her and was her only family now.

This time he didn't stop her but kept pace. "So now's your chance to tell me what you changed your mind about. I won't..." he paused, seeming unsure for the first time about what he wanted to say. "This is new to me too. I've never asked a woman to become my mistress who I once wanted for a wife."

"You tell me what you were talking about." She was afraid now, terrified he no longer wanted to wed her. It had taken so long for her to understand the difference in the proposals, mistress versus wife. Now when she came to a decision what the devil was he thinking?

"Well," he paused as if thinking, his handsome and oh so debonair grin giving her hot chills. "I've decided since you are so adamant about becoming my mistress instead of my wife, I'll oblige you. I've found that keeping my hands to myself when you're in bed with me is becoming nearly impossible. I also know I want you sleeping next to me for the rest of my life. What choice do I have? I guess one could say that you called my bluff."

She pushed back the moisture filling the back of her throat and threatening to pool in her eyes. She wasn't going to cry, ever. "I think you once told me there is always a choice."

He pulled her close, pushing flyaway hair behind her ears. "I want you and you know it and I think you feel the same way. Correct me if I'm wrong."

She was shaking her head; her usual accurate assessment of a situation had gone horribly wrong. She had weeks to tell him how she felt and she kept it to herself. What was she to do now? She didn't dare tell him about her change of thought.

"I want you too," she admitted, unable to breathe. "Need you as much as I need to breathe."

"Good, then we can agree. Tonight, we can finish what we began a few weeks ago in my bedroom. Will you like that?" He didn't give her a chance to answer. His lips met hers in a magical and enchanting kiss promising so much yet not enough.

The assurance of her future vanished with his words. Her dreams evaporating just as the mist did on a heated morning. She needed to tell him the truth but she couldn't find the words.

His lips met hers again, the kiss long and slow while she melted into him the sweetness overwhelming her. He could do this to her, take all rational thought from her head with just a kiss. She ran her hands up his back in an attempt to pull herself closer yet not even a breath of air separated them.

He drew away. His forehead rested against hers. She watched him moisten his lips, the tiny gesture somehow erotic. "We should go back to the inn before I take you here on the water's edge where anyone could see us. I want our first time to be magical," His breathing was heavy, his voice raspy.

She bracketed his face with her hands. "You know I'd never tell you to stop but I don't think I can walk that far. Your kisses have this way of unraveling me one tiny strand at a time." Closing her eyes, she felt the soft touch of his lips against her, moist gentleness, caressing her.

"I can remedy that." He scooped her into his arms, cradling her close and striding down the narrow path.

She rested her head on his shoulder, her fingers toying with the buttons on his shirt. "Can we do this slowly?" She was suddenly unsure and the rapid escalation of her emotions terrified her.

The games she played with Brett as well as her past seemed to accumulate and grow. It was all true, everything she told him. She'd watched whores with their johns and Jocko had tutored her in the ways and wants of men but she never experienced anything like this.

"Anything you want, little imp but after the weeks of wanting and waiting..." He paused seeming to recognize the fear in her eyes. "What is it? You've never been afraid of my touch. You've welcomed everything I've done."

"Set me down, please." She started to speak then stopped, thinking of the right words. "I think I was in a different world. I was playing a game I thought you needed me to play. You've pampered me and I've seen how other people live. When we have sex, when I become your mistress, I want you to have the greatest pleasure and even with what I've seen and done, I don't know what that is. I've no idea how to bring you pleasure."

"Let me get this straight." He chuckled softly, his smile wide and infectious. "You want to give me pleasure."

She nodded several times, feeling the rush of embarrassment result in heated cheeks. "Is that wrong?" She was only his mistress for a few minutes and she was messing everything up.

"Nothing is wrong, sweet darling. We will do this slowly. Perhaps with some food and a little wine."

"It doesn't have to be as soon as we're back to the inn?" she asked, wishing she had some idea what to say to him.

"Let's just walk back and see what mischief Rogue has gotten himself into since we've been away. I half expected to see him running after you when we walked but he's nowhere in sight."

"He's most likely in the kitchen trying to steal some food, and if he's on his good behavior, he'll stare at the workers until they toss him something." The thought gave her serious thoughts a lighthearted boost.

He wrapped his arm around her waist while they retraced the path they took earlier. She tried to focus on him.

"I've booked the rooms for you and Miss Piper," their driver said, handing over the keys to the rooms, "and I've arranged for dinner to be sent to your room. Did you want a bottle of wine or tea?"

He looked at her then and making their arrangement clear, "Both. And we don't want two rooms. Not tonight." It seemed there was no longer a need for pretense.

She might want some brandy. It seemed an eternity since that first night when the house was broken into and he touched her so gently and so very intimately. "Could we get some brandy too?" she spoke up, knowing he would agree to her request.

He roared with laughter. "I don't think I want you drunk, sweet imp." He bent close to whisper in her ear. "A little more relaxed than you are now but I want you to remember tonight. I've waited a long time for this to happen."

"And you've been a very patient man." She laughed too, realizing he didn't expect her to know everything from her whorehouse tutorials.

"But now I'm eager and taking this slowly will be difficult." He smiled at her, his fingers squeezing slightly.

"I'll try and reward you for your patience, but you might have to tell me what to do." She also realized she'd never really seen this side of Brett. With the decision made, he seemed more carefree than ever. Of course they were on his land, Scottish land. His clan was only a few hours away. Indeed, the owners of this inn were his clan also.

"Here we are." He swept her into his arms and after unlocking the door he walked across the threshold. She didn't understand why, but it was nice and before he set her on the floor, his lips brushed gently across her. The caress was soft and even a slow deep kiss. One that didn't demand a response yet mercuric heat rushed through her at the brief contact.

Waiters appeared with food and drinks. They were alone now, and again he'd expect certain things. She watched as he loosened his shirt. During the days of travel, he dressed more casually than when they were in London. Today he wore buckskins and a white shirt that laced in front.

She smoothed her skirts, wondering what was expected of her. He helped her with the cape she wore. Now she stood in front of him, her fingers winding into her skirts. Her heart raced in anticipation.

"What are you afraid of?" he asked, unfastening a few buttons on her dress. "Hmm... Maybe one more. There I like it that way, reminds me of when you used to dust my library."

"Aren't I supposed to seduce you? What does a mistress do?" She tried to remember what she'd seen in the whorehouses, but they were mostly unclothed when she watched them.

"Whatever feels normal and natural. Come sit down and have a bite to eat." He poured them wine.

She sat across the table from him, sipping her wine and watching him over the rim of the goblet. "Can we just do this now? Have sex?" she asked suddenly believing her shaking hands would calm when they actually had sex and not a moment before. "I want to get it over with so I don't have to think about what's going to happen next."

"Aw...my little imp, that is not the way I want my first time with you to happen. Are you impatient or terrified? Just a few minutes ago you wanted to go slowly."

"Both maybe," she said, downing the glass of wine then pouring herself another one. "I just don't know what to do or what you expect me to do."

"If you keep that up, I'll have to ring for a second bottle and you won't enjoy what I've planned." He spoke smoothly, his voice low and deep.

"I need to make the plans. Remember, since I'm your mistress, it's my job to give you pleasure. This isn't about me." She recalled how the whores stroked the men and ran their lips along their sex to the tip and back. Would he like her to do that to him or would it repulse him? The men certainly seemed to enjoy it.

"In my mind tonight is about you. Tomorrow night or the next one we can make it about me if you'd like but not tonight." He relaxed against the back of his chair, two fingers on the stem of the glass, twirling it slightly.

"It's just I'm so worried. I'm afraid I won't do this right." She squirmed in her seat and fiddling with the buttons on her dress two more burst free.

"Don't be nervous or over think this. There is nothing you can do wrong." Standing and walking to her, he pulled her from the chair. "Come, let's sit on the bed with our wine and see what happens, or would you rather sit in front of the fire on the fur rug?"

She licked her lips, looking from one place to the other then squinting her eyes at him. "What would you like to do?"

"That's not entirely fair putting the question back to me. But if I were to be honest, this first time I think I prefer to sit in front of the fire for a short while. It might be considered romantic to watch the flames."

"The fireplace then," she said too quickly, moving in that direction.

He set their glasses on the hearth. "Lean against me."

"If that's what you want."

"What are you thinking now?" he asked as she let her head fall against his chest and enjoyed the feeling of his fingers roaming along her ribcage then higher as he unbuttoned more of her dress.

The caress of his lips on the back of her neck surprised her, sent heated shivers down her spine. Soft lips, hard teeth, exploring her while it seemed her bodice slowly slipped off her shoulders.

"What are you thinking?" She was mindless as his fingers cupped her breasts and played with the hard tips.

"You've done it again but I'll answer first. You are so soft, and smell so sweet and I want to learn about all of you tonight, leave nothing unturned. I crave to touch and caress every inch of your beautiful body."

She pulled her arms from the sleeves then turned. Now was the time to tell him she no longer wanted to be his mistress. But what if he stopped, what if he agreed to this arrangement because he didn't want her as a wife. Better to stop this now then. "Brett," she trailed a fingertip between the lacings of his shirt.

"What." His teeth closed gently on her earlobe.

She shuddered, her mind going blank for a second. Then she blurted, "I don't want to be your mistress. That's what I changed my mind about." Her breath rushed out then it didn't seem she could inhale another one.

"You don't want sex with me? I'm going to have to see what can be done about that," he said as his lips softly traveled from her ear along her chin to settle so close to her mouth yet not touching while his fingers continued their exploration of her breasts.

"I didn't say that." She moistened her lips and her touch caressed his mouth. She needed more than the slight distance between them.

"What are you saying then?"

"You're not going to make this easy for me, are you?" she asked as his lips claimed hers, their tongues meeting in a primal dance creating a molten inferno sweeping within. Her heart sped while blood pounded through her.

"I don't want to make it difficult. I just wanted to know what you were thinking." His teeth tugged gently on her lip. "What is it, Piper? What is on your mind?"

She clung to him, her body spinning out of control. "I...I want to be your wife, not your mistress."

"So." He pulled slightly away, only a whisper of air between them. "You've changed your mind. How do I know you won't change it again tomorrow after you've had your wicked way with me?"

"Does it matter?" she asked.

"It does for me."

She pushed away from him, irritated once more with him. "Why would I change my mind again?"

He lifted his broad shoulders in an indifferent gesture before slipping the straps of her chemise from her shoulder. Her breasts were full and the tips hard, seeming to need his touch. "Really, at the moment, your decision doesn't matter in any case. Once we're legally married you can't change your mind and it has no affect what so ever on what is going to happen tonight." He drew a nipple into his mouth, sucking and biting gently until her body moved in the rhythm he set.

The sounds emerging from her were soft moans of pleasure. She clung to his head now, pulling him toward her, needing him so very much. Tugging his shirt upward, he distanced himself from her so she could take it off. Then her breasts touched his chest, enticing and arousing her.

She wanted to give him pleasure and except for what she'd seen, all she knew was how she experienced her pleasure. Settling her mouth over his nipple she licked and nibble enjoying the deep groan springing from him.

"I want to see you, all of you." She stared at him, her gaze riveted on his darkening eyes. Eyes that seemed filled with passion and desire.

"As I do you," he spoke slowly, lifting her so she could shimmy out of her dress and underclothes. Except for her stockings she was naked. "Leave them. There is something erotic about a woman dressed in only her lacy stockings."

She sat beside him, unfastening his buckskins and watching as he tugged off his boots then his pants. "Can I touch you?" she asked hoping he would like her caress.

"Not this time," he said holding her hand. "I think we should move this to the bed." Carrying her to the bed he set her there then slowly came down on top of her, her legs spread wide for him.

For the longest time, he gazed at her. It seemed all of her, his brows crinkling together for a moment. His changing expressions unnerved Piper. She wasn't sure at all what he was thinking.

"We are on the bed, now..." she reminded him.

He lightly stroked her leg, from the tips of her toes, to the very center of her desire. A second and a third time as he watched her and she could not help it but her hips moved as in silent invitation. Yet still he gazed upon her until he followed the path of his fingers with his lips, seeming to leave no part of her untouched.

Heat built inside, burning her, promising so much yet she was unfulfilled and she knew she wasn't giving him pleasure. Although when she gazed upon his sex, he was aroused, just like the other men she'd seen. But he didn't look like the other men. His stomach was well muscled and hips narrow. Every part of him was beautiful as raw power emanated from him.

"Brett." She moaned softly unable to find relief from this mercuric need he enveloped her in. "Please."

He found her lips with his while he caressed her intimately and seemed to bring her higher and higher to a pleasure she couldn't describe, a burning need that couldn't be appeased. She closed her eyes tightly, reaching for something she didn't understand, while her hips moved to meet him.

"This will hurt for just a moment then I'll make sure you are well satisfied."

She watched the lines on his face deepen as he slowly entered then thrust quickly. The pain intense, she let a cry escape but he held her, "I didn't think..." She moistened her lips but the pain vanished as quickly. He filled her and made her one with him. Heat could not rise so swiftly and yet it did. Mounting, sweet, thundering, unrestrained, it rose as if a warm summer storm swept within her, brought her to an intense and shocking climax and cast her down tenderly and amazingly to earth once again. He gave her no reason to question what they did and no chance to wonder at the beauty now that he possessed her. Still holding her so very close, still entwined with each other, he rose above her.

"Tell me again you want to be my wife not my mistress and I will see that the vows happen tomorrow. Say the word, sweet imp. Reassure me that your promise to me true. I need to hear it again."

She gasped, stunned by the ferocity of his voice, knowing she had never truly understood the depth of her feelings for this man or what the proposal had meant to him. Now   she could be positive of nothing.

"I spoke true," she said her words whisper soft while she lightly touched his face. "But if you don't want to wed me..."

"I didn't say that. I just need to be sure of your intentions before we carry this further and I present you to my clan as my wife. You have to be sure."

~ * ~

Avery Bainbridge paced the small room he rented for meetings such as this one. He couldn't tolerate fools and it seemed fools were precisely who he'd been dealing with the last month. A message would have to be sent to the Goldwyns post haste. They would need to know the real heiress was no longer in his custody. Although he regretted the loss of the blackmail money, he didn't intend to go to prison for this deed or meet his executioner. What the Goldwyns didn't know was that Piper wasn't the man's brother's daughter. He used her as a ruse in his attempt to get even with someone else. They also didn't know the child was a boy, not a girl.

He should have drowned the baby the day he killed her father and poisoned the unsuspecting mother of a different child, but for some odd reason Melanie Goldwyn wanted the child kept alive or at least she didn't want to be responsible for the murder of an infant. So, he kept both babies alive waiting for the right moment. As time passed however, he found another way to use the girl. She was such an adorable child and he knew she would grow into a beautiful woman. He had plans for the boy as well.

"Do you have any idea where MacLachlan took Piper? Of course you do. The problem was you let her get away in the first place." His anger threatened to overcome his common sense. Days ago, they hashed over this very thing and Jocko swore he'd get her back, promised. "You'll pay dearly if you don't find her and bring her back to me."

"I'm sure they left for his home in Scotland. It wasn't until his entire household departed that I learned of their travel. It seems they left in silence. I would have reported it sooner." Jocko's voice shook.

Yes, the man should fear for his life. Yet Avery waved his hand in the air, spittle flying from his lips. "Get her back." That was all he could say, anger overwhelming him. He'd never lost in this game he played simply because everyone understood their lives were in jeopardy if they failed him.

"Sir, her worth seems overrated to me. She's just a lass, nothing more. If you were lookin' to bed her, I'm sure you can find another woman just as lovely. I'm not understanding..."

"Of course you don't understand. You're hired help, not paid to make decisions or understand my reasons."

"But sir..."

"The information surrounding her and her value are not privy to you and never will be. All you need know is that she is a valuable asset, one that needs to be regained." He thought on all the years he made sure Piper stayed alive. Even had men watching her to make sure she wasn't violated. And now this, an upstart Scotsman gets directly in the path of his plans. Why would the MacLachlan take such an interest in a commoner?

"It will be more difficult to retrieve Piper from the Scotsman's home. But my boys and me will be more than willing to give it a try for the right price," Jocko offered, seeming to relax into his chair as he sipped the brandy Avery offered.

"It's just as well you and your boys stay away. MacLachlan's no idiot. He sees you coming and you'll be in chains in the dungeon in Edinburgh before you can blink." Avery paced the room now spinning one idea after another, each seeming worse than the second.

"Don't know why you'd say that," Jocko said. "Don't want to lose the lass either. Seems if I'm in for a penny I'm in for a pound. Thinkin' I should understand the risks you keep eluding to."

"Better you don't know anything. Now go on with you. If I need you again, I'll send a message."

"I'll get her back for you." Jocko slipped the empty glass in his pocket, leaving the room and cursing the gentry and the uppity way they talked to the men they hired and should trust.

Avery poured himself another glass of brandy then, gazing into the fire he began to slowly form a plan. He knew he had to take offense in this game of intrigue or he'd end up drawing his last breath at Tyburn's

Tree. He didn't relish the stay in Newgate prison then the ride via horse and cart to embark on a journey through St. Giles then down Oxford Street only to arrive at the hanging tree. Nor did he relish the people who would line the streets and the hours it would take to arrive there.

He chuckled though. Jocko would make a fortune at the event if it happened. With all the people watching, his little tribe of pickpockets would certainly benefit from his execution. Too bad the drama wouldn't happen. He didn't intend to get caught and there were no longer executions at the Tyburn Tree, only Newgate prison.

Avery downed his brandy before sitting at his desk and penning a letter to Melanie and Bertram. They would need to be told of the possible disaster waiting for all of them. Didn't matter this was a different child. All their lies could topple all of them.

Melanie and Bertram,

Due to no fault of my own, I've lost contact with the child we've both had great interest in over the last eighteen years. It seems a Scotsman decided to give her a home with him. I've no idea in what capacity, as a servant or a mistress or even his whore. In any case we need to take grave care. If there are any incriminating papers you might still have, get rid of them. Our situation is no longer as secure as it used to be. I had plans to wed Piper thus making sure her identity would remain secret forever. Presently, that is not possible.

Sincerely,
Avery

What he didn't tell them was he had plans to use Piper for long waited revenge. He despised her family, especially her father. When he sold her to the highest bidder he would feel heaven on earth. There was really no way for anyone to prove he helped the Goldwyns. Really, Melanie shouldn't have had remorse about the killing of babies. Without Piper now... He'd helped keep her alive because he wanted revenge.

Chapter Four

Brett whistled as he dressed in more formal clothes than his buckskins and white shirt. After all he was getting married today. Today he was wearing his kilt with the dress plaid of his clan, the sporran and knee-high socks. Also, a velvet double-breasted jacket of deep blue decorated with lace around the neck.

He gazed at his sleeping soon to be wife, having kept her up most of the night with many different ways to make love, some he initiated and some she witnessed in the whorehouse. She pleased him, pleased him greatly and he didn't believe he would ever tire of her. He wanted to make this day one she would remember with pleasure the rest of her life.

In a few hours she would be his wife and a few more hours after that he'd be showing her their home, his home. He sent a message. A celebration would be waiting for them. Kissing her on the cheek and leaving her a note he was pretty sure she could read, he closed the door to their room behind him.

He took the steps two at a time, eager to set up the arrangements for the wedding as well as meet with his longtime friend Collin Stewart. Grabbing a bite to eat and arranging for a breakfast to be sent to their room in two hours, he strode to the stables. A few minutes later he was headed to the village church.

The day was sunny, the sky a bright cerulean blue with few clouds. Piper put a song in his heart he didn't understand. When he was with her everything seemed more beautiful.

"Welcome, Brett," Collin greeted him. They embraced, slapping each other on the back. "The message you sent implied you're getting wed today? What makes you think I'll bear witness to such a dastardly thing and preside over the ceremony?" he laughed as they strode into the church. "Usually banns are read and..."

Brett interrupted with a chuckle. "Because this is my land, my clan and you're my friend."

"So, you found a lass worthy of your station who you can love forever," Colin said lightly seemingly in disbelief. "I'm surprised."

"I found a lass who intrigues me and is never boring. Don't know if I love her, but I don't want to live without her. She has a secret I mean to discover but for now," he paused, "if she's in my bed every night, I'm a happy man."

"Sounds like love to me," Collin laughed. "So, what's her story? She some rich heiress you met in London?"

"Hardly, not sure if I should tell you everything. I might have to kill you."

"Now you have to tell me," Collin said. "What did she do, rob you?"

"Her dog picked my pocket and stole my purse. So, I suppose if you get technical you can accuse her of the deed. Best day of my life when I caught up to her and took her home."

"Bloody eyes, why'd you do that?"

"Not too sure. At the time I thought she was a he. Finding out she wasn't a lad is another story altogether."

"Perhaps I'll have to sit down with you and have a pint. You can tell me the story in its entirety," Collin said.

"So, you'll wed us today in a couple of hours. She's still asleep but as soon we're done here, I'll get her. Don't want anything fancy just something that will be official and binding. Don't want any questions later."

"You consummated the marriage before the wedding. Not something that is advisable," Collin guessed.

"Couldn't keep my hands to myself. Asked her weeks ago but she refused to be anything but my mistress. Said she wasn't suitable for me."

"I take it you didn't agree with her."

"Because she was born a commoner..."

"And a pickpocket I'm assuming from St. Giles..."

Brett waved his hand in the air dismissing Collin's statement. "...Made no difference to me then and still doesn't. She challenges me, makes me a better person. And like I told you there is something else about her that intrigues me."

"You think she has another story but you have no proof." Collin sat down in the church, beckoning for Brett to follow suit.

"She does. There is no reason Avery Bainbridge would be so preoccupied with her unless that was true. Jocko and his boys broke into my home to abscond with her. There is something going on here that needs to be figured out."

"Avery you say... You think marriage to you will keep her safe from Scarface? His reputation is felt even here in the Highlands and I've heard many stories that echo his name," Collin said.

Brett let out a heavy sigh, "It can't hurt. Should we plan on noon for the ceremony? I'd like to sleep in my bed tonight and introduce her to the staff today. I think you'll like her. She's a bit different though." For some reason he wanted everyone to like Piper. To him, she was such a breath of fresh air.

"Whenever you get her here. You said she was still asleep. I'm sure my housekeeper will want to do something for the two of you, but I'm guessing you won't want a celebration until you're home."

"I want to get home tonight. I've had a feeling someone was following us for a long time." He did leave her alone in their room but he felt it was secure. Still the sooner he returned and they were married the better he'd feel.

"Go on then, I'll see you soon," Colin rose and extended his hand. "I'll let my housekeeper make a cake and we'll open a bottle of wine just to send the two of you off in good style."

They shook hands, and Brett left, once more feeling his life was beginning to fall into place. When he opened the door to his room, Piper was eating the food he ordered for her, greeting him with a smile.

He sat beside her and with a cup of tea in hand, "Are you ready to get married?" He kissed the back of her hand, wishing he had time to take her to bed before they left.

"Do you still want to marry me," she asked setting her fork on the table, gazing at him with her deep blue eyes, her hair sticking out in too many places to count.

"Only if that's what you want. You haven't changed your mind, have you?" he asked, his heart in his throat, waiting for her response.

"I want to be your wife." She spoke without hesitation. "No, I haven't changed my mind."

"Good then, let's get you dressed so I can wed you then undress you again." He looked through her things, finally coming up with the dress he had made especially for this occasion before he left London and underthings as well. "Would you like help?" If he assisted, he might not get her dressed fast enough to get married and travel the distance to the church.

"Just with my corset then you best leave or we won't accomplish your," she paused thoughtfully, "our plans for today." She turned her back to him, offering the laces. Then, "I've never seen you in a kilt."

"Do you like it?"

"Yes," she smiled. "What's under it?"

He chuckled, ignoring the question. "Come downstairs as soon as you are ready. I'm eager for this to be official." He couldn't help himself. Before he left her to finish dressing, he trailed a line of kisses across her shoulders.

In the lobby of the inn, he paced. Every few seconds he stopped to look at the stairs and when he didn't see her, resumed his walking. When she finally stood at the top of the steps, his heart caught in his throat. Majestically, as if she was a queen descending the steps, she walked to him, an impish smile on her face, her eyes shining and filled with passion.

"You're so beautiful you stole my breath. You enhance the dress." He reached out for her hand. The pale blue silver lame over a blue satin slip created an enchanting picture against her porcelain skin and dark black hair. Other exquisite details combined with Belgium lace made the dress gorgeous, but it was the woman who wore it that was the most beautiful. And it was the fact the colors represented the Scottish flag that caused him to choose this dress. After she wed him, she'd be Scottish and he hoped she'd embrace his clan and the culture.

"When did you buy this dress for me? It's beautiful. Thank you." She turned for him to see the back. "I've never owned anything so delicate and fragile."

"A week or so ago. I've other things for you, but they are to arrive with the rest of our belongings in another week. I hoped you would marry me, and I wanted you to have a beautiful dress." Bloody eyes but he felt as if he rambled, his words rushing from his mouth, almost without thought.

"I don't know what I did to deserve this but," she paused in thought, "wearing this makes me feel like a princess. I don't think I ever want to take the gown off." Her hands holding the sides of her skirt, she twirled several times.

"After we are wed, you will have a title. Did you know that?" Of course she didn't, "You'll be a baroness and everyone except close friends will need to address you as baroness or milady."

Her hand went to her throat, "A title? I knew you were a lord, but I truly didn't have any idea you came with a title. I don't know what that means."

"That's what makes your desire to become my wife so refreshing. I know you're not after anything; money, power or title. You care for me and that's all I could ever ask." Actually, her love would be nice, but he didn't dare hope. Having her in his life was all that mattered to him.

"Do you care for me?" she asked as he escorted her from the inn and into the carriage awaiting them.

"I wouldn't have asked for your hand if I didn't care. You're a challenge to me and you intrigue me in ways no other woman has ever done. I need to know all of your secrets." He knew she wanted more from him, but now wasn't the time. And one of those secrets was the scar on the inside of her leg.

Silence between them on the way to the church seemed normal yet he noticed her fingers, winding in and out of the fabric of her gown. He relaxed against the back of the carriage, his arms spread wide, watching the play of emotions across her face. And giving thanks this gown had no fastenings in the front. "You don't need to be nervous. I don't want you to be anxious today."

"I can't help it. I've never done anything like this. If you were asking me to pick pockets in Vauxhall Garden, I wouldn't feel a bit of anxiety."

He chuckled softly, "Of course not, not unless you saw me. I remember that day so well and how you tried to escape from me."

She looked down, hiding her expression from him. "I'm glad you caught me."

"Me too." Closing his eyes, his senses seemed more honed to the smells and sounds surrounding them. His fingers wound around the pistol he wore, even to his wedding. He didn't anticipate trouble so soon, but they were dealing with Avery Bainbridge and some of the darker elements of St. Giles, living and surrounded by men who would stop at nothing to gain what they wanted. He didn't understand his gut instincts in this, but somehow he knew Piper's secret and the small scar might give him the answers he was looking for.

"What are you thinking and why is your hand resting on your pistol?" Piper asked, her eyes wide.

His eyes opening, he sat up quickly. "Didn't think you'd notice." Yet the reflex to remove his hand didn't kick in. He should tell her the truth, but at the moment he wasn't entirely sure what that was.

"I didn't. Rogue did. He's staring at your right hand. He's smart, knows what a pistol is and what it can do."

"Just a gut feeling," he murmured. "Thought I might have heard something that shouldn't be there. Need to be ready for anything."

"I always trust my gut, or the hairs on the back of my neck. For some reason the day you found me they didn't speak to me." She reached toward him, touching the top of his leg.

"We're almost there. Let me get out first and make sure it's safe." His heart in his throat, for the first time in his adult life he was afraid, not for himself but for Piper. He prayed this was nothing and they would laugh about it tonight, but he wasn't going to leave anything to chance.

"Be careful," she whispered, her deep blue eyes wide. "I don't want you to get hurt either."

Out of the carriage he quickly looked over the land in front of him then was surprised, "Stop right where you are." He pointed his pistol in the direction of two young men who were now holding up their hands, very familiar men.

"Don't shoot," Billy said, "Don't mean you any harm. Just knew we had to get out of the city if we was going to stay livin', if you get my gist."

"Why are the two of you here? The real reason."

"That was the real reason. But we also thought we could be of more use to Piper if we could protect her than sitting in London waiting for Scarface to murder us for not bringing her to him. We spent most of our lives protecting her, and we decided we wanted to end our lives, ifn' they was going to end soon, doing the same thing for Piper. Always thought she was a he though," Bobby said. "You turned into a right pretty girl."

"Speak for yourself. You're a bloody fool and a blind idiot ifn' you don't mind me saying so," Billy said. "Didn't fool me. Always knew he was a she."

"Liar," Bobby shot back.

"Billy and Bobby." Piper nearly fell from the carriage. Would have landed on her hands and knees if Brett didn't catch her. She stood dusting off her hands. "Do you really mean that? You want to protect me with your lives? I'm beholdin' to you. Thank you."

"Not sure I trust these two blokes." Brett paused, thinking over all the encounters with these two men. "They could be here on behalf of Jocko and Scarface." Bloody hell, but he understood what was coming. Piper was going to ask him to trust these two fools and if he was honest..."

"We can trust them, Brett. I'm sure of it. They've never lied to me."

"When pigs fly," Brett murmured.

"Well, they're here. What other choice do we have?" she asked, her voice sounding indignant. "Pigs will never fly."

"That was my point," Brett said.

"Well, you're not very generous with your trust." Her hands rested on her hips. "Why would they want to hurt me?"

"Money. We can send them back." One eyebrow rose when Brett spoke, wanting that very thing but realistically knew it would never happen. Piper needed a friend and if those friends had to be Bobby and Billy, so be it. He'd sleep with his pistol under his pillow. Wasn't about to take any chances.

"We'd just turn around and come back here," Bobby said, grinning. "Can't get rid of old B&B so easily." They laughed, slapping each other on the back as if they'd made a good joke.

"They can witness our wedding," Piper said, letting out a long slow breath she'd been holding onto while she seemed to wait for an answer. "It would be nice to have a friend or two when I say my vows."

"You don't need friends like these two," Brett muttered. "They're the kind who would slit your throat in the middle of the night."

"They took care of me, watched my back for as long as I can remember. I don't think they mean me harm and other than you they are my only friends." She stepped close to Brett, placing her hand delicately on his chest.

When she looked at him, her eyes wide he couldn't refuse her. "They have one chance to prove themselves and yes they can sit in the church when we are wed, but if they do anything to harm anyone I love, I'll hand them over to the constable without blinking."

"Thank you." She jumped into his arms wrapping hers around him. "Thank you. I'll repay you somehow."

"Sure, and she will tonight, I'll be bettin'," Billy said while Bobby punched him on the arm.

"Ouch, why did ya do that?"

"Enough of that kind of talk, the priest is waiting for us." Brett held Piper's hand. Entering the church with B&B behind them and his driver bringing up the rear seemed surreal to Brett. Not the kind of wedding he would have planned if there had been time, but of course there wasn't.

"Never been in a church before," Billy said. "How about you, Piper? You been in a church?"

"Never..."

Brett heard the trepidation in her voice and squeezed her hand. "Collin, we're here," he called out. "Everything's going to be fine, Piper. You don't have anything to be worried about."

Collin and an older woman emerged from a door in the rear. "I see you have your lovely bride with you. I drew up the papers and documents to make this wedding official, but I didn't know your last name."

She scrunched up her face then shrugged her delicate shoulders. "No one does. I'm just Piper, nothing more nothing less."

"And who are these two unlikely fellows?" Collin asked, his head tilted slightly as if he examined them and found them out of place.

"Friends of Piper's, they can bear witness to the nuptials." For the first time since these two presented themselves, he felt as if perhaps their presence was a good thing. If Jocko or Avery Bainbridge questioned the marriage, these two reprehensible fellows could vouch for them.

"Are you ready for this wedding, my friend?" Collin asked, his voice more serious than Brett had ever heard him. He must fear for his sanity and if he looked on this entourage and the woman who had no last name, he would question the marriage also.

"I've never been more ready." He turned to Piper. "And you, you still want to be my wife?"

For a moment she stared at the floor then bringing her gaze to meet his. "Yes, if you still want me."

"We're both ready." He tried to reassure Collin with the steadiness in his voice. "Time to make this official."

"Good then," Collin proceeded and it seemed the vows were said quickly, his mind spinning. "Do you have a ring?"

Brett grinned at Piper, "I do have one for Piper. I purchased this in London in hopes I'd convince her to say yes. To my utter delight she has obliged me." Brett reached into his pocket and held it up.

"Blimey," Billy said, "that would bring a pretty penny in certain..."

Bobby elbowed him in the side and he quit talking. Collin drew his brows together in obvious disapproval.

More words were said.

Brett slipped the ring on her finger; pleased she seemed to like the symbol of their vows.

"I now pronounce you husband and wife," Collin spoke. "And now the two of you can sign the documents. You may kiss the bride."

Those were the words he'd been waiting for. Slowly, he pulled Piper close, his lips brushing across her, briefly then for a moment he deepened the kiss, enjoying the fact she returned the kiss. When he pulled away and looked at her, her eyes were sparkling with heated passion and desire.

"Can you write, Piper?" Collin asked.

She nodded, a pleased smile on her face. "Brett taught me how to write my name and some other things too. Yes, I can sign the proper documents." Her words sounded practiced, yet Brett was glad she'd wanted to learn.

With that said all Brett could think of were the things he and Piper taught each other last evening and the continuing education tonight. He craved his home and his bed knowing the celebration planned for them when they arrived would take up much of the evening.

While they signed the papers, the older woman who also witnessed the wedding disappeared for a few moments then reappeared with a small cake and a bottle of wine, as well other necessary items. "We must cut the cake and celebrate your marriage." She set the cake on a table. The glasses and knife were sitting on the table.

"Go on," Collin said, with a nod and the first smile Brett had seen during the wedding.

He held the knife and nodded to Piper, her eyes wide. Then seeming to realize she had no idea what they were doing here, "Together we're going to cut a slice of cake then feed a bite to each other."

"Why would we do that?" she asked, her voice hesitant. "Doesn't make any sense to me. I can feed myself as I'm sure you can."

Brett chuckled, "Tradition. You'll enjoy it, I promise."

"Promise? I've never eaten cake. What if I don't like it?" Yet, she placed her hand on his and together a slice was cut.

"And neither of us have ever been married, a whole slew of firsts," Brett said.

He held the slice in one hand, wondering if he dare. Of course he wanted everything to be perfect, and he wanted to find out how she tasted with cake on her face. Close to her lips, he said, "Take a bite." And he smeared a small amount around her mouth.

"Brett!" She stepped back but he kissed her, licking the icing from her lips.

"Hmm... You taste just as good as I remember." He kissed her again then pulled away, feeling the silly grin on his face grow and hearing the clapping and cheering behind him. He was quite pleased with himself, and he wondered if she would follow suit.

"Do I get to feed you?" A wicked glint seemed to possess her eyes and he understood she would reciprocate, looked forward to it.

She held the slice to his lips and seemed to wait for him. "You can do whatever you want." She returned his actions.

"Thank you," he murmured as he pulled her into his arms, kissing her deeply, touching the frosting with his tongue then felt her sweet tongue on his lips. Her strokes were tentative at first then it seemed she started to enjoy herself.

"Way to go, sir. That's a real kiss," Bobby called out. "Bout time you kissed her like a man."

Brett pulled away and with a napkin from the table he wiped the remaining frosting from Piper's lips then his own. "Are you ready to see your new home?"

She nodded several times, her eyes sparkling with delight. "Yes."

"Thank you, Collin. I assume you will file the papers in the appropriate places. I'd also like a copy as soon as possible." He turned to Pipers friends. "I hope you'll follow the carriage at an appropriate distance. We don't want to be interrupted."

Piper blushed, seeming to understand what he implied.

The two nodded, grinning. "Yes, sir, of course, sir. Wouldn't want to intrude on nothin', sir."

With that taken care of, he took Piper's hand, walking for a few steps. Then he scooped her into his arms and strode quickly to the waiting carriage, his lips trailing kisses along her neck.

Inside, with the carriage moving, Brett whispered close to her ear, "I didn't think we would ever get out of there. Didn't think I could wait this long to have you again." He pulled her onto his lap, his mouth descending on hers, his lips tasting and exploring. His hand cupped her breast, through the fabric, teasing the hard tip nestled beneath.

"Brett." She whispered his name, pulling away slightly from him. "Should we do this in here? What if...?" then, "Billy and Bobby?"

His hands were in her hair, his fingers sifting through the growing silken strands. He kissed her again, a long drugging kiss, pulling at her lips with his teeth while he turned her so she straddled him. Her core pressed against him and he knew she would be wet and ready for him.

"Billy and Bobby wouldn't dare interrupt. They know what we're doing."

"How?"

"Trust me."

Bloody hell, he needed to control himself at least until they reached his bedroom. That would be too long. He needed her now. The tiny sleeves that barely rested on her shoulders were easy to slip down her shoulders until her breasts were bared to his gaze. The sight of the pale white flesh and soft pink buds made his belly hurt with need.

"Do you want me as much as I need you?" He licked the tip of her breast then bit gently and listened delightedly for the tiny sound of desire he could always count on hearing surfacing from the back of her throat. "Bloody eyes, but you taste so sweet."

"I don't know." She could barely speak. "I think so but we're in a carriage and what if..." it seemed she couldn't stop thinking of the repercussions if someone came upon them, yet she pulled his shirt from his waistband and her hands found their way beneath the fabric, caressing, exploring.

"No one will see you but me. I won't let that happen, promise." Running his hand along her leg, he lifted her skirts then with intricate maneuvering, pulled her underclothing from her.

She was naked beneath her skirt and open for him. He needed release but didn't dare, reminding himself he didn't trust the men following them, didn't trust what could be around the next curve. Yet she was so wet and her folds so hot, calling to him. He found the tiny bud that would bring her such pleasure. He would have to wait for his own release. He slid his finger inside her. She was small and tight, just as she felt last night when he claimed her virginity. The thought pleased him immensely.

Her hips were rising, jerking, actually anticipating what was about to happen. She now knew how a climax felt, what startling pleasure he could give her. What she didn't know was that he could give this gift to her without coming inside. He would finish that part when they had more privacy. "Open your eyes, little imp. I want to watch them when you climax."

Finally, she let out a small cry, seizures seeming to ripple through her again and again until they finally slowed. He pulled her to him, soothing her, running his hands along her back. "That was good, very, very good. I'm pleased."

"What about you?" she asked as he rearranged her bodice and pulled down her skirts.

"You would do that for me?" He laughed softly. His sex was hard and pulsing beneath his kilt. He thought of her hands on him and her soft mouth caressing him. He couldn't stifle the groan.

She didn't answer. Her nimble fingers lifted the fabric until she found him, touched his rod. "I didn't really look at you last night. It's...you're amazing and hard. I want to please you."

"You don't have to do anything you don't want to do," he told her, watching her eyes while her fingers touched the tip of his shaft.

"You're wet..." she said almost reverently while her fingers closed around him, moving gently, up then down, tantalizing, teasing yet so damn erotic he could not hold back.

He closed his eyes, his fists clenched, understanding if he watched her, he wouldn't be able to stop himself from pulling her on top of his lap, with her legs straddling him and burying himself deep inside her. This would have to do for now. This evening would come and they would have all night to explore their passion.

He jumped, startled when he felt her lips and mouth enclose him. His thoughts were ripped from him at the sensations and her boldness. Bloody hell, but this was not something he ever expected. She ran her tongue along his length, sucked and nipped lightly.

"Am I doing this right?" she asked and he opened his eyes long enough to see her hands around his sex moving up and down, stroking caressing.

He couldn't answer because she didn't wait for an answer. Her mouth surrounded him again, sucking him deeper until he thought he would explode. He cried out and lifted her from his shaft as he spilled his seed. He would rather have his seed inside her but there would be plenty of time for that.

"Are you alright?" she asked, running her hands along his chest stroking him again.

"Never better." He pulled a handkerchief from a pocket before cleaning himself. Then mischievously he tucked her underthings into the small valise they packed for this evening. She would be naked beneath her dress. That pleased him.

"I should put those on." She looked to the valise.

"Why? You never wore them before." He grinned, thinking of her nakedness beneath her skirts. A secret only they would share. "I don't want you to wear anything other than your dress."

"I feel a bit naked and still craving you." She licked her lips, watching him as he adjusted his clothing.

"Good, that's exactly how I want my wife, naked and wanting me deep inside her. It's something only the two of us will know."

"But..."

"Hush, don't argue with your husband, and master." That sounded autocratic, but if she'd let him get away with the comment he wouldn't argue again. After all she was the master of him not the other way around.

"Wives aren't supposed to disagree with their husbands? Are they just supposed to obey?" she asked, seemingly surprised. "I don't understand why."

"It's a waste of time. The husband's word is final." He smiled at her, stroking her cheek and enjoying the crease of her brows, which told him she was mulling over his words and would argue with him.

"Doesn't seem fair to me."

"You're right. It's not fair but it's just the way things are." He wondered at that and the reasoning because a man is stronger and more intelligent than the weaker sex. He was pretty sure Piper survived more than any person man or woman should have to. She would have to be strong in many ways as well as intelligent. He'd have to think a bit more on this idea.

"We're almost to my home. Let me look at you." He rearranged her hair, then realized there was nothing he could do about her obviously kiss swollen lips. He didn't think anyone of his clan would say anything to her, but he couldn't be sure of the gossip behind their backs.

~ * ~

Thinking about meeting his staff caused her entire body to shake. She was not ready to be a baroness, did not have the skills, had not a clue as to what was expected of her. Picking pockets in London didn't qualify her for the things she needed to learn here. Brett would tell her what the responsibilities were, she reminded herself. During the last part of the ride he skimmed over the duties she would have.

"You can do this, Piper. Hold your head high and if you have questions, ask me. Your ladies' maid will help you to the best of her ability. There is nothing for you to worry over. Everyone will love you," he told her. "If I'm not around then make the decision from your gut. Do what seems logical and you will be fine. Mrs. Pickery and Angus will arrive in about a week, and they will both help with any questions."

She nodded several times, as if that tiny gesture would make everything right then inhaled long deep breaths of air for more courage. When he helped her from the carriage, he assisted her with adjusting her skirts and smoothed some of the wrinkles before they stepped around the other side to see eight people lined up on the steps to greet them.

"There are eight servants. You didn't tell me there were so many," she whispered.

"These eight are the ones who will be the most helpful and around the most often," he told her. "They will all like you. I promise."

"Don't make promises that can't be kept. I'm sure someone will hate me just for being here."

When they walked up the steps, the people curtsied politely. He stopped at each person, shook their hands and introduced them to her and her to them as his wife, the baroness. She tried for a polite smile with each stop. Until the lady he introduced to her as Siubhan.

Siubhan seemed to look down her pointed little nose at her before turning her attention to Brett. The smile she graced the baron with changed from wicked to purely angelic while her eyes darkened with what Piper could only assume was passion. Piper took an immediate dislike to this woman who set her attentions on her husband and was suddenly sure this woman and her husband had once shared a bed.

She hugged him, clinging to him, running her hands along his arms. "I've missed you, Brett. So much, I can hardly breathe thinking of you." It seemed she made a point of touching him with her breasts, her hand resting provocatively on his chest before traveling lower.

Brett gently removed her hand from his person, setting her aside. "It's nice to see you again, Siubhan. You should get back in line and wait for directions." His voice was curt and she looked surprised.

"Of course, whatever you say," she murmured, looking contrite, yet her smile seemed flirtatious as if she didn't believe him. "I'll see you later then. Perhaps a walk in the gardens later tonight?"

What was that supposed to mean. *I'll see you later.* Well, she survived St. Giles and emerged as a baroness. She would best this Siubhan, servant that she was. Brett was hers and she wasn't going to let anyone take him away.

"Would you like a tour of our home?" Brett offered his arm to her. "We'll start with the first floor and proceed from there." They walked through the parlor and the dining room then the kitchen and scullery. He reminded her who worked in each place and gifted her with some tidbit about each one to help her remember their name.

"Do you have a library? I'd like to see it next if you don't mind." She wanted to practice reading. Sometimes at night when they were in bed, she'd read to him. He seemed to enjoy it; at least he told her he did. She wondered how well Siubhan read, she thought pettily before reminding herself it made no difference. After all, Brett chose her to become his wife, not Siubhan.

"I do. It's upstairs along with my office. The library is in the west wing. Our chamber is in the east wing. Let's go outside first. I want to show you the gardens." He headed through a pair of French doors and across a covered patio to a pathway lined with roses.

"The gardener, what was his name?" she asked, frustrated with herself and her terrible memory. "I'm horrible. I can't remember anyone."

"You'll learn. The gardener's name is Douglass. You'll like him and he might let you help him cut the roses if that's what you would like."

"I'd like that, I think. Never done anything like it before but I used to love the flowers in Vauxhall Gardens." She thought about those days that seemed so long ago. Most days she feared getting caught and most nights she feared for her life. Billy and Bobby did keep a look out for her and she always knew where to run if necessary. They kept her safe and she owed them.

"Good, I'm sure Douglass will enjoy the company and he won't even care if you forget his name."

They strolled through the grounds, and he pointed out the gas lanterns that would keep the grounds light in the evenings as well the gazebo. Bending close to her, his breath whispered across her ear, sending an inferno of chills down her spine. "We can have a tryst or two here. Not tonight though. There is too much to do and we won't have the privacy we need."

"How would we ever have privacy out here where anyone could see them? You have so many servants that I would always fear they would suddenly appear, and I assume they have free access to all the areas."

"That's where you're wrong. They have duties in certain parts of the home. Only the gardener has access here. If I give him the afternoon off, we'll be alone." He waggled his eyebrows at her. "And we can do whatever we want."

"You're horrible," she laughed, thinking she liked everything he said, "Is that all you think about? Sex?"

"When I'm with you, yes. You know what I'm thinking about right now?" He pulled her close, wrapping his arm around her waist and squeezing gently.

"Probably, but you can tell me." She wanted to know about Siubhan and what she meant to him. The woman certainly insinuated herself to him at the greeting. Had they had sex? Would they have it again?

"I'm thinking about the way your eyes darkened when I gave you your woman's pleasure this afternoon in the carriage and how I'd like to see you look that way again. I'm remembering you have nothing on beneath your skirts and that you're probably hot and wet just ready for me. What are you thinking?"

Now was her chance. She meant to always be honest with him even though he wanted to hear other things. "Who is Siubhan and what are her duties?" *Who is she to you?* She should have asked.

"Is there a problem?" he queried, seeming surprised. "I thought you would like all of the servants."

He was astute. "I don't like her." So much for tact. "She has this way about her that annoyed me the moment I met her."

He paused, stopping to look into her eyes, crease lines on his brows. "She is your ladies' maid but after you've been here for a few days, you can go into town and you can find someone you like."

"Do I have to have a ladies' maid? What do they do?" She didn't want to wait one day to get rid of Siubhan. If she didn't see the woman again, she'd be wonderfully happy the rest of her life.

"For starters, when I'm not around your ladies' maid will help you with your corset, and God knows I'd rather take it off you than put it on. A ladies' maid will lace your corset and help you dress. She'll get you your bath in the morning, set out your clothing for the day among other things. Sometimes she serves as a confidant."

She would never confide in that woman and she realized suddenly she missed Molly, wished she would forget her fiancé and come with Mrs. Pickery. "Except for lacing my corset, which I don't want to wear anyway, I can do all of the things you've listed without help from a woman who obviously despises me." Anger and frustration swept through her then she spoke adamantly. "I don't want her anywhere near me." *Or you.* She wanted to ask him what she was to him but bit her tongue to stop the question, understanding it would all come out soon enough.

"Such strong feelings and you only met her today. Why?" He pulled her close, his forehead resting against hers.

She felt the whisper of his breath against her face and she prayed he'd understand. While she might be innocent in so many ways in other's she was worldly. "You're willing to listen to what I have to say?"

"Always." He kissed the tip of her nose then pulled back, gazing into her eyes. "What is it that has you so concerned about Siubhan?"

"She's a backstabber and she's after you, resents me for having what she covets. I've known many women like her and they think only of themselves and act only with their own best interest in mind." Inhaling a breath of air. "She wants you at any cost," she repeated.

"What makes you think that?" He brushed hair from her eyes, gazing at her tenderly, seemingly concerned. "I never got that impression of her."

"The looks she gave me before she flaunted herself on you. She's a whore even though she doesn't frequent a brothel. She gives herself to men for money and she wants you for your wealth and position." Piper spoke plainly, understanding that was the only language he would understand.

"Perhaps I should find another position for her. Maybe..." He paused, roughing his hands through his hair. "I don't know what to do with her. I can hardly send her away. The family's been with us for decades."

"You're too sweet and kind, Brett, and you always see the best in people. Try to think of something that won't hurt her feelings too much, a position that might be more important than a lady's maid. She's the kind of person who will seek revenge, but you won't know what she's doing until it's too late. I also don't trust her. She would give me to my enemies without even blinking."

"There really isn't anything more important than being the maid to the baroness," he spoke softly. "The only job I could give her after this would offend her."

"I can't abide her." Her stomach was rolling, fear for her life suddenly taking over her common sense. Women were harsher than men, and this woman would stop at nothing to give her away if she could get what she wanted.

"I will keep everything you've said in mind. Should we go back inside? I was told there would be a celebration in our honor. Indeed, I believe I hear the pipes playing already. Have you heard the pipes before? Should I don my kilt again? Are you willing to dance with me?"

So many questions... "Only if I won't make a fool of myself and of course you should wear your kilt. I would love to see you in it again."

"Of course you would. It's akin to you wearing nothing beneath your dress. A kilt is traditional Scottish dress for men."

"I think I'd like that." She grinned at him, thinking how vulnerable he would be to her searching fingers. She could take advantage of him as he did to her.

"Then you should have what you want but not tonight. There is no time. People are already celebrating." He kissed her nose, tightening his grip around her shoulders.

Arm in arm they walked along the pathway, the gaslights beginning to shine. Inside the estate was lit up, but outside was also lit. It seemed the servants and their spouses were dancing and the pipes were playing.

"Look they are dancing across from each other." She'd love to learn how to dance. Even now her fingers tapped to the rhythm. This was just one more thing she had no experience with. She could run from the law, hide, do any number of illegal things but dance? No, she couldn't dance.

"It's called a country dance. It is fun. We could join them." He seemed to watch her for a reaction and hoping she'd say yes.

Before she could say yes or no, Siubhan was tugging at his arm, smiling flirtatiously.

"Brett, we must dance. Come on..." She tugged again. "It will be so much fun. You and me just like before you left for London."

It seemed Brett remembered Piper's words about the woman. "Siubhan." He took her hands away from his arm. "I'm a married man. I'd like to share my dances with my wife, not you. What we shared is in the past." He paused thoughtfully, "I've no recollection of ever dancing with you."

"You can't mean that," she said indignantly, a scowl on her otherwise lovely face. "We danced many a time."

"Piper?" He held her hand in his. "Just try to copy what everyone else is doing and you'll manage just fine," he spoke gently, reassuring her.

"She doesn't even know how to dance. What kind of woman did

you wed?" Siubhan screeched. "A guttersnipe?"

Piper felt the need to cover her ears, instead she straightened her back and followed Brett. She didn't intend to let this woman ruin the celebration of her wedding. Together they joined the line of dancers. And facing each other she tried to mimic Brett's steps.

It seemed they danced for hours. Most of the dances were lively. The music slowing, Brett pulled her into his arms. She stumbled a bit, but he kept her upright. At times her feet didn't touch the ground.

Then they were in a darker place in the garden. His lips found hers briefly for a tender kiss. "I had to do that. It's going to be a long night. We won't find our bed most likely until the sun begins to rise."

"It seems we've been dancing for hours, but I've enjoyed everything." She smiled at him, "kiss me again."

"You don't have to ask me a second time," he whispered as his hungry lips found hers one more time. Then, "We need to return before we're missed and someone comes looking for us."

On the covered patio, food was served, the aroma breathtaking. The guests from inside the home seemed to have made their way outside to join with the commoners who were invited as well the servants. She found she was hungry, her stomach rumbling. When they reached the table, there was food she'd never seen before and some normal looking things.

"Try a bite of everything? Show our people you want to be one with them." Brett said holding something out, "Haggis."

She licked her lips several times, pondering his request and understanding she wanted to please him, "But, I don't know. What is it?"

"I won't tell you until you try some. Be brave. Take a wee bite."

"That doesn't sound too promising. Be brave," she repeated.

Brett laughed then bit into the food and smiling slowly chewed. "It's really good and see, nothing will happen to you if you eat some haggis. I won't ask you to try something really strange."

There were so many foods she'd never seen before, but that was true no matter where she was. She grabbed his hand holding the haggis, and bringing it to her mouth, attempted a small bite.

It seemed he was holding his breath waiting for an answer to the unasked question, do you like it.

"It's good."

"You would like to finish this?" He handed the haggis over to her.

She accepted then, "You need to eat one too."

They tried more of the foods on the table and talked to the various people who came from the house to celebrate with them since it was clear they wanted to be outside. The weather was warm and pleasant. A light filtered through the leaves making them dance and shimmer with the candlelight. The dancing was loud and boisterous, filling the air with good fun.

He poured her a glass of champagne and bending close, "I'll be over there. I need to speak to that man for a moment. He's a tenant and before I left for London, he had some issues with his crops. Will you be alright?"

"Yes, of course. Go speak with him." She enjoyed watching the dancers and trying to take in everything around her. These were her people now and while she didn't quite understand everything that meant, it pleased her.

She sipped the champagne, her toes tapping in time with the music. She hummed the tune, thinking she'd heard some version of it in London.

"You won't keep him, you know that. You have no idea what he wants or needs." Siubhan stood beside her. "He's mine, always has been. You're just a fleeting thought in his head."

Piper stiffened, searching her mind for the right words to use with this caustic woman. "Time will tell the true story. In any case you won't have him either."

"You're nothing but a guttersnipe," she said, her voice strident. "He will see you for what you are then he'll leave you."

"And he married me anyway. Maybe that's why. He understood I didn't care about the title or the wealth. In fact, he knew from the moment he met me where I came from." She was pleased with that answer.

"You admit to be a guttersnipe?" she asked, a look of shock on her face.

"I'm no more of that class than you are. Haven't you heard? I'm a baroness and you're a commoner. Now why would he want to lower his standards for the likes of a bitch like you?" she said, walking away, no longer wanting to engage with her.

Siubhan grabbed her arm, pulling her backward with such force she landed on the ground. Her glass flew in the air, the liquid landing on Siubhan.

"You whore," Siubhan shrieked. "You did that on purpose."

"What? I did what?" Piper was shocked at the scene this woman created. "You pushed me to the ground." Piper tried to stand, but Siubhan stood over her and she had to back away.

"Piper? You all right," Brett was beside her, pulling her to her feet, maneuvering Siubhan away from her. "What happened?"

"She attacked me." Siubhan pointed an accusatory finger at her. "She pushed me and tossed her drink in my face."

"A simple accident, that's all." Piper wanted to shrug off the incident and hoped nothing more would come of it. She knew now, Siubhan wasn't going to give up on her quest for Brett.

"You can tell me later tonight. Right now, we have another cake to cut and another icing kiss." He pulled her close, and Piper hoped Siubhan understood she'd lost this round between them. Piper knew though, this wasn't the last she'd see or hear from this woman.

"Again? How many cakes are we going to have to cut before everyone will be satisfied?" She smiled, remembering the quick kiss they shared earlier today and the sweet taste of his lips on hers.

"You just going to take her side when she attacked me?" Siubhan asked, her hands on her hips, a scowl marring her face. "She ripped my dress. See." The sleeve had been pulled down and Siubhan's breast was almost completely revealed.

Piper turned her attention to the woman, shaking her head in disbelief. "How? I was on the ground and before that I was trying to walk away. I never touched you." Piper knew how to street fight, but this subtly was new to her. In a real contest, this mad woman would never stand a chance against her.

"Milord, she ripped my dress. Unprovoked, I might add. What are you going to do about it? You must punish her."

Brett appeared frustrated and angry. "I'll buy you a new one." His sigh was long and heavy.

"Is that all? She should have to pay for it. On top of that she threw champagne in my face."

"I'll buy you a new dress. From what I saw you pushed her and when she fell, her glass flew in the air. It's a coincidence the liquid landed on you. As to the dress, I never saw her tear it. She was on the ground when it happened. But nevertheless, I'll be happy to purchase a new one for you and put this despicable incident behind us. I'd like you to leave now. It seems you've overstayed your welcome."

"This isn't the end of this, baroness." Siubhan turned away, leaving the celebration. "You and I have more to discuss."

"Bloody eyes." Piper reverted to her street language. "I'm sorry, Brett. I tried to reason with her." Then to Siubhan, "There is nothing for us to talk about. I tried to be nice but no longer." This was not the way she hoped the party would go, but it seems there was nothing to do about it now.

Bret took Piper's hand in his then guided her away from the horrible scene as well as Siubhan. "Forget it. I believe everything you've told me about her. I'll find her something that will save face if I can, but I want her away from the estate."

"She's still going to be a threat to both of us. You know that don't you. She would give me up to Scarface without a second thought if she believed she could get her hands on you or just for vengeance sake." Piper clung to Brett's arm, exhausted from the long day as well as this incident and desired nothing more than to disappear upstairs to their bedroom.

"More cake and more celebration. I need to drink champagne and hold you in my arms while we dance." Brett laughed. "The evening has only just begun and I mean to make the most it. Don't want to let one moment slip by without enjoying every second."

"Really, and all I want right now is to leave." She gazed up at him. "When can we leave?" she asked. "Somehow I'm not feeling the celebration any longer."

"Not for awhile." He kissed her forehead. "I've a few more friends to see and a few more dances with you. For the rest of the night, I'm going to keep you by my side. I'll introduce you to everyone even though I doubt if you'll remember the names."

"I'd like that. How many more women am I going to have to defend myself to?" She wanted to laugh, hoping to make light of the situation, but she understood this feud between Siubhan and herself was not over and she prayed there were no other women who'd set their sites in Brett's direction.

"Unfortunately, I can't answer that. I didn't know Siubhan would react this way to our marriage. If you're asking if I've slept with other women, the answer is yes. I haven't been celibate since I was fifteen. And yes, there are women in the village I've taken to my bed, but never Siubhan. I've no idea where she got the notion I might wed her."

"She wants to be in your bed as well as have the title. She's not going to stop until she has them both. She should find someone else to marry. Someone who will give her so many children she doesn't have time to cause trouble. Do you know of anyone who needs a wife and might be a candidate?"

He let his head fall back and roared with laughter, "Perhaps I could help with that. A husband you say. As head of the clan, I can arrange marriages. Tomorrow I'll look into appropriate suitors for Siubhan." Taking her hand in his again, he directed her to the cake. "Now, my baroness, the second and last cake to cut."

"This time I know what I'm doing," she whispered. She picked up the knife and let him set his hand on top of hers.

The cake cutting proceeded as planned. She tasted the icing on his lips when he kissed her and loved the cheers and applause during the kiss.

I love you Brett MacLachlan and I'm never going to let you go. 'Til death do us a part. With that thought a shiver slipped down her spine. No, this was her imagination. Nothing was going to happen to them. So why did she think those horrible words?

"I see you found a lovely bride."

The words surprised Piper. Seemed to come out of nowhere. She whirled to see who was speaking, afraid her past in St. Giles was already coming back to haunt her.

"Charles, what are you doing here?" Brett asked, once again, protectively bringing Piper closer to his side.

"I was nearby and heard the clan was having a wedding celebration. Didn't know it was your wedding we were celebrating. Who is your beautiful wife?"

"Piper, my name is Piper," she spoke up. "Until I married Brett, I didn't have a last name." She wasn't ever going to pretend to be anyone but herself. If people didn't like where she came from and how she grew up, they could go to the devil.

"Well that's a story I'd like to hear. You are very lovely and you remind me of someone. Someone in my past, now who could it be?" Charles tapped his chin, "I'll think of who but it might take some time. Yes, you are a very lovely lass."

"Piper, this is Charles Hepburn. He's Ella Montgomerie's father. You remember Ella?" Brett asked.

"I saw Drake a few times. Did I meet Ella?" she asked, thinking back on the conversations and the visitors to Brett's home.

"Now that I think about it, I don't believe you ever met Ella," Brett said. "But you spoke of her teaching reading at the orphanage."

"Your voice reminds me of someone too. Can you sing?" Charles asked. "This woman who I can't think of her name could sing like a lark."

"Never really tried other than a few bawdy tunes I heard in St. Giles." She felt her heart thunder in her chest. This man might know where she came from or provide a clue to help locate her family.

"Bawdy tunes in St. Giles?" Charles laughed. "I'm intrigued and you are very beautiful. Is that part of why you have no last name?"

"It's a long story, Charles. Piper's an orphan who was taught how to pick the pockets of the wealthy. I caught her, picking my pocket, and now I've wed her. Scarface, Avery Bainbridge, is interested in Piper, which brings up a wealth of questions as to who exactly Piper is. I'm guessing she comes from a wealthy family or the viscount wouldn't care a fig about her."

At the name Scarface, Charles inhaled a deep breath. "That puts both of you in danger. I hope you're taking precautions."

"Why do you say that?" Brett asked.

Charles rubbed the back of his neck, his brows drawn tightly together. "Just rumblings of gossip from the past. He's a dangerous man, but I know you understand that fact. It's the idea he's interested in Piper that bothers me. You need to get to the bottom of this mystery quickly and before anything happens to your wife. If that man is after her, running to the highlands won't keep him from finding her."

"I'm trying and I've questions for Drake as well as Piper." He pulled her closer.

A second time this evening a chill swept down her spine. "I understand how dangerous the man is, but he's never been anything but nice and courteous as well to me," Piper said. "Although I've only seen him a few times."

"If that man was nice to you, he has ulterior motives and there is a reason behind the niceties. I've a feeling he's cultivating you for something. Take care and listen to your husband where your safety is concerned. If I remember who you look like, I'll send a message to Brett. Until then, I've some business to conduct. Enjoy the rest of your wedding and of course the night." He walked away, tapping his hand on his leg.

Piper leaned her head against Brett's chest, her body shaking, yet his strength seemed to flow into her. "Is it time yet?" she asked, wishing they could walk away from all of this, leave it behind them forever.

What she thought she escaped in London seemed to have followed her to Scotland. The danger she flirted with in St. Giles now loomed in a different form. She wrapped her arms around her waist.

"Perhaps it is time. I know you're tired."

"It's been a long day but I'm not so tired as I'm frightened. Charles said some things that bothered me. I look like someone. You know what that could mean."

"Most likely nothing. Yet he gave me ideas to think about. Do you care if you ever know who you are?"

"Not really. I've everything I want right here with you. If who I am put's me, us, in danger then we need to find out the truth and that's the only reason I care."

"I'm glad you said that. On another note, would you like a child, Piper? Have you ever thought about a baby?"

"No, never, staying alive was pretty much my everyday thoughts as well as staying out of a whorehouse. If I ended up in one, I knew I'd have babies but also understood that they would be taken from me before I could see them. So, I never much thought about it."

"You realize what we've been doing, well, you might already carry our child." His hand rested below her belly.

"I think I understood that but I've not thought about what we did and a child. This is all so new to me."

He held her, her back to his chest and they watched the dancers and the celebration from a distance. She closed her eyes, humming and enjoying the warmth of Brett's body as they slowly rocked to the music.

"Brett." Charles stood in front of them.

"What is it?" Brett's arms tightened around her.

"I remember who Piper looks like."

"Who?" Brett asked.

"The Duchess. Piper's the spitting image of that woman at eighteen."

Brett's hands tightened even more then he ran them up her arms, soothing her, trying to calm her trembling body. "The Duchess," Brett said.

"Yes, rumor was the father died trying to defend her. But her daughter was only a few months old and she vanished. The Duchess was so overwhelmed and incapacitated for so many months, she lost the trail and was unable to call in favors. No one knows if the child lived or died but she was never found."

"The father died and the daughter disappeared."

Charles cleared his throat. "Vanished, eighteen years ago. The Duchess would have never given up her child. She doted on the babe."

~ * ~

Melanie lounged on a couch in the parlor, eating bonbons and watching her fat husband waddle around the room, a whiskey in his hand. She deplored the man, married him for his money, which she soon discovered he'd gambled away. As far as the bedroom was concerned, they parted ways years ago. They both found lovers in other quarters and it suited them both.

"Why are you here, Bertram? It isn't like we've anything in common these days." She rose, her negligee, she knew, accented all her curves. While noting he did aroused her, she knew seeing her almost naked would provoke him, "I've company coming soon. You need to leave before he arrives. I wouldn't want him to think I was having sex with you."

"One of your playthings?" he asked with a demeaning sneer.

"Don't talk to me of playthings. You probably have the pox from all your whores. Now get on with it. Why are you here?" She walked, conscious of the sway of her hips as she strolled to the sidebar and poured a glass of brandy aware too that he was staring at her. Then she turned, leaning against the furniture, her breast pushing against the fabric of her sheer robe.

Bertram, looked away then clearing his throat, pulled out a piece of paper. "I've a letter from Avery Bainbridge." He slowly unfolded it. "We need to take care. There have been developments."

Hearing the name Avery, Melanie stiffened, afraid her worst fears were coming to haunt her. Lyssa's baby would be eighteen now if she still lived. She downed her brandy before pouring another one. She needed to sit down. Looking back on everything, she should have had Avery drown the child as he intended. She'd never understood why it had been so easy to sway Avery to her side. But she was beginning to see the reasons now, that is, if the child looked anything like either parent.

"What does it say?" Inhaling a deep breath, she sat, her hands shaking. Praying this wasn't her worst nightmare coming true, she waited for the words that could change her life forever.

Bertram read the letter out loud then handed the paper to her. "Seems he's lost track of the little girl who would be a woman grown, don't you think? What are we going to do?" He asked, his voice quivering.

She waded the paper into a tiny ball, letting it fall to the floor. "Nothing for now. Even if someone thinks the child might be the heir to the Cameron estate, there is no proof. She lives because of our generosity, no other reason. We've nothing to worry about unless you start moaning and groaning about this. Don't tell anyone, not your whore or your mistress. No one can be trusted." She stood, smoothing the folds of her gown. "You may go now."

"No," Bertram was backing up, shaking his head. "Have you forgotten what we have to lose? I haven't. If this is discovered, all this," he waved her hand in the air, "will be gone."

"Don't worry about anything yet. I'm sure Bainbridge has the situation all in control. He'll find her, retrieve her and no one will learn anything about our misdeed so many years ago. He'll keep blackmailing us but life will go on as normal. Scarface is a resourceful man, as you well know." Melanie sipped the brandy, realizing she didn't feel as calm as she sounded, reminding herself there was no proof, nothing at all that could tie the girl to them.

"I can't help but worry." Bertram sat down, head in his hands. "We'll go to Newgate and we'll hang. Can't bear the thought of hanging. Nasty way to die I'd rather shoot myself and be done with it all."

"Bertram," Melanie rose, setting her hand on her husband's shoulder, "Calm yourself. We'll take this one step at a time. Nothing is going to happen today or even tomorrow. We aren't going to die, at least not anytime soon."

He was sniveling now. There was nothing else to be said about him, drool running from his mouth, tears from his eyes. Why had she ever married that man? Money, she reminded herself.

Money that vanished.

"I set up the accident that killed Lord Cameron, your sister's husband." Then he sat up. "This was all your idea," he shouted. "You poisoned your own sister. I would have never done anything like this if you didn't goad me."

"We did the misdeeds together and do you remember why?" she asked, turning in a full circle. "For all this, the estate, the wealth, the title. Have you forgotten you're the duke now because of me?" she sneered at him. "We both wanted the money as well as the power and the expense was not too great, at least not for me."

"You sure no one's going to find out what happened so many years ago? How do we know this little chit is the child, your sister's baby? No one even knew if it was a boy or a girl. All we have is Scarface's word." He wiped his nose with the back of his sleeve. "I don't want to lose everything."

Bloody eyes, Bertram was such a simpering man. She would take matters into her hands and visit Avery, an innocent visit of course. She'd think of some excuse. Then she shuddered wondering how the man would react to a visit. Probably not wise to be seen with the man who stole the child in the first place. She didn't want anything to lead to her and Bertram. Avery could turn everything back on them and escape, with a slap on his hand. If Bainbridge twisted the truth, everything would be their fault. She had to keep the secrets and keep Bainbridge as a friend and not a foe.

She'd have to think on it. Right now, she needed her husband to vanish before he went to the constables and confessed everything. "Bertram, time for you to leave. Don't you have a woman waiting for you in some hovel."

"My mistress doesn't live in a hovel."

"No, I suppose she doesn't. It's our ill-gotten gains that have provided the source to keep her set up nicely."

"What ill-gotten gains?"

"Alaric, what did you hear," she nodded for Bertram to leave and walked slowly toward her latest lover.

"Just the last part," he smiled. "You have secrets for me to uncover," he said, walking toward her. Pulling her to her feet and to him, his lips found hers. Then, "We'll have to talk about this later," his hands delving beneath the silken lingerie she wore just for him.

Chapter Five

Brett rose from the huge four-poster bed where he and his beautiful wife Piper spent their wedding night. A week had passed since their wedding. As usual he kept her awake most of the night and now she slept peacefully. Walking to the window, he looked out on the land he loved then back to his wife. She would do well here. Her soul would grace this land along with their children, God willing. He had made the right choice bringing her to the Highlands.

He realized this was the life he'd been hoping for, waiting for and he never thought possible until now. His family would grow and he intended to nurture the land as well as a family that would come sooner, he hoped, rather than later. His tenants would prosper and live good lives. This was his home.

"Your bath is ready," Angus stood in the doorway to the bathing and dressing room, a large bath sheet draped over his arms.

"Thank you, I'm glad you and Mrs. Pickery arrived earlier than expected. Piper needs some friendly faces. She's been lonely over the last weeks with only me to talk with. I also need you to think of something Billy and Bobby can do so they don't become bored and get involved in something they shouldn't. Would you stick around here and make sure Siubhan doesn't appear here this morning? Don't know who will get the bath and take care of Piper, but I'll find someone."

"Certainly, sir, can't tell you I'm surprised the lass doesn't like Siubhan." Angus turned into the other room. "That one has only her interest in mind. Has always had an eye turned in your direction."

Brett followed then settled into the hot water, his head resting on the back of the tub. "Why do you say that? I always thought she was a nice girl. That is until the night of our wedding celebration and the unprovoked encounter with my wife."

"Everyone here has noticed how she's had her gaze riveted on you." He cleared his throat seeming to pause to think then repeating himself, "She's had her sights set on you since she was a teenager. Think her mother set the notion in her head that she could become a baroness and all she had to do was make herself available to you. Thought she could do better with you than the local lads."

"I see," but he really didn't understand anything. Siubhan inherited the position of lady's maid to the baroness when her mother grew too sick for the duties, even though until today there was no longer a baroness, he assumed Siubhan would continue to show up ready to perform the duties. And he would have to turn her away again.

"What would you like me to set out for you to wear today?" Angus asked, effectively changing the subject. "Perhaps that velvet jacket and matching pants along with a cravat."

"No, Angus, I need something casual. I'll be spending most the day on my horse visiting the surrounding farms. Wish Molly would have come with you. She would have made a wonderful helper for Piper. I think they like each other." Brett rose from the tub, water sluicing on the floor as he stepped out.

"She did, sir. Molly's beau decided to bed another girl before we left. Can't say Molly was entirely heart broken. Seemed she recovered quickly enough. Said she wasn't going to be cuckold before they were even married." Angus chuckled softly, "Didn't like that fellow much. Glad she changed her mind."

"Then find Molly and tell her to draw Piper's bath. Tell her she needs to address her as milady or baroness unless Piper directs her differently. I'll see if I can find Siubhan and tell her I've got a husband in mind for her and her services at this estate are no longer needed." Brett wrapped the bath sheet around his waist after towel drying the rest of his body.

"Who do you have in mind to wed the lass, sir, if you don't mind me asking. By the way that's a fine idea. That's what the lass needs; a fine man to keep her in line and gift her with as many children as she wants."

"Duncan Erskine. His farm is prosperous and he told me before I left for London, he was looking for a woman to share his life with. I believe he's a fine selection for Siubhan." Brett was pleased with his choice. Duncan was broad of shoulder, lean hips and was fair to look at. They would make handsome babies together.

"The lass will have to agree." Angus reminded him. "After the night you told me about, she might be in a snit if you don't mind my saying so. And you've sent her away every day since it all happened."

"She will agree to my proposal or I'll send her to Edinburgh. There are homes there of need of maids of her stature and knowledge." Brett felt certain the incentives he would proffer Siubhan would be accepted. He also planned on offering more land to Duncan even though he was well aware Duncan would accept Siubhan as a wife without the added enticement.

"You can be so sure? She doesn't have to agree to any of this," Angus asked, stepping aside. "I'll put out your buckskins and a white shirt along with your riding boots. Is there anything else you'd like?"

"A hot cup of coffee and whatever Mrs. Pickery has prepared for breakfast. I'll eat downstairs in the kitchen. Want to be on my way before the sun gets very high in the sky." Already he was thinking of getting back as soon as possible to be with his wife.

He heard the door close softly behind Angus. On a different note, bloody eyes, but he needed to be alone with his thoughts and he also needed to find out what that damn scar on Piper's leg meant. Determined to see not only Duncan but a few other of his tenants, he hurried. There were rumors about thefts of their produce and he needed to get to the bottom of this before sunset so he could eat dinner with his wife and ask her about the scar.

The last week with all that happened between Piper and Siubhan and the words of Charles Hepburn, he didn't want to dampen the mood any more than it already was. And despite everything, Piper responded with the passion he'd come to know.

Out of the bath and dressed he glanced into the bedroom. Piper was still sleeping soundly. Whistling and feeling as if he solved the immediate problems, he made his way downstairs to the kitchen. "Good morning, Mrs. Pickery. It's a find day is it not?" He kissed her on the cheek before sitting down at the table.

"What has you in such a good mood, Master Brett? You must have had a fine night with your lady." She pulled a plate of eggs, bacon and potatoes from the warming oven and set them down in front of him along with a hunk of freshly baked bread.

"I did and thank you for this wonderful breakfast. Where is Molly?" he asked while he ate. "I've something to discuss with her."

"Angus told Molly she was to be promoted to lady's maid. She was thrilled and she rushed upstairs to wait for milady to wake up." Mrs. Pickery cracked a few more eggs into the frying pan along with two pieces of bacon.

"Good, good. If you see Siubhan, tell her she needs to go home immediately. I'll meet with her this afternoon, earlier if possible. I don't want her anywhere near Piper. Have you seen Billy and Bobby?" The list of things in his head that could not be put off seemed to be growing at the minute.

"They were just here checking on Piper. I do believe they mean well and want to put their past misdeeds behind them." Mrs. Pickery appeared busy preparing another plate he assumed was for Piper. "They told me they would be outside near the stables if anyone wanted them. Think they were speaking of you, Master Brett. The pair of them told me they wanted you to give them a job to do. Didn't much like charity or sitting on their behinds."

"Not too sure what I could trust them with besides robbing houses and picking pockets." Brett chuckled, forking in his last bite of food. Yet thoughts of their faithfulness to Piper loomed in his head. They'd spent a lifetime with the lass protecting her, perhaps they could spend the rest of theirs doing the same thing, making sure nothing happened to her.

"Do believe they can be trusted to guard Milady. Seems the gossip is ripe this week about the goings on the night of your wedding. Heard all about the confrontation between Piper and that little harlot. You could send them to guard her door and make sure Siubhan doesn't show up to cause more trouble.

"You really believe that don't you?" Brett stood, searching his cook's face for the truth.

She smiled at him, nodding her head. "Your sweet missus needs someone she can trust. Those two fellows are the only link to her past for good or bad. She needs them by her side, and I believe they will come through for her if times get challenging. They both are good blokes in an odd sort of way."

"I appreciate that. I would have never sent them to guard Piper, but everything you've told me makes sense." He left going over the pros and cons of taking Mrs. Pickery's advice and decided he would give the young men a chance.

Brett found them sitting on the grass by the stables using the side as a backrest. At his appearance both stood.

"Sir, MacLachlan sir, we're here for you. What can we do for you? We've decided we like Scotland and the folks. Your clan has been real nice to me, to us." He looked at Bobby as if to see if he agreed with him. "The stableman let us sleep in the loft. It was real comfortable and warm up there. Not used to such nice lodgings," Billy spoke for both of them.

"Glad to hear that. Mrs. Pickery told me you would like a job. Is that true? Would you like to do an honest day's work and get paid for doing it?" He stood with his feet planted apart, his arms crossed in front of him, watching the pair and liking the change that seemed to have come over them.

"It's true enough," Bobby spoke up. "We could muck the stalls and haul hay, whatever you need. Wouldn't even mind becoming a farmer if you had a bit of land we could learn on."

Brett shifted slightly, a smile ticking and threatening to break through his stern demeanor. "I'll think on the land but it will depend on how you do with the job I'm offering right now."

"What is it? We'll do anything," Bobby said. "You don't want us to rob or kill anyone do you? We wouldn't do that. No siree, we've changed out ways."

"Glad to hear that," Brett did laugh. "Part of the terms of this job was that nothing would disappear from my house."

"No, sir," Billy said. "We won't take anything. Don't need it now.

Never did before except Jocko had to make so much to give to Scarface or things would get real bad for all of us."

"What is it you want us to do?" Bobbly asked.

"Well." Brett stroked his chin thoughtfully. "Two things. I need the two of you to guard Piper and to make sure Siubhan doesn't go near her. Siubhan doesn't have good intentions or thoughts where it concerns Piper."

"You want us to be her bodyguards?" Billy asked in seeming disbelief. "Think we might be qualified for something like that."

"No one's ever asked us to do such an important job before. Jocko asked us to watch out for her but that's not the same thing as being her official bodyguard." He turned to look at his brother, "What do you think, Billy. We can guard the lady, right."

"So, you want to do this." Brett continued searching their eyes for the truth. Then remembering the scar and Charles' Hepburn's words, "This could get dangerous. Are you prepared for that?"

"Lived our whole lives in danger and looking over our shoulder. Yes, we want to make sure nothin' happens to Piper. Seems like life will be safer here than in London."

"Milady or baroness, you must try to remember to call her by her proper title. The clan won't like it if you disrespect her and they won't understand that you knew her before all of this happened," Brett told them sternly. "Can you do that?"

"Yes sir, when do we start?" Bobby asked. "Tired of sittin' on my arse."

"Right now, but you forgot to ask what you get paid," Brett said, beginning to think the pay didn't matter to these two.

"Don't really care, Master Brett. Know you'll be fair. Gotta go. Got an important job to perform."

"Wait, no pistols unless Piper's life is in danger. You can carry them hidden as well as your knives. And don't hover over her. She doesn't have to see you all the time, but you have to see her. Understood?"

"Yes, sir." They dashed to the house and through the kitchen. In a few minutes they stood in front of him again. "Where do we go?"

Brett gave them directions telling them to wait outside her door and not to go inside. Molly would give them further instructions when she came out and knew what Piper was going to do next.

With that accomplished, he headed for the stables looking forward to riding his stallion and making a mental note to himself to teach Piper to ride. He wanted to show her MacLachlan land; the lakes and the hills and even the small cottage, all places where he'd like to make love to her.

Duncan Erskine's land was about a thirty-minute ride from his estate. He didn't remember seeing Duncan at the celebration last night but he never had the chance to say hello to all his guests. He supposed the man could have been there, but he also remembered that once a long time ago rumors had it that Siubhan and Duncan were sweet on each other. Perhaps they had been lovers long ago and this trip would be successful.

Still morning, the sun and the slight breeze made the ride comfortable. Green leaves shimmered with the play of the sun's rays against them. As he rode, he noticed the crops on either side of the rode that were almost ready for harvest. These were Duncan's crops. Not today but soon he would summon Duncan to the estate and learn if he knew anything about the crop failures and thefts.

At the small cottage where the man lived, he dismounted and was surprised to see Duncan stride from his home, hand extended in greeting. "Good morning, sir, what brings you out this way?"

"Two things," Brett took off his riding gloves. "Half expected to find you in the fields supervising your crew. Does all go well?"

"It's Sunday morning, sir. Just got back from church. Don't usually work on the Sabbath and I sure don't ask anyone else to go out in fields unless there's an emergency. As you can see for yourself there's no need. The crops are fine. Planning on harvesting them soon. Got extra men available to help out."

Brett slapped his gloves on his leg. "Forgot what day it is. I've been on the road so long and the celebration lasted late into the night. For the last few days didn't know what was happening."

"You said there are two things you wanted to see me about?" Duncan sounded a bit irritated to Brett.

Ah well there was nothing to do about that now. He decided to proceed as if there was nothing untoward with his question. "First, I wanted to know if you needed anything and if all is going well. I'm checking on all my tenants, by the way. Just getting to you first because of a question I have for you."

"The crops are thriving and the harvest will be more than the last few years. I'm pleased and I believe you will be too. What else can I do for you?"

"Do you have a romantic interest at the moment?" Brett wasn't quite sure how to broach the subject of Siubhan.

"Would you like to come inside, a cup of coffee or tea?" Duncan laughed. stepping inside while Brett followed. "No romance on the horizon at the moment, but I'm open to finding someone to share my life with."

The inside of Duncan's home was tidy, everything in its place but Brett noticed dust on the shelves and infrequently used furniture. "Coffee for me, thank you." Brett sat down at the kitchen table, drumming his fingers on the table.

"Why do you ask?" Duncan poured two cups of coffee.

"As Laird, I've the right to arrange marriages, but I'd never do that if you already had a sweetheart." No, he'd look for someone else to take Siubhan off his hands.

"Had a sweetheart once, until she set her sights higher than a farmer. I was disappointed at first but I've come to accept that fact," Duncan said, bringing the coffees to the table.

"I see, so there is no one else. No lady who sparks your interest?" He wasn't sure how Duncan would react to a new lady in his life now. Supposed all he could do was ask and if Duncan said no he'd have to try someone else.

"Do I have the right to say no? Or is this set in stone?" Duncan sat back, his legs outstretched sipping the drink. "At this point I'm not real particular, but I don't want to crawl into bed with...well you must understand. Heard your wife was real beautiful, short hair and all, her eyes compelling."

"She is and her hair is growing out. It was short because it helped her survive the streets." He smiled thinking of Piper and her life in London before he was fortunate enough to have her pick his pocket.

"Who do you have in mind? Might as well put it all on the table and when do you want us to wed if I do accept the proposal. I'd just as soon have as short a courtship as possible. Don't really have time for all that nonsense, not during the harvest."

"Siubhan O'Leary." Brett waited for a reaction and watched as Duncan's face paled then a slow smile lit his face. Perhaps he'd chosen the right man for the job. He certainly hoped so.

"Did you know that sometimes one's destiny or maybe fate can come full circle?" Duncan asked. "I'm sure I wouldn't mind that feisty lady in my bed and a partner in life, someone to bear my children."

"So, you're pleased with the proposal," Brett said, wondering what was behind Duncan's broad grin.

"Does the lady have to agree? We both know she might not and I'm guessing you could have trouble with that. Siubhan is a strong-willed woman with a mind of her own. She can't be easily swayed once she's set her plans in motion."

"In this case her plans have already been stopped."

"Then this might be an easier procedure."

"I expected as much but probably not for the same reasons as you." Brett studied him closely.

"Think we need something stronger than coffee." Duncan strode to a cupboard. "Brandy." He lifted the bottle and the glasses in a silent salute before pouring each a drink.

"I hear a story coming. The two of you go back a ways, I'm guessing." Brett was eager to hear the tale assuming Siubhan was his earlier sweetheart and not someone he rejected.

"We do. We were sweethearts since she was thirteen and I was sixteen. Siubhan was my first and only love. I believed she loved me too and we would marry as soon as we were old enough." He shrugged down the brandy then slammed the glass on the table. "Bloody cycs, she gave me her virginity when she turned sixteen and we had plans to marry then something changed and, well, she left me."

"What happened to the two of you?" Brett knew, he heard part of the story, until she set her sights higher.

"She thought to become the baroness. Told me there was no one else for her. I wasn't good enough for her and she found a way to move into the house when her mother could no longer perform her duties. She used to come by after work, tears in her eyes complaining that you never paid her any attention." He looked at his bedroom. "We'd make love then in the morning she'd go back to work."

"Do you think she loves you?" Brett asked, thinking if she did it might be able to convince her this was the right choice.

"I thought she did, but now..." he paused. "I heard what happened last night. I'm not surprised you're here asking for someone to take her off your hands. You can't trust her with the baroness."

"I can't keep her in my home. She hates my wife and is trying to undermine her at every opportunity. I'll talk to her and give her some incentives. Perhaps she'll see things our way."

"That won't be easy. All she wants is the title and I can't give her that." Duncan seemed resolved that this would not be solved.

"Don't have the ability to bestow a title on you but a bit more wealth might make you more appealing particularly since she liked you before she thought she could get more out of life. I'll give you another tract of land and bestow a dowry on Siubhan she'll have to say yes to."

"That might work and if it were any other woman, I wouldn't take you up on the proposal, but I love her and despite her obvious flaws, I always will." Duncan rose, pacing the confines of the kitchen. "Just not sure what to do."

"You might not have to do anything." Brett rose, setting his empty glass on the table. "I'm going to see Siubhan now even though... You should come with me, make your case."

Duncan chuckled, seeming to see a bit of humor in this strange situation. "To keep you safe from her? Whatever it takes for her to say yes. I might even try a bit of seduction. It used to work. I'll get my horse."

When they found Siubhan, she was in bed, moisture staining her face but when she saw Brett, she sat up wiping tears from her eyes and adjusting her clothing.

"You came to see me? You're tired of your..." Then it seemed she saw Duncan standing behind him.

"You should get dressed and meet us in the parlor," Brett said. "It would be in your best interest."

"If you're not there in five minutes, I'll retrieve you from wherever it is you've decided to go. Perhaps we'll take a trip together," Duncan said.

Brett grinned. He didn't think he'd have too much to say when Siubhan finally showed herself. If she didn't say yes to the proposal, he was sure Duncan would keep her in bed until she agreed to marry him.

Five minutes to the second, Siubhan appeared in the parlor. Both Brett and Duncan were standing, and they watched as she slowly made her way to the sofa and sat, her hands folded primly in her lap.

"What is it?" she asked. "Why did the two of you barge into this house and demand my presence. I don't believe you have the right."

Brett began, "As laird I do but I'm not going to argue that fact. As you most likely know you are no longer employed by me. You made a terrible impression on the baroness the other night. You can seek employment anywhere except at my home. After last week you are not to step foot anywhere near the baroness."

Thankfully Siubhan chose to remain silent. She looked at her hands then to Duncan, eyes shimmering with moisture.

"You have one chance, Siubhan. I want you to become my wife, always have. Don't blame you for wanting a better life than I can give you, but now those possibilities have been quenched. Take me or leave me as I am, a farmer. I'm not a nobleman or wealthy. You know my body and I know yours. I want to marry you."

To Brett's surprise Siubhan didn't argue. She looked at Duncan with huge eyes, her lips tight. Yet if Brett wanted to bet, he would side on Duncan's side.

"You'll obey me and my wishes, Siubhan. I won't ask much of you and you won't have to work except in my home. Even though I'm not a wealthy lord I've enough coin, to clothe and feed you. I've enough to provide for any children we might have. You'll have a comfortable life."

She was still silent, scrunching her skirt in her hands, her breasts moving more rapidly than normal. Duncan seemed to be growing impatient.

"What do you say, Siubhan? I won't wait much longer so make

your decision." His voice was stern and it seemed to Brett he wasn't going to tell Siubhan his offer to make the acceptance easier.

She looked up then. "Fine," she said.

Duncan roared with laughter as if he found something amusing in her answer. "You're going to have to do better than that or I'll walk out of here and not look back."

It seemed Duncan knew his woman very well.

"I told you yes," she said in a huff.

"No, sweetheart, you said fine. And it was in an insulting tone. My wife will have to want me not just accept me. No, she'll need to crave me in her bed, desire my touch and fill my nights with passion."

She snorted and looked away. Then turning to stare at him, "What about my cravings and my desires? Do they mean nothing to you?"

"Of course not. Remember that night in the hayloft when you gave me your virginity and vowed to love me for the rest of your life? Did you forget that when you decided you wanted to be a baroness?" He kneeled beside her, touching her chin and lifting it so she had no choice but to look at him. "Do you remember?"

She licked her lips, "I remember."

"Was your vow an empty promise? Did you even then intend to leave me for the baron just because you wanted more than I could give you? The laird MacLachlan can't ever give you what you crave at night because he doesn't love you, never will. His heart belongs to someone else."

"The promise was not empty. It's just..."

"You're greedy?"

"Yes, I suppose I am," she told him indignantly. "Is that so bad to want a better life and go after someone who can give that to you?"

Duncan's lips molded over Siubhan's, and Brett decided it was time for him to leave and let these two finish making up. His mission here was accomplished and he would have good news to tell Piper upon his return.

Mounting his horse, he set off to meet with the tenants who were having trouble with their crops and to discover the reasons why.

He whistled, enjoying the sunshine, impatient to get back to his wife and trying to think of all the things she could be doing.

She was probably long past bath time as well as breakfast. Molly wouldn't know what to do with the remaining day anymore than Piper. If he had to bet his last dollar, he would guess both were in the kitchen talking Mrs. Pickery's ear off, Bobby and Billy too.

Or perhaps she'd be in the rose gardens with Douglass and Rogue would be barking and making a nuisance of himself.

When he finally reached his home, he dismounted and handed the reins over to the stable boy before striding inside.

In the kitchen, Brett leaned against the counter, finding a freshly baked cookie. "Mrs. Pickery, have you seen Piper?"

"I did, finally got the lot of them out of my kitchen so I could get something done. Bobby and Billy are doing their jobs just fine. Nobody's going to get close to the lass, but they're not giving her room to breathe. I would have thought you would have directed those two not to hover." She cut carrots before tossing them into what appeared to be a stew she was preparing for dinner.

"So where are they now?" he asked, laughing at his cook's indignation yet knowing the woman enjoyed every moment. "Did Piper help you with the cookies or is that flour dusting the floor your doing?"

She huffed a moment but then, "Believe they're in the garden with Douglass. I'm sure they are tormenting the poor man near to death. You should definitely give him the rest of the day off."

~ * ~

"Fetch." Piper tossed a ball into the air so Rogue could chase after it. The dog clearly loved that part of the game but when he caught up to the object, he sat down and stared at her. "Bring it here, Rogue. Be a good dog." Piper called out, knowing the dog would wait for the chase. He didn't seem to understand that until he brought the ball to her, she couldn't throw it again.

"Well that's just not right," Billy said indignantly and tried to take the ball away by grabbing at Rogue who quickly dashed away. "The dog always brought the handkerchiefs to you, didn't he? Then why's he so obnoxious now? He should bring the ball to me."

"The people he stole from almost always chased him. It's a game to him, one he enjoys," Piper said, laughing at all the antics. "If you chase him, he'll most assuredly bring the ball to me."

Rogue, enjoying the game, dashed away, swerving and maneuvering just as he did when he picked a pocket. Brett chuckled at the game as Bobby joined in with Rogue, eluding all of them.

Piper sat on the grass, her legs curled beneath her, laughing hysterically at their antics. Molly stood beside her, grinning too.

He approached, trying to make some noise so as not to startle anyone. B&B were sadly unobservant at the moment so caught up in the game of chase they didn't know he was there, which didn't bode well for their ability as her bodyguard.

Loudly, he cleared his throat then again. Piper heard him first. Turning she tossed him a huge smile. "Brett." She stood, rushing to him, her arms open wide. Throwing her arms around him she hugged him then leaned back, gazing into his eyes. Quickly he met her lips with his for a quick kiss.

Breathless after the sweet kiss, "You're back. Did everything go as planned?" she asked, touching his cheek and enjoying the stubble. "I missed you."

"I see you couldn't figure out what to wear but you look fetching," he told her, seeming to look her up and down.

"On the contrary, I wore exactly what I wanted to wear. Mrs. Pickery helped me before we left for our trip. She found these in the attic of your townhouse in London. Haven't worn britches and a shirt for what seems like forever." She laughed, loving the expression on his face, deciding to try to surprise him with something every day.

"I do prefer a dress but you do look eye-catching." He offered an arm, nodding to the others in the direction of the kitchen. "I'd like some time alone with Piper. Unless it's a matter of life and death, I don't want to be interrupted."

"Are we going to the gazebo?" Piper wasn't at all sure she wanted to trust any of her friends to leave them alone. If he had making love in mind, she might protest but if he was going to tell her about his day, she wanted to listen.

"You guessed my intentions." He squeezed her arm. "But I need more privacy for what both of us are thinking about. I don't trust B&B not to hang around you. Mrs. Pickery said they've been hovering. Does that bother you?"

"Not today. I liked the company and while I don't want to be reminded of St. Giles, I appreciated the familiar faces while you were gone. Did you accomplish what you set out to do?" she asked once more, sitting down beside him inside the gazebo and running her hands along her legs.

"Everything, plus a little bit more I didn't count on, but it was all for the best." He pulled her onto his lap, his lips meeting hers, tasting her, exploring while the heat he fanned slowly burst into flames.

His lips were soft and she loved the way they felt against hers, but she sensed he didn't mean to seduce. She pulled back, touching his face. "What is it?"

"We need to talk about several things." He pushed her flyaway hair away from her face and behind her ears, his gaze focused on her lips.

"Important things?" she asked. He left this morning without leaving a message, but she trusted he had work to do and now that they were here living on MacLachlan land he would be gone more than she was used to.

"Important to both of us, perhaps more so for you. I found a suitable match for Siubhan. She won't bother us any longer." His hands ran the length of her rib cage then back down.

"She accepted what you proposed? I've a hard time believing that but if it's true, I'm more than grateful. You're a magician, a wizard a..." Truly this news seemed too good to be true.

"The man I chose was very convincing when he presented his case to Siubhan. Seems the two were lovers only a few years ago; had plans until Siubhan decided she wanted to become a baroness. I think her mother must have put the notion into her head. It's a pity too because they wasted a lot of time."

"Who is this man? If I ever meet him, I'd love to thank him." She had never bargained to have a title, truly didn't care, but here she was a baroness with no idea what a baroness did with her day. Molly was no help either. It seemed they were both ignorant of their duties.

"Duncan Erskine. They were lovers and now they will be married. He'll send me notice as soon as they are wed, and I'll send a dowry that both will appreciate. I also intend to present Duncan with more acreage. He's a good farmer and will, I'm sure, continue to turn a profit."

"That news lightens my heart. I hope she'll be happy." Piper leaned against Brett, soaking in his warmth as well as his strength. His arms were wrapped around her, his hands settling possessively on her belly.

For several minutes she soaked in the silence and wondered what the second thing was he wanted to talk to her about. She listened to the breeze as it shuffled through the leaves on the trees. The scent of the rose garden filtered through the latticework in the gazebo.

"Piper?" he asked, setting her on the cushioned seat, his visage grim. "We've more important things to talk over."

One look at his face told her this was more serious. "I don't like the expression on your face. What is it?"

"That's just the thing, Piper, I'm not sure." Facing her he stroked her arm, lingering at her pulse point. "I really don't want to bring it up, don't even know if it means anything, but..."

"You're worrying me more by your silence than what could possibly be bothering you." She swallowed hard, her stomach constricting.

Inhaling a long deep breath before letting it out slowly. "Did you know you have a scar on the inside of your thigh?"

She blinked several times, "I have a scar? No, I didn't know. Is there some significance I should know about?"

He placed her hands in his, "Yes, and I'm not surprised you didn't know. It would be very hard for you to see."

"What does it matter?" she asked, her heart seeming to beat double time, worried that he would find fault with her.

It seemed he guessed her fear. "Not what you think. It makes no difference to me if you had a hundred scars, it's just that it is so unusual, and I believe it was put there on purpose."

She stared at him, feeling blank and worried as well. What was he trying to tell her? "How is it so different it has you worried? Tell me, explain before I go crazy with anxiety."

"It's the shape of a crest, an English or Scottish crest, one or the other if I'm not mistaken. I've drawn it but I've missed a few important details. I've only seen it briefly and perhaps tonight you'll let me get a closer look."

For the first time since she could remember, he didn't look at all confident. "A crest of what? I'm not at all sure I understand what you're trying to tell me, and I don't know if I'm comfortable with..." Bloody eyes, but he'd touched and looked at every part of her. Why would she feel apprehensive about this?

"A family crest, I think. It could tell us part of your story. If I possessed an accurate picture of it, I could find out what family it belongs to. Perhaps discover the history behind the family and if it does belong to The Duchess' family. I don't want to approach her, if it's not true. After all it's been a long time since The Duchess was young and Charles' memory might be faulty."

She was shaking her head, disbelieving what she thought he was trying to tell her. "You are attempting to say that some family...that I might belong to a family with this crest. Why would someone scar me then pretend I'm an orphan? I wouldn't want to know them at all if they were so calloused."

"It might be more than that. Look at what we do know and all that we don't. It all seems nefarious."

"I was raised by Jocko, and I'm an orphan and that's the god honest truth. This scar is some kind of mistake. It doesn't make me a daughter of some duchess," she protested in disbelief. Her life had already been turned upside down. Did she need more questions and did she want the answers?

"Didn't you tell me that Jocko said Scarface brought you to him when you were a baby? Scarface is an aristocrat with ties to many of the families in England and Scotland. What if someone plotted against your mother and father to gain their title as well as wealth?" he asked her.

"What if they did? Doesn't mean anything to me now. With you

I've more than I ever wanted or needed." She was tired of all this intrigue, the running and hiding. After marrying Brett, she thought it was over. "This knowledge could put me in danger. That's why you hired Bobby and Billy as bodyguards isn't it?"

It seemed he ignored her question. "If you let me get a better look at the scar, I'll send the drawing to Montgomerie and see if he can tell me what family the crest belongs to. If he can do that, we can investigate further."

"Do I have a choice?" she asked, realizing every time they made love, he would look at her. It seemed she couldn't catch her breath, her body shaking, terrified of what they might discover if they pursued the truth.

He kissed the back of her hands. "I can tell by the look on your face you realize that I will see the scar every time we have sex. It can't be helped and even if I were to try and close my eyes when I touched you, kissed you in that very spot, I would never be able to keep from looking at you and wondering what danger lurked just beyond my estate and threatened you. We have to discover the truth and the lies as well or we will be forever looking over our shoulder."

Her lip tucked beneath her top teeth, she nodded her understanding. "It just feels really strange to think about you looking at me intimately then drawing a picture of something on my body in such a private place."

"This drawing could save your life." He wrapped an arm around her shoulders, pulling her close before kissing the top of her head. "We need to do this, Piper, but if you tell me no, I'll honor your decision."

Quickly, she distanced herself from him, pushing away slightly so she could see the expression in his eyes, "How so? I've a hard time believing a drawing could save my life."

"It won't be long before both Scarface and Jocko know I've wed you. They know you have my protection, but if they did something eighteen years ago to you that could be traced back to them, your life is in jeopardy. We have to learn who you are."

"I'm nobody," Piper insisted, refusing to believe this story Brett presented to her. She'd rather believe her parents died, with no relatives who could take care of her and the authorities stepped in to place her in an orphanage. Only it wasn't the authorities, it was Scarface.

Thinking her parents had been subject to foul deeds and she might find herself in peril because of it, didn't sit well with her. She was happy with her life just the way it was and didn't want anything else. Finding out the truth wasn't necessary to her, but it seemed to be for Brett.

He touched her tenderly, "You are somebody and very important to me. I don't want anything to happen to you. Even if we discover your real identity, it doesn't mean that discovery needs to change your life."

"Don't you think that if you do nothing, all the excitement and speculation will be over before it's really begun?" She thought her point a good one. "If Scarface or Jocko don't think you know anything, they'll ignore the fact I've left London."

"Not if there were crimes committed eighteen years ago that people thought would be kept secret forever. The fact that you defied the odds by escaping St. Giles means you might have become a threat they can't forget about, the risks might be too great. These secrets could mean life or death for both men."

"I never asked for any of this. What could anyone possibly have taken from me that I would want now?" Piper needed to dismiss all this foolishness in her head. She craved the peace she thought she'd found. Running and hiding was supposed to be something left in her past.

"I know you didn't, but we have to address the issues and find out the truth or you'll have to live your life waiting for something bad to happen, as will I. Do you want that?" he asked, his voice harsh. He seemed to notice the shock on her face. "I'm sorry. None of this is your fault."

"You know I don't want the problems or care about meeting my parents, never bargained for these men to have control over my life." She paused, pushing her hair behind her ears, a soft sigh of resignation following. "When do want to draw me?" she asked, her voice matter of fact. She was ready to get this over and behind her.

Brett laughed softly. "I'm not going to bring out the pen and ink right now, but we can stroll to our chamber and perhaps do a few other pleasant endeavors after I have what I need or perhaps before if that makes you more comfortable."

She couldn't help but think on all the times he made love to her. Moistening her lips, she nodded to him, trying not to grin too broadly. "What are we going to do with the bodyguards?"

"Give them to Mrs. Pickery to keep a watch over?" he asked, standing and holding out his hand for Piper to take. "That might work and keep them busy for a short time. What they really need are...they each need someone to love."

"I think Mrs. Pickery will quit if you give her too much accountability with B&B. Maybe you can give them some project out of the house." She accepted his hand, walking along the well-manicured path to the main house. "Something that will keep them occupied when I'm with you."

"They might be of a mind set to talk to the farmers who've had produce stolen. There's a thief among my tenants, and I need to discover who it is before they rob the rest of them blind. Duncan had no idea who it could be."

"They lived on the streets, survived and managed to better themselves in the process. If the situation was explained to them, I'm sure they can ferret out the perpetrator and maybe even the reason." The sun was beginning to set and the gaslights flickered, giving the growing darkness a soft glow.

"The reason makes a difference?" he asked, sounding skeptical. "But I'm glad you think they'll be able to do the job."

"I wasn't a willing participant in the crimes Jocko expected of me, neither were Billy and Bobby. The reason is always important." They stepped into the house, which seemed too calm under the circumstances.

B&B suddenly slammed through the doors. "Where you all going?" Billy asked, his hands on his hips. "You two shouldn't be leaving us without telling us where you're going."

"Not nice of you to give your bodyguards the slip." Bobby finished for Billy. "This job's too important." He set his arms across his chest.

"Private things," Brett said. "When I'm with the baroness, you need to keep your distance lest you embarrass Piper. However," he began, watching heat stain both men's faces when they realized Brett was talking about sex, "I'm going to add to your jobs. Not right now, I'll have the details later. Try to have some fun. You could both use some free time and perhaps a woman of your own."

"You shouldn't have put that suggestion into their heads. They can get into a lot of trouble with free time and women. I've heard some stories about their sexual encounters." She laughed, smiling to herself.

"They won't hurt anyone?" Brett asked, seeming suddenly concerned. "I thought perhaps after her heartbreak Molly might find comfort with one of them."

"Most likely both of them," Piper said. "They like to share, but I've never heard of any complaints and they always got call backs."

"Both of them you say?"

"That's what I've heard."

Up the stairs and into the bedroom, silence seemed to reign. In the bedroom, Piper sat on the bed her fingers, winding into the bedding. She inhaled a deep breath, letting it out slowly as Brett seemed to be gathering things. He brought her a ring and sitting down beside her, held it up to her.

"This is the size of your scar and it looks something like this with some notable details that are different. It's very small, and it's very difficult to make out anything pertinent. These rings aren't used so much anymore, but the ring was used as a seal for letters. When heated, the metal would melt the wax which closed the letter showing the crest so the recipient knew who the missive was from," he explained.

"So, someone heated a ring and branded me?" she said in disbelief, stunned that someone would do that to another human, a baby at that. "I can't imagine why someone would do something that would hurt so badly."

"I can, and the reasons all point to someone who was desperate to keep a baby girl's legacy as well as her life intact," he told her. "I believe there are some reprehensible things going on here. If you lie on your stomach while I draw, the process won't be quite as intimidating. I need to get as many details as possible into the drawing. I've a magnifying glass to help me out." He sat down on the bed, waiting for her an encouraging smile on his face.

Piper held back, hesitant and so unsure of herself she felt as if she walked into the flames of hell. "Perhaps you could make love to me first then I won't feel so self-conscious or maybe you could take all your clothes off too." She fiddled with the fastenings on the britches she wore, staring at him, unable to continue without some kind of assurances.

"Either scenario works for me." Brett pulled her close, his lips melding with hers. Then, "I'd be happy to remove all my clothing."

Not too many seconds later they were naked and Brett was making sure all of Piper's concerns vanished. She lay beneath him now, her breasts and legs bared to his view, her body quite naked. The shyness disappeared as she wound her fingers through his hair, pulling him closer, the kiss amazing. She remembered that first night and she didn't seem to have any inhibitions where Brett was concerned.

"Are you ready for this? We could make love first then... Never mind," she told him, the sheet settling around her waist. Getting this over with would make her life a whole lot better. "I know I am. What do you want me to do?"

"Turn over." He hesitated, seeming to wait. Then clearing his throat...

"You showed me where the scar is." She spread her legs apart so he could locate the scar. "Can you, is this enough of me..."

"More than enough, I promise to finish as quickly as possible. I don't like the discomfort I see in your eyes although I don't entirely understand it."

Closing her eyes, she tried not to think about what Brett was doing and why, tried not to believe someone would brand her or that her life was in danger if anyone figured out who she was. She was Piper from St. Giles, that was all, except now she was a baroness and Brett MacLachlan was her husband.

"Are you cold?" he asked, his voice filled with concern. Before she could answer, he covered her everywhere except for the scar.

Time ticked by and Brett drew. She tried desperately to keep her mind away from all the things Brett told her could happen or the what if's he presented to her. This was all so ridiculous to think that someone might have been killed to keep her safe or even some other possible scenario.

For a moment Piper must have dozed. Back in St. Giles, she saw Jocko. He was bedding his favorite girl. When they were done, he rose, stark naked, unconcerned that she watched. On a chain around his neck, he wore a ring. She jumped, startled. Now wide-awake she realized the room was growing dark and Brett must have covered her with a blanket.

She rolled over then sitting up and looked for Brett. "Where are you?"

"Didn't want to wake you." He rose from the desk near the window. Then walking to her and sitting beside her, he lit a candle then held the drawing out for her to look at. "With the magnifying glass I created a few more details, including the raven at the top of the shield. The raven on the shield is definitely not Cameron, and I still can't make out the words written below it."

She pulled the sheet high, covering herself, "So now you are sure I'm not a Cameron. So, I might be related to this duchess? What does all that mean to me?"

"I don't know, is my answer to both questions," he told her honestly. "I'm sending this to Montgomerie, and I'm going to let him ferret out as much information as possible. I might also send a copy of this to Charles Hepburn. Charles seems to think he might know something, he does know who you remind him of."

"Someone called The Duchess. What are we going to do now?" she asked, pushing hair from her eyes. "I'd like to eat and perhaps a glass of wine would be nice." His bare chest fascinated her as usual, but for some reason she didn't want to make love and she didn't want to tell him how beautiful he looked. All these new things that happened to her made her life in London seem non-eventful.

"I'll ring for Molly. I'm sure Mrs. Pickery has something warming in the oven. Molly can bring it to us."

Strangely, no one appeared and Piper wondered if B&B had taken Brett up on his suggestion of wooing some willing lass and could that young woman be her lady's maid? Molly needed some happiness after her beau in London betrayed her.

"I'm thinking Molly and the boys found something else to do,"

Piper said, laughing. "You did put the idea in their heads, and Molly is a beautiful woman who's had her share of heartbreak."

"I'll go down and see what Mrs. Pickery has left warming and bring up some wine." He slipped on the shirt he removed earlier but neglected his boots, making his way down the stairs barefoot.

Piper rose from the bed, clearly feeling at a disadvantage. Her nakedness had never been an issue with Brett, but she'd never been without clothes when he was dressed. It seemed so out of the ordinary. She found a negligée he bought her and a matching robe and slipped them over her head.

Sitting down at the desk, she studied the drawing he made of her scar. This tiny brand was changing her life and she didn't like that fact. Bloody eyes, but she wished she could recall something, but of course her mind was a blank.

Jocko told her she was naught but a babe when she was delivered to his doorstep in the middle of winter. He always wore that ring on the chain around his neck. Could that be her ring, her family's crest? She didn't know if she wanted it back, didn't want to admit it could lead her to knowledge of her past and she especially didn't know what she wanted to learn about the beginnings of her life.

With a fingertip she traced the letters of the name. "It was a raven," she murmured, suddenly feeling a deep connection to this unknown entity. Shaking her head, she stood up quickly knocking the pen and ink over.

It spilled across the bottom of drawing even though she quickly righted the bottle. Her body shaking, she sat back down. Closing her eyes, she understood the ramifications of this drawing. Everything she held dear could be in peril.

"Piper, can you get the door?" Brett called out, knocking with must have been his foot. "I've not enough hands."

"I'm coming." She opened the door and helped him by taking the wine and the glasses from him. "You've out done yourself. This smells amazing."

"No, Mrs. Pickery did this. I see you're wearing the negligée I bought you. You look wonderful." He graced her with an all-knowing smile. Drake Montgomerie had suggested the seamstress and the shop, telling him he should buy one in all Piper's favorite colors.

She wasn't sure how to respond. "I've some things... Well," she set the glasses on the desk and poured the wine.

"What is it?" he asked.

Piper held up the drawing, "I spilled the ink. I was looking at it, thinking about it and... I've some things to tell you. Something I remembered when I dozed off a few minutes ago."

"After we eat. Whatever you have to say can wait that long. I find I'm famished for two things. You and this food. When we finish with all this and I've tasted you again, we can talk."

"Perhaps we can talk while we eat. Would that be too hard?" There were so many thoughts rattling in her head she was afraid she might forget something. She watched him heap the two plates with food. "I can't eat half of that."

"What is so important to tell me that can't wait until morning?" He sat down beside her, sampling the food then the wine.

Fiddling with the wine glass, "I fell asleep while you were drawing the brand and the dream I had was one of Jocko wearing a ring that dangled from a long chain. He always wears that ring. Don't remember ever seeing him without it. Do you think he's wearing the ring, that ring?" She nodded toward the drawing, inhaling a long breath of air. "Do you think he knows who I am?"

He set the glass of wine down then thoughtfully, "There is a good chance he does. At first, I believed he was just one of Scarface's pawns, but I'm beginning to think he's more of a role in that man's plans."

"Now you don't believe he's innocent." Her voice shook, "I trusted Jocko all my life, put my very survival in his hands. I was even willing to become some man's mistress for him."

"Not after what you've told me, I don't trust him." He sat back, seeming to stare at her for the longest time.

Once again, she was left with no clear thoughts, her mind in turmoil. "So, what does it mean if I'm the daughter of this duchess? Who is she and where does she live? I believe Charles must know more than he told us the other night, and I'm guessing the people who might be my parents lived somewhere close to him, lowlands I presume or they were good friends. We have to find out everything we can and as soon as possible." She told him downing the glass of wine. Suddenly and faced with no other choice, "I want to learn about what or who I might have been."

"This is dangerous ground we're treading. You have to be sure and fully behind all that we choose to do. Think I'll ask Drake to visit Jocko and ask him about the ring. Perhaps he can even retrieve it and we can see if the crest on the ring matches my drawing. As soon as that happens then we'll have to be even more careful. Each step needs to be thought out carefully before we proceed."

"Agreed."

~ * ~

Molly stood by the side of the barn, wondering why the message from the boys and what they wanted. She was only going to wait two more minutes, tapping her toe with impatience. *A possible bit o' fun they said, if I was willing. What was that supposed to mean?* Of course she was always ready for a bit of fun.

"You came?" Billy stood in front of her, his hair damp, sounding surprised she was there.

"You took a bath. Whatever for?" she asked, seeing a tiny bit of humor in his slicked back hair. "Thought baths were for Saturday nights."

"For you, my little darlin'. Took the bath just for you and the fun we might have. Are you a bricky lass tonight? You want to dally with two instead of one?"

"What are you talkin' about, Billy? Can't say I'm fearless or courageous. Seen my fair share of scary things in my life and don't know what you mean by dallying with two." She placed her hand on her hips, tossing her hair back in what she hoped was a flirtatious manner.

"I'm starvin' for a kiss from your sweet lips. Been that way since I first saw you in London. Couldn't believe you were goin' to run off with that snake. Glad to see you figured out who he was before it was too late," Billy said, running a lose strand of her hair through his fingers. "Your hair's mighty soft, feels like silk. Silk and fire all mixed together."

"Why do you think you deserve a kiss, Billy?" She smiled at him, her breasts pushing from her bodice meaning to entice him. She thought for a moment to unfasten it at the top so she could breathe better. "Besides, don't know if I want you or Bobby. Why do you think I should kiss you?"

"You can have us both ifn' you want. Two of us is more fun than just one of us. We try to do everything together, but if you object...you can pick one of us," he said, taking her hand before leading her into the stables. "Got a place I want to show you. Think you'll like what we can do there if you're a willin' lass. Are you willin', sweet Molly?"

"That remains to be seen." She touched him under the chin, enticing him to kiss her, she moistened her lips, letting her lashes fall across her cheeks. "How good are you?"

"Ah, little Molly dear, you do that and it makes me think you want that kiss I offered. Do you? I won't be taking anything you don't want." He pulled her close, lowering his head so his breath brushed across her lips. Then sucking her bottom lip into his mouth, he cupped her bottom with his hands, bringing her against his pulsing rod.

She squeaked when two more hands cupped her breasts form behind then unfastened her bodice, the fingers slipping inside to explore her aroused flesh, touching her nipples, tugging on them.

"Do you want me too, Miss Molly?" Bobby asked as he squeezed her nipples and Billy's hand caressed her legs beneath her skirts.

She had no idea when he pulled her skirts to her waist. Her breath caught in her throat as Billy deepened the kiss, his tongue plunging inside. Bloody eyes, but she'd never felt anything like this. Then Billy turned her and Bobby was gazing at her. His lips so close to hers all she could do was say, "please."

"Ah, little Molly I'm going to please you so much," Bobby said as all the fastenings on her bodice were suddenly free and her breasts were exposed for easy access.

"Pick up your feet," Billy told her but she was so mesmerized and mindless she couldn't do what he asked her. Bobby was kissing her, over and over again. She felt the fever of his mouth upon hers and she clung to him, stunned by this new ferocity of passion yet willing to ride the soaring force of it. She met his lips again and again, returning the passion.

Bobby lifted her off the ground and she felt her underclothes slide the length of her legs and she was suddenly naked beneath her dress, a sudden an intense inferno sweeping within her. She didn't know who was doing what and she didn't care. It seemed one or the other or both were touching every part of her.

"We could take this to the loft where we'd all be more comfortable," Billy whispered in her ear before he gently bit then swirled his tongue inside. Bobby's hands possessed her breasts, rolling the nipples between his fingers. Then Billy swept her over his shoulder.

"Just going to climb up the ladder. Don't want you to fall," Bobby told her. "You just relax now. Don't move a muscle just yet, not until I set you down."

Bloody eyes, she didn't want to fall either, and at the moment she didn't think she could walk let alone climb a ladder. At the top he set her down on a blanket before pouring her a glass of ale.

"Thought you might like something to drink. Your mouth might get a bit parched by the time we're done here."

She no longer knew who was talking to her or whose hands belonged to who. She didn't care. Both boys were naked now. She stretched her hand out to touch one. Hot, wet and swollen, she needed relief from the ache they created so easily.

"Not so fast. You've got to be naked too before you can touch. Is that going to be alright with you? It's a rule we have. Everyone's got to be naked or we don't allow liberties."

She nodded, hands fumbling with what was left of the fastenings on her dress. It wasn't necessary, the boys were adept at removing clothing and before she could blink, she was naked between them.

"We always share." He was kissing her, lying slightly to the side. One whispered against her lips as he explored her further.

The other was on top of her and between her legs, kissing and sightseeing the length, caressing her intimately then nipping his way to her breasts. One man caressed and kissed one breast and massaged her most intimate lady places while the other's tongue was deep inside her mouth and his fingers were tugging on one nipple.

She moaned, her hips bucking then he surged intimately within her, moving slowly at first while her spasms of pleasure spiraled within then out of control while she cried out into the other's mouth.

Lying on the blanket, spent, she was surprised when the one who had filled her and brought her to a place she'd never been before slipped beneath her so she straddled him. "Now it's Bobby's turn ifn' you're still willing. We'll make you feel mighty fine again, a bit of agony and a bit more bliss if I do say so myself."

She licked her lips, wondering how she could possibly survive another bout with these two but she was willing to try. "I'm spineless and I doubt if I can move but I'm willing. The two of you will have to do everything."

"That's not gonna be a problem, Miss Molly."

Billy pulled her so he could suck her nipples into his mouth while Bobby kissed and licked her bottom, spreading her feminine folds with his fingers. Then Billy was kissing her, his tongue inside her mouth. Bobby held her breasts in his hands.

From behind her he drove inside. The boy's hands and mouths were everywhere, exploring arousing and bringing her to another point where she had no control of her body. Tremors once more encompassed her, took over her body. Then a deep guttural cry came from him and he emptied himself inside her.

When they finished, she found herself curled up next to one of the men, the other one's body protectively sheltering her back.

"Did you like that, Molly? If you did, we can do it again, anytime you like. Maybe as soon as you're rested?"

Chapter Six

Before Brett left the house the next day, he wrote two letters, one to Drake Montgomerie and the other to Charles Hepburn. Both missives requested information and spoke of the urgency of their situation. He sent a copy of the drawing as well as what they learned about Lyssa Cameron but included the fact the crest was not the Cameron crest. Also, the fact they were searching for more information from various servants. There were rumors.

The need to know how Jocko got the ring he wore consumed Brett's waking thoughts. A trip to the Hepburn estate might be prudent yet he didn't want to uproot his household again, especially Piper. She was just beginning to settle in, and he didn't intend to go anywhere without her. Any trip could prove dangerous to Piper's health. These hours on the road he spent not being able to see her and protect her left him eager to return to his home.

Today was to be the wedding of Duncan Erskine and Siubhan. He asked Piper if she wanted to attend and her first answer was an adamant no then with further thought she agreed. He can still hear her words that she wanted to see the woman happy with her young man just as she was happy with him.

The sun had risen a few hours ago. He wanted to ride his land and talk with a few tenants. So far he'd not seen Molly or B&B. Molly should have been at her post when he left their bedchamber, but she was nowhere in sight. When he strode through the kitchen, Mrs. Pickery hadn't seen the trio either.

The boys should be in the kitchen eating by now and ready to work. He couldn't leave if Piper didn't have her bodyguards nearby.

Drumming his fingers on the kitchen table, he looked to Mrs. Pickery and the back door several times.

"They're not going to come if you keep lookin' at the door," Mrs. Pickery admonished, shaking her finger at him.

"Won't come if I'm not looking at the door either," Brett mumbled while Mrs. Pickery poured him another cup of coffee. The sun seemed to rise higher in the sky at an astounding rate while the wait turned to what seemed like an eternity.

The cup of coffee he drank turned into two then three. He finished his meal and was suddenly ready to find new employees. Then Molly rushed inside, her body shaking from what must have been a swift run. She should have been inside her room upstairs. So why was there straw poking from her hair?

"Sir, sorry sir. It won't happen again." Molly rushed through the kitchen spewing more apologies. "I'll have milady's bath waiting for her and her breakfast." She looked at Mrs. Pickery who nodded. "I didn't mean to be late." She curtsied, "It's just that, well...I've no excuse. It won't happen again."

"I'm sure she'll like that, Molly. A bath and perhaps some breakfast would be nice for her. I know she likes hot chocolate instead of coffee. I'm sure Mrs. Pickery has both. Are B&B coming to work anytime soon?" he asked, believing there must be more to the story and hoping to discover the truth without prying, sensing the boys were involved. Molly had never turned up at work so disheveled before. He grinned, his imagination running in too many directions to count.

Molly's face turned a deep shade of red. "Oh, I'm sure they'll be along in a few minutes. They thought we should wait a few minutes for them to appear, for decorum 's sake you understand. So people won't talk." Her hand flew to her mouth. "Oh, my, I didn't say that. You didn't hear that, sir."

"No, of course not. That's a very bricky lass taking on two men in one night." He chuckled softly wondering if she'd take the bait.

"Not so much. They made it so wonderful, I..." With that Molly fled.

Brett rested his forearms on the table, his gaze riveted on the door, and just as Molly told him a few minutes later the boys sauntered into the room looking more pleased than they should if a normal night's sleep preceded this morning. Had Molly truly been with both men all night? Bloody eyes, he'd heard of such things but never met anyone who participated.

"The two of you are late. Don't let it happen again," he said, his voice dry yet he was having a devil of a time commanding anger.

"Sorry, sir, we'll be up directly to guard milady," Billy said as he snatched a piece of bread off the platter.

"Won't happen again," Bobby said following in his partners wake before heading to the door that would take them upstairs.

"What? Your tardiness or having your way with Molly?" He tried not to laugh at the expressions on their faces.

"Howd' you know?" Billy asked.

"Molly can't keep a secret, never been able to. I'll be back here at noon then I want to know everything the baroness has done and anything you think is out of the normal. Keep your hands to yourselves during working hours." He rose then set his napkin on the table and took a last look towards their chambers.

"Of course not, sir. Never would do such a thing, sir. Playing is for when there's the time then you got to take what life's willing to give you," Bobby said over his shoulder as the two men disappeared upstairs. "Never can be too sure what's around the corner so to speak."

Brett paused midstride for a moment, realizing their attitude came from living on the streets and surviving. One has to find pleasure and take it whenever one could. In his sheltered life, he'd never really thought about things like that.

Striding to the stables, and thinking on all he'd learned about Piper, he had the suspicion she wasn't the child of Lyssa Cameron but she was Charlotte Leighton's child who vanished that day eighteen years ago. He'd also wager Charlotte Leighton must have hidden the ring in the babe's swaddling. Jocko would have found it. The only question he had now was whether it was Scarface who picked up the child or was it Jocko? Did either of them have anything to do with William Leighton's death? The raven on the crest seemed to be the key to Piper's parentage? Yes,

Piper was probably the daughter of The Duchess, but he still had a few doubts.

He spent the better part of the day on a mission that led nowhere. None of his tenants were willing to talk to him and he suspected the only way he'd ferret out what was going on with the stolen produce was to have B&B infiltrate this tight community. What he did learn was that the problem began when he left for London. Because of that he didn't believe this had anything to with the secrets surrounding Piper. And what if anything did Scarface have to do with Lyssa Cameron's death and the disappearance of her child.

The time was fast approaching noon and he promised himself he'd be back by then, so he gave up on his mission and turning his horse, headed home. Duncan's wedding was to begin at three o'clock in the small parish church nearby. He supposed most of the villagers would attend. It was his duty as laird to appear, and he hoped Piper would accompany him. It would be their first official duty as baron and baroness.

Once again, he found Piper outside near the gazebo, playing with Rogue and the boys. Molly stood by watching, her hands clasped tightly in front of her, clearly in distress. This time, however, Piper was dressed in preparation for the wedding. The gown was a beautiful shade of blue, very nearly matching the color of her eyes.

Molly or Piper, she didn't know which, had pulled her hair back and piled what little of it that was there on top of her head, dressing the coif with pearls, his mother's pearls. He made a point to gift Piper with all the jewelry his mother left behind. Little tendrils dangled around her face, accentuating her deep blue eyes. She wore a light dusting of powder as well as blush on her cheeks and color tinted her eyelids as well as her lips and she darkened her lashes.

"You are absolutely fetching. Every man in the village will be jealous of me when they see you." He pulled her into his arms, brushing his lips across hers, careful not to mess up the makeup.

"Sir, don't do too much kissing and such. You'll ruin all the work we did this morning and it wasn't easy to keep the baroness sitting still." Molly sighed in a huff, her voice strained. "I've had the devil of a time keeping milady from soiling her dress while she's playing and the boys aren't helping either." She squinted at them as if trying to send them a message.

"Thank you for your patience, Molly. I appreciate your efforts. The boys are just bored and need something more to do. That is my job. You all have the afternoon and evening off unless you wish to attend the wedding," he told them thinking they might have a dalliance or two planned with the extra time.

"I'd like to go to Duncan's wedding. He was always the kind of man a woman could be proud to call hers. Never understood what he saw in Siubhan. He was always goo-goo eyed over her though." She turned to Billy and Bobby, tapping a toe, seeming to wait for at least one of them to speak up and volunteer to escort her. Both remained silent staring at their toes.

Silence surrounded them for what seemed like hours until Piper decided she'd heard enough of nothing. "Well, after what the two of you did last night, at least one of you should escort Molly or do you need an engraved invitation. You need to treat her like the lady she is, not some..." she stopped seeming to decide she'd said enough.

"Thank you, milady. I was thinking I'd bribe them but I think you made your point. If neither of you take me it's going to be a long time before..." she paused. "Well, the two of you know what I'm talking about. I won't fall into your bed of straw anytime soon and not so easily as I did yesterday," She turned to leave, lifting her skirts, "I can walk I suppose. It's not all that far."

"Of course, you won't walk," Piper spoke up. "You can ride with Brett and me. Can't' she?" She leaned against Brett, seeming to know her breasts were provocatively pushing up from her dress. Bloody eyes, but he could see the deep V of her cleavage and almost her pretty tits. He groaned in the back of his throat, understanding he'd give her anything she asked for.

He grinned at her, trying not to focus on the beautiful round globes, so large they filled his hands. She seemed even larger than before. In London the dress had been fit meticulously to her. Perhaps it was too soon and this was just his imagination, but he hoped she carried his child.

"Of course, we wouldn't want to use the carriage for anything except transportation." He pulled her close, enjoying the blush rising to her cheeks and thinking of another carriage ride when they made love.

"Milady showed me the drawing you made." Molly spoke up before anyone could comment on Brett's outrageous statement. "I think I might know something about it and the Camerons." She spoke as they walked to the carriage.

Brett felt the hairs on the back of his neck stand on end at her words. "You know something? How?" He helped both ladies into the vehicle then hopped in behind them.

"My mum was the duchess' lady's maid. She loved Lyssa Cameron as if she was her sister. They shared everything, well almost everything. I'm sure there were aspects of her life after her husband died she didn't want to share." Molly folded her hands in her lap, seeming to wait for a question.

"Miss Molly," Billy was knocking on the carriage door. "You didn't wait for an answer about the wedding. Well, in any case, Bobby and I had to discuss this matter before we could say yeah or nay. We want to escort you but we don't have a carriage or a horse. You can ride with the baron and baroness and we'll walk."

"We'll meet you there," Bobby said.

While Brett was eager to learn more about Lyssa Cameron, he didn't want to share the carriage either to the wedding or on the return. "The three of you can use the smaller carriage if you promise to behave yourselves. No shenanigans, if you get my drift," he told them.

"I'll be right back, just give me a few minutes." He looked inside at his wife, enjoying the view. "Don't go anywhere."

In the stables the three men prepared the small curricle. "It's going to be a tight fit. Since the two of you like to share perhaps one of you can sit on the other's lap."

"Sounds like a right fine idea to me," Billy said, rubbing his chin as if pondering what he said.

Molly appeared in the doorway, sunlight shimmering on her red hair, making it look like a sunset.

"There now, who's going to drive?" The horse was hooked up and there was just room enough for two of them. Brett wondered just how they were going to manage but he didn't have any doubts the trio would figure it out.

"I'm going to drive. Don't trust these two not to head somewhere else. I know what they've got on their minds, and it's the only reason they want to come with me." She chuckled, leaning over and kissing Billy on the lips, implying with the added wink they could have whatever they wanted after the wedding. "The two of you are not going to dance with me together but one at a time," she added, giving the horse the go ahead. "And there won't be walks in the dark to some shadowed place. None of that tonight while we are at the reception, do both of you understand?"

Brett rocked back on his heels, watching them leave and wishing Molly luck with the two men before heading to the carriage and his wife. Once inside, he tapped on the roof signaling the driver to go.

"What do you think about what Molly said?" Piper asked, touching Brett's hand, her eyes filled with anxiety. "Her mother was Lyssa Cameron's lady's maid. Do you think she could have administered the poison?"

"Lyssa Cameron? I don't know what to think and it's not wise to guess about anything. We need to hear more of what she knows. Is her mother still alive?" Piper asked.

"She is but her memory is not that great. She's forgetful and seems to dwell in the past, which might serve us well. Don't you think though she would put something so horrific as the murder of a newborn in the back of her mind? Still I'm thinking we need to look in a different direction too," Brett mused. Clearly, he could recall his father who suffered with a diminishing memory. The past was all he wanted to talk about. He remembered his teenage years as if they were yesterday but very little about the present.

"Perhaps Molly and I could go to her home and talk with her tomorrow. Two women would be less intimidating than a man she might not know."

"I would go with you," Brett said, determined not to let her out of his sight unless her bodyguards were present.

"She might be more at ease with just Molly and me," Piper said again, resting her hand on his then seeming to notice her bodice. Looking down, "I don't understand what is wrong with this gown. It fit when we left London."

"I like it. Reminds a bit of that dress you wore the first day we met. You were spilling out of it, and I couldn't keep my eyes off your pretty bubbies. Wanted to see if your skin felt like satin and if you'd moan with delight when I sucked your pretty nipples into my mouth."

"And what did you find out?" she asked, flaunting herself and seeming to forget the problem with her dress or perhaps using that problem to her advantage.

"That I can't resist you, silk and satin. Sometimes I can't keep my hands from you and I'm not speaking of your dress but the way you feel beneath my fingertips. Don't worry about your dress. It's quite in fashion. Perhaps the seamstress, can't think of her name now, cut it a little lower than the norm because it's an evening gown." He smiled trying to reassure Piper. It was too early to broach the subject of pregnancy while her mind was on so many other things.

Seemingly unconscious of her actions, she pulled on the dress, trying to bring it higher to no avail. "I'm afraid to bend over or eat. I might fall out of the gown," she sighed softly, looking to him as if he could fix any problem.

Chuckling to himself then unable to hold the laughter back. "I'll be more than happy to catch you when you fall out. These tiny little embroidered sleeves, well they could slip down your arms and then..." He touched the edge of her bodice tracing the Belgium lace to the sleeves. "We could stop along the road here...we don't have to go to the wedding."

"Stopping on the road is one thing and we're not going to do it. But if I fall out of my dress well, that wouldn't make you happy and you know it. Don't think you're at all like the boys. I don't see you as a man who wants to share his wife. Although Molly's not a wife to them." She sat back, leaning into his chest.

He stroked her arms, wishing they were at home and alone in their bedroom. At least for a few hours he was going to have to share his wife to some degree. Tonight, however, he didn't need to worry about Siubhan asking for anything from him. He generously gifted them both and he knew Duncan at least was thankful.

"What are you thinking?" Piper pushed away from him, gazing into his eyes. "You look so serious. Your brows are drawn together and lips have thinned while your eyes are so dark."

"That I'd like to be at home and alone with you. The wedding is something we need to attend even though no one will care tomorrow. I'm certain Duncan will have other things on his mind this evening. But it's a courtesy we need to observe."

"How long do we have to stay?" she asked settling back and making herself comfortable in his arms. "We can't always be thinking of sex you know."

"I think the general rule is until after they cut the cake." He groaned, thinking of all the wasted time. As laird he'd have to get used to these times. When he was single the evenings like this would be spent drinking with friends he'd grown up with and looking for a willing lass. That all seemed so long ago.

"Will we be expected to attend all the weddings of the people in the village?" Piper asked. "I've no idea what a baroness does. You should make a list for me and I'll try to be dutiful."

"Dutiful?" he asked, trying not to laugh, "Piper from St. Giles as a dutiful wife and baroness, hmm... I like that thought for at least a second. Would that mean you'd no longer be impulsive and unpredictable?"

"I don't believe I've been either impulsive or unpredictable for a long time," she sighed. "I've finally learned that life now for me is more than survival. I've a future to look forward to."

"You'll learn your duties, I'm sure. Like I said, trust your instincts. And the answer is yes, the weddings as well as the funerals we will be expected to attend, christenings as well."

"The births?" she asked, seemingly still curious.

"Only if you bring skills, midwife skills. Have you ever delivered a child?" Brett asked, wondering if she sensed what might be happening to her body.

"Never seen a child being born, never wanted to see such a thing. When those events happened, all the men were sent away. They'd go drink, some would find a willing woman and I'd go with them." She lifted her shoulders in a delicate shrug he was beginning to adore. "For obvious reasons no one let me into help with the birthing."

Anger and frustration suffused him, yet he realized he would have never met Piper if not for the circumstances that sent her to London and the dubious care of Jocko. "I wish that part of your life never happened, but then I'd be wishing away our life together. But for your unfortunate circumstances I would have never met you."

"I'm not going to look backwards except for the immediate danger threatening, that of my heritage. Thoughts of St. Giles are best left in the dark shadows of my memory. What happens if it is true, that Charlotte Leighton or Lyssa Cameron was my mother or someone else for that matter?" Her fingers wound into the fine blue crepe of her gown leaving tiny creases.

"Let me see." He pulled her closer, trailing a fingertip along her arm. "You will be a duchess and will out rank your husband. Your title would be inherited and your duties more extensive. As a duchess you'll have to answer more closely to the crown."

"Would you become a duke by marriage?" she asked, "The beat of your heart is strong and steady. The sound of it gives me comfort along with the knowledge you will never leave me."

"No, I would not. None of what I just said is true," he laughed, tickling her ear now. "Women don't inherit titles, but your birth would have been to a duke and duchess. Wouldn't want more responsibilities in any case. Seems I'm having enough troubles discovering the thefts on my land and handling this tiny estate in my part of the highlands."

"I'm sure you'll figure this all out," she told him, wishing for the umpteenth time all this intrigue was finished so they could get on with their lives. "Perhaps the boys will learn something at the wedding. They have a way of fitting in with the people. Your clan won't know they didn't grow up in the same village."

"I think we're here," he told her as the carriage pulled to a slow stop. The door was opened and Brett helped Piper down. "Try to enjoy the wedding and when we get back home, we can pretend it's our wedding night," he whispered close to her ear, sending shivers down her spine.

Duncan was popular in the village, a leader and a man with a strong opinion. When they entered the church, it was very nearly full.

They sat in the front designated for the laird and his family. To Piper this all seemed surreal. She'd never been to a wedding except her own and she barely remembered anything of the ceremony. In deed she didn't know anyone who was married.

She watched with avid interest both Duncan as well as Siubhan while they were saying their vows. Both seemed inordinately nervous, yet Duncan's smile when the priest told him he could kiss the bride was broad as well as when he announced them as husband and wife. Siubhan seemed hesitant throughout the ceremony, but when all was said and done, she looked pleased. Piper sighed a breath of air, relieved she would not have to look over her shoulder to see if Siubhan had something planned that would be unpleasant.

Outside the church, tables had been set for food and drinks and lots of chairs for seating had been arranged. Piper guessed there had to be at least one hundred guests in the church and more now that they moved outside.

"Did you pay for all this?" Piper turned to her husband, smiling and beginning to appreciate all Brett did for his people.

"It was part of Siubhan's dowry, but these fine people all brought something for the celebration and Mrs. McDonnell made the wedding cake. She owns a bakery in town." Together they watched the festivities.

Pipes played, people dance, they ate, they drank and laughed. The musicians changed the songs to fit their moods and the dancers responded in kind. The boys took turns dancing with Molly and plying her with food and drink. She laughed and flirted as if she wanted a repeat of the night before. Mrs. Pickery and her husband showed up. Piper didn't see them during the ceremony but now they too danced.

Piper tapped her foot in time to the music but wasn't eager to try dancing again. Her wedding night she had not been graceful, and Brett didn't seem too eager to have his feet stepped on once more. She was content for the time being to watch the others, clapping her hands in time to the lively tunes and humming during the ballads.

Duncan brought his new wife, Siubhan to talk. "Thank you for all your generosity," Duncan said, holding Siubhan close as if he didn't dare let her go. Yet the woman smiled at them and was strangely silent, not her usual demeanor.

"I'll be in touch soon," Brett told Duncan, eager to learn about the clan and what was happening to the crops. "Two of my best men will be working with you." He clasped Duncan's hands, the gesture warm and friendly.

Suddenly Piper's breath caught in her throat, her heart stopping for a moment. She could barely breathe. Her fingers tightened around Brett's arm. He didn't seem to notice, his conversation with Duncan overshadowing everything else.

"Brett," she whispered, her distress clear if he would only listen. For a moment she looked at her feet then back to the apparition she saw a few seconds ago. The man was gone just as quickly as he appeared. She searched the area but he had truly vanished.

Closing her eyes for a few seconds, she decided this was just her imagination. They had been thinking about Jocko and Scarface so much she was bound to see him around every corner.

"What is it?" Brett seemed to acknowledge her for a moment, looking at her and waiting for a reply.

"Nothing, just my imagination playing games with me," she murmured yet she was sure she saw him. He had no reason to be in this part of Scotland unless he intended her harm or was trying to find out what she knew.

"You sure?" He bent close, seeming to hear the distress in her voice. "I know I wasn't listening before but I'm paying attention now. What's bothering you, lass?"

"No, but I'll let you know if I see him again. I'm sure it's nothing," she told him, searching the dancers for Molly who could now be in as much danger as she was just because of her mother's relationship with the Duchess of St. Aubries, Lyssa Cameron. Even though Brett seemed sure the scar on her leg was from the Leighton family crest, it seemed intrigue surrounded the Camerons as well.

She found Billy, downing a pint with a few other men and women then tried to get his attention. Waving several times, Billy finally seemed to notice and sauntered her way. He seemed distracted though when a buxom blond caught him by the arm then tried to tug him away from the party. She whispered something in his ear and Billy laughed. Piper felt a surge of anger at the man. Didn't he have any loyalty at all toward Molly and the things they did the night before?

Trying to keep her movements subtle, she waved at Billy again, who finally seemed to comprehend the urgency of her situation. He signaled at her as if he understood what she wanted then holding on to the blond, he sauntered her way.

Still hanging on to Brett's arm, she spoke quickly and quietly to Billy. "I'm sorry," she addressed the blond, "but Billy's working tonight. Maybe you can have some fun some other time." Piper waited for the girl to leave, but she stubbornly held her place until Billy kissed her and whispered something in her ear. With a huff she left, her hips swaying provocatively.

"So, what is it?" Billy clearly forgot her new station. "You keepin' me from a little dalliance."

"You need to change your tone of voice," Brett interjected as he finished his discussion with Duncan. "You're an employee in case you've forgotten and you are always on call, despite what you might want. If you have objections to that, I can pay you now for your services and you can be on your way."

"Sorry, sir, of course. I want to work for you. Don't want to go back to what I was doin' before. What did you need me for?"

Piper didn't want to concern Brett when she wasn't positive about what she thought she saw, but now she would have to let him hear what she'd meant for Billy. "I saw a man who looked a lot like Scarface. It was dark and he was in the shadows."

"Was that what you meant by nothing? Scarface?" Brett said, obviously annoyed with her silence.

"I didn't want you to worry and I wasn't sure. I thought I saw him then he vanished." She tried to defend herself. "In any case that doesn't matter right now. If Scarface played a part in the adduction of Lyssa Cameron's child, Molly is in danger too. We have to protect her. I don't want her to lose her life over something that happened to me ages ago."

Brett slowly stroked his chin, seemingly thinking. "You're right about the danger for Molly, probably more so than for you at least at the moment. We haven't given any indication we know anything about the events of eighteen years ago, and we've made no claims as to your inheritance. Scarface will want to stop Molly and her mother from talking to you if he was involved in Lyssa's baby and the child's kidnapping."

"Can we move her mother into the estate, along with Molly of course?" Piper asked, believing they would be safer there. "It isn't as if we don't have the room? There's an entire wing no one lives in. Not quite sure what it's for."

"Guests," Brett said laughing.

"Guests, that's exactly what they'll be. Do you think Mrs. Pickery could be in danger?" she asked as an afterthought.

"Yes, to the first part of the question. We need to make sure they all stay safe. And we'll ask Mrs. Pickery. To my knowledge she has no connection to Lyssa Cameron or Charlotte Leighton, but she can decide for herself. We must think of a good reason for the move, however. You say Molly's mother can't remember anything?"

"She can't. Molly says that sometimes she doesn't remember who she is."

"Her safety is a good enough reason since Molly can't be there for her all day and all night. The move is logical because Molly is your lady's maid and her mother needs extra care."

"Go get Molly," Piper turned to Billy, "And of course Bobby. Make sure Molly gets to the MacLachlan estate safely and we'll pick up her mother."

~ * ~

When Piper and Brett stopped in front of Molly's home the tiny cottage was nearly dark. It appeared one candle burned in a back bedroom. Eerie shadows cast from the moonlight seemed to dance on the outside walls.

"What do you think, Brett? Seems as if..." she paused. "Not sure but why is there a candle burning? It's late. Everything should be dark, shouldn't it? My skin is crawling, and I can't seem to rid my arms of the goosebumps," Her heart raced as she felt a deep apprehension at the thought of entering the house.

"If I was alone, I'd probably keep a light burning until my daughter returned."

It seemed Brett tried to calm her but knowing Scarface might have been at the celebration troubled her deeply. That fact also meant the man could be inside Molly's and Kate's home.

Firsthand experience told her how dangerous the man was and Brett's recounting of some of his misdeeds hit home right now. Even if the man had nothing to do with the death of Richard and Lyssa Cameron or something to do with the death of Charles Leighton, he was lethal. The inhabitants of St. Giles feared and avoided him. She inhaled long and deep before letting the air out slowly, understanding this woman's safety was the responsibility of the laird MacLachlan, Brett's more to the point.

"You're right of course. I'm still terrified," she told him, bracing herself for what needed to be done. They had a better chance of convincing the older woman of going with them, if she was there, if Molly had come with them. Brett could be intimidating, by his size alone let alone the fact he was a man and if the lady's memory was diminished. She might not realize he was the laird and had her interests at heart.

Brett set his hand on top of hers. "I understand but you'll be safer with me, no matter the terror you feel at having to walk inside that cottage. Besides I need to know you're breathing." He pulled two pistols from beneath the seat, handing her one. "Do you know how to use one of these?"

She pulled her lower lip beneath her teeth, "I should but never had the chance to learn. I do know how to use this. "She pulled a small stiletto from her pocket. "I can use a sticker. Always carry one."

Brett chuckled softly, "I remember that first day and your bath. You pulled one of my carving knives on me. The only problem with a stiletto is that you have to be close to use it. If you recall, I disarmed you without much difficulty. Use the pistol. All you have to do is point and pull the trigger, keeping your distance in the process. Just promise you won't hit me."

"I don't want to hit you," she murmured as she looked at the weapon in her hand then at Brett. He was grinning and she didn't understand why.

"Don't want you to shoot me either, but I trust you and don't think you'd point the gun at me. Hold it this way." He showed her the pistol he was holding. "You've only got one shot. If you have to use it, use it wisely."

A few seconds later after mulling over all the random thoughts filling her mind, she nodded. "We should do this before I lose my nerve."

"Good." He stepped from the carriage before helping Piper.

"Wish I was wearing my britches," she told him while she picked up her skirts with one hand and held the pistol with the other. "I can barely move with all these skirts wrapping around my legs."

"Hopefully, no one but Kate is inside and you won't have to move very fast. We'll walk in and convince Molly's mother to come with us. Before you can blink, we'll be at the estate and safe. Worst case scenario is that we'll have to do a good deal of convincing to get her to come with us."

"We can make sure she understands the danger Molly is in if she doesn't come. Molly will insist she return home if her mother isn't safe beneath our roof. Problem is Molly has no idea how treacherous Scarface is and how easy it would be to kill both these women."

The door was slightly ajar when they reached it. Piper slanted a cautious look Brett's way while he motioned her to silence and to stay behind him. Appreciating the human shield, she wasn't sure why she felt slightly more at ease. He was certainly a bigger target than she was and in the dark, he would be a great deal easier to hit.

Inside they waited. She wasn't sure why but she trusted Brett to approach this in the safest way possible. A scuffling sound came from the room where the candle was burning. Brett walked cautiously toward the light.

Pushing open the door, he called out, "Hold it right there."

One of his tenants held a knife to the elderly woman's throat. "Don't come any closer or I'll slit her throat," he threatened. "She doesn't mean anything to me. Don't care if she lives or dies."

"If you do, you'll hang. You'll never get out of here, Callum. You know as well I do that I know where you live. What will your wife say when she finds out what you're about to do? You're not a murderer. What brings you to these circumstances?"

"He's threatened my wife and my children. Unless I kill her, they'll kill all of them." The man had tears running down his face. "Don't want to lose my family."

"You should have come to me with this. I could have helped. Still can for that matter."

"No one could have helped," Callum said.

"One death doesn't make another one right. I'll do everything I can to make this right for you and yours but there are no guarantees. Put the knife down, Callum."

Brett felt the barrel of the gun to his head before the man in front of him had the chance to set the knife on the floor. "Piper?"

"It's not me..." She couldn't breath, her heart in her throat as she watched the scene slowly unfold in front of her. The man stole the gun from her before she even realized he was there. Still she had her sticker in her pocket. She meant to use it as soon as she got the chance.

"Set your gun on the ground and kick it away, or I'll kill the lass." The voice behind him was ice cold.

"Don't do it." Piper felt the same terror she'd known several times in St. Giles but now she felt empowered, no longer weak. The man holding the gun to Brett's head didn't consider her a factor in this. He underestimated her and she meant to use that to her advantage. What he didn't know about her would get him killed. She didn't have the same sense of terror she used to have when cornered. Her identity was intact and she wasn't concealing anything.

For a second only she thought of the repercussions. Then she pulled the weapon from her pocket and pushed the stiletto into the man holding the gun to Brett's head. The weapon fell to the floor with the agony filled groan from the man involved. Quickly, she picked up the pistol, her hands now trembling.

"Do you want your friend to die?" Brett asked, slowly moving toward the farmer whose hands were quivering so hard, he feared the man would accidentally slit the ladies throat.

"No, didn't plan or want any of this. The man with the scar told me it would be easy, just an old lady and her daughter. Kill them or bring them to him, he didn't care."

"If you let her go, you can see to your friend and I promise you as soon as I get home, I'll send someone to your farm. I can bring your wife and children to safety until we catch whoever is responsible for this or the man with the scar. Did he give you his name?"

"I don't know. He sounded as if my family was dead the moment I failed him."

"Ma'am, your Molly is safe. This man is going to let you go." Brett sounded confidant, perhaps too much so.

"Molly is fine, you know," Piper tried to reassure Kate, "She wants you to come with us so you'll be safe too. As soon as this man sets down his knife, we'll get you to your daughter." She walked forward staring at the man. "You've got to let her go. There is nowhere for you to hide if you don't. Scarface will kill your family whether or not you do this for him. You know that don't you? The laird is the only man who can protect you from Scarface's wrath. He doesn't abide failure, you know."

"No," his voice wavered as he seemed to think over her words."

"She speaks true," Brett said, as he walked closer. "Your friend is bleeding out even as we speak. He won't live if you don't help him. What about his family, what will happen to them if you let him die?"

"Don't want to let him die. Known him since we were kids. He's married to my sister," he said, nearly sobbing. "This shouldn't be happening to us. Didn't do nothin' wrong, always minded our business."

"It shouldn't but it is," Piper said wishing she had more strength. All she had was cunning and the right words, words that would sway the man. "I've known Scarface since I was a little girl. He's ruthless and he rarely keeps a promise unless it's in his favor to keep it. Give your laird the weapon. Go home and collect your family then bring them to the laird's home. We will keep all of you safe. I promise."

"She's right," Brett said, as he reached out to take the knife from the man's hand. Once he disarmed Callum, he crumpled into a ball sobbing while Molly's mother struggled from the bed and into her arms.

Piper held the elderly woman, stroking her back in hopes of easing the trembling. Her body was paper thin and frail. She could feel the woman's bones beneath her nightgown.

"Can you get a few things together to bring with you?" Piper asked after a few minutes. Brett was busy with the fallen man, trying to stop the bleeding. Piper didn't feel a bit of remorse at stabbing him. The man intended harm to Brett. She told herself she did what was necessary yet she was terrified she would be put on trial. The man wasn't dead. Piper learned long ago where to stick someone to disable them not kill. Jocko taught her, trained her.

"When we get home, I'm going to send for the constables. I'll tell them everything that happened here. Don't want any rumors or gossip to get out of hand. I'm afraid we've a long night ahead of us."

"We don't even know where Scarface is or what exactly he wants. What we do know is that he won't give up," Piper said.

"You're the key to whatever it is he wants. This lady and Molly are also part of it, and he's willing to blackmail my tenants to get the information he's looking for," Brett spoke through clenched teeth.

Piper didn't think she'd ever seen him this angry, or angry at all.

"I'll send the constables to your home to help you get your families to the estate. I hope the two of you choose not to run but decide to confront what you've done and why," Brett said.

Riding in the carriage now, with Molly's mother, Piper wasn't sure how to approach the subject. Brett stole the decision from her.

"You worked for Lyssa Cameron?" he asked, leaning forward, his forearms resting on his thighs. "Can you tell me anything about that time?"

Piper was amazed at Brett's patience. She would have asked about those days leading to Lyssa's death. "Was Lady Cameron pleased to have the child?"

Kate suddenly appeared to be far away, perhaps reliving another time, "They were both so happy. When the baby was born, they seemed to grow even closer together, if that could be possible. Richard and Lyssa were in love, so in love and they wanted that baby more than life itself."

"Do you recall Richard's death? What happened? I've heard it was a horrible accident," Piper asked, understanding she might be rushing this conversation but she needed to hear the truth.

The older lady started shaking, her hands quivering. "It was Richard's awful brother, Bertram." She looked out the window of the carriage for a few seconds before turning back to them. "They craved the title and the wealth more than anything else. I remember one night, it was late, and Bertram was arguing."

"They?" Brett asked, picking up Kate's hand and kissing the back. "Who are they?" It seemed he didn't want to leave anything unasked, even the obvious.

"Bertram and his wife Melanie talked about what they would do if Bertram had been born first and how unfair life was because of it. I used to hear them plotting against the duke and duchess but I never really took them seriously." She leaned back, closing her eyes, the lines in her face more pronounced than before.

"In hindsight you probably should have," Brett said.

Piper thought Kate had fallen asleep, but after a few minutes she opened her eyes. "Richard was an excellent sailor. The day was sunny and barely any wind to fill the sales. He didn't let himself get hit in the head by the boom. That was a lie Bertram made up to suit their purposes."

"Is that how Richard died?" Brett asked, leaning back against the seat. "And Lyssa committed suicide, I've heard."

"Milady never did such a thing." Kate sat up her voice fierce. "She would have never abandoned her beautiful little boy. The babe looked like his father, the reddest hair, just like a sunset and his eyes were a deep dark green." She paused for a few minutes, staring at Piper. "Did you know you're the spittin' image of milady. Why, if the babe didn't die, you could be her daughter." Then she closed her eyes again, heaving a long sigh.

"What do you think?" Brett asked Piper. "Are you the legitimate Cameron heir? Does what Kate just told you tell you anything?"

Piper laughed, shrugging her shoulders. "Well, he had red hair and green eyes and I'm the spittin' image of him while I've got black hair and blue eyes. There is also the fact that I'm a she and not a he. It seems the evidence keeps piling up in a different direction. So, Lyssa Cameron is not my mother, but I'd still love to find out more about her. She obviously had a son who could be working on the streets of St. Giles." Piper leaned into Brett, taking comfort in his arms. "When I was little, I used to wish for a mother and a father. Of course none of the children I knew had parents. We were all the same," she paused. "Orphans. Doubt if we'll ever find this other child, an adult now."

"I'm sorry for that. If I could change your past I would. Even if we discover all the truths here, and discover the Cameron's child, he will never know them. We can't be sure of anything though, Charles Hepburn did say you reminded him of The Duchess when she was your age. The crest will most likely be the deciding factor."

"Or feel their love. If we ever have children, I want to make sure they're protected from Scarface or anyone else who might want to take advantage of them." She pushed away from Brett, "How can one protect against such horrible people. Bertram killed his brother. Didn't he care about the child?"

"The child stood in the way of his inheriting everything. He had to get rid of everyone if he were to succeed."

"I..." She was at a loss for words, her stomach churning.

"Yet he would have been the guardian. With a bit of creative money managing he could have maintained the wealth in his name and left the child penniless."

"And he would have the title, but I suppose getting rid of the infant made everything simpler." Piper placed her head back on Brett's chest, running her hands along his shirt. "I don't know what I'll do if I truly am anyone's lost child."

They rode the last mile or so in silence. Kate was asleep and perhaps able to fill her head with more pleasant thoughts than what had occurred in the last hour. The next few days might be a surprise for all, and Piper wasn't sure she wanted any more revelations. The last year changed her life in too many ways to count.

"We're home," Brett whispered close to her ear, his breath tickling as it floated across her sensitive flesh. "Wake up, sleepy head."

She must have dozed in his arms, sitting up and realizing dawn would be here soon. Between the wedding celebration and the intrigue at Kate's cottage, the night seemed to have wasted away, her exhaustion far deeper than the surface.

"Did you fall asleep too?" she asked as she pushed hair from her eyes and stretched, feeling her muscles begin to wake up.

"No, but I enjoyed watching you sleep, the slow rise and fall of your breasts. Kate is still asleep as the evening must have been traumatic for her also. I can't imagine being ripped from my home," Brett said.

"I can, but in my case it was necessary and everything turned out for the best. Don't know if we can say that about Kate."

"I did that to you, didn't I? Ripped you from your home," he spoke softly, almost nostalgic. "I suppose it wasn't well done of me."

"As I told you, it was for the best and I don't want to return to that life. Who would? Even Bobby and Billy are happy to be away from St. Giles."

The carriage pulled to a stop in front of the big porch that welcomed guests and family to the laird's home. "I'll get Molly to help with her mother and maybe the boys," Brett said, "I'll be right back." He kissed her quickly.

Piper sat back on the leather seat, closing her eyes and trying to sort through the events of the night. Waiting for something to happen didn't sit well. Scarface was in the vicinity and what did he have planned for her? Jocko told her he wanted her, for his mistress or wife? She always assumed mistress but if she was Charlotte Leighton's daughter, perhaps he meant to force her into marriage. Perhaps Scarface held the proof needed to secure the title.

Billy, Bobby and of course Molly appeared at the carriage with Brett, ready to help Kate to her new lodgings.

"Brett told us there were men at mother's home trying to do god only knows what," Molly said with a visible shiver. "Thank you for bringing her to me."

"In the morning, you will explain everything to your mother," Piper said. "I'm not at all sure what she understands, what happened or why we brought her with us. When she's up to it, find out as much as you can about the duchess as well as the days leading up to her death."

"As soon as she's slept and eaten, we can talk." Molly watched as Billy pulled her into his arms and walked with her to the upstairs room she'd been given.

"You look tired," Brett said, wrapping an arm around her before walking with her to their rooms. "How are you holding up?"

"Not so tired now that I've had a little cat nap." She smiled, gently touching him on the chin. "You worry too much about me and it seems you forget where I hail from. I'm not a delicate flower that needs to be coddled."

"No, you're not but you're still not as strong as a..."

"Man." She laughed softly, relishing this side of Brett. "Pound for pound, I'll bet I'm stronger than you. My life hasn't been easy as you well know. There were many nights I spent with one eye open, hoping no would find my hiding place. Those events molded me into who I am now. In case you haven't noticed, I can take care of myself."

"You hid from the constables?" Brett asked.

"Yes, and those in St. Giles who wanted to rob me before I could hand over my ill-gotten gains to Jocko. The gangs always roamed together and if I got separated from Billy and Bobby before reaching Jocko's apartment, then I was at risk." She held her breath waiting for Brett to say something else about her fragility.

Instead he swept her into his arms and carried her the rest of the way to their rooms. When he set her on the bed, "How do you feel?"

She smiled at him, wondering what he was trying to find out. "How do you feel?" she asked him in return. "This couldn't have been any easier on you."

For a moment he looked away and with a sigh, "Terrified for your life and afraid I might lose you. Can't lose you."

"I'm not easy to get rid of," she told him, pulling his head to her lips and letting him wash away his fears with a long deep kiss that she didn't want to end. By the time the kiss was finished they were both naked and beneath the covers, exploring each other again.

"I'm going to make love to my wife right now then we're going to sleep until noon if we want. What do you think about that?"

"Anything you want, husband."

~ * ~

Ella Montgomerie sipped the tea Alma, her lady's maid, brought her while she watched Drake pace the veranda of their country estate. He was thinking, she knew, and she didn't dare interrupt his thoughts, but damn it she wanted to know what was in his head. The dark shuttered look had taken over his expression.

She would wait. Eventually he would tell her what she wanted to know. A few minutes earlier he had wadded up a piece of paper and tossed it onto the ground.

Drake swore under his breath then picked up the crumpled ball of parchment before pacing again. Stopping, he opened it and stared at the paper once more. "Blessed hell, I would never believe the little guttersnipe Brett turned into a lady could be related in some manner to The Duchess."

"Auntie?"

"Did she have a daughter?" Drake asked.

"Not that I know of. Auntie Charlotte keeps many things secret. She's never spoken of one. Suppose David or Charles would know."

"Like what?" Drake sat down beside her. "What secrets does she keep? This is important, Ella."

"No one I know of knows how her husband died, the Duke of Ravenswood, William Leighton. She's never spoken of his death. Whenever someone brought the subject up, she turned pale and would leave the room."

Drake rose, pacing again, silent for so long she began to question everything he'd told her.

"You know you can tell me everything that's bothering you," she told him pleasantly before setting her cup on the table and walking to him. Wrapping her arms around her husband, she pulled his head down for a kiss, a very unsatisfying kiss. His distraction overwhelmed his thoughts but she tried. "I guess you're too preoccupied to kiss me properly." She returned to her large cushioned chair where she'd been sitting and sipped her tea, watching him over the rim.

"It's Brett MacLachlan and Piper I'm worried about. When he married the little pickpocket, he never thought he'd be embroiled in intrigue that began almost two decades ago. We all thought she was a hoyden from St. Giles and nothing more. By the way, your father is involved in this too."

"He is? My father, Charles?" She was astonished at that fact. He always kept to himself, grieving for his wife. In the last year though he'd taken a step outside what felt comfortable to him, "You mean he's not mourning his life away any longer. What happened to change that? I'll be forever grateful to whoever or whatever is responsible for the turnaround." Her father was in such a depression because of the death of her mother, his wife, he didn't attend her wedding. She'd missed her father and assumed she might never see him again. Thought he would die pining his life away for Sadie.

"From what I've heard, The Duchess happened to him. She visited him and convinced him Sadie, your mother, wouldn't want him to mourn her death any longer. Charlotte told him he should get on with his life."

"Auntie does have a way about her. I'm not surprised. It's impossible to say no to her. Charlotte was very upset he didn't come to the wedding, and I was sure she meant to visit him and make her point known." Ella continued to peer at her husband over the rim of the delicate porcelain teacup. "What are you thinking?"

He ran his hands through his hair before focusing on Ella again. "Nothing specific or anything I can make some sense of."

"Back to my father and this intrigue. You've peaked my curiosity. What could he possibly know?" She laughed softly, thinking of all his wasted years "But then it doesn't take much these days."

"No, and this is something I want you to stay away from. It involves Avery Bainbridge, better known among the thieves and whores of St. Giles Parish as Scarface. He's an extremely dangerous man. You don't know Piper or Brett so this is not your fight. You must promise me not to let your curiosity overrule common sense. Think of Ashcroft if he were to lose his mother."

"You make it sound dangerous," she paused, shrugging her shoulders as if that gesture would make him tell her more. "Why would I consider this my fight if I don't know anyone involved?"

He inhaled a long deep breath before proceeding. "Because you might be closer to the story than we ever excepted. We watched Brett catch Piper in Vauxhall Gardens that first day we kissed. We talked about my brother trying to get rid of me so he could inherit the title and the wealth that goes along with it and we lived through the murder attempt at our wedding along with your abduction."

"I'll never forget that day in the park and the way Auntie Charlotte hit you with her walking stick." She couldn't help laughing, knowing she digressed form the immediate problem, "You knew she'd do it and you kissed me anyway," Ella said, a satisfied smile filling her at the memories.

"It wasn't the kiss that had your auntie whacking me on the back for." His arrogant grin gave her heated shivers, delight sweeping through her. "It's because of the other places my hands were wandering."

"It wasn't that day we talked about your brother and coveting your title," she corrected him thoughtfully. "It was when we thought your brother might have our demise in his thoughts." She adjusted her skirts with a subtle wink, an invitation she hoped for later pleasures.

"I remember you telling me about someone living nearby you," he paused seeming to think, "The husband died in an accident and the wife committed suicide, so some would have us believe, and the child vanished. What if the husband died but not in an accident and the child vanished but the mother still lives and in her own way searches for the little girl she lost?"

"Seems pretty simple when the brother inherited everything because he was the next in line. What was their name and do you believe what you've learned about Piper might be related to this long-ago incident somehow?" She gazed at him as if he could give her the answer she looked for.

"According to the letter Brett sent me that would be the duke and Duchess of St. Aubries, Lord and Lady Cameron, but the crest is not theirs. It is someone else's."

"So, I'm going to ask the obvious. Why is Brett concerned about the Camerons? He's a Scottish Highlander and not a relation that we know of." She set her hands in her lap, a stern expression on her face trying to challenge Drake to break through his secretive nature until he told her all the truth.

"Believe it or not, I mean to tell you everything and probably enlist the help of Addie and Hamilton in ferreting out the truth. They might be in need of adventure again. The more who know this story and the perpetrators of the murders the less chance they will have of getting away with two more murders. Before we pursue any of this a visit to your aunt is in order."

"So..." Alma, Ella's lady's maid brought a tray of cheese and bread along with a bottle of wine and glasses. "I was thinking the two of you might be hungry. All this talk of conspiracy and secrets must be exhausting."

"Thank you, Alma. I do need something stronger than wine," Drake said.

"It's a welcome thought that finally you think my knowing something won't be detrimental to my well-being and I appreciate being included." Ella watched her husband over the rim of the crystal glass, waiting patiently for him to tell her more of the story.

Slowly he smoothed out the crumpled paper before handing it to her. Words seemed unnecessary at the moment, but he would have to explain soon. She stared at the paper, acknowledging the fact the drawing was of a crest, the Leighton crest not the Cameron crest. She handed it back to him, sucking in a gasp of air. "What does this drawing have to do with anything?"

"I've good reason to believe Piper is the lost daughter of Charlotte and William Leighton, Duke and Duchess of Ravenswood."

"The good reason then?" Ella asked her brows rising in speculation knowing full well Drake would never make an assumption unless it was grounded in fact. Still, she needed to wait until he decided to explain how he received this.

Drake cleared his throat, "Brett copied the drawing from a scar on the inside of Piper's thigh, a very intimate place. The scar is the size of a ring."

Ella inhaled a sharp breath of air before letting it out slowly, "Branded," she paused, "Only a mother terrified for her baby's life would hurt her child in such a horrific way." Her stomach turned over as she set her glass on the table unable to take one more sip until the churning subsided. "How did William die? Was it an accident as everyone said?"

"No one really knows. I suspect your aunt Charlotte covered it up in order to protect the little girl who was kidnapped. The rumor was that he died in a riding accident, absolutely preposterous idea," Brett spoke quietly. "I'm sure the duke was an excellent horseman. Before we confront anyone with our suspicions, we need to figure out everyone who was involved."

"I suppose... I just don't understand how anyone would come to these conclusions about Piper. How could Aunt Charlotte's baby end up in St. Giles? That fact seems preposterous too. She should have been doing what she does best, calling in favors and threatening everyone she thought were perpetrators. This doesn't sound at all like The Duchess."

"You must remember she would have been in mourning. She loved William so very much. The trail might have vanished before she could make contact."

"I can't imagine losing Ashcroft."

Drake walked behind her, massaging her shoulders, "Two things," he murmured, kissing the back of her neck. "One, Charles recognized Piper. He told Brett she looks exactly like Charlotte. Saw her at their wedding celebration and while it took him a little while to recall who she reminded him of, he finally figured it out."

"And the second thing," Ella prompted, trying to speed this up. She loved her husband but he had this way of taking his sweet time when it came to stories of intrigue.

"Always impetuous. While making love to his wife, Brett noticed the scar and realized it was a crest. Later he drew the exactness and sent a copy to me. Yet we've no way of proving anything. It's one person's word against another's."

"You can hardly present her to the usurpers and show them the scar. Considering its location. Yet I'll wager Piper doesn't care whether or not she meets a mother she never knew existed."

"Brett didn't mention anything in that vein, but I suppose you're right. She didn't seem to want money and power when she agreed to marry Brett. She didn't even know he was a baron when she said yes to his proposal. The few times I saw her she was content with what she had."

"Finding a way out of St. Giles," Ella said. "I can partially identify with what it could be like to live your life in the slums of London. That short time I spent..." She looked away, unwilling to relive the horrible hours she spent in the whorehouse waiting to be sold to the highest bidder.

"You don't need to think about that night or compare it to the life Piper led before she met Brett. I'm sure she doesn't think on that much either. If we do solve this mystery, and she is the child Charlotte lost, Piper's life will change again. I'm not really sure what Brett will do or how he'll handle this situation."

"Brett is the least of our concerns. Who are the pretenders?" Ella asked.

"There are no pretenders that we know of. A delving into William Leighton's family seems to be my first order of business. Don't really see the motive in this scenario, but I'm sure we can uncover the truth."

"Without telling Aunty what we think or what we are doing? I don't want to get her hopes up if Piper isn't her missing daughter."

"I'll put out the necessary feelers. For now, I need to talk to Brett so perhaps a trip to see your father would be in order? Would you like to visit your childhood home?"

Chapter Seven

"Rise and shine, my beautiful wife. Time for your first riding lesson." Brett leaned over giving Piper a quick kiss on her cheek. The plan he meant to put into practice this morning was to divert attention from everything but having fun. Over a week had passed since Duncan's wedding and the household was beginning to settle into a normal routine, visitors and all. In that time there had been no sightings of Scarface. Today he would take every precaution.

"Tomorrow." Piper rolled over, pulling the covers over her head. Then mumbling, "Please let's put this torture off another day. I'd be happy with just one more day with my feet grounded to the earth."

"I'm not teaching you how to fly." The pleasure he felt was all-consuming.

"You might as well be trying something just as preposterous. I can't ride a horse. I know it."

Brett laughed, understanding his wife's ploy. "We've put this off for over a week now. I'm not going to allow any further stalling. Today is the day you're going to learn how to ride a horse."

"You've put it off because of business. Now it's my turn." She turned over, smiling at him while he sat on the bed. "It seems we've done everything your way. Besides, I'm exhausted. I can't seem to get enough sleep."

"I'm not going to let you sway me from this endeavor with a flirtatious blink of an eye and the promise of more pleasure in our bed." Striding to the window, Brett pulled the curtains apart, letting brilliant sunshine filter through the bedroom. Truth be told though, he was a bit worried about her. It seemed the last week or so she'd been abnormally tired.

"Seduction always worked before. Why not now?" She grinned lazily, lowering the covers to tempt him further.

He cleared his throat realizing it would take all his control to keep from undressing and joining her in the bed. "You're new riding habit is ready. Molly set it in the dressing room and I've been to the stables. Your mount is saddled and waiting for you also." He needed to laugh at her antics, yet refrained. "Would you like help dressing?"

"Of course." Stark naked she rose from the bed before slipping on a sheer robe. "Are you volunteering?"

He opened the door and before he left, "Molly is waiting for you in the dressing room." He winked at her then, "I'm not going to let you seduce me into forgetting about the ride. I'll be downstairs. I'm sure Mrs. Pickery has a small breakfast waiting for you. I'll partake of my second cup of coffee while I wait." He did have to admit, he taught her the fine art of seduction well and her innate sexuality was obvious. Before he left, he had to take one more look.

She stood near the bed, her hands placed delicately on her hips. "So, if I'm not mistaken you've eaten already. How long have you been up plotting my demise by the hand of a horse?"

"I have eaten and I let you sleep away half the morning. You should thank me." He needed to keep her mind away from Scarface and Jocko, away from her real identity, whoever that might be. There were repercussions to whatever the truth was. Today was meant just for fun.

As he strode down the steps, he recounted the letter he just received from Drake Montgomerie. The gist of the missive pointed out Piper's probable connection to Charlotte Leighton, most often known as The Duchess. Drake mentioned the direct relationship to Portia Leighton's, Piper's, kidnapping and the death of William Leighton, the Duke of Ravenswood, Charlotte's husband. He also pointed out he needed to delve more into this new scenario since there were few accounts of that tragic homicide. Few even remembered the lost daughter; she had been a newborn and the Leighton's kept Charlotte's pregnancy private.

Brett's heart sped at the thoughts swirling in his head, anger simmering, racing through his veins. If this scenario was true, their lives would take a new direction and create a new family, and he didn't relish becoming part of the Leighton dynasty even by marriage. Too many tales abounded about Charlotte Leighton, The Duchess. He felt as if they were pawns in a game that began over eighteen years ago. Ending this had become essential to him.

"More coffee Master Brett? It's still nice and hot. Will the missus be wanting any?" Mrs. Pickery asked when he strode through the kitchen door.

Sitting down at the table, "A cup would be nice. Piper will be down shortly. I assume you've made a plate for her and she'll probably prefer a cup of tea."

"That I have. Her breakfast is in the warming oven, and I'll put a kettle of water on the stove to boil." She nodded in that direction. "The tea is on the table."

"Go on home then. With the lunch packed, we won't need you until dinnertime. Enjoy your afternoon." He sipped the coffee, sitting back in the chair and studying the scene outside the window. The day was sunny and the sky a beautiful cobalt blue. He wanted to bask in the warmth of the sun and perhaps take a moment or two to discuss Piper's possible pregnancy. She had all the common symptoms, and he was pretty sure she had no guess as to why she was suddenly so tired.

Mrs. Pickery thanked him and busied herself with a few things in the kitchen before leaving. She smiled at him then, "You better watch out for Billy and Bobby. They're just not used to a regular job. Fill them in on what you expect from them and they'll do better work."

Brett drummed his fingers on the table, wishing he knew all the facts and thinking about Mrs. Pickery's words. The helplessness he felt was not a feeling he needed. Perhaps a trip to London and a visit with Drake Montgomerie was in order. He just didn't like sitting and waiting for something to happen. Before he saw Piper, the subtle scent of her perfume wafted through the kitchen as she entered.

She poured herself a cup of tea before sitting across from him. "What has you looking so intense and apprehensive? You've drawn your brows together and I always worry when you do that." Tilting her head slightly it seemed she waited for an answer. "It can't be the riding lesson.

So out with it. We said no secrets."

"We did? I don't recall." His gaze followed her.

"Well, don't you think it's a good idea? What's bothering you?" she asked again, seeming to think if she repeated herself, he would tell her.

"Just waiting for you and hoping you'll like riding. I've got a picnic planned near the river and perhaps a swim," he told her, sure she understood the ploy and hoping she wouldn't call him on it.

"With you as my teacher how could I not like riding? You understand though, I also don't know how to swim. I can paddle around with my head out of the water, but that's about it. Certainly not something anyone would call swimming."

"Mrs. Pickery left you breakfast. It's in the warming oven." He drummed his fingers on the table, energy pulsing through him.

"We ate so much last night I'm not hungry. My dresses seem to be getting tighter by the second. Even this riding habit, which you just bought for me, is tight around my waist and bust. Think I'll forego breakfast and wait for lunch. If you're ready to teach, I'm ready to learn." She smiled sweetly at him.

"You need to eat something," he told her, realizing she didn't know she was pregnant and wondering when he should tell her she should be eating for two. Perhaps Molly would notice and say something.

"I'm sure I won't waste away if I miss one meal. Goodness knows I've lived through worse." She pushed a few stray tendrils of hair from her face. "There were times..." Her voice faded away as the memories resurfaced.

He liked the little tendrils of hair that framed her face. Her hair was finally getting longer and it was so beautiful and soft. He stood and holding out his arm to her, he realized the secrets he was keeping from her seemed to be mounting. "No, you won't waste away, but missing one meal isn't going to help your dresses fit either," he muttered, hoping she didn't call him on the last statement he blurted without thinking.

She graced him with an odd expression, her hands resting on her hips then, "What aren't you telling me? Out with it, Brett MacLachlan, tell me what's whirling around in your head."

He ignored her, instead decided to enjoy the warmth from the sunshine. With her hand linked in his arm, they strode to the stables. The horses ready he noticed the hesitancy emanating from her. Yet she drew in a deep breath and graced him with a strained smile.

"You'll do amazing." He laughed at the expression on her face. "Really, it's as easy as walking, and I'm sure you're a natural." If she'd lived the sheltered life with the Leighton's, she would have learned to ride at an early age, and you never would have met her.

"A natural hoyden, I am and can't say I know how to do anything else. Not sure I want to learn." She touched one of the horses on the nose then quickly withdrew her hand as if the slight caress burned.

"She likes to be petted. Here." He brought a sugar cube from his pocket. "Keep your hand flat and let your little mare take the lump. Her name is Aingeal," Brett told her, watching her natural curiosity come into play.

"So," she paused, "you're telling me she's an angel and won't buck me off." Piper eyed him skeptically.

"Aingeal's not going to buck you off unless you ask her. Whisper sweet nothings to her and she'll always be yours." He chuckled at that idea, pulling her close, molding his lips to hers. "Just as I succumb to the sweet nothings you whisper in my ear so will she."

"Brett." She swatted at him.

Minutes later, Piper sat the horse and Brett guided the mare around a small area outside the stables for several minutes. He led the two back to the stables where he mounted his horse.

"Where are we going?" she asked, her voice wavering. "I'm not sure how far I can ride Aingeal. My legs are already starting to feel tired."

"Down the road a ways then we're going to cut cross countryside and have a little picnic by the river. You won't be on the horse for very long. Mrs. Pickery packed us an amazing delicious lunch. Promise me you'll eat and not think about the way your clothes are fitting."

"When I can barely breathe because they are so tight, it's hard to think of anything else," she retorted, her nose tilted slightly upward.

"I'll buy you more clothes that do fit," he promised

"A picnic you say." She watched him, seeming to look for some indication of his plans or perhaps ulterior motives. "I might like that. What did Mrs. Pickery pack? Not going to eat anything I don't like and if this dress gets any tighter, I'll have to unbutton it before we ride home."

He smiled at her, enjoying the peaceful moment and hoping she wouldn't ask questions that weren't any more prying than the last one. "Don't know what's in the basket. Hoping perhaps she added some of that chocolate cake we had for desert last night and a bottle of wine."

Piper groaned softly. "That's why my dresses aren't fitting. Never got chocolate cake or three meals a day when I lived in St. Giles Parish. I was lucky to get one meal a day if that and it seems I was always running from someone. Now all I do is sit around the house and eat."

"I haven't noticed, except..." he paused, not wanting to be suggestive even though when he was with her, her body and sex seemed to be the gist of the majority of his thoughts. Now that her breasts had grown, he couldn't keep his eyes from focusing on them.

"Except what?" It seemed she didn't want to let this go. "Except for what, haven't you noticed?"

"Let's move on to another topic." He sat up straighter, clearing his throat, watching the leaves as they flitted on the tiny tree branches, silver melding with green shimmering as the breeze wafted by. He didn't have another topic to move on to though, at least not one that was less uncomfortable.

"Then you could tell me what Drake said in the letter he sent you." She pressed him with another topic he had no desire to elaborate on. "I would read it myself but you know that's impossible."

"Nothing definitive." Those two words were the truth. Everything Drake mentioned created another question, answering nothing. "The brand on your inner thigh seems to be the best clue we have to your identity. But there are still hundreds of concerns that need answering."

"That many," she said, slanting him a look that left him running a finger around his collar. "How about you tell me one question that has been answered. I deserve to know."

"You ride very well for a beginner." He laughed at her strange expression but decided to say something that might appease her curiosity for a little while. "The most important clue we have is the brand on your leg. It's the crest of the Duke of Ravenswood not St. Aubries."

"So, I'm not inheriting the title of duchess, or am I?" To Brett she looked relieved, little did she know that becoming The Duchess' daughter would turn her life even more upside down than it already was. She would now have a mother, a very formidable mother.

"In either case, as the daughter you don't really have a title, just responsibilities," he sighed. "Really Piper, all we have to worry about right now is how far it is until we stop and enjoy the day and this picnic lunch Mrs. Pickery spent so much time preparing. I don't want to dwell on your heritage right now."

"Neither do I but I can't keep from thinking about what's going to happen to me when all this is solved." She ran her hand across her forehead before glancing his way, her eyes dark with worry.

"You will still be my wife, a baroness." His voice was curt, he realized needing to change the tone if he wanted the day to proceed as planned. "I'm sorry. Let's not talk about this anymore today."

"I can't stop thinking about it."

"I'm having the same problem, but I truly hoped a pleasant outing would reduce the stress and let us dwell on more pleasant things, at least for the afternoon." He needed to change tactics and considered her possible pregnancy as the best way to take her mind from the intrigue surrounding her identity. He for one wanted to know for certain and he assumed she would too.

Reaching the spot by the river, Brett helped her from Aingeal, reveling in the brief feeling of her body against his. It seemed in her present state, her body was more evocative, more enticing. Her curves abounded and didn't go unnoticed by him.

He spread a blanket on the ground near the riverbank and beneath a tree before retrieving the picnic basket and bottle of wine. She sat down, seeming exhausted by this brief ride. That fact concerned him. Piper always had an abundance of energy. The last few weeks had been different though. Perhaps that was another symptom of pregnancy. He'd never really paid attention before Piper.

After letting the horses drink and tethering them, he returned to find Piper rummaging through the basket of food. "What's in there?"

She grinned staring up at him. "Looks like roast beef sandwiches, berries and I think I see some cheese and bread."

"Are you hungry now?" he asked, watching her as she pulled out two crystal glasses Mrs. Pickery packed. Then she poured wine for them. He sat down beside her, leaning casually on one arm, watching.

"I was hungry when I woke up. Now I'm famished," she told him, sipping the wine before finding a nearby spot where she could set the glass. "Seem to be hungry all of the time these days."

"Why?" He twirled the liquid in his glass, watching her over the rim and hoping she would come to some logical conclusion so he wouldn't have to broach the subject. "Why do you think you're always hungry and tired?"

"Never was hungry before. Maybe that was because I never really had any food so I didn't know what hungry felt like." She popped a piece of cheese in her mouth before chewing thoughtfully.

"Believing you weren't hungry was simply a way to keep your body and mind from thinking about something you couldn't have," he said, once again wishing she'd not had such a difficult life.

"Well," she paused briefly. "I don't like the fact my new clothes don't fit." She spoke before slowly biting into one of the sandwiches. "I don't want to go the dressmakers and buy more. There's simply no need so I'm going to stop eating so much."

He plucked a piece of grass, turning his attention to the river and its swirling currents before he focused on Piper. Trying to keep a measure of calm to his voice, he said, "Have you considered that you might be carrying a child? That these symptoms you have are because you are pregnant?" He watched the changing expressions as they quickly flitted across her face.

"What are you saying?" The hand holding the sandwich fell to her lap. "What did you say?" she repeated. "Pregnant? How can that be?"

"Yes, you might be pregnant. At least I hope so. It isn't from lack of trying." He choked on the words. "I don't know. You're going to have to tell me."

"How?" She coughed then drank half her glass of wine. "Why would you say that?"

Roughing his hair with his hands, was she truly that innocent? She had seen the sex in the brothels, had watched men as they had sex with the whores, had been trained to do just that. "Because we've..." He wasn't sure what to tell her. She obviously didn't know anything about sex and babies. He couldn't tell her it was because he'd been deep inside her every night and some days for weeks now.

"Because..." she prompted, appearing truly curious.

"Piper," he held her hands in his, "when we make love, every time there is a chance you will become pregnant. Every time I leave my seed inside you. I believe that's why your clothes don't fit and why you're exhausted and hungry. It's just your body preparing itself. Those are all common symptoms."

She looked down at her folded hands then, focusing on him, her eyes squinted slightly, "Do you want to have a child? We haven't really spoken about it."

"Of course I do." He wasn't sure about the question, but again his thoughts turned to possibilities he was confident she'd never think of. "Why would you think I might not want an heir?"

"I guess I'm glad. I don't want you to toss me out if I don't provide you with an heir." Her voice grew softer still. "What if it's a girl?"

"Why would I do something like that? Toss you out if we have a girl?" His mind spun, one striking scenario after another hitting him in the gut.

She inhaled a long deep breath, "The men I've seen and known don't want children," she paused, "The women don't either. Children are burdens where I come from. The women can't work if they're with child and when the children are born, they go to orphanages. Some try to get rid of the babies before they are born."

"And many women die when they try." He didn't know how to convince her life for her was different from that.

"So, you want this child and I will have to go to the dressmaker. But Brett, "she looked at her belly, "I really don't believe I'm eating for two, at least not two of me."

"Are you trying to tell me you don't have to eat for two?" He laughed, realizing she did have a point. "I will stop insisting you eat two plates of food."

"What is going to happen to me?" She stood, walking toward the river, her gaze focused on the water. "I don't know anything about babies or children and less about having them."

He followed her and wrapping his arms around her he let his hands settle on her belly. "You're going to grow much larger. Of course you know that. You probably have about seven months before the child is born. I'll make sure the best midwife in this area will be here to attend to you and the infant." In his arms, her body trembled and he knew he'd effectively changed the direction of her thoughts.

"You've known for how long? And you didn't tell me?" she asked, pushing away from him before turning in his arms, her expression fierce.

"I've been expecting this to happen. My first guess was at Duncan's wedding when you seemed to be spilling from your gown. My second was when you didn't have your woman's time." He just wasn't sure what she would be comfortable with and guessed this didn't fit in with what she wanted to talk about. After all, she'd never had anyone to talk with about her sexuality. Billy and Bobby certainly wouldn't be a wealth of information for her and he was sure Jocko didn't bother with much except her visits to the viewing rooms at the brothel.

She pushed from his arms and walking along the bank, she seemed focused inwardly. When he caught up to her, he wasn't sure what else to say.

"I never even considered children were a part of what we did yet I'm not stupid. When I first started to become a woman," she paused unsure of herself, "you know, Jocko had a lady talk to me. He swore her to silence about my gender but I never put the two together."

"Are you happy?" he asked, drawing her close, watching her even more diligently. This had been the needed diversion he looked for but it wouldn't last.

"I think so...I really don't know. If you're happy then I can be content and we can go on with our lives. Let's just forget about the brand on my thigh and who I might be. I'm your wife, Piper. That's all I want to be."

"If other people would let us forget I'd be more than pleased to oblige you in every way. But that's not going to happen. Even now Drake Montgomerie is pursuing more information, and we know Scarface is out there. We don't yet know exactly what he plans or why he has so much interest in you."

"I wish we could go away where no one could find us. Start a new life somewhere..." she said, her voice whisper soft. "Why does all this have to be so confusing and difficult?"

"Because you were ripped away from your rightful family. Because I found you and changed your life, and if you hadn't picked my pocket, Scarface would have you doing something..." He paused, wondering what that something really was. If Scarface knew who she was, he might have intended marriage. What better way to collect from The Duchess if Piper were indeed Charlotte Leighton's daughter?

"We should finish the food Mrs. Pickery worked so hard to pack for us. I'm suddenly very hungry." She turned to walk back to the blanket and the food.

He watched as she sat down, her expression unreadable. Unexpectedly, the hair on the back of his neck stood on end and a subtle shiver ripped through him. The weather had not changed, the sky still blue, the sun still shining, but a strange chill took over the idyllic scene.

"I think we should return home, now," he told her, searching as far as he could see for some reason that all his instincts cried out for him to run.

"I've..." she hesitated, moistening her lips. "I..." Once more she stopped, seemingly unable to voice her opinion.

"It's a bad feeling, nothing more. A long time ago I learned to trust my gut, and I'm not going to change now." He packed everything away then folding the blanket, he started for the horses.

"It's Scarface, isn't it?" Piper pointed to a form on a hill some distance away. "He's watching us. What do you think he wants?"

You. "I see that." If he'd been alone, he would have pursued the man, but now he had too much to lose. Piper was carrying his child, and he couldn't afford to confront the man and risk losing either his wife or their baby or both.

"Don't do anything you'll regret," Piper said. "I need you now more than ever. You have to stay with me."

"Come here." She stood beside him and her horse. He helped her mount. "If anything happens, just let Aingeal take the lead. She knows the way home."

"Brett..."

"I'm not planning on leaving your side but things happen. Just know your sweet angel will make sure you arrive home safely. And if B&B are doing their job, they're close by watching." He didn't want to tell her Scarface might have stopped them and at this moment they could be dead. "Do you understand what I'm saying?"

She slowly nodded, her head seemingly focused on his eyes. "I understand you're going to go after him. I don't like it. But then," she paused, "don't suppose I've a say over what you do."

"You're wrong on that score," he said, gazing at the hill where Scarface had been spotted to find he disappeared. That fact didn't surprise him, but now he would have to be even more cautious.

"Good, I can rest more easily if I know nothing rash is going to happen." She looked up, seeming to also notice the man had vanished. "Where do you think he's gone?"

Brett sat up straighter once again letting his gaze roam the horizon. "Wish I knew," he muttered. "What I want you to know is that his real name is Avery Bainbridge, and I've heard rumors that he was acquainted in some way with the late Duke of Ravenswood."

"Charlotte Leighton's husband?"

"Yes, you should know his name and possible connections. If you are The Duchess' daughter you can find just about anyone in London who will take you to her."

Out of nowhere a shot rang. He felt the ball hit him in the chest then the world spun while he clung to his saddle. "Run, Piper," he whispered. "Let Aingeal get you home before he can grab you." He had just enough time to swat her horse on the rear and pray she didn't fall before he landed on the ground.

In his heart he knew Avery would catch Piper before she reached home, and he also knew his injury wasn't life threatening. While he struggled to sit and breathe as well, he tried to think of the man's motives. Avery wouldn't hurt Piper simply because he wanted her for himself and perhaps revenge.

Bobby suddenly hovered over him, "Billy's gone after her. Sorry we weren't any closer. Wanted to give the two of you your privacy, if you get my drift." He was unfastening Brett's shirt in an effort to see the damage.

"You have to stop the bleeding then we need to make sure Piper stays safe. Have to stop him from doing something that can't be undone." Brett let Bobby pry the ball from his chest with a hunting knife while he gritted his teeth against the pain.

"Just as soon as I get this fixed up, we'll be on our way. You got any whiskey in that basket? Need to clean the wound. Why do you think ol' Scarface wants her?"

"Can't you do that any faster? And yes, there is whiskey," Brett told him, watching him for a few minutes before he closed his eyes.

"Here it is," Bobby held up the tiny ball. "Didn't do much damage. You'll be good as new in no time. Gonna stop the bleeding now and pour some of that good stuff you got into the wound. A waste if you ask me, but it's got to be done." He ripped part of his shirt to make a bandage, finishing his doctoring.

"Only after we get Piper back." Brett pushed from the ground and using one hand, mounted the horse.

"I'll just run along behind. Don't you worry about me. Got to be pretty fast on my feet when I was dodging the law. Maybe Billy and I should have been takin' riding lessons while we've been here."

"You're going to have to learn fast. I need the two of you with me, and we can't take the time for a carriage." Time here was more important than Brett wanted to admit. He prayed Piper would find some way to slow the man down.

"Don't much like carriages and always wanted to learn how to ride. Billy and I did our best on the way here, so sitting on top of a horse isn't as foreign as you might guess," Bobby said.

Brett urged his horse forward, grimacing each time the hooves landed on the earth. He swallowed back the dizziness threatening to overcome him. This was far too important a task. His heart leapt and careened to his belly.

What seemed like hours later, he rode down the lane to his home. He prayed when he entered the stables, Piper's horse would be tethered there. It was.

"Get me a fresh horse, one for you and another one for Billy, hoping we see him soon." Then he turned to Bobby. "Any ideas about where they would be headed?"

"Back to London for sure. A long time ago I heard some rumors I never quite believed."

"And?" Brett didn't have the inclination for guessing games.

"Everyone thought he wanted Piper for his mistress, but I heard it was really a wife he wanted. Heard the word 'revenge' bandied about too. So maybe it wasn't a wife he wanted either." Bobby mounted the horse the stable boy brought him.

"Impossible. Piper's wed to me." Brett hoped it was a mistress he intended. That was much easier to attend to.

"You and I both know that with enough money and power one can annul a marriage. Scarface has both."

"Not as much as The Duchess. If we don't catch up to them before London, I mean to pay a visit to Charlotte Leighton and discover what she knows." Brett just couldn't abide thoughts of Piper with another man let alone a man such as Scarface.

Somehow Piper was able to touch him in a way he had never imagined. Touch him with her innocence and yet evoke the most pagan and sensual thoughts that had ever come to plague him, to scorch him. Now she was in the hands of a mad man.

~ * ~

Piper nudged her horse forward, but her fears as well as her riding skills kept Aingeal from moving fast enough to outpace Scarface and his stallion. When she saw him from the corner of her eye, she wasn't surprised. He reached out for the reins and brought her horse to a stop. She focused her gaze straight ahead, unwilling to give credence to him or the fact he bested her.

What to do now?

"Thought you could run from me, did you? Never a good idea, running from this man." His smile sent chills slithering down her spine. "Not when you're outmatched in strength as well as cunning."

"Just hoped. I'm not very good on a horse. There weren't any in St. Giles." She swiped hair away from her face as her eyes filled with moisture. She straightened then inhaling a deep breath, "What are you doing here? Why?"

He laughed, "Why you ask? Vengeance."

"You don't even know Brett," she said, baffled by the man's strange words. "He's not of your world."

"Our world," Avery said. "I've waited eighteen years for this day to lord over The Duchess. I'm not going to be denied. A long time ago, I lived in the same world, lived and prospered among the gentry. Until the Duke of Ravenswood ruined everything for me."

"You talk nonsense."

"Enough of this." He waved a hand in the air. "We've got to keep moving now that I've got you, I've some people to show you to, some bartering to do. Hopefully you will please one of them."

"Why? I'm exhausted and don't think I can ride very far. Brett will catch up with us," she said even as she turned to look over her shoulder, hoping she'd see Brett's form on the horizon.

"You're husband's dead. He's not coming for you. You best start looking out for your best interests, because he can't take care of you any longer. I'm going to make your life one of ease."

Those words struck her with fear and desperation. Her husband wasn't dead. She would know it if Brett had died. Then, "I'm not the same girl who lived in St. Giles and picked pockets to make you rich. I'm not going to be your avenue to more riches at my expense. I'll refuse whatever it is you've in mind for me," she told him while he grabbed the reins of her horse and headed toward a road.

"No, I don't suppose you are, Portia." He grinned at her, the white line of his scar highlighted by the gesture. "But you no longer have a choice unless you want to die. I educated you to be a mistress, and that's the role you're going to fulfill for the rest of your life."

Her stomach churned at his words even while she wondered how long she could stay on the horse. Brett told her she would not be riding far today. He was obviously wrong and Avery was deadly, Piper realized with a sinking heart. He was cold as if no blood flowed through his veins. She'd never seen him like this, never seen him so unyielding.

"I can't ride far." She groped for any reason to dissuade him even though she understood just how useless this ploy was. He would see that she did his bidding.

"I've a carriage waiting at our first stop, so you won't have to ride. I'm going to take very good care of you, my dear. Your health is of the utmost importance to me."

She was shaking her head, disbelief rolling through her. "I can't stay on for much longer. What good will it do you if I fall off and break my neck?" He was revolting, from the white scar across his face to his icy blue eyes. He made her skin crawl and filled her with loathing. Now, her teeth chattered in terror of the unknown.

Suddenly, two more men joined them. One swept her off her horse, settling her in front of him. His arm wrapped around her waist holding her. She had thought to fall off the horse to slow them down. They approached the carriage and she found herself inside with Avery sitting across from her. She assumed the men followed.

It seemed like hours before they stopped. Miles back, they had turned off the main road and now they rode down a tree-lined drive. A magnificent home loomed in front of them.

"We'll spend the night here." Avery dismounted, then, his hands on her waist he helped her down. "If you're thinking of running, there is nowhere for you to go where I won't find you. You would only make yourself sick."

Running was on her mind, but she meant to wait until she was either desperate or she held an advantage of any sort. Brett might find her, or not. She understood she couldn't wait for rescue. Just as her life had been like in St. Giles, she would have to fend for herself.

Avery gripped her upper arm tightly, leading her up the steps to the large front door. A servant met them. "Good afternoon, sir. I've a room prepared for you and the lady. Follow me."

Up the winding steps, ones that were not too different from the ones in Brett's home, they walked down a long hallway. "Here you are." The door was open, the room inviting if she wasn't a prisoner. At the threshold she hesitated.

Avery ushered her inside before locking the door and placing the key in his pocket. "You should have a bath waiting for you in that room," he nodded, "and a clean set of clothes. I don't mean you harm, my dear. I've plans for you and if you're bruised or injured in any way, you won't bring top dollar."

"Vengeance," she muttered as she watched him, wishing she could see some sign of weakness in the man.

"Yes, my dear, but you must be in impeccable condition for me to collect the highest possible price. While revenge is my first motive, I don't turn down money when it's under my nose." He stared at her then, and she understood real terror. If she'd never left the slums, this would just be another piece of her life, but now that she knew something different, she didn't think she could go back.

"Can you at least tell me why?" She sat down in a fireside chair. "I deserve to know who I am and how you know. I need to understand why you hate me so much you'd take me away from my husband to sell me to some man I don't know."

"Refresh yourself first then join me in the room next to this one. All you have to do is knock. We'll have something to eat and I'll give you as many details as possible. You of all people will enjoy the irony." He rose then and left the room, leaving her alone with her thoughts.

Piper watched his departing back, shuddering when the key turned in the lock. For a few minutes, she waited, watching the door then she strode to the only window in the room. Looking at the ground below, she realized she could jump. Perhaps the fall would break a bone, perhaps it wouldn't. Willing to chance it, she tried to open the window, but it was painted shut. Closing her eyes, she inhaled a deep lungful of air. Not tonight but maybe tomorrow she could find a way to escape him. There would be so many opportunities on their way to London. If indeed that was where they were headed.

Resigning herself to Avery's company as well as an explanation, she bathed and dressed. Unluckily, the dress did not accommodate her expanding form although the bust had more room than she expected. So, Avery's visits to St. Giles had not left her unnoticed by him. Perhaps this was the type of dress he wanted her to wear. It revealed and would tempt a man, but what kind of man?

Piper knocked on the door between the rooms and a few seconds later Avery opened it, a grin on his face. "Welcome. You look beautiful tonight. The gown fits just as I had hoped."

"You didn't give me much choice. Don't you think the bodice is too revealing?" A few lights around the room cast small shadows and a merry fire danced in the fireplace belying her somber mood.

"The gown becomes your new situation. It is perfect."

"As a mistress?"

"Of course. As I explained to you earlier, that is my intention. Whoever can pay the most is the man you will belong to. Sit down, eat, drink and ask any questions you like. I'll answer what I can." He sipped a drink while he seemed focused on her bodice.

She sat down, accepting the plate of food he offered as well as the glass of wine. Sipping the liquid, she watched him over the rim of the glass. "What do you want from me? I knew you were grooming me to be some man's mistress, and at the time it made sense. I was pleased I wasn't going to a whorehouse. Now, nothing makes sense to me and the information no longer gives me any type of pleasure."

He shrugged his shoulders, and this time his smile was almost appealing despite the scar that stretched from his forehead across his nose to the corner of his mouth. "I think I spoke of that earlier. Your compliance, Portia, just your compliance, nothing more is what I want from you and I'm glad you appreciate the fact I'm not sending you to become a prostitute in such a dirty place where you're bound to get syphilis within the year. You should really be thanking me."

"So, you want me to do whatever you ask of me and give thanks to all your generosity as well. That's likely not going to happen," she told him, with her fork turning her food over on the plate.

"You must eat not play with your food. This is your first task." He casually leaned back on the chair. "Men like to have plenty of curves to play with. Your breasts fortunately are very large and compelling to any man."

"Not so easy, your presence makes me sick to my stomach," she told him but she did take a small bite.

His smile changed, his brows drawing together in distaste. "You're too much like your mother and you don't even know her."

"Will I ever?" she asked, thinking he might be referring to Charlotte Leighton, the Duchess of Ravenswood.

"Not if I have a say in what your future holds." His smile was now a sneer on his face. "Need I remind you I hold all the cards?"

"Who is she? My mother?" she asked, deciding she did need to eat more food. Strength to escape this man and his plans was too important to let her distaste for him make it unbearable.

"I'm guessing you know the truth, so my saying her name is simply a formality." He downed his whiskey before pouring another. "But I'll indulge you since the fact you're here with me makes me pleased that all my endeavors are coming to fruition."

"I'd like you to say her name, my mother's and why you kept me from her, stole me away." Her body thrummed with anticipation of this moment and discovering more about herself. Yet somehow, she'd have to come to terms with whatever the truth was going to be.

The diabolic grin as well as the ice in his eyes chilled her to the bone. When he spoke, his voice changed. "Charlotte Leighton is your mother. I stole you because I craved revenge, and I wanted to see them suffer."

"What did The Duchess ever do to you that would create such a need?"

"William didn't deserve to be the heir apparent. He was a womanizer, a rake. I was the good son. I did everything right and William, well, William was always their favorite just because he was born first."

"The good son?" That statement was hard to believe. She knew there was much more to this story than he had divulged as yet.

"Ah, but she wasn't The Duchess back then. She was Charlotte or the duke's wife, sometimes the duchess. But Charlotte really had nothing to do with anything that happened to you. You might say she was a victim also."

"Then who?" She finished her wine then poured another glass, sipping while she tried for patience. "Who is William?"

He swirled the contents of his drink several times, seeming to watch the amber liquid. "My dear brother William, the heir to our family's wealth and title, your father. I was the second son, nothing more."

"You're my uncle? How could you?" Disgust with him filled her. "You don't mean to wed me or...rape me..."

"Oh no, my dear, that would be repulsive even for me. No, like you understood when you were merely a hoyden in St. Giles, you would be some man's mistress. I was grooming you for a suitable position when you vanished. I had to come after you. I couldn't allow you to have a respectable life of ease. There's much you need to tell me also." He leaned forward seeming to wait for her to divulge certain facts.

"I don't know what. I'm sure you know everything via all your numerous informants." Her body seemed to shake uncontrollably. She swallowed trying to relieve the dryness in her mouth. Sickness washed over her in waves.

"So, true. Nothing of import happens in St. Giles that I don't know about. I knew nearly the second the Scotsman caught you." Once again, he was twirling the liquid in his glass, a sneer on his face.

She tried to recreate that day in her mind she was kidnapped as a babe and tried to forget what was in store for her now. All this new information left her mind in a daze. "I was guarded, I'm sure. How could you abscond with me without anyone preventing or trying to stop you? Where was my mother and father when all this happened?"

"You've learned a few things with your Brett, and I'm sure all your newfound education will come in handy when you are trying to please your master. My brother was too arrogant to put guards on his daughter. They were all trailing your big brother, Richard. Your mother was visiting a friend and left your nanny, Scarlett to guard you."

"You were after Richard then, not me."

"I was but once your brother eluded my grasp, I realized your potential. I only regret I couldn't watch William suffer these long years until you grew up a whore then a mistress. It would have killed him instead..."

"You killed him..." Her glass slipped from her hand, wine spilling on the floor as well as her dress.

"Mores the pity. It's the only thing I have for you to wear until our next stop since we're traveling light. You'll have to try to clean it yourself. There are no maids here."

"He gave you the scar..." This time she picked up the glass and poured more wine for herself.

"True and truer. If you bring that up, I will deny any knowledge of what we've talked about." He laughed, his eyes raking her with chilling disdain. The gaze seemed to strip her of her clothing to lay her bare and naked. A sizzle of mockery touched his eyes while he watched her reaction.

"You didn't brand me though, so how..."

His browse furrowed together, and for a brief time she thought she might have surprised him with her statement.

He cleared his throat, "I would know about this brand you speak of."

"Why should I tell you?" In a small measure of defiance, she sought courage where there was none. "A lady needs a secret or two."

Slowly his gaze raked the length of her. "Because I will rip your clothing off and search you until I find what you speak of."

At his words her heart nearly stopped. Indeed, it might have for a second as she tried to breathe again. "I've been told I was branded on my inner thigh with the crest of the Duke of Ravenswood."

"Did anyone tell you how?" His intensity increased, as did the simmer of anger in his eyes.

"Who would know?" she asked, stunned by the fact he knew nothing about the scar.

"Scarlett did this, the old biddy," he mumbled. "I'll have to pay her a visit and seek out another small measure of retaliation."

"I don't understand."

"You already know more than you should. Have you had enough to eat?" He rose then, seemingly ready to dismiss her. "You should get some sleep. One way or another tomorrow will be a busy day."

She didn't want to leave the room, not yet, not while she was so much closer to the truth about herself. This man was her father's brother, and he was well-known as one of the most dangerous man in London, one to be feared and to leave a wide path between him and you. Until now, she'd never been afraid of him. She'd known him since she could remember, but fear had never been a part of her thoughts.

"My father gave you the scar and you killed him before you kidnapped me," she ventured a guess.

"Your mother was too distraught after her beloved husband died to search for you, and I don't think she understood the power her deceased husband had over the ton until much later. It didn't take her long to learn though, but by that time you were buried deep inside the bowels of London, so deep she couldn't find you."

"Portia is my name then? Portia Leighton..." She mulled the name over in her head. Her mother cared more for her husband than she did for her. That was a heart stopping thought.

"Yes, Portia. Nice name, don't you think? Perhaps I can present you as Portia instead of Piper. It does have a bit more of sophistication. Portia doesn't sound like a hoyden," he told her.

"I'm not feeling well. I'd like to go to bed now." She rose, slowly walking to her room and wishing she could go backwards in time. All this information made her sick to her stomach, all the things Avery did to her and to her family she could never get back.

He stood beside her, "There's no way for you to escape me. You do know that? There's nowhere you can run I won't find you. Best you resign yourself to your fate and make the best of it."

She nodded her head several times, understanding how true his words were. Brett would never find her unless she took matters into her own hands. If they were in St. Giles, she could hide from Avery. She didn't doubt that for a second. This short time she had with Brett would be the best part of her life, and she would have to hold on to those memories.

He would never find her, not if Avery stayed on the back roads and had places to rest that weren't inns. In London, Avery had ways to disappear where no one would even think to look and so did she.

"I understand what you're telling me." If she were to change her future, she could not wait for rescue.

In her room, she heard the lock turn. She was alone with her thoughts as well as her fears. Tears welled in her eyes, but she forced the moisture away with the backs of her hands. Crying was for fools and the weak. Walking to the door, she tried the handle, which didn't budge. Piper sat down on the bed, raking her gaze along the walls in search of some route of escape.

"And where would you be going if you did get out? He'd find you before you got ten miles down the road, and you don't even know what direction to go. You know how to ride so well you could steal a horse and then what? The steed would most likely buck you off.

"If you tried to get away and didn't make good on the escape, he'd make sure to tie you up before he left you alone again." She stood and walking to the walls, she ran her hands along them, searching behind the paintings and in the armoire, finding nothing.

The noise behind her startled her. "You should try to get some rest." Avery stood in the doorway, leaning negligently against the frame. "There is no secret passage. You could look all night but you'd never find anything," he chuckled softly, "At least not from this room."

"I don't want to sleep. I feel as if someone is watching me," she told him, once again searching the walls, this time for a peephole. "You've, well, you do know that even if you sell me to someone, I won't stay with them. I'll find a way to escape. Besides who would pay money for someone like me? A hoyden from the ghettos and bowels of London."

"Have you looked in the mirror lately, Portia? If you weren't my niece, I'd bed you myself."

"I'm not beautiful..."

"Of course you are and your body...your breasts will fill any man's hands and over flow most. You will bring a tidy sum and when your pedigree is revealed, I'm sure the price will triple."

"Triple?"

"There are many who would love to know they bedded The Duchess' daughter. They would revel in the knowledge. Now go to bed.

Rest assured there is no way out, so don't waste your time looking."

"Alright then, maybe you're right." She sat down on the bed, watching and waiting for him to leave the room. It seemed to Piper the man protested too much. This time, before she searched, she would give him time to fall asleep.

When the door closed behind him again, she blew out the candles in the room. Moonlight shimmered through the window. In the bed, she could see the moon. It was full and would light her pathway home if she could find a way out of this room. Perhaps Brett was watching the same moon and thinking about her.

She woke to Avery's hands shaking her awake. "Time to leave." His voice sounded too urgent to her yet at the same time held a hint of anger.

"It's still dark." Outside the window the moon had vanished while no light filtered through the sheer curtains. For a moment she thought she was at home in bed with Brett. All she wanted was to pull the covers over her head and tell him she wanted to sleep a bit longer.

"We have to get on the road now." He pulled the covers away from her, standing with his feet braced apart.

Piper sat up, pushing hair from her eyes. "Why? It's still dark outside." she asked even though she understood the repercussions of arguing with him and hoped the reason for this hasty departure was because of Brett.

"He's not interested in a pregnant lady. Didn't tell me that," he sneered. "This changes things. Not so sure anyone's going to want you now. Going to have to keep you hidden away until you birth the child."

"If it's finances now and not revenge, I'm sure either Brett or The Duchess would pay you more than anyone. Why don't you let them bid on me?" She thought her logic impeccable yet knew from everything he told her last night where she was concerned, he wanted more than monetary gain.

"Never let either of those two have a hand in this," he muttered as he tossed her clothes on the bed. "Get dressed. I'll be back in five minutes."

She realized he wouldn't allow her, her own way in this. If she didn't dress now, he'd walk in here and probably help her into the clothes strewn haphazardly on the bed in front of her.

His words about a man not wanting her created more questions in her mind. How would some man know she was pregnant when Avery did not? Her hands settled on her belly and she suddenly realized there must be a peephole in the wall somewhere as she had guessed. It had not been her imagination. A brief moment of outrage swept over her to be replaced with acceptance of her situation. At least now she was beginning to understand his intentions.

Quickly finishing with her clothing, she tried the door only to find it locked. One could hope. Sitting on a chair, she waited.

She heard the key turn in the door. "On to the next place. Perhaps it will prove more beneficial than this one," he told her as he stepped inside.

"You're thinking another man would like to have sex with a pregnant woman," she said as she rose, walking toward him. "You know your first thought of keeping me hidden until the child is born seems to be the most logical."

"I'm thinking the knowledge that little bundle you're carrying inside you is the granddaughter of the Duke and Duchess of Ravenswood. That gives the gentleman who wants you untold power once the information is divulged."

"No one would dare disclose something like that. Not unless they were just as powerful as that woman."

"Ah, you're beginning to see why the child is a liability to my purposes, but there are always possibilities. I'll have to give this more thought." They strode from the house and to the stables. Outside, the carriage waited for them while Avery helped her inside.

Chills ripped through her at his words. If this next man wasn't willing to pay Avery for her, she wasn't sure what would happen but didn't like the thoughts filling her head. Her stomach churned. The man would do anything for revenge against the Leighton's.

"You wouldn't do that again?" she whispered, the words barely audible. She looked at him her eyes wide with fear for her unborn child.

When he grinned, the scar seemed to grow. "I would do anything as you well know. Your life in the parish is proof of that, and I'll relish watching MacLachlan and The Duchess trip over their heels trying to find you and the baby."

Thoughts of a girl growing up as she did, fending for herself and for every bite to eat, but a boy... A boy would be subject to deportation or death if caught stealing. She tried to push those thoughts to the back of her head. That was a long ways from now, and she wasn't about to remain a prisoner long enough for the child to be born. No one could hold her. No one!

She turned her attention to the scenery passing by, trying to memorize the minimal landmarks. They travelled a road that was not well used, and by the time they finally stopped, the sun sat high above the ground. Clouds dotted the sky and seemed to grow darker as the seconds past.

"We're stopping to eat. Behave yourself," he told her, narrowing his eyes at her as he helped her from the vehicle.

"What else would I do?" She tossed him a smile she hoped would tell him she wasn't afraid of him.

"I'm sure your agile little mind can come up with a host of things. You can't run when you don't even know where you are." A cloud floated between them and the sun, dropping eerie shadows across his face.

She'd spent most of her life running and hiding. There was little difference between the days in St. Giles and now, except she meant to start out on a full stomach.

~ * ~

"Is Scarlett here?" Drake Montgomerie asked Charlotte Leighton as he entered the parlor of her townhouse, determined to discover the truth.

"Upstairs, I'll send for her." She turned her attention to the maid. Then The Duchess focused on Drake. He felt her gaze burn through him. "Why are you here and why do you and Ella both look so distressed. What has happened?"

"When you hear what I've got to say, you'll need Scarlett by your side, plus I've a question for her and you as well. I'll wait for reinforcements." Drake looked to the stairway, hoping to see Charlotte's companion of over twenty years walking down the steps. He cleared his throat, nodding to Ella to sit by Charlotte.

"Now you're scaring me," Charlotte said, looking from her niece to her husband and back again. "What is it the two of you aren't telling me?"

"You might want a drink, Aunty," Ella said as she poured a full glass of brandy and handed it to Charlotte Leighton, The Duchess. She poured one for herself and Drake as well.

"Probably need a lemon bar more than a drink," she told them as she tapped her cane on the floor with her gaze now riveted on the door to the parlor and the staircase beyond. "Scarlett was taking a nap. She really shouldn't be awakened abruptly. Not good for the health."

"Neither is a shocking revelation," Ella murmured.

"What is so important you had to wake me up from my afternoon sleep?" Scarlett, a bit sleepy eyed walked into the room, standing behind Charlotte, her hands clasped in front of her.

Charlotte turned, her expression unreadable, "Do you have any idea what all this is about. It doesn't bode well when I look at my niece and I see such a somber expression on her face. I'm afraid someone has died."

"I'm sorry, Charlotte. I can't tell you anything until Drake finishes with all the details. You do understand I'm usually the last one to know anything, never the first."

The Duchess waved her hand in the air, "Then get on with this. I've got things to do and I don't want to waste any more time on guesses."

Ella placed her hand on her auntie's knee, nodding at Drake to begin. Shadows flitted around the room as clouds passed across the sun, a somber omen of the words he was about to utter. Drake understood the repercussions here and wished this was over. It was good and bad news, or bad and good news, however one wanted to interpret this. In any case Charlotte would be devastated to learn the information he was about to share. Yet she would still feel joy that Portia still lived.

"Charlotte," he cleared his throat, his gaze now penetrating

Charlotte's then he paused taking time to breathe deeply, "we believe we've found your daughter."

All color drained from The Duchess' face while her eyes closed momentarily. When she opened them, she looked stronger than the previous moment yet more fragile than he'd ever seen her.

"You must be confused or it's a cruel joke. She died. I searched every available lead and couldn't find her." It seemed she held her breath while she waited for him to deny the fact.

Drake walked toward her, moving his head in denial as he kneeled in front of her. He took her hands into his, "Your daughter was branded with the Duke of Ravenswood's crest on her inner thigh. There was no mistaking the design once her husband discovered it. Either you or Scarlett did that to protect her or identify her."

Scarlet's sharp indrawn breath startled him, catching everyone's attention and diverting the focus of this conversation from Charlotte, "No," she moaned softly. Then, "I knew she had to be alive. I would have felt it if sweet little Portia had died that day. What has happened to her?"

"So, you branded her?" Drake asked, thoroughly glad she had thought so carefully and quickly, "How did you know her life was in danger?"

Scarlett folded her hands in her lap, gazing at them then at Drake and back. She moistened her lips before she spoke, "Avery was always such an evil man. Several times he tried to bribe me to hand over Portia to him. After Charlotte and William made sure Richard was out of reach, he set his sights on the little girl. When I saw him that night and only the duke and I were in the house I found the ring on William's desk, heated it and placed it on little Portia's inner thigh. Then I wrapped her up in a blanket. I held on to her, determined to never let her go. But..."

Drake meant to pursue the part of the story he had no answers to, "But..." he prompted.

"I don't know. That's just the thing. I saw the duke slash Avery across the face. He was bleeding and it was awful. Blood everywhere. Thinking the fight was over before it had really begun, William started to walk toward us and Avery rose from the floor and stabbed William in the back." Tears slipped from her eyes. "He died on the spot, and there was nothing I could do for him."

"Do we have to relive this again?" Charlotte asked. "It was the most painful day of my entire life. We all know Avery killed my husband, but there was no real proof. It was a servant's word against his, and Avery had an alibi."

"Did you see what happened to the child?" Drake asked Scarlett, turning his attention to her.

Scarlet was wiping tears from her eyes while she was shaking her head over and over again as if she watched the scene unfold in her mind. "No, I was hit on the head and that's one of the reasons no one believed me. I don't remember anything except Avery must have taken her. There was only Avery and two of his men. We looked but could never find her."

"I mourned both my daughter and my husband. Some thought I didn't care about the little girl because I was so devastated by William's loss. Everyone knew he was my life, but the truth was I mourned them both equally. It was then I vowed I would learn how to use all the resources William left to me, everything he knew about the evilness of mankind, all the blackmail possibilities he documented and left in the safe. But I couldn't find Portia no matter how hard I tried. It seemed to me she vanished into the deepest and darkest part of the earth." Charlotte brought her glass to her lips with a shaking hand. Suddenly, she slumped forward, the liquid in her glass spilling onto the floor.

"Aunty," Ella cried out as she knelt beside the unmoving form of her beloved aunt. "Someone get the smelling salts. Hurry!"

Ella held Charlotte in her arms, rocking her and trying to soothe her. Ella kneeled beside her, holding her hand in hers. "We will find Portia if she's still alive." Then Ella looked to Drake. "You know where she is, don't you?"

Drake nodded, "believe I do."

Scarlett arrived with the salts and a few second later Charlotte was sitting up and breathing deeply. She looked as if the world had fallen on her, yet there was hope in her eyes; a vibrant shimmering that had not been there before she fainted.

"Are you alright, Aunty?" Ella asked, stroking her arm as if that tiny gesture would make everything right. "Let me help you sit and I'll pour you another glass of brandy."

"I will feel much better when I hear the rest of the story." She inhaled a long deep breath, letting her gaze touch everyone in the room. "I'm assuming you know where my daughter is or none of you would be here shocking me near to death."

Drake stepped back, wishing he could give her the news he understood she craved, "We do and we don't."

"What the bloody hell does that mean?" Charlotte seemed to regain strength by the second.

"It means..."

"Yes." She tapped her cane on the floor. "Out with it. I've a need to start searching for my daughter now."

"Aunty," Ella stepped in, "Portia is known as Piper and she..."

"Piper! The little pickpocket who married Brett MacLachlan? I'll have him skinned alive if he knew anything and meant to take advantage of this family." The Duchess seemed to be herself once again.

"He married her. He didn't know she was your daughter. Indeed, he fell in love with her believing she was nothing more than a pickpocket from St. Giles Parish. Brett was innocent in all of this. The only thing he is guilty of is loving Piper," Drake said. "We've been corresponding for some time now and it was with Brett's help we've uncovered her true identity."

"Pshaw," The Duchess waved her hand in the air. "He's only after the money and the power I can give him."

"Aunty, we all believe you're wrong about that. We believe he truly loves her. Don't you think you should give your daughter more credit? After all she is your daughter and William's," Ella said indignantly.

A noise from the foyer caught everyone's attention.

"Avery kidnapped Piper two weeks ago from her home in Scotland. I've searched for her and can't find my wife anywhere. I've come here for any help all of you can give me," Brett stepped into the parlor. "I trust you'll catch me up on all this information, and I can assure you I love Piper as well as her dog." He addressed Drake while Rogue raced into the room, seeming to believe he was the center of attention.

"If you loved her, you would have found a way to stop that evil man," The Duchess accused. "What have you done to find her?"

"My misfortune has nothing to do with love or the efforts I've put into that task. Avery did not take a normal route to London, which is where I assumed he would be traveling. I should have caught up to him, so I can only accept the notion he took back roads and stopped at homes of friends instead of inns. He left no trace."

"That man doesn't have friends, only scums of the earth." Charlotte muttered, downing her drink.

"Now what do all of you intend to do to find her?" Once again, she waved her hand in the air. "I'm going to call out some favors and pressure a few low lifes into giving up what they know."

Chapter Eight

The bullet hole in Brett's chest throbbed while he fought down the nausea welling into his throat. As he rode, he closed his eyes, pushing the pain from his thoughts as he focused on the task at hand, finding Piper.

Bobby rode by his side for several miles without saying a word. Then, "If you don't mind my saying so, sir, you appear to be fallin' off your horse. You're not going to do Piper any good if you die now are you?"

Brett forced Bobby's words to the back of his mind and urged his horse to a faster gait. He wasn't going to die. The wound was nothing he couldn't handle. "Piper needs us and Avery's not waiting for this bullet wound to heal."

"That's all there is to this?" Bobby asked incredulously, staring at Brett. "Piper needs you alive not dead. How's she going to feel if you die trying to find her? You've got to realize that little lady is capable of rescuing herself. She has skills a normal woman wouldn't have as well as grit and determination. She's a bricky lass."

"You're wrong, on all counts. She is a little lady and as fragile as a kitten. She needs me," he repeated as if he was trying to convince himself. Piper wasn't as fragile as he sometimes thought, but she had the baby to worry about now, and he knew she wouldn't take the same risks.

"She needs you to be there for her, but she doesn't need you to escape from Avery Bainbridge. Avery doesn't think a woman's got a mind or heart. Believes she's only good for one thing, if you get where I'm going with this. He'll never expect her to outsmart him. Piper's been thinking on her feet since the day she could walk."

Brett didn't like the moan of pain he accidentally allowed to escape his lips and immediately glanced Bobby's way. He bit down on his lower lip, his heart pounding and his breathing in short pants. "I'm not going to stop looking for her until I find her." And with those last words he slid from his horse. He felt the air beneath him for a second before he hit the ground. Then the world went black.

"Well, I told you that you weren't in any condition to pursue this endeavor but just like all aristocrats, you weren't listening," Bobby muttered as he dismounted and checked Brett's pulse. "Now I've got to figure out how to get you back on that bloody horse and home before you wake up and start out after Piper again."

Bobby stood up, feet braced apart trying to figure out the logistics of this enterprise and wishing Billy would show up soon to help. "Well, you got yourself into another fine jam now, haven't you?" Bobby told himself, still wishing he'd see Billy sauntering over the hill ready to help.

Grabbing Brett beneath his arms, he pulled him toward the horse, stopping with an idea. He let Brett lie on the ground. With the reins of the horse in hand, he tugged, "Down, now you can get down and help me get your master on your back." To his amazement the horse did lie down. "Good job." Bobby stroked the horse's nose after Brett lay across the back. "Now you can get up."

Leading the horse, Bobby started back to the house hoping Brett wouldn't slip off the horse again.

"Hello there," Billy called out. "What happened to master Brett? You be needin' any help?"

"Got himself shot then insisted on going after the little gal. Kept going until he fell off the horse. I'm taking him back, and so it's your job to figure out where Scarface took Piper. I'm guessing they didn't stay on the main roads, but the master insisted so that's where we are."

Billy pushed his hat back then muttered, "Getting dark. They're probably settled in for the night."

"Since when has the likes of you been afraid of the dark? Times wasting away and for Master Brett's sake, we need to find her and bring her home," Bobby told his brother. "You get going or the next time I'm with Molly I'm not going to share."

"How long do you want me to look for Scarface?" Billy was

scratching his neck and staring down the road with a mournful expression. "Don't really want to leave before daybreak."

"Until you find him and Piper," Bobby said over his shoulder while he made a trail back to the house. "You don't come home until you've got Piper in tow and we know she's safe and sound."

Billy nodded then turned down the road, his back disappearing in the distance while Bobby set his sights for the MacLachlan manor house. Before the sun fully set, he pulled up in front of the stables, calling out for the stable boy to help with the master.

Together the two young men carried Brett upstairs to the bedroom. "Go now, get Mrs. Pickery. She'll know what to do. Don't' waste any time. There's a good lad. I know you'll hurry back."

The injury seemed worse now than when he dug the ball from his chest. With no internal damage, Bobby had been fairly certain Brett would be fine. At this moment he was no longer sure.

Brett tossed on the bed groaning, his eyes closed. A fine sweat had broken out on his face. Bobby sat down beside him, trying to remember what he'd been taught on the London streets about saving a man's life. Not much though; every man had to fend for himself. Calling a doctor had never been an option since any gunshot would have been attained during a crime.

He marched into the bathing room and found a pitcher of water as well as a bowl and a rag. Filling the bowl, he brought it as well as the cloth to the bedside. Staring down at Brett he prayed a moment for him.

"Sure hope this works master Brett. You need to bring down the fever. Suppose there's some infection setting into your wound that we need to treat, but I'm going to wait for the cook before I do something more stupid than prying the bullet out with a dirty knife. Don't know where it's been, and that fact could cause you some problems.

Bobby dipped the rag into the cool water before placing it on Brett's forehead. He set about unfastening Brett's shirt so he could see the wound. It was red and hot to the touch, swollen too. Bobby ran his fingers through his hair, thinking.

Truly, he didn't want to do anything until Mrs. Pickery arrived, but he understood the necessity of quick actions. Examining the room, he found a bottle of whiskey on a sideboard near the bed as well as wine and a few other spirits. He chose the whiskey and opening it, he swallowed a large portion for courage, he told himself, before moving back to the bed.

"This is going to hurt like the devil, master Brett, but I've got to do it or I'm afraid you're going to die. First time must not have been enough. Heard this stuff cleans out the wound and keeps away infection." He swallowed another portion before pouring the alcohol on the wound.

He was happy to see there was no reaction except another groan from his patient. He knew first hand it could sting like hell. Bobby sat by the bed, for how long he had no idea. Darkness descended and the clock in the hallway ticked away the seconds. He now had second thoughts about giving the stable boy the task of fetching Mrs. Pickery.

The knock on the door startled him awake. He rubbed his eyes before he stood to open the door.

"It's me, Mrs. Pickery. How's the master doing, Bobby?" She walked into the room not waiting for an invitation. "Tell me what you've done and I'll know if I have to undo any damage."

"Took the bullet out then poured some whiskey in the wound. It looks better now than it did an hour ago. I'm hopin' he'll wake up and we can get going first thing in the morning." He moved away from the bed to allow Mrs. Pickery a better look.

"Too bad you didn't clean that knife before you poked around for the ball. No, you didn't tell me, just knew it had to be true. I've seen that wicked knife you always carry," Mrs. Pickery muttered as she worked. With his shirt off, she bathed his chest and finding soap, she cleaned and poured more whiskey in the wound.

"Is he going to be in a lot of pain when he wakes up?" Bobby asked, bending closer. "Seen worse wounds and heard men screaming in pain before they died from the aftermath of what appeared to be nothing serious. That's what I thought. The wound didn't do any real harm."

Mrs. Pickery reached out and covered his hand with hers. "He's going to be fine. You did the best you could under the circumstances. Now tell me what happened to the little missus. The stable boy didn't have any idea where she was but told me her horse returned without her. Just told me the two of them went for a ride and only you two came back."

Bobby gasped for breath, his inside churning and whirling, thinking little Piper was really gone even though he'd tried to convince master Brett she could take care of herself. Few could take care of themselves against Scarface. She was in dire trouble and most likely headed to be some man's mistress. That was the strategy for her before she was caught picking Brett's pocket so why would Scarface change his plans now?

He inhaled several times then again before he could actually speak. Swallowing hard, "Scarface shot him and grabbed up Piper. Took her with him, he did. I know he wants to make her some man's mistress. That was his intent before master Brett rescued her and made her his wife. Thinks he's goin' to make some money off the sale." It seemed he couldn't stop talking. Words rushed out in a jumbled up mess, but Mrs. Pickery seemed to understand.

"And you left her to fend for herself to save Brett," she said as she continued to cool the fever that seemed to be keeping him unconscious. "Not sure that was the wisest choice, but I'm glad you did."

"Billy went after her and I brought the master home. Didn't know what else to do. Got every confidence that Piper can rescue herself. She knows the best ways to get out of a scrape, and despite how evil Scarface is and how much everyone fears him, he doesn't know anything about us. Doesn't understand the life we've led. Can't comprehend what it's like in the most seedy and darkest parts of London where we all grew up and learned how to survive. She's a fighter, that's what she is."

"Us?" Mrs. Pickery pursued Bobby's words.

"Us, as in those who've lived by any and every means possible since we could walk."

I agree with you. Piper will find a way out of this mess."

"Unless he kills her first," and Bobby didn't think Scarface would kill someone who promised to be a gold mine for him. "He wants the money she'll bring him, but also he's got some other reason for keeping her safe. Piper's always been granted a few more privileges than anyone else has and it's because Scarface had another reason for doin' so."

"And I'm guessing you know what this Scarface wants from Piper besides the money. What is this other purpose?" Mrs. Pickery said.

"You've got to tell me so I can try to help."

"Nothing you can do for Piper now. Only Piper can do for herself. Like I said before, the rumor was that before Master Brett caught her pickin' his pocket, Scarface was training her to be some man's mistress. He was going to make a fortune on her. Some say she was the daughter of a duke or some wealthy gent, but there was no real proof. Could be he's lookin' for revenge. That was the other rumor."

"Well, what we've got to do now is keep Master Brett alive so he can find her. He's not going to like this set back at all, but there's nothing to do for it now. I've got to figure out just how to keep him sedated until he's well enough to start looking for her again, or the two of you will be back here with the baron in this bed again and still without his wife."

"How you going to do that?" Bobby asked. "Seems to me as soon as he wakes up, he'll be hightailin' it out of here. Words of caution won't make a damn bit of difference. If he hadn't fallin' off his horse, we'd still be out there riding."

"You're right of course, but I've got some wonderful tea that will aid his sleep until I'm satisfied he can sit a horse for an extended period of time, I'm going to keep giving it to him." She bustled around the room, Bobby watching her and wondering about all she said.

Bobby sat down on a nearby chair, hands folded across his lap. He watched his new boss as his breathing seemed to ease and his color slowly turned normal. Mrs. Pickery had done what she told him she meant to do. The only question remaining was just how long Brett would be in the bed.

Brett was aware of the conversation around him as he fought his way out of the deep fog surrounding him. All his body seemed to ache, but to save his life he couldn't remember why. He tried to repress the groan emanating from his chest but was unsuccessful. Bloody hell, but he couldn't move, not even an inch.

Through the narrow slits in his eyes, he watched the bedroom swirl and churn. A light sifted through the window. Mrs. Pickery bent over him, placing a cool cloth on his forehead.

"Seems his fever has finally broke. He should wake up soon," Mrs. Pickery said as she set a tray on the bedside table.

"And there's going to be hell to pay when he discovers just how long he's been in this bed," Bobby said.

How long he'd been in the bed? Brett tried to open his eyes wider to no avail. He tried to sit up and found the feat impossible. Why wasn't Piper in the room, by his bedside? His heart lurched to a brief stop. Avery had taken her. Where was she? Someone must have gone after her, but Bobby was in the room.

He moistened his lips, his eyes a bit wider. "Piper?"

Mrs. Pickery stood beside the bed. "Now you don't be worrying about her. She's got nine lives just like a cat, I'm sure. Right now, if you're going to do her any good you've got to get stronger. She'll be just fine when you come for her."

His eyes were wide open and now he remembered everything. Then, "Avery? Help me sit."

Bobby was helping him up and propping pillows behind his back. "Avery ran off with Piper," he blurted out.

"And I'm here in bed?" He didn't want to think about how long but the question was there and he had to ask. "How long? How long have I been sleeping when Piper's been in trouble?"

"Now that doesn't matter right now," Mrs. Pickery hedged. "You got to finish healing before you can help Piper, and that's going to take a few more days."

He tried to swing his legs out of the bed but didn't have the power. He fell against the pillows, groaning again. "Have to go after her."

"You will. As soon as you're strong enough. Right now, you've got to get your strength back." Mrs. Pickery held a bowl of steaming liquid in front of him. "You can start with some chicken soup."

She tried to spoon a bit of the broth to his lips. "I can do it myself."

It seemed to Brett she almost laughed. "Suit yourself." She set the bowl on the table beside his bed before she walked from the room leaving him alone with Bobby.

Brett eyed the soup and attempted to reach for it, managing to knock the spoon from the bowl. At least he didn't spill the contents.

"Want me to help you?" Bobby asked from across the room. "Won't do you any good if you don't get something to eat. You haven't eaten anything for a week now. Only had the tea Mrs. Pickery kept you sedated with."

So that was the way of it. "It was in the tea and yes, she is right. I need to eat. Hope it's more than chicken broth."

Bobby pulled a chair beside the bed. Until Brett finished the soup, they didn't speak. He understood the necessity for patience but given the situation, he had none.

"Help me dress." Brett directed his attention to Bobby. "I need to find Piper. Where's Billy?"

"Told Billy to find Piper and not to come home until he did." Bobby rummaged through the armoire pulling out clothes for him. "Even if I help you, odds are you won't be able to sit your horse more than a few minutes at best."

"So, Piper is still missing." Brett slipped his arms through the sleeves of the shirt and with a great deal of effort, pulled it over his head. By the time he finished he was breathing hard and a layer of sweat coated him. Resting against the headboard, he closed his eyes, waiting for his heartbeat to return to normal. Nothing he could remember had been this difficult.

"Either that or Billy hasn't the means or the wherewithal to return here. He's probably holed up safe and sound in some obscure place in the parish." Bobby grinned, seemingly pleased with his conclusion.

"And that's supposed to make me feel better?" Brett swung his legs off the mattress, wishing that dressing didn't seem such an unobtainable task. At this rate and just like Bobby told him, he wasn't going to be able to ride a few feet without falling off the damn horse.

"Don't really know how it's supposed to make you feel, but Billy and I've been charged with keeping the little lad safe for years and now that she's a lady, the task is more important than ever. Need any more help or can you put those britches on by yourself?" He stood back arms crossed over his chest, waiting for a reply.

"Get the carriage ready and have Mrs. Pickery pack a basket of food and find Molly. Have the stable boy hitch up two horses to the back of the carriage for when I'm strong enough to sit a horse. We're going to London. Come back here when all's ready and help me down the steps." Brett watched Bobby's departing back then set himself to the task of putting his clothes on.

Finished, he sat on a chair in by the window staring out at the road, thoughts of Piper and all that could have happened to her flitting through his head. Too many times to count, he told himself she was strong and could think on her feet. She would find a way to outsmart Avery.

"Sir? We're ready. The carriage is packed with everything we'll need for a few days. Do you want me to pack a valise for you?"

Relief at finally doing something swept through him. "Mine is by the door. Give me your arm and help me with the steps." Frustrated, he needed help to walk. He took solace in knowing he was indeed gaining strength by the minute. An hour ago when he woke from his weeklong sleep, he was unable to sit up and now he walked down the steps. He was going to London and he would find Piper.

Bobby had pulled the carriage so it rested near the front porch. Molly was inside waiting for him and two horses were tied to the back. He half expected Mrs. Pickery to be inside too but she wasn't.

~ * ~

They were headed to another home and a man, another revealing she supposed. She wouldn't give him the pleasure of seeing her naked. The thought made her skin crawl and she understood this wasn't going to be easy.

At the next home, Avery followed the same protocol as the first and everyone after that. He brought her to their respective rooms, bade her don fresh clothing then left telling her to knock when she'd bathed and dressed.

Each time he left, she searched for the peephole, finding nothing. They all must have been hidden well, perhaps in a painting. Today, sitting on the bed she waited until she thought enough time had passed for her to accomplish everything Avery ordered her to do. The slow tick of the clock set her nerves on edge. She truly didn't know what she thought to gain by this little show of defiance. Avery would make her disrobe and bathe, in order to show her off to the man who lived here.

She knocked on his door then opened the door not waiting for a reply. Stepping inside, "I'm ready now." She inhaled a long deep breath, feeling her nerves unraveling one thin strand at a time.

Avery looked up from something he'd been reading. When he noticed her, his expression changed to a sneer. "What do you think you're doing? I expected to see you clean and in the new garments I purchased for you."

She smiled before sitting down at the table that was piled high with food. "Coming to eat. I would like a glass of wine then we can discuss my clothing."

As if in slow motion, he stood and walked to her. Grabbing her by the arm, he lifted her from her seat. "How dare you presume so much? You are not the queen of the castle. No food, not until you bathe then dress in the clothes that were set out for you. Obey me or I'll rip your bloody dress off you."

"I don't want to," she spoke again, but the grip on her arm tightened until she cried out in pain.

"I suggest you do as I say. I shouldn't need to repeat myself. If you don't, I'll undress you and make sure you bathe. Do you want that? My hands on you?"

"No more than I want some man peering at me. If I could find it, I'd cover it up." She wanted to stand her ground but understood all too well Avery would do what he said and if she covered the hole, Avery would allow the man access to the room. At least this way she could pretend she was alone.

He led her to her room, pushing her inside none to gently. "I'm going to wait right here while you make your decision. The bath is getting cold by the way."

Piper glanced around the room, staring at the walls and understanding it made no difference what she chose. She could pretend no man was watching her and judging. Perhaps if whoever meant to pay money for her saw she was with child, he would lose interest just as the first man had.

Slowly, she walked into the room, shedding her clothing as she stepped through the room. Naked, she settled into the water, taking solace now that whoever watched her could see less of her.

She stayed in the tub until it turned chilly and her fingers were wrinkled.

"You going to stay in there all night?" She jerked. Avery's voice behind her penetrated her thoughts.

"If I could," she muttered, trying to cover herself with the washrag she'd used.

When she peered at him over her shoulder, he was nonchalantly leaning against the doorframe and the smug expression on his face spoke of owning his little part of the world and he seemed to be enjoying the view.

"You're a quick learner, Portia. I'm sure you'll find some way to turn this to your advantage, but escaping is not an advantage. I'll never let you go or escape me of your own devices. I've taken great pains and spent a lot of money to make sure that will never happen."

Words eluded her and hatred for Scarface grew in her heart. Allowing some man to violate her was not an option she wanted to consider. If that happened, she didn't know if she could go to Brett with an open heart.

"Let's just get this over with." She rose, water sluicing from her then reached for the bath sheet resting on a table nearby. "I'm sure he won't want me either, at least not in my current condition." Turning, she smiled at Avery. "This pregnancy might work to my benefit."

"We could get rid of the baby. It wouldn't be hard. I know people." His voice assumed a dark edge. "Aborting the child would not be all that difficult."

"And you would risk my life when revenge is so important to you. Don't believe my death would give you what you crave." She slipped the new chemise over her head then pulled her stockings on, hoping whoever this man was who was watching her would decide to keep her. Truly, she thought anyone would be easier to escape from than Avery, who had part of himself in London's underworld and the other part in the seedier side of the aristocracy.

"Your ploy won't work, sweet heart. He doesn't care about purchasing you for himself. Instead, he wants you for his daughter. It seems she needs a female plaything having grown tired of her last lover."

Her startled gasp made him smile. He enjoyed taunting and tormenting. "Daughter? No..." She wasn't innocent and she'd heard of and also watched women make love to women in the brothels as well as men together.

At the thought her stomach churned, disgust filling her. She felt the blood seem to drain from her body as the room started to spin. Clinging to the chair she sat on, she tried desperately not to fall.

When she next opened her eyes, Avery stood over her, slowly stroking her cheek. "You will get used to the notion. Indeed, you might even find that you enjoy a woman's company as well as her touch. In any case, these people need to be the highest bidder if I'm to sell you to them. Know for now they are interested in you."

She tried to sit up.

"No, don't move, not yet. Your face is still as white as a sheet. Perhaps your new young lady might want a child, the child you carry. After all she's been deprived of a baby for a number of years. The two of you can raise the little tyke together. Now won't that be fun." He sat back on his haunches, seeming to study her, gauging her reaction and laughing at what he saw.

"I'm sure she could have purchased an orphan," Piper shot back, struggling to regain her composure. Yet his hand rested on her belly, possessively, and she tried to shake it off.

He laughed at her words as well as her feeble attempt to remove his touch upon her, "Ah, but an orphan would not have the same pedigree as your child." He chuckled again as if he thought of something wicked.

"Hurry now." He turned to leave but stopped at the doorway. "You need to eat. You're eating for two now, and we must keep you fed and healthy if we want to gain top dollar. I believe the new gown will fit you much better than the last one. Now that we know your condition, it's much easier to send word ahead and have suitable clothing purchased for you."

"We're going to another place?" She must have misunderstood, thought this was agreed upon, this place would be her new home. A tiny wave of relief swept through her but was replaced with the fear of what would come next.

"Of course, we've three more residents to visit before I ask for the final bids. I still need to make sure all know who you are and the identity of the child within your womb as well. It will make this process so much more enjoyable when all are apprised. Who knows what will come of all this?" He moved away from her yet kept his eyes focused on her. Then spinning on a heel, he left. She heard the soft sound of the door as it closed.

"I'm not finding anything enjoyable about this process or you," she muttered as she sat up and finished dressing. Walking into his chambers, she found herself alone. A bountiful amount of food had been brought to the room along with two bottles of wine.

Sitting down, she poured herself a generous amount of the liquid hoping for courage. Waiting for Avery set her nerves on edge and she was terrified if these people rejected her, they would be in the carriage within seconds and on their way to the next man, or woman, she amended. She tried to make sense of what he told her. Three more men would see her and perhaps bid on her.

Toying with her food she ate a few bites, everything seeming to stick in her throat. The hour grew late, her eyes drooping. She supposed Avery found entertainment somewhere else and she should go to her room. Exhaustion filled her and every part of her ached from sitting in the carriage. It was strange how she could be so tired from doing nothing.

Slowly, her head fell forward. She jerked awake, searching the room for Avery. Downing the wine that was left in her glass, she picked up the bottle and walked into the bedroom. Slipping from her gown, she put on the nightdress that had been left for her before pouring more wine. The alcohol seemed to steady her nerves and ease her breathing.

Now that she was in bed, she was wide-awake and alert. All the fears from the days with Avery settled in her gut. Escaping from Avery seemed to be a more difficult task than she'd first anticipated. She had never expected the man to keep such a close eye on her.

Well, there was nothing to do for it until he made a mistake, and he would. She meant to sleep now, even though it seemed to elude her at the moment. Thoughts of Brett and the way his hands felt when he touched her ran rampant in her mind.

Staying strong now was a necessity. Determined, she rose and made her way back to his chambers. Scooping as much of the breads, cheeses and meats she could fit into two table napkins, she meticulously folded them and brought them to the room.

At the last home, he'd given her a small bag for her to keep the clothing he gave her. She stuffed the food inside, hoping to find a way to get away from him tomorrow. Well, she was always hoping. Tomorrow they would be in the carriage again and one never knew.

She dressed and stuffed the nightdress into the bag then she curled up on the bed and waited for Avery to come in the morning to wake her up. Her dreams revolved around Brett. At one point she woke, thinking he was holding her in his arms and she was safe in his home in Scotland.

The next time she woke sunrays slanted through the window. When she rose and walked to the window, the sun was shining through a tiny portion of black clouds. In the distance dark shadows crept from the clouds to the earth. Raindrops began to pelt the ground around the house. Leaning on the windowsill, she watched for a few minutes mesmerized, by the sounds of the storm.

"You ready to leave?" Avery asked, his hands behind his back as he rocked on his heels. "You look fetching in your new gown. The color suits you. I'll have to keep that in mind when I purchase new things. The Duchess would be pleased with the way you look right now. Too bad she's not going to see you. Ever."

Piper looked to the scene outside then back to Avery. "I'm hungry. Can we eat before we leave?" she asked, hoping he had a basket of food waiting in the carriage or in his room.

"You can eat later. I'm sure you won't starve." He turned, seeming to expect her to follow.

"I thought you wanted me to eat for two."

"I did say that, didn't I. Well, there's no breakfast to be had. It seems we are alone in the house this morning."

She watched him, her hands clasped in front of her, fury building that she knew she needed to get under control. Slowly she followed him, picking up her bag as she made her way from the room then down the staircase.

"Did the lady not find me satisfactory either?" she asked him, hoping to distract herself from the rumbling in her stomach.

"On the contrary, Madam thought you would be perfect for her. She enjoys younger women because they have so much more energy in the bedroom. I'm sure she'll put in a hefty bid when it comes time." He turned and placed a hand on her shoulder, stopping her. "You need to come to terms with your future, the sooner the better."

"I see," younger women... "How old is she?"

"Let's just say she could easily be your mother. By the way she has known Charlotte Leighton most of her life. The Duchess is responsible for her husband's death, suicide that is, threats she made to him to get something she wanted. Not that she cared particularly but she did enjoy his company and he enjoyed the fact she didn't protest his dalliances and supplied him with the needed funds to gamble. The arrangement was perfect for the two of them. She wants fulfillment now and believes she can teach you how to be a willing partner."

Piper gagged, forcing the nausea down. "No, that won't ever happen. Best you tell her that before she demands her money back when I fail her. I can't imagine being with a woman." This nightmare could not be happening to her. She didn't really care what other people did. There were all kinds in this world, but this particular scenario wasn't for her.

"I see you still haven't learned you have no choices in this matter. You're going to have to learn to become more willing to do and try anything. If you rebuff her advances to the point where she wants her money back, I'll have your child. You know what that will entail. They will grow up in the parish and you understand very well what can happen to a child there. What happened to you there."

She inhaled a swift deep breath, wishing for power to call him out, but she had nothing to hold over his head. "I'll do my best," her voice a whisper in the silent foyer. "I'll make sure she or whomever buys me is happy."

Stepping onto the porch, a stiff gust of wind caught her cloak, pushing the fabric against her legs. She gritted her teeth against the next gale, reaching for the railing to hang onto. Avery collected her hand in his, helping her down the steps and into the vehicle waiting for them.

Piper braced herself for the start of the carriage ride. Closing her eyes, she tried to think of pleasant thoughts, things that would give her a ray of faith on this increasingly dreary and dark day. She'd hoped to see Brett by now, tailing her or confronting Avery. The man only had two bodyguards. With Billy and Bobby at his side, it wouldn't be too difficult to overpower them, but he'd told her Brett was dead. She wouldn't believe that lie.

"How long?" she finally asked, needing to stretch her legs.

"A few more hours," he smiled. "You really should find a way to relax. It would be much better for the baby."

"As if you care."

"Every time I think about The Duchess and the fact I hold her grandchild's fate in the palm of my hand, I care. I care a lot. I will truly enjoy this scenario, watching it play out and it wouldn't be nearly as much fun if either one of you was hurt."

Searching for words, she came up with nothing. The power was his and as long as that was a fact, she would have to do things his way. Rain continued to pound the rooftop and it seemed the cheerless day was affecting her mood. Moisture clogged her throat, but she refused to shed tears, refused to give him any reason to think he was breaking her.

He leaned forward, his forearms on his thighs. "You must resign yourself to your new life, Portia. I shot Brett, so he won't be coming after you even if he survived. No one is going to rescue you."

"I don't need rescuing," she bit out and, "He's not dead. I would know it."

"Seems you do, sweetheart. You're mine for the rest of your life. You would fare so much better if you accepted the fact."

"Never." She straitened her back, holding on to the armrest as the carriage lurched and skidded on the muddy road.

Avery's brows drew together, his eyes shimmering with what seemed like anger to Piper. "Compliance will get you much farther. You'll have nice clothing, jewels if you please your master or mistress if that becomes the case. They might even allow you outside if you're biddable."

"There is nothing I can say."

The carriage lurched again before sliding and sliding some more. She was thrown against the side of the cab. When the door flew open, she clung to whatever she could find. Avery disappeared outside. As the carriage skidded to a halt, a loud cry of anguish filled the rain soaked air.

"Avery?" Piper scrambled out the window to find the driver had been thrown from his seat and was unconscious. On the other side, Avery as well as the driver were pinned beneath the carriage.

Despite her desperate need to flee, she bent over, touching Avery's neck for the heartbeat. It was weak but there. "Avery..." she whispered but he didn't open his eyes. The driver didn't move, and she didn't take the time to check on him. "You were wrong. I am going to escape you."

Reaching inside the carriage, she was able to grab her bag as well as a blanket.

"Good bye, Avery," she whispered. "I hope..." she didn't want to speak the words prevalent in her mind. "I guess I just hope for the best for both of us and I pray I never see you again."

She had listened to the man when he spoke to her about the places they were going to visit. He was headed to London. At least two more men were on his list of possible bidders. In any case, she wasn't sure if she should stay on the road or try to parallel it. What she couldn't figure out was where the two guards were.

Then she walked back to Avery and reaching into his pockets, took his coin purse and everything else of value he carried on his person. She slipped the items inside her bodice. "You won't need this Avery but I will."

With that said and done, she started down the road, hoping to find an inn or someplace she could stay the night. Hours later though, she'd not found an inn to take refuge from the storm. Exhausted, she stepped to the side of the road. Trees and bushes would provide some shelter. Because of the cloak Avery gave her, she wasn't soaked through to the skin, and the blanket she grabbed would provide some warmth in the dead of the night.

She found a thick grove of trees with low-lying branches. Breaking off the largest pieces of the trees that she could, she set them against a tree trunk, making a hollow she would fit into. At times she'd had to make similar sleeping tents when the law was too close. Before she pushed her way inside, she wrapped the blanket around her and grabbed her bag.

Looking at the food she packed the night before, she realized it would have to last her until she reached London or found an inn. Portioning out five days worth of food, she settled into her shelter eating and trying to savor each bite for as long as she could chew.

This pattern continued for five more nights. She didn't dare knock on a house; besides they were few and far between. One night she found shelter in an old barn; another night she was able to stay in a dilapidated old house.

The food shortage terrified her, not for herself because she'd been through worse in her life but for her growing child. The miles she could travel grew shorter each day, and she spent more time sleeping than walking. Despair, deep and absolute, hung over her head as she trudged down the roads, having lost track of the days.

A sign at a crossroads indicating London was only three miles from where she stood lightened her heart, giving her hope. Finding places where she used to haunt and people who would recognize her in her current condition seemed impossible. Yet she said a prayer. Placing a hand on her belly, she knew she had to maintain courage to survive. Giving up was not possible now.

She had alternatives that she mulled over in her head, none of which seemed prudent or compelling. Going back to St. Giles was not an option. If Jocko found her, he would give her back to Avery, that is if he survived the crash. She'd been terrified for days that the next carriage passing her by would be the man she was running from, but so far she'd been lucky.

She could find out where Charlotte Leighton lived and knock on her door. What would she say? Oh, by the way I'm your long lost child. She wouldn't even guess at how she looked right now. Mud streaked her gown, and her hair hung in limp strands around her face, which she was sure was as mud streaked as her dress. When the food was gone she abandoned the valise.

Hunger gnawed at her belly as she placed one step in front of the other. Sure she would collapse, she took refuge by the side of the road. A few trees provided shelter from the elements as a breeze sifted through the leaves and a harsh sun dried the ground from the drenching it had taken for the last few days.

She slept, visions of Brett passing through her mind, the hours making love, the moment when he found her in Vauxhall Garden. All those times, some pleasant some uncomfortable, filling her soul. She relived everything. Groaning, she stirred, her body reacting painfully to the movement. Her eyes opened, blinking several times before she pushed from the ground, willing her feet to move forward. The baby deserved a life something better than she had.

Deciding to take refuge in the place she'd sheltered in numerous times in Vauxhall, she made her way in that direction. Billy or Bobby could find her here if they looked and if Brett still lived, he might think to search in the spot where he found her that night when Rogue picked his pocket. She wished for her dog's company, had so several times in the last week or so.

Time had passed slowly and while she tried to keep track of the seconds and minutes, the feat had proved useless at best.

The walk over the bridge to Vauxhall Gardens seemed to take an eternity. She passed by people she knew from another life, but no one recognized her. Remembering the coin she stole from Avery, she disappeared into a secluded area and pulling the smallest coin she could find, made her way to a stand that sold meat pies. Licking her lips, she held out the coin.

"Who'd you steal that from, you little guttersnipe. Never mind. You're looking hungry and at least you're paying not stealing." The man held out the food to her and she dropped the coin on the counter, nearly swooning with the possibilities.

As she turned to leave, "Wait up." He handed her several coins. "You're going to be needin' something smaller if you want to get food without someone calling the constables. No one will believe this is rightfully yours."

"Do you know who I am?" she asked the man who'd given her

free food so many times she couldn't count it on her hands as well as her feet.

For a second he looked at his cart then backed to her. "Heard you married some fine gent. Doesn't seem that's the way of it. If there's anything I can help you with, Piper, just come to me. You helped me out when I was having a hard time even though you most likely got punished for it."

She looked down and for the first time since Avery abducted her, she shed actual tears. "Thank you. When it's possible I'll make sure you never want for anything again. When the MacLachlan finds me, I'll be fine again. Just promise me you won't tell anyone you saw me. No one."

"Now, I don't see that happening anytime soon, but I appreciate the thoughts. You take care of yourself, Piper, and nothing about you will come from these lips."

She nodded, walking away from the cart and onto the vast trails in Vauxhall, knowing she could lose herself. After she walked about ten minutes, her favorite hiding place loomed in front of her. She scooted inside, wrapping the blanket around her and finishing the food she bought.

Summer had passed and now the nights were getting longer and colder. She understood she had to find better shelter but couldn't risk showing herself in St. Giles, and she didn't want to go anywhere she wasn't familiar with.

Her thoughts wavered to include Avery, and she wondered when he was rescued, and he would be. After that how long it would take before he came for her again. She understood the motive. Vengeance against someone was powerful, and where Avery was concerned it seemed to be all consuming. He'd sought revenge for over eighteen years now.

She closed her eyes, letting herself relax, yet keeping her senses tuned into the sounds emanating around her. Lovers strolled by as did children as they played at losing the parents in their lives. Crickets chirped and she was sure she heard the hoot of an owl. Sheltered in this spot, life seemed to stand still for her even while her body tensed at every unusual sound.

Would The Duchess, she wondered, be happy to see her, to know she had a daughter or would she shun her because of the life she led. And

Brett, would he accept her back if he thought she'd been given to the men Avery presented her to. She would be used and unacceptable to a baron.

She must have dozed. Now with her eyes open the sun was down and her shelter was cloaked in darkness. Sleep was a necessity but she was afraid to succumb. A rustle of branches nearby and the snap of a twig sent her heart racing. She pulled the blanket closer as if that meager barrier could protect her from the predator beyond.

"Piper?"

Her name was a whisper in the night, quiet yet reassuring. Tensing, she waited, trying to recognize the sound of the man's voice.

"Piper, you in there? It's just me, Billy. Came to rescue you but as usual if you're in there, you don't need saving, at least not by me."

"Billy, yes, I'm here. Where's Brett? Is he all right, the gun shot..." She waited for him to maneuver into the tiny space.

"Brett should be on his way to find you. Can't really say how he's doin' 'cause I've been lookin' for you since that day. Bobby told me not to come home until I found you." He sat down cross-legged beside her. "Once I picked up Scarface's trail, wasn't too hard to keep track of you."

"And now you've found me. Should we head home? I don't want to be in London any longer than I have to," she asked, unable to stop smiling. She reached out, touching Billy on his cheek, relieved to see a friend.

"Can't go home until you meet your mama," he said, a purely masculine chuckle following. "I wish I could see the look on The Duchess' face when she sees you for the first time since you were a baby."

"And Avery, have you heard anything about him? Is he alive?" Her body shivered when she recalled his white face when he was trapped beneath the carriage and the strange skew to his leg.

"Scarface is alive, more's the pity," Billy said. "When I ran across the vehicle turned on its side and saw Avery on the ground pinned underneath the carriage, I feared for your life. Was thrilled when you weren't inside. Knew you got nine lives and rescued yourself. Knew, too, that you would hightail it to Vauxhall where I'm sure you feel safe. Nowhere else for you to go except..." he paused.

"I'm glad you're my friend, Billy. Now all we've got to do is figure out where we're going next. The weather is changing and we can't stay here forever."

"Got that one figured out, Piper. We're going to go in the back way to the MacLachlan townhouse, and you're going to stay there until Brett comes for you. We won't turn on any lights. Don't want anyone figuring out someone is staying where they don't belong although if anyone belongs, you do."

"You sure that's wise?" she asked. "Won't Avery think to look there for me even if it's dark at night?"

"Thought about that too. Tomorrow morning after I get you settled, I'm going to pay a visit to Charlotte Leighton and tell her about you. If all goes well, she'll invite you to stay in her home which could have been yours all these years."

"Avery might have the house watched, both houses. You don't know how much he wants revenge against the Leighton family. I heard him brag about his deeds against his brother. The duke was Avery's brother. Scarface is not going to stop until he's dead."

"I'm sure that can be arranged," Billy said. "I'll take great delight in doing the deed. Just let me at him."

"What about Jocko?"

~ * ~

Jocko paced the room he'd purchased for Avery to stay in while he healed. He knew where his loyalties should be, and he'd never risk having Scarface turn against him. Valuing his life and making choices to that end had served him well the last forty plus years.

"You going to keep walking around the room or are you going to find the girl?" Avery said, his voice pleasant but Jocko had heard that tone before and knew the underlying meaning. "I can make your life heaven on earth but also a living hell," Avery told him while he seemed to study his fingernails.

"I'll find her. Got a pretty good start on that as we're speaking."

"What have you done? I want you to keep me apprised of everything."

Jocko stopped his pacing, turning to face the man who'd made his life better than he'd ever expected. Scarface had given him protection from the law several times. Now his obsession with Piper was a puzzle to him. What had the girl done that would cause such animosity?

"I've several of my boys watching the places in the parish she favored." Unfortunately, Billy and Bobby knew more than anyone else and they'd never shared, never been a reason for that.

"And they know this how?" Avery's voice was harsh, demanding.

More demanding than Jocko had ever heard before. "Just making some guesses. As you know, Piper kept to herself mostly. Didn't want to give her real identity away." Jocko understood he needed to figure something out and find Piper before Brett could protect her again.

"You need to have The Duchess' home watched."

This struck Jocko as very strange. "Why?" Before the question was out, he questioned his sanity. Scarface didn't like to be questioned. "Never mind."

Avery waved his hand in the air. "You should know the tale from its beginnings. That ring you've been wearing around your neck for eighteen years tells the entire story."

He dug beneath his shirt and pulled out the chain holding the ring. "I always knew this could be important. Why you allowed me to wear it is beyond me. So, what does this ring tell me about Piper?"

"It speaks of Piper's identity and my vengeance. I let you wear it because I was sure you'd never betray me. Had no idea I'd already been betrayed by The Duchess' wet nurse."

"I'm not sure I understand anything you've said. What does Charlotte Leighton have to do with Piper?" Yet Jocko felt a sudden slide of knowledge. His gut tightened while he focused on the ring. The crest told him nothing even though he knew he'd seen it before. He looked to Avery.

"My name is Avery Leighton, not Bainbridge. William, the Duke of Ravenswood, was my brother."

"And..." Jocko knew Avery left much of the story untold. He'd always guessed Piper was an heiress of some sort. Rumors had abounded around Avery and his penchant for helping out those who were unfortunate enough to be the second son. "You were the second son, but you didn't inherit the title after William died because he had a son. Why didn't you abscond with the boy?"

Avery's laugh pierced Jocko's heart. "Because I couldn't get to him, understood barring an accident taking Richard's life, I would never be the duke so I sought revenge." Avery finished the story, leaving out the part about taking William's life, stabbing him in the back. "William gave me the scar across my face."

"Piper is their daughter," Jocko said in awe. "Bless my soul and she was under my protection all these years. You planning to ransom her?"

"To the highest bidder but The Duchess will not be part of the bidding. Piper is going to be some man's or woman's mistress. Unfortunately, with the carriage accident I lost the opportunity to show her off to some potential buyers."

Jocko's heart caught in his throat. Piper didn't deserve that but no one went against Scarface, no one who wanted to survive to see another day. "I'm sure you'll find a way to get what you want."

"You having second thoughts?" Scarface asked. "If you are, I need to know now."

He'd be crazy to tell Scarface his feelings. Having his throat slit in the middle of the night was not the way he wanted to die. "I'm always on your side. I'll do whatever I can to secure Piper for you.

"Good, I'm glad to hear that. So, why are you still standing in this room? You need to set the wheels of St. Giles Parish in motion and find the lass. If anyone holds back or is protecting her, you need to make sure they don't see another day."

"I understand," Jocko said, letting out a long breath of air. "I understand exactly what you're telling me."

Chapter Nine

Brett spent the night in his townhouse with Bobby and three of his men standing guard at the two main doors and windows. In the morning he meant to send Bobby deeper into London in order to find Piper.

Sitting at the breakfast table, he watched a small sliver of sunshine penetrate to earth through the dark clouds as Brett sipped his coffee. Molly prepared a simple breakfast for them, maintaining that Piper, if she was in London, would come to the house. Brett didn't think so. Piper would find the places where she felt the safest and where she didn't think anyone would look for her. This place, although it was their home, was not a safe haven for her.

He tried to remember exactly where she'd been hiding when he found her in Vauxhall the day she picked his pocket. Rogue would know. He rubbed the dog's ears and realized the animal was whining, clearly missing his master. "Do you know where Piper is, big guy?" He watched Rogue move to the door then look back to him, seemingly eager to get on his way and find his mistress.

Bobby strolled into the kitchen pulling out a chair and sitting down at the table as if he wasn't a servant. "The dog knows everywhere she's ever hid," Bobby said as he heaped the eggs and potatoes Molly had prepared onto his plate. "We didn't. Piper kept most of what she did a secret, but she knew people, vendors in the gardens who would help her out when she needed it."

"As soon as you finish eating, we'll head out. I don't plan on returning until Piper is in my arms and I know she is well. We won't stop looking." Brett felt his insides turn over again and again. He rubbed the spot on his chest where Avery's shot hit him. It had been sore for days now, but when he checked it there was no infection. Bobby cleaned it twice a day and must have emptied several whiskey bottles into the wound to ward off infection.

"Don't need to finish. Been eatin' more than I'm used to. Got to find the lil' gal." Bobby grabbed a chunk of bread and downed a gulp of coffee. "Let's go. The sooner we find her the sooner we'll both have peace."

"Where to first?" Brett followed Bobby and Rogue. He decided to take a carriage to wherever Bobby decided to lead them.

They spent most of the morning searching what seemed like every nook and hollow in St. Giles Parish. Sweat beaded on Brett's forehead, dripping down his face, frustration building inside him. He wasn't sure of anything anymore.

They headed to Vauxhall Gardens still hoping. He let Rogue lead the way. In a small hollowed out area beneath thorny bushes he found traces of what he hoped was Piper, but no Piper. She'd left a blanket and a food wrapper, which gave him a small measure of hope that at least she wasn't starving. By late that afternoon he reached the end, having searched every inch of Vauxhall. His hopes of finding her doused.

"I'm going to see The Duchess. It's my last prayer for now. If nothing else the woman can call out some favors and help find her. By now Charlotte should know she has a daughter and that people are looking for her."

"You just going to quit?" Bobby asked, a pained expression on his face. "You said we wouldn't go home until we found her."

"Never, but we can't keep going in circles. We need more information and The Duchess is the only person here who could give us some clues."

What seemed like hours later the carriage drew to a stop in front of the Leighton townhouse. Another carriage waited in front of the home.

His heart pounding beneath his ribs, Brett strode quickly up the steps, eager for whatever assistance he could get here and waited to be let inside. In the parlor he saw Drake Montgomerie and the woman sitting beside him on a settee he assumed was Ella. The Duchess sat on a nearby chair along with another woman.

At his appearance, Drake rose and made introductions. "Do sit down. We've a lot to talk about. I'm sure you've a story to tell as well. Have you found Piper? If so, Charlotte is eager to meet her."

"No, I haven't found her. Do any of you have any ideas as where to look for Piper?" Brett asked as Drake stood by, waiting. "Bobby and I have exhausted all the possibilities that came to mind."

"You mean Portia? No, we haven't seen her," The Duchess said then pointedly, "Are you holding something back from us? It would not be wise."

Brett felt anger begin to simmer from deep inside, ready to explode. Yet he tamped it down, understanding no good would come of showing his emotions. "With her dog, we explored all the ins and outs of St. Giles. We found nothing. After that we went to Vauxhall where I found what looked as if she had been there with a blanket and some food. I was sure Piper had stayed in the shelter but she left. By the way," he turned to Drake, "Avery has men watching this house. If she does appear here, they will have her. And I pray she doesn't try to go to my home because I suspect the same scenario. Avery is clearly not careless or a fool."

"We know it's Avery's men outside. Saw Jocko in the shadows and he does everything Avery asks," Bobby spoke up, pushing his hat back from his forehead. "Got to be careful."

"I've men also," Drake said, "and we were made aware of Avery. He's now at his home, healing from an accident. The one I assume allowed Portia to escape."

Brett would never be able to call his Piper by her given name. The name didn't fit her. Perhaps if she'd been raised in this family, she would be a Portia. He knew, however, he would have to get used to hearing it.

"She has nowhere to go if everything is watched and the nights are getting colder." What to do now? "We have to find her, preferably before the sun sets." He turned to Bobby. "Do you have places where you and Billy hid from the constables? Would he take her there?"

"If Billy is with her, they might..." Bobby paused, seeming to think things over then shook his head, running his fingers through his hair. "Jocko would know most of the places we hid. It would be too big of a risk. Never kept anything from him."

Brett felt a small amount of hope, thinking Billy might have caught up to her and was with her now. Billy would protect her with his life if he had to. He prayed it would not come to that and prayed too they would find her before another nightfall. He couldn't bear to think of her cold and hungry.

"Between all of you, you should be able to find a little slip of a girl," The Duchess spoke, slowly tapping her cane as she seemed to think. "Do I need to call in favors and do we know if she is still safe from Avery? She might not have escaped the carriage accident that injured Avery. She could be at his home now."

"I'm sure his men would not be outside your door, if Avery had found Portia," Drake said calmly. "My intelligence has given me no notification that it could be true. But calling in favors would be prudent as well as wise. Whatever you can find to hold against Avery can be used to our advantage."

"He took her because he wanted revenge," Brett spoke up, "revenge for something that was out of Piper's control. She's a victim and thank god she's not a bloody debutante who would have swooned."

"My Portia would be a fighter, would never give up even if she'd been a debutante. She is strong. I know it," Charlotte broke down in tears.

Ella strode to her, wrapping her in her arms. "We will find her. Drake has everyone he can call in searching. Perhaps even now we will have news. What will you do when you meet her? It's been eighteen years."

"I suppose I'll have to figure that out. She doesn't know me, or remember this house, Scarlett or her father." She looked up then, hope in her eyes. "I trust you, Drake Montgomerie. Find her and bring her to me. Give this old lady the happiest day of her life." Then she turned her attention to Brett. "I've been told you love my daughter, so I'm going to trust you also. You did come after her despite the bullet wound."

"I'll do my best," Brett said.

"His eyes narrowing, Drake looked up to see one of his men at the door. "Perhaps there is news."

Drake motioned for the man to come inside. "Sir."

"What is it?" Drake asked seemingly impatient.

"Avery has men at MacLachlan's home also. Only two but I think someone is inside. There was a flicker of light before Avery's men arrived. I was headed here to tell you but the presence of the two men stopped me from leaving. I needed to make sure everything was in order before I started here."

"At my house?" Brett spoke, his heart in his throat, thinking of Billy and Piper. "How did they get inside?"

"Billy can get in any home including yours as you well know. Done it before ifn' you remember," Bobby seemed to be delighted. "If they are there, what are we waiting for? Let's go get them."

Brett felt the same but he was sure Drake would caution prudence in this situation. He wouldn't want to leave this home unguarded, rushing to his without taking the proper precautions.

"It could be a trap." Drake said. I'm sure Jocko can also get into any home he wants also. We need to make sure if they are there, we reach them first."

"I'll go by myself or take one person with me," Brett said. "I'm sure I know where we'll find her if she is in my home. Someone should get the constables. I'd like to see Avery punished for this transgression as well as the ones in his past. He deserves to rot in Newgate."

"I'm sure that can be arranged. If Avery sees his world imploding, he will probably flee the country. Perhaps he's already left," Drake said as he stood. "I'm going with Brett."

"Bobby can retrieve a constable to meet us at the Bainbridge home. After we've established Piper's safety, I'll send Billy, with Drake, assuming Billy has rescued my wife."

"The rest of the men we'll leave here to guard your place." Drake turned to the man who brought him the news. "I want you to go with Bobby."

"Sir," he nodded and the two men headed out the door.

"Shall we?" Drake asked.

During the trip to Brett's home there was little to no conversation. Brett's mind was focused on Piper and the condition she might be in. He had Rogue by his side, idly patting the dog's head as they rode through the residential section of London.

Brett's heart was in his throat as they stepped from the carriage making their way into the home. For a moment he held his breath, letting his eyes adjust to the darkness. Getting his bearings, he picked up a candle near the door and quickly lit it.

"Piper? It's me Brett are you here?" He listened but heard nothing. With Drake behind him, he strode to the library. Pushing open the door he held the candle high, searching the area.

"She's not here. Anywhere else she might go?" Drake asked, roughing his hands through his hair.

"My bedroom, perhaps or hers which is on the third floor. This doesn't bode well at all. Rogue would be at her side by now if she was in the house." Brett felt the steady slide of despair. If Piper wasn't here, it meant one of two things.

Drake placed his hand on his shoulder, shaking his head. "Avery doesn't have her, I'm sure of it. My men saw the accident and all signs pointed to Portia escaping on foot."

"We'll search the house then go find Bobby. If they aren't here and Avery doesn't have her, then she's in one of their hiding places."

"We'll find her and she'll be safe," Drake said with a good deal of determination as they made their way through the house, leaving nothing unexamined.

It didn't register in his mind. He had to find her, a burning need to do just that possessed him since he was free of the drugs Mrs. Pickery had given him.

"It was my fault, all my fault. I knew Avery was nearby and I took her for a ride anyway. Blessed hell, I should be skewered through for not thinking of all the possibilities. Thought Billy and Bobby were enough to keep us safe. I'm a bloody fool."

"Had that feeling a few years back too," Drake said. "Ella was kidnapped and I didn't take enough precautions when I knew she was in jeopardy. We will find her."

They were back at the front door, no Piper or Billy in sight. "What now?" Brett asked, sitting with his head in hand, tears in his eyes.

"We go to Avery's home and see what is happening there. It's just a short trip from here. Then we repeat the process, go everywhere we think she could be."

"You know there is probably another victim in the slums of St. Giles. There was talk of the St. Aubries infant vanishing suddenly around the same time. The brother inherited. Perhaps this investigation should continue on," he paused, "after we find Piper."

Bobby met them when they pulled up in front of the home. "Avery's not here," Bobby said. "It appears he left quickly, taking few belongings."

"Piper?" Drake stepped forward taking charge of the situation.

"No sign of her. Constables searched the house," Bobby told them.

"As Scarface, it is well known the man has built hidden passages in every place he frequents. I'm sure he only left when he realized all was lost," Drake said. "Go back inside and search the wall in his bedroom then all the other rooms until you find out how he got out of the home so quickly."

"We should search too."

"My men are trained in things like this. Send Bobby to the Leighton residence to bring two more men. I doubt if Avery is still a threat to any of us."

Drake strode into the home, Brett following, still wondering if Avery had her or if Piper was safe somewhere with Billy. The breath he inhaled was long and deep before he began his search in the Library, Drake taking the stairway two steps at a time.

Brett ran his hands along the walls, tearing off paintings, uncaring if they were damaged when they fell to the floor. Avery would never return here. All he found were peepholes, which had to lead to passages behind the walls. Thoughts of what he used the peepholes for disgusted him and reminded him of some of the tales Piper told him about the whorehouses.

When he finished with the library he strode to the man's office, repeating the process. If Avery had eyeholes in his house, he...no he wasn't going to let his mind wander in that direction.

"Brett, come here."

Drake's voice startled him but sent him racing up the steps. When he stopped at the doorway, he saw a secret door open to a passage. The two men stepped inside, following the darkened hallway. A few feet from the opening they found a candle and lit it.

"Where does this go?"

"Past all the bedrooms then downstairs. There are spyholes in the library as well as the office," Brett said.

Together they strode through the dark passageway in the house to the lower level then lower still. Finding a stone tunnel, they continued. The silence inside was deep and eerie. There was no sign of Piper here or in the house. Surely, she would have thought to leave some clue. She was smart and she would think of some way to tell them she had been here.

When the tunnel finally stopped, a set of stairs wound upward. At the top they emerged into a stable.

"There are no horses or even a carriage."

"He could be halfway to Scotland by now or Dover, that is if that's where he is going. I believe he would head for France. From there he could go on to Spain, no one the wiser."

"What do you know of Avery Bainbridge?" Brett asked, wishing he'd thought to learn more when there had been suspicions about the man. "Does he own any ships?"

Drake raked his hands through his hair. "Don't think so but anything is possible. He has a network of spies, men working for him. He could leave England and we would always be looking over our shoulders. The man has always been elusive. He would go somewhere he felt safe," Drake said, striding outside. "Just don't know exactly where that is."

"This isn't even the stable next to his home. It's not good, not good at all. Have to find Piper. The viscount could be anywhere and we've no clue as where to look for him."

"We also don't know where to find Piper," Drake added. "Do you know if there are any of these tunnels and passages in your townhouse?"

"Didn't think there were." His gut told him she would go to Vauxhall, but would Billy allow it, providing Billy was with her. But there was no reason to assume Billy wasn't beside Piper. He'd been instructed to follow her, make sure she stayed safe. Bobby and Billy had proved themselves loyal to Piper.

"We need to look there also. If Piper was in one of the passages, she might not have heard us calling for her," Drake started for the carriage.

"Your men are here." What to do now? He was beside himself with worry and the need to race in three different directions.

"I'll send two to the docks and Bobby can take Rogue to Vauxhall. Maybe the dog can sniff her out. We will find them," Drake reiterated again.

"Sir, if you're going to your home to look for a hidden passage, there is one. It's how Billy and I got into your house that night you caught us and sent us on our way with a few of your valuables to appease Jocko. It' comes out in the library behind one of your bookshelves."

"So, that's how you got in so easily, been wondering how you did it. I'll have the door fixed so it only goes one way. Now, could she be hiding there, in the passageway?" Brett asked.

"Don't think so, never told her about it, but if she's with Billy, he knows where it is. They might have gone deep into the cellar to stay safe, particularly if they saw Jocko waitin' for them in front of your house. In that case they would not have heard you when you were there."

Brett was shaking his head and walking to the carriage, mulling over old as well as new information. "Bobby, take Rogue and go to Vauxhall. You might be right. It's quite possible the two of them are in the townhouse, shivering and starving but not nearly as cold as they would be if they were in that tiny little hole I found Piper in the day I caught her. Cover every possible hiding place. I'm sure that one is not the only one."

"Take the carriage. Brett and I will ride to the townhouse, assuming you don't ride," Drake said, eyeing Bobby as if he knew him, understood him. A man from St. Giles would have no opportunity to learn how to ride a horse.

"Getting better by the day. Been learnin' ever since Billy and I left London to follow Piper. Wasn't nothin' here for us so we took the chance and it paid off. Thought maybe the baron would take us in and give us a job since he didn't turn us in to the constables the night we broke into his house."

Drake glanced his way as if to confirm the story.

Brett lifted his shoulders slightly then to Drake, "Everything Billy said is true. I trust both of them and pray Billy found Piper along the road somewhere."

The streets, lit only by a few gas lamps were dark as Drake, one of his men, and Brett rode to his home. Rain started falling in a soft mist, yet by the time they reached the stables, they were drenched through to the bone. The rain was unexpected and sudden. Thunder punched the air in the distance, lightning flashed toward the ground, more thunder following.

Shivers wracked his body. Now he had one more reason to worry about Piper.

Leaping from his horse before letting the reins fall to the ground, he raced to the library, knowing Drake would take care of the horses before joining him. Piper might have known of the passage. When they lived here, she spent an inordinate amount of time in the library, dusting. They shared their first kiss here. She didn't need Billy to help her find the opening. She had been trained as a boy, as a pickpocket and pickpockets moved up in the ranks to robbing houses as they got older. She would have learned a lot about those things.

He was more and more certain that was where she was; the tunnels or perhaps curled up in their bed, waiting for him to join her. The thought brought a smile to his lips.

"She's here. I can feel it in my gut." He stood in the library, in front of the bookcases, running his hands along the rows, searching for a latch of some sort even while a sinking feeling of despair swept through him.

Yes, she had been here, but he was more certain than ever she left.

Drake began work at the opposite end, probing for the latch or some small thing that might cause the bookcase to swing open. After two many minutes, they reached the middle, unable to find anything that would allow them access to the other side.

"Would Bobby lie?" Drake asked, seemingly just as perturbed as he was. "You trust the man, but I don't. All my experiences tell me a man doesn't change his colors so easily."

"I don't believe he would lie about this," Brett said, stepping back to take in a broader spectrum. "Why the devil can't we find it?"

"Perhaps we were looking in the wrong places. Piper used to dust in here and she complained that it wasn't enough work. That's why she started looking inside the books and wanting to learn to read. Perhaps one of the books when pulled out will open the panel."

"So, you think it's a book that is the latch. Are there any books here that aren't really books?" Drake asked. "Something with no meaning or just decorative?"

"Not that I know of, but the books came with the townhouse when I purchased it. Owner never spoke of a passageway, secret or otherwise." He shrugged, trying to remember if he ever saw something when he surprised her walking into the room. Nothing came to mind.

The two men proceeded to pull out books that might leverage a door to open to no avail.

"What is this?" Brett found an oval object and turning it the bookcase slowly swung open.

"He didn't lie," Drake sounded surprised.

"Piper must have dusted this and if she tried to pick it up..."

"It would have stayed in place."

"And she's a very curious woman." Brett laughed, feeling the first relief in hours. "Shall we proceed?" He stepped into the tunnel and just as the one in Avery's home, a candle sat near the entrance.

Brett and Drake followed the tunnel until they arrived at a nearby building. The shed held rakes and shovels, more gardening tools and unlike Avery's escape route, this one sat on Brett's property.

"She's not here. I'm going back to Vauxhall Gardens. The pathways are lit and I'm going to keep looking for her. I can't leave her or trust that Billy found her. Truly, I thought she was here or in the house." He didn't understand why she'd leave the safety of their home to venture outside. If she was afraid and found her way to the townhouse, why didn't she stay where she would be safe from the elements and Scarface's minions.

"Portia must be terrified," Drake murmured, roughing his hands through his hair. "I remember that night I chased after Ella. It was raining just like it is tonight. When I found her, I vowed I'd never let her out of my sight.

"A daunting task I'm sure but I feel the same way."

"You're right, Ella didn't like my hovering then and still doesn't appreciate it. Calls me out on it."

"Well, I can hardly wait to have that same opportunity. Got to find her first though."

Do what you must, I'll stick by your side. Before we leave for the gardens, let's stop at the Leighton home. I keep getting the feeling that we are just missing her by minutes, possibly seconds. She's going to want to settle somewhere for the night. Perhaps it will be there."

"She knows better than to be running around London in the dark. All kinds of bad things can happen to a woman at night. She used to have the protection of her disguise but no longer."

~ * ~

Billy and Piper left their shelter at dawn, leaving the blanket behind. She wasn't going to need it if all went well and if it didn't, they'd be back here tonight. No reason to carry it.

The day was slightly overcast and the rising sun created a brilliant display on the horizon. Piper stopped for a second to appreciate the beauty then realizing she needed to be on the move, she set her steps in the direction of the river.

"I need to wash," Piper smoothed her mud soaked skirts, laughing under her breath as she checked to make sure the purse she stole from Avery was still safe in her pocket. "This gown was nice once not so long ago. Now I look like the hoyden I was raised to be. Wish I had my britches and shirt to wear. I'd just walk into that water and rinse everything off. Wearing this dress, I'd most likely get sucked into the current and drown." She watched the river sweep by, looking for a protected area where she could rinse some of the mud from her clothing as well as her face.

"You're a beautiful lass no matter what you're wearing, Piper. But you're right, a bit of refreshin' for both of us would be in order." Billy stretched, his muscles bulging beneath the shirt he wore. His had seen better days too. He'd lost weight over the last few weeks, having always been a bulky, well-muscled man.

"How long has it been?" Piper started for the river, a place where she knew would be safe. "And what are we going to do when we look presentable?"

"Don't know if we'll ever look presentable, but half way clean would be nice. Why, Molly would toss us out of the house if she saw us lookin' like this." Billy looked over his shoulder before casting his gaze down the narrow path.

"So, what are we going to do first?" she asked again as her stomach rumbled. Without conscious thought, her hands settled on her belly. She had to get something to eat for her baby's sake. One meat pie last night would not do for the rest of today.

"I've still got a few coins from the last time Master Brett paid me. We can buy something from one of the vendors."

"Money is not a problem. I stole Avery's purse when he was pinned under the carriage."

"Good then something to eat and a hot cup of coffee would be in order."

"After that?" Piper shivered as she rinsed her face with a handful of water. "We can't keep hiding. We could go to the constables and present our dilemma, but I don't think they would believe us."

"True, that's a possibility, but I for one don't want to step into the home of the constables. They might lock me up for past crimes."

"Then we should see if we can find a way into the townhouse."

"You know I could pick the lock of his townhouse, but I've a better way inside," Billy said as he splashed water on his face and chest. "Don't know why I didn't think of it last night. My head must be addled." He dried himself with the cleaner side of his shirt before slipping his arms into the sleeves and buttoning it.

"And what way is that, Billy?" She thought she might have the same idea. When the boys got into Brett's house, there was no damage done to the doors or windows. She'd thought more than once when she'd been in the homes Avery brought her to that if she could find the secret door, she might be able to escape that way. The chance never presented itself.

"Tunnel leading from an out building to the inside of Brett's home. Don't think Master Brett knows about it though. Most of these older homes in this section of London have secret passages." Finished speaking, he sat down to wait for Piper, averting his gaze when she lifted her skirts and waded into the water.

She was standing, her skirts damp from the water she brushed across them trying to rid them of the mud stains. Sighing heavily, "This isn't working and I'm just getting colder by the second. My hair is a tangled muddy mess and I smell."

"Like you've been running for your life," Billy said as if trying to lighten the mood, a hint of laughter in his voice.

"I suppose I'll have to make do with the way I look. Food should be next. The man at the meat pie food cart is friendly. He made some change for me yesterday and told me he'd help anyway he could. We should go there first."

Slowly, they walked along the paths, hoping not to draw attention to them. It was good. The few people they saw paid the pair little to no attention. If it had been a summer evening, they would have seen the opposite.

"I see you're back for another meat pie," the man said as Piper and Billy stood at the cart.

"We are," she told him handing over the exact number of coins. "Tasted good last night. Can you give us two apiece and do you have coffee? We'd each like a cup if that's possible."

"See you picked up a friend. Seems I know this bloke too. You better be takin' good care of this one. And yes, I've got what you want." He handed the food and drink over to them.

"That's my job," Billy said, protecting the little lady. "And don't you be tellin' anyone you saw us here."

"Except Brett," Piper spoke up. "My, er..."

"Scarface is lookin' for Miss Piper. Has plans for her, but Master Brett wants to keep her safe. Just don't be tellin' Scarface or Jocko about us. Neither have any good wishes for this little lass."

"Promise I won't say a word about the two of you if anyone comes asking."

Eating they walked in silence for a while. Then, "I've enough money to hire a cab, but I don't know Brett's address. Do you think anyone would accept our money without asking any questions?"

"Don't know. Lookin' at the two of us, they might think we're out to steal from them," Billy said, eyeing the nearby row of cabs waiting for fares. "But we got money. A cabbie might take us to the constables instead of where we want. Seeing the way we look, we shouldn't have coin."

She stiffened her back, taking in a lungful of air. "Suppose all we can do is try. Avery's purse might prove more detrimental than helpful."

"You never give up do you?" Billy asked following along behind her. "Do you want to let me hold the purse in case someone takes exception to our having money? If I've got it, you can say you didn't know anything about it or where it came from."

"Nope, don't give up and if we're caught with this, we'll just have to muddle through the best we can. I'm not going to let you take the fall for something I did." She stepped up to the first cab. "We've money and we'd like you to take us to..." she turned to Billy who gave the driver Brett's address.

The man eyed her critically before looking away for a second. Piper was about to move on to the next cab when he looked back at her. "Take you anywhere you want. Your money is as good as anyone's. Climb on inside and relax. Bloody eyes, the two of you appear to need it."

Inside, Piper leaned back, closing her eyes, thankful the man didn't ask more questions. "Don't know what we're doing here. Don't know if Brett has even come for me. He could be dead. What do we do if he's not there?"

"We'll go see your mother. She'll take you in, take care of you and be thankful you're still alive."

Piper laughed, yet in a few seconds the laughter turned to hoarse sobs. She didn't want to give up, didn't want to admit failure, but she was exhausted to the bone and hungrier than she'd ever been when she roamed the streets of St. Giles parish. The strength she needed seemed to vanish with each clop of the horses' hooves.

"My mother would take one look at the hoyden I've become and toss me out on my arse. She holds all these cards and calls in favors to get what she wants, but she didn't do that for me. If I lost this child I'm carrying now, I'd never stop looking for the babe."

"Maybe she hasn't stopped looking for you, lass. I don't think she would do something like toss you out on your arse, not from what I've heard about The Duchess."

"What have you heard?" Curious, Piper looked up, wiping the tears away with the backs of her hands. "She's formidable and ruthless. That's what I've heard. There is nothing tender or forgiving about The Duchess."

Billy took her hands in his, not seeming to care about the dirt still embedded in her fingernails and the callouses on her hands. Lord, but she didn't ever remember being this filthy.

"Aye," he began slowly. "That she is, formidable and ruthless, but I've heard she looks after family with a vengeance. You're her family, her daughter. I've heard so many tales about the things she's done for her nieces, how she protected them from anyone wishing them harm. I think when you do show yourself to her, to your mother, you'll be pleasantly surprised. If someone stole her child, I believe she would keep looking for her even when the trail went cold."

"Billy, I'm terrified. I want to believe everything you just said but..." Her hands were shaking, her entire body quivering.

He wrapped his arms around her, holding her, giving comfort. "Now lass, we're almost there. You've got to pull yourself together. Gave our driver directions to drop us off a block before the address I told him. See, he's slowin' down as we speak. Wipe the tears away and stiffen that back of yours. Your agile mind and determination got you through a whole lot worse back in the day. It hasn't been that long since you were running the streets of St. Giles dressed as a lad. Get those memories back in your head and pretend you're Piper from St. Giles, not a Scottish baroness."

"You're right. I can do this, together we can do anything, Billy." She rubbed her arms, goose bumps rising on them. The day was chillier than the last, and the sun seemed to have disappeared behind grey clouds.

They needed to find shelter in the townhouse.

Billy helped her from the carriage, ready to catch her if she fell. "Stay close to the trees and hunker down. We want to use the natural shadows to our advantage. Too bad it's daylight, but we'll be able to tell if Avery has put any men out to watch the townhouse.

She didn't see anyone, but that didn't mean anything. Inside the outbuilding she sat down on a small stool while Billy lifted a trap door. Closing her eyes for a moment, she wished for a soft bed. The ground had not been her friend over the passing days.

"I'll go first," he whispered, giving her a thumbs up. "After you get inside, close and latch the door. Ifn' someone else who comes in here doesn't know there's a passage, we don't want to give anything a way. When we're in the tunnel, try not to make any noise and don't say a word."

Piper nodded agreement, slowly following Billy.

Once inside, Billy lit a candle. She wondered at the convenience of that but after a few seconds, didn't give it anymore thought, just grateful for the light. They traveled for a while through the damp tunnel, the walls sweating with moisture, the chill in the air reaching into her soul. She thought she was cold earlier, now her hands and feet seemed so frozen she could barely wiggle her fingers and toes.

"I'm so cold." She didn't know she whispered the words aloud. "Don't believe I've ever been this cold before."

"We'll get you a blanket when we're in the house," Billy said, looking over his shoulder, concern clearly etched on his face. "Keep on going. Don't give up now when we're so close to the finish. Your Brett is going to be here and everything will be fine. You're a fighter, lass. You've proved it time and again ever since you were brought here."

Nothing had been fine for weeks now. So many days had passed she'd lost track of what they were. "What if..." she swallowed. "Never mind. I'm only going to have positive thoughts from now on."

"That's good, very good, Brett would be proud of you. I'm proud of you." They walked up a flight of stairs and the walls in front of them were no longer stone but one side was made of wood. They had reached Brett's home.

Once inside the library, Piper felt a bit of deja vu. Wrapping her arms around herself, she turned in a full circle, smiling for the first time in so long she couldn't remember.

This was where she first fell in love with Brett. She was foolish for him, she admitted. Foolish from the moment she first saw him in Vauxhall Gardens. Had acted in ways she didn't understand. The brief thought gave her reason to smile. The library was where he first kissed her, touched her in ways that made her dizzy with longing. Where Drake Montgomerie made the crazy suggestion that Brett marry her to keep her safe from Scarface. Even marriage did not accomplish that feat.

"Did he leave blankets or clothes here?" Billy stepped from the library, dousing the light from the candle.

"Mrs. Pickery was in charge of packing. Seems there's a lot she would have left behind. Don't think we took all my clothes but maybe we did. I didn't have much to start with. I might have my old britches and shirt in my room upstairs."

"Heard Mrs. Pickery threw them out. Burned them."

"Most likely, maybe the dress she loaned me from someone, don't remember who is still here. Would like to have something clean and fresh to put on even if it's a bit too small for me." She started up the steps. After the first floor, she had to stop and rest she was so exhausted. She'd give anything for a full night of sleep in a bed, maybe twenty-four hours would be in order. The stairs to the third floor seemed daunting to her. Deciding she'd check out Brett's room before she tired herself more, she turned down the long hallway.

Billy didn't follow her. He was checking out the rest of the house, walking through the rooms. Below her she heard his footsteps. In the master chamber, she walked through it, thinking a bath would be nice but knew they didn't dare heat the water. Still she could clean herself, wash her face and hands.

She sat on the bed then lay back on it, closing her eyes, nearly falling asleep in those few seconds. Forcing her eyes to open, she wound her fingers into the heavy quilt, wishing for life to return to normal. She couldn't take this with her when they left and somehow she knew they would leave. If they could get inside, if Billy knew about the tunnel then

Jocko would know too. There was no escaping that fact. They would have to leave if Brett didn't find them here in the next few minutes or so.

This house wasn't safe for her unless Brett was here to protect her. If Avery was still alive, he'd be watching it, he'd have Jocko stationed outside. Jocko was his man in St. Giles. Jocko would do anything for Scarface, including keep a child alive until Scarface could use her for revenge.

Brett's large mirror hung on the wall. She looked at herself, cringing inwardly. No mother would want this child, not even one who hadn't seen her daughter for over eighteen years. The Duchess would most likely kick her off her doorstep if she tried to present herself to the Leightons. Thinking back, she was shocked the carriage driver gave them a ride.

The knock on the door sent her heart racing. Her hand on her chest, "Who is it?"

"It's just me." Billy poked his head inside. "Found the dress you were looking for, and I'm hoping Master Brett left some of his clothes behind." He set the dress and tiny shawl on the bed. "They won't fit well, but at least they are clean."

"That's good, Billy. Thank you."

"I can bring up some water for you to bathe. Won't be hot but it might give you a little boost to your spirits to get cleaned up. I'm going to wash up downstairs best as I can. There is a small standing room only tub in the scullery."

"Just to get dirty again. We've got to go back to Vauxhall. You know that." She found a bottle of brandy left at the home. Pouring two glasses, she offered one to Billy. "Jocko's going to know how to get into the house. Probably gave the two of you directions when he was searching for me the first time. If he senses even for a second that we're in here, he'll send his men through the tunnel."

"Of course, you're right on all counts, but we've got to get cleaned up. I'm willing to take that risk if you are, both with the bath and stayin' the night. I'll get you the water and we can talk about what you just said. Don't be thinkin' we should be out in the elements this evening. If my good sense of the weather is tellin' me anything, there's going to be a downpour tonight. Best we stay where we'll be dry. I could sleep by the panel and if I hear anything...maybe we could latch it from the inside to keep any one out whose tryin' to get in."

"There is always the front and back doors. We have no way to defend ourselves, Billy."

"Hate to admit anything but you do have a point. Just not lookin' forward to sleepin' outside when I could be dozin' in a warm house."

"Don't want to be anywhere Avery is going to come looking for me. He terrifies me more now than ever. That man has no scruples, no sense of right from wrong. He's pure evil and he enjoys it. I won't tell you what he put me through, but I'm sure you've got a pretty good idea."

"Not going to give up on our lives right now. You're right. We need to get out of here," Billy said as he was backing out the door. "I'll be right back up with the water. Will take me a few trips to fill the tub, but I'm gonna do that for you. You deserve more but for now a tepid bath will have to do."

Piper pulled out the tub, leaving it where Billy could fill it easily. Thinking of the water, tepid, not hot, still uplifted her. She watched as he made several trips, the last one leaving sweat on his forehead.

"Thank you, Billy." She sat on the bed; hands folded in her lap. "Thank you for staying by my side."

"You enjoy now. I brought you two extra buckets to rinse your hair and a large bath sheet." Nodding he backed out the door.

"Thank you," she said again, standing and walking slowly to the tub filled with water.

Quickly she stripped, shedding her filthy clothing. She slipped into the water, feeling a moment of peace. When her eyes closed, she floated in a dream world. Brett was searching for her. He was in Vauxhall Gardens peering into her hiding place. She bolted up, splashing water over the side of the tub, her heart in her throat. Gripping the sides of the tub, she willed herself to calm down. It was just a dream, just wishful thinking.

Billy had thought of everything. He'd even brought her lavender scented soap. She had to get back, had to find Brett just in the case the dream could turn out to be true. She didn't want to risk losing him again.

He was there now. If only she and Billy had waited for him to find her instead of coming here.

Billy would have argued that we didn't even know if he was alive. She had to save herself and that was what she was trying to do. But they were going back and it was too late for Brett to find them at least not tonight.

She would deal with that and in the morning make a new plan, one that would end in success instead of failure.

Piper finished quickly, washing and rinsing until she was nearly close to squeaky clean. She smiled inwardly, praying she would find Brett soon. He remembered her hiding place. That gave her hope. Dressing in the gown that nearly left her popping out of the bodice, she attached the modest shawl with the same pin Brett used the first time she wore it.

This time when she looked in the large mirror in the bedroom, she didn't cringe as much. She was still pretty close to revealing most of her breasts and without the shawl, one would be able to see her more intimately than she wanted anyone except Brett seeing her.

Billy was knocking on the door again. "Piper, you dressed?"

"Come in, suppose we should have that discussion again." She knew he was right, understood they had to leave. "We're taking the brandy with us." She handed him a just filled glass and anything else that might be useful.

He stepped inside, a smile on his face. Brett's buckskins as well as his shirt were too tight for him, but at least he wore something clean. Brett was a large man. She never realized how strong Billy and Bobby were, how large they were. No wonder Molly found them both intriguing.

"Found us two rain nappers. Might keep some of the wetness away tonight. Got two blankets. We could put the old one on the ground and wrap up in these to keep warm."

"If we're not too late, we can buy more meat pies and hot coffee," Piper added with a heavy sigh. "I'm going to miss sleeping on this bed." She bounced on it for a moment.

"Awful sorry, Miss Piper. If I wasn't so sure Jocko could find us here, I'd fight to stay indoors. Don't know anything else we can do unless you know the address to the Leighton house."

She was shaking her head, despondent. "Don't know and Avery is bound to have people watching that home too." She downed the rest of her glass, slipping the small crystal into her pocket. Probably not a prudent idea but the thought of drinking out of the bottle didn't appeal to her. Nodding to Billy, "Why don't you take your glass too?"

"Perhaps we should leave them here. Don't want to get nabbed with the purse as well as the crystal."

"In for a penny in for a pound. Didn't tell you the purse has the name Avery Bainbridge engraved on it. If anyone stops and searches us, we're goners. We'll be on our way to Newgate or Australia before we can blink." Piper almost laughed at the expressions washing over Billy's face as he stuck the crystal into his pocket.

"Shall we?" He gallantly offered an arm and she accepted until they were at the staircase. "I've put the rain nappers by the secret panel and the second blanket as well. You get this quilt here. It will keep you nice and warm." He pulled it off the bed, folding it into a something easy to carry before handing it to her.

"Won't we look strange walking through the gardens with the blankets?" She didn't ever recall watching anyone with just blankets. They would usually have picnic baskets also. Of course she never really paid attention to the lovers. She always looked for men with pudgy stomachs and short legs, people who couldn't run fast. She didn't understand why Rogue decided on his own to steal Brett's purse.

"Not at all, people have picnics in the gardens all the time," Billy said with a hesitant chuckle.

"We shall see, don't want to bring attention to us but guess we don't have a choice," she said, having too many regrets and very few choices. "If what you say is true and it's going to rain tonight, there won't be many people there to see us."

In the library, the pair gathered the items Billy found for them and making their way through the tunnel, they emerged to find a mist falling from the sky. Billy checked out the surrounding area, finding only one man watching the house, Jocko.

When he returned, "We're going that way." He pointed in a direction that would take them away from Jocko's line of sight. "Jocko is guarding the house. Don't know why he didn't try to go inside, but I'm not going to question our luck right now."

"How far do we have to walk before we can find a ride?" To Piper it seemed she'd been walking for days on end, never stopping with no rest even though she knew it wasn't true. Her hands on her belly she prayed she could last this night and whatever else would come her way. There didn't seem to be an end in sight.

"A few blocks," Billy said, placing a reassuring hand on her back. "You going to make it?"

She pushed damp hair from her face, wishing she knew how to put the unruly hair in some kind of chignon to get it out of her way. "I'm not complaining, but my feet hurt as well as my back. Seems like every part of me aches."

"You just hang on a little bit longer. When we get to the gardens, we'll get food and coffee then hole up in your hiding place for the night. Everything is going to be fine. In the morning I'll inquire about the address for The Duchess; got to be someone who knows and is willin' to turn over the information for a few coins."

She nodded, inhaling a long deep breath of air, searching inside for the strength she needed. "Can't say I'm excited for that, sleeping on the ground. Right now, though, the thought of sleep and a place where I don't have to walk is better than the alternative.

~ * ~

Avery laughed as he leaned against the railing of a ship taking him to Calais. He had resources in the Paris countryside as well as money in the banks. If he acted quickly, he would be able to transfer his London funds without anyone concerned raising an eyebrow. At the moment, London was a deathtrap for him.

Before he left, he stopped by his mistress' home, thinking he would miss her but nonetheless he wanted to say goodbye and pose a question to her. He was delighted when she agreed to journey with him.

"What are you thinking?" She nestled in close, the wind from the ship had her body shivering. "Like to know what's in store for us when we land."

He turned toward her, running his hands along her sides, enjoying the way she trembled with his touch. His scar never seemed to bother her. She genuinely liked him. Probably the only person in all of London he could say that about. "That I'm a lucky man. Didn't think I would get out of London alive and shocked you wanted to come with me. We're here and about to embark on a new life."

"London would be boring without you." Her hands rested on his chest. With her head tilted slightly back, he could see the swollen curve of her breasts as well as the rosy aureoles. He needed her but he was a man of control and he could wait.

"Is that the only reason you agreed to this trip?" he asked, running his hands further up her body to cup her breasts, delighted in her swift intake of air.

"Of course not, I've always cared for you. Never too sure why but," she lifted her shoulders, "that's just the way of it."

"I want to watch Dover disappear from view. Then we can go below and explore each other more thoroughly. My only regret was that I was unable to exact my revenge." He tried to imagine the look on Charlotte's face when she finally met her daughter but it escaped him. He never had children, never wanted brats under foot.

"Calais and wherever else you want to take us will be nice."

"Portia might not have survived. My best men never found her and before I fled, neither had Brett. All I know is that she lived through the carriage accident."

"One can always hope." She shivered when his lips traced a path down her neck and across her corsage. "You are very naughty."

"And you love all this attention. I believe I will call you Jolie. It is very French, you understand. We will have to find a way to blend in with everyone else. Buy a small cottage outside the city and pretend to be farmers."

"Whatever you want, Cheri. I'm malleable. Do believe I've proven that fact over the years."

"Do you speak French?" he asked, thinking of asking her to marry him. There were no other prospects and the thought of spending the rest of his life alone suddenly was not appealing. Over the years she was loyal to him, and he wanted to leave her well-taken care of if anything happened to him. Marriage would be the only way he could secure her welfare.

"*Mais oui*," she told him, laughing at her horrible accent. "Not fluently though. Suppose I can learn." She graced him with a flirtatious smile.

He hardened, thinking about the night to come as well as the following days. "Perhaps someday when no one is looking I can return and exact the revenge I sought."

"You would risk your life for vengeance?" she asked. "If that is your choice, I'll stand by you."

"Only if I thought I could get away with it."

"Shall we go downstairs to our cabin? Seems the white cliffs have vanished in the clouds."

"And make plans for our future."

Chapter Ten

Brett and Drake entered the Leighton home, "Any news?" Drake asked, taking his coat off before hanging it on the coat stand.

Brett followed behind him, wishing he would look up and see Piper sitting on the sofa, sipping the fine French brandy he knew they served at the residence.

Charlotte walked through the parlor to meet them at the door, Ella behind her. "We were hoping you would have some. We been waiting not so patiently, tapping our fingers and staring at the door."

"It's not much fun waiting and worrying, not knowing anything," Ella said as she gave her husband a hug and a quick kiss in greeting. She accepted his arm, strolling into the parlor.

Brett looked at the happy couple, wishing Piper was there and he could hold her in his arms, feel her breath against his cheek and her heartbeat close to him. "No, nothing. It seems we just missed her at every turn. They have been all the places we've looked except here and we were hoping..."

"We don't know if she understands who she is yet. The only way she'd know for sure is if Avery told her," Ella reminded them. "But now you must believe she is alive and trying to find someone to help her. Portia is going to be fine. She's a Leighton after all."

"She is cautious and wily," Bobby said stepping forward. "If she wasn't at your house, then she's somewhere safe, and I'm praying still that Billy is with her. He wouldn't shirk on his duties. No, sir, not Billy or me. You hired us to protect the little lady and that's what he's doing."

"When we left my townhouse, only one man watched that we could tell. I'm going to assume it was Jocko." They could tell him a thousand times she was fine but the words didn't help. Nothing would until he could hold her in his arms. Brett accepted the drink that was offered as well as some food that was set out, wishing Piper would have food. Fear for her growing every second he couldn't find her.

"Avery fled London without looking back." Drake accepted the brandy offered, sipping slowly. "The hasty departure was evident in his townhouse when we raided it. Gut instinct tells me he left for France rather than Scotland and at some point, he'll find someone to send the necessities he left behind."

"He could lose himself in the States. We'd never find him," Brett said, pacing and raking his hands through his hair. "The land is vast and much of it is not inhabited."

"Too provincial for my brother in-law," Charlotte said. "He would never survive without all the comforts of European cities. Even New York city would not give him the life of leisure and decadence he is addicted to."

"Why is this the first time we've heard about Avery?" Ella asked. "I never knew he existed and for that matter, I never knew how your husband died. If the man is your brother in law...William's brother?"

Charlotte appeared exhausted with worry. She lifted her shoulders in a small shrug, "Never talked about him or the fact he killed his brother and kidnapped my daughter. Couldn't prove anything. Seems the reasons are obvious. He was always a strange man, unpredictable. My husband thought him crazy at times. Don't think William ever realized the depth of the man's hatred toward him. He always just thought of him as his strange little brother."

"We should have known about him, about what happened, so we could guard against him," Drake said, striding to the window to peruse the landscape. He stood looking out for several minutes before he spoke again. "If we'd known, perhaps we could have found Portia before this."

"The trail turned cold years ago," The Duchess said. "There were no favors that could be called in when she was first kidnapped. I had no idea the extent of information on the members of the ton William had collected, the tidbits on people or where he kept the information. Honestly, no one knew of her or had heard anything. If they did, they weren't talking for fear of that man."

"Perhaps even then they were more afraid of Avery than anything you could hold over their heads. Your threats and promises of blackmail were nothing compared to Avery's diabolical promises which more than likely would end up in murder." Ella said.

"But did you understand his contacts in the underworld of London? Probably not, your knowledge grew with time," Drake said, turning to address the group once more. "Perhaps..." he paused seeming to think. Then waving his hand in the air as if to punctuate his thoughts. "We don't need to dwell on the past. All we can do now is find Portia. Since we are the only ones looking for her, the task will be easier. Avery will not get to her first."

"But Jocko might still be looking for her. Scarface might have charged him with the task of seeing that the plans he conspired for her would be carried out," Bobby reminded all of them.

"What if," Charlotte began, pausing for breath, "what if when she learns about me, she thinks I didn't care enough to look for her. Avery must have spoken to her of this time. He would have tainted her feelings toward me, her mother. He would have told her I didn't look for her and wouldn't now. She could believe his lies."

"I'm sure that man would have said all those things and worse," Brett said, thinking he needed to leave, impatient with this time he was spending out of the rain in a warm home while Piper would be freezing and wet. "From all Piper and the boys have told me about him, he would lie with impunity. While Piper never understood the perfidy of that man, she never harbored negative feelings for him until he threatened her. She didn't know who he was and from what she's told me he made sure she had a room to herself as well as people around her who could get her out of any trouble she found herself in. Perhaps after he kidnapped her for the second time, he told lies."

"Until she met you, he kept her out of trouble," Bobby said.

"Can't say I was trouble though," Brett recalled that day with clarity.

"And Piper wouldn't believe everything. She's sharp that one. Nothin' gets by her, Bobby said, confirming everything Brett said. "Were there any signs of Billy where you went? Was he with her?"

Brett had not given a moment's thought to the man other than praying he was beside Piper as ordered and keeping her from harm's way. "Nothing to indicate Billy was with her. However," he paused, "I believe he found her, believe too she would not have ventured from the first hiding place without his encouragement."

"When you go to Vauxhall Garden, I assume that's where the two of you are headed, would either of you object if I trailed along behind you?" Bobby seemed just as eager as he was to set out. "Want to see the lad and make sure he's fine."

"As long as you're not needed here," Drake said quickly, not seeming to have any reservations about him leaving. "It's getting late and I doubt if Piper will show up here."

"Then we should leave," Brett said, exasperated with the wait.

"You will let us know everything as soon as possible," Charlotte said, standing and reaching a hand out to Brett. He accepted, kissing the back.

"Of course, I'll ride my horse," Brett said. "One of you needs to take the carriage. If we find them...when we find them..."

"I'll be takin' the carriage. I'd just slow the two of you down if I tried to ride. I'll meet you there. You got to promise me, you'll wait," Bobby said.

Brett was shaking his head as he headed out the door toward the stables, the two men following him. "No promises on that count. I'll make sure Drake knows where I'm looking and he can wait for you."

Mounted, Brett and Drake raced through the city, dodging vehicles. Seconds seemed like hours, but hope filled Brett's heart and mind as he tried to absorb all they learned. He was going to find her. Avery had left the country. Their lives could return to normal, as long as she was healthy and well.

The two men left their mounts tethered in a sheltered spot. Drake stood beside his horse, gesturing with his hand. "Go on, get out of here. I know where you're going to look. Bobby and I will join you in a few minutes. If you find them, whistle."

Bret left at a trot. The place he was looking for was a half-mile or so away from here. He headed down a wide path before veering to the left and a less used trail. Rain sluiced from the sky. Even with his slicker on, he was chilled to the bone. She would be frozen through.

With the next turn, no more gaslights lit the path. He slowed to a brisk walk, cautiously watching the route for obstacles that could trip him. Then he saw it. The sheltered nook where he first found Piper, where he'd been this morning.

His heart leapt to his throat when he heard a small sound then a low grunt and the softly spoken words.

"Hush, lass, we don't know who it is."

"Piper." His voice was gruff, his throat raw from lack of oxygen. "Piper...it's me."

"Brett!" She pushed from the foliage covering her, a smile on her face, racing toward him, arms outstretched.

He was frozen in time as she seemed to slowly move toward him, seeming to melt to the ground before she reached him. The sight of her falling spurred him until he was beside her.

He picked her up, looking to Billy who just emerged from the shelter. "'Bout time you got here, sir. Ifn' you don't mind me sayin' so."

"What's wrong with her?" Holding Piper in his arms, he was sick with worry. Her eyes were closed, her body limp yet she was breathing, soft and even. He stroked damp hair from her face, gently moving it behind her ear.

"Nothing food and a lot of rest won't cure," Billy said. "Let me get the rain nappers and blankets and follow. You go on, with the little one. I'll be right behind you. It's good to see you. Mighty good to see you, sir, wanted to find the Leighton's residence but decided we'd try that tomorrow."

"You sure nothing is wrong with her?" he asked, gently cradling her against his chest as he walked with her.

"She's not sick and Avery didn't do anything untoward to her. Just showed her off to some men and a woman he was hoping would buy her. She wasn't hurt in the carriage accident either, which I'm sure you all heard about already."

Billy disappeared into the shelter emerging with the things he brought from Brett's townhouse before catching up with him. One turn later they met Drake and Bobby.

"Finally," Drake said a smile on his face. "Glad to see you were right about where your wife would go. Had my doubts but should have trusted your judgment."

"Just want to get her home safe and sound. You can go to The Duchess and explain to her where we've gone." Brett's strides lengthened as he drew closer to the safety of the carriage.

"Charlotte's going to want to see her tonight. If not tonight, she'll want to know when or she'll take matters into her hands," Drake said. "She's been known to show up unannounced."

"I can't tell you what you want to know, at least not right now. Obviously, Piper is exhausted. She isn't ready to see anyone, at least not tonight and tomorrow is questionable." Brett had never had an extended family, used to doing things on his terms not someone else's. "I'll send word when it's acceptable for Charlotte to come see her daughter."

"She's been known to show up when she wants, but I'll tell her," Drake reiterated, "Perhaps she will abide by your wishes, one can always pray."

Brett didn't care about The Duchess, or Charlotte. She could visit or not. It didn't mean he'd present Piper to her until she was rested.

"Tell her in two days, not tomorrow but the day after she can come after lunch, not a moment before. If she comes before, she will have wasted her time."

"I'll tell her," Drake said with a bit of a chuckle. "She's also not too used to anyone telling her what to do."

Behind them Bobby and Billy were exchanging tales. Brett didn't care about that right now either.

Piper moaned softly, her eyes opening. She reached out, touching his face. "You found me." Then her eyes closed again.

Brett smiled, looking at his wife, wishing she was awake and could talk to him. "Always," he murmured. "But don't you ever leave me again."

He watched Drake and the boys ride away. Billy and Bobby would go to his townhouse and sleep upstairs. Drake would most likely end up at his own townhouse with his wife after appraising Charlotte of what transpired here.

Brett held her close during the ride. In his home he carried her up the steps to the master chamber, setting her carefully on the bed before stepping back to look at her more closely.

She could sleep for a while, after he got her out of her wet clothing. While he wanted to be with her, he had things to do downstairs, preparations for his staff. Mrs. Pickery should arrive tomorrow sometime. Molly was here, and had emptied the bath water left by Piper.

He was a contented man. The only thing wrong was the fact Avery, Scarface, escaped and would spend the rest of his life estranged from his home. The man should have been ensconced in Newgate and hung.

Before he closed the door, he took a long look at her, covering her with a quilt. She was beautiful. With her smudged cheeks and disheveled hair, she reminded him of another time not really so long ago. This was not what he expected when he took her to Scotland. Didn't expect her to be the daughter of the legendary Duchess. Didn't expect to almost lose her to Scarface.

Walking down the steps, he could hear the boys talking in the kitchen. He decided to join them for a few minutes.

"The two of you can find a room on the third floor. You can share or not. It's up to you."

"We share most everything but generally not beds," Billy said.

"Not unless there is woman we like in the bed," Bobby laughed, sipping the brandy he poured. "Too bad sweet Molly is exhausted from the trip."

"Looks like one of my bottles as well as two crystal glasses have disappeared," Brett said, wondering what the story behind this was.

Billy shrugged, "Wasn't my idea but the lass wanted to take the brandy with us when we left for our hiding place, the little spot where you found us. Guess she didn't want to share the bottle with me." He held it up. "She took the glasses with her."

"As well as the bottle?" One eyebrow lifted in speculation.

"Like I said, sir, not my decision or idea. Just tryin' to make the lass happy," Billy seemed contrite. "Thought you might be on the way, knew you'd question me, but she..."

"You're right, whatever she wanted. I'm glad you did what Piper asked. Can you tell me anything about the days before?" He swallowed hard, wondering if he wanted to know.

"Not much, found her in that little hiding place. She made it all the way to London on her own. After I saw the carriage tipped over on its side, I was pretty worried. I was close enough to see that Scarface was still alive and hurting. Piper was nowhere to be found, but there were footprints leading into the woods. I would have thought she'd stick to the road. Piper's a city girl so I was surprised she got off the main pathway."

"So, you found her..."

"Not right away, sir, but I did find her because I knew where she would go. I never left her alone."

"Where have you been today?" Brett asked, sitting beside them at the kitchen table and pouring a drink for himself.

"Well, sir, we were at the shelter in Vauxhall for a while. We were able to buy meat pies and coffee from a vendor who promised secrecy if Scarface came looking for her. Piper stole Scarface's purse so she was never out of money."

Brett laughed, thinking once a pickpocket always one, but he was happy she had the foresight to grab the purse. "Just somewhere to keep her warm and dry. Did she ever think of renting a room at an Inn?" Brett asked, mulling the pros and cons of doing something like that.

"Scarface owned many of the proprietors of places she could afford. It wouldn't have been safe for her."

He tossed back the two fingers of brandy then poured more. "You're right of course. Street smarts kept her safe. Thank you and if there is anything either of you need, just ask."

"We'd hope Molly would be a willin' lass tonight now that were back to London," Bobby said with a laugh. "We both kind of miss her."

"We do appreciate Molly," Billy agreed with his friend. "But she wanted to sleep by herself."

Brett rose, intending to head upstairs and lie down beside his wife, wrap his arms around her. "Molly and Mrs. Pickery should be here in time to prepare dinner for all of us tomorrow. Does that make you happy?"

"Much obliged, sir," Bobby said. "Suppose we need a bath before tomorrow night, hopin' she's more willing then."

"I'm sure you are." Energized, Brett took the steps to his chamber two at a time.

When he stepped inside, the sound of the door opening must have awakened her. Piper sat up, pushing disheveled hair from her eyes and smiling at him.

"How are you feeling?" Brett sat down beside her, picking up her hand, stroking it tenderly.

"Tired and hungry. Don't suppose there is anything to eat in the house," she asked, touching her belly.

"Of all the things I prepared for, food was the last on my list but..."
"But...?"

"Your mother, The Duchess, Charlotte, sent food. Bless her soul, she thought of things I did not. There was food in the kitchen when I went downstairs. I'll get some for you."

"And a glass of wine? I know I don't need anything to help me sleep, but the wine would be a nice touch."

"It would just taste good? I'll be right back."

"You don't mind?"

Never." The knock on the door stopped him, "Come in."

"Brought you some of the food Madam Leighton sent to the house. It's real good and her cook came along then stayed and warmed everything up," Bobby stood at the door a tray in hand.

"Is there any wine?" Brett asked before he saw the bottle under his arm.

"I was told by the cook it's a Chianti from a vineyard in Tuscany and that it's very good but if you prefer a Bordeaux I can go downstairs and bring one up."

"The Chianti is fine, Billy. Thank you for everything you've done."

"You're welcome, Piper. Wouldn't have gone against Scarface for just anyone, you know." He set the platter on a side table before leaving the room.

"After we eat, can I have a hot bath?" She looked to the tub. "Billy fetched me water for a bath earlier, before we left, but he couldn't heat it. Then I want to get into one of your shirts and sleep all night. You do have some extra shirts here. After that I want you to make love to me."

Brett laughed enjoying the sound of her voice. "Whatever you want, Piper. I'm foolish for you, always have been." *Foolish for Piper.*

~ * ~

Two days later, Piper lay in Brett's arms, completely recovered from the ordeal. He was stroking her back, murmuring silly things in her ear and she was very happy. It seemed to her, the horrible days with Avery and those after never existed. She knew Brett would make love to her again, before he called for a bath and she was pleased with the idea.

"I sent word to Charlotte that you would see her today, before lunch if it pleased her. I hope that's all right with you. We cannot put it off forever, you know." He placed tender, gentle kisses down her back.

Her shivers of pleasure seemed to spur him to continue. If she could, she would put the meeting off forever. "Charlotte will have to wait if she's downstairs now."

"I've been told no one leaves The Duchess to wait, but Charlotte is different. She seems to have a tender, soft side to her." He turned her over, his lips exploring more sensitive spots. The tiny sounds coming from the back of her throat could not be stopped. She heard his chuckle as he continued, settling her on top of him.

"You make me foolish, or have you already figured that out?" His hands moved up then down her ribs, touching the undersides of her breasts.

Her head fell back as she rose and fell on him with the rhythm he set. She wanted to tell him the same, she was foolish for him too but at this second, she couldn't form the words. This was heaven and as she closed her eyes her body responded to his as she spun outside herself. Just as suddenly he turned them so he was atop her, pushing inside until it seemed he touched her womb.

She stared up at him. His face was taut, there was sweat on his brow, and he groaned, his powerful back arching. He came down over her, balancing himself on his elbows. The look on his face was that of intense satisfaction.

"My God, it just gets better with you. You are mine, Piper, always will be and this child in your womb, we will take great care of him. His hand rested possessively on her belly as he enjoyed the small baby bump. We'll never lose track of the child. I promise you that."

"Or her," she smiled, touching his lips with her finger, tracing the line of his mouth and wishing they had all afternoon to lie in bed together, but her mother waited, quite possibly already downstairs.

"Or her," he agreed, "but I really do believe you carry a boy. Are you ready for this meeting today?" He tenderly brushed hair away from her face.

"I don't think I'll ever be ready, but I've decided the sooner I go down those stairs, the sooner it will be over with. You don't think she'll want to make up for lost time, do you? I don't think I could do that. Or she is overbearing and decides she must come here everyday to see me."

"Charlotte is probably just as worried as you are about this meeting. It means just as much, possibly more, to her."

"Doubt if you're right. From everything I've heard, that woman is afraid of nothing." She wanted to be just as fearless as her mother. "I will tell her right off that I won't be called Portia."

"I'm sure Charlotte will agree to any terms you want, but don't be surprised if she has trouble with that one. Together with her husband they named you Portia. The name must have meant something to them. Perhaps you will need to compromise on a few things. What would it matter if she called you by your birth name?"

"It is not her life that has been uprooted," Piper shot back, feeling angry right now. "Mine has taken two drastic changes in less than a year."

"Both for the best," he reminded her.

"I never asked for a mother, at least not a powerful and wealthy one, not one who controls the ton." She sounded defiant and petulant as well, and she wasn't surprised to see Brett's eyebrows furrow together in seeming concentration.

"We won't even be living in London, so I don't think you need worry too much about surprise visits or an overbearing new mother. Charlotte Leighton has twelve nieces, and it seems until now she's treated them as hers. None of them have mothers, you realize."

"I just don't know how to act."

He rolled off her, touching the pulse at her neck. "You're heart beats too fast. Calm yourself. By the end of today you will have spoken with a mother you didn't know you had."

"Nice advice." She sat up, the sheets falling to her waist, one hand resting on his chest, a thought to seduce him rising to the forefront.

A knock on the door had her pulling the sheet up and scurrying beneath the bedcovers.

"It's probably Molly come to help you get ready for this meeting you seem hell bent on putting off." He laughed, smoothing his hand along her side until it rested on her bottom.

He squeezed and she squirmed. Perhaps he would seduce her, not the other way around.

From beneath the covers, "You haven't helped at all. We didn't have to make love this last time."

"Everyone decent in there?"

It wasn't Molly. She was going to poke her head from beneath covers but chose to stay put. "He can't just walk in here?"

"Come in."

Bobby walked thought the door with a tray. "Brought you and the little missus coffee and croissants. The Duchess had the food brought over this morning, saying she doubted if your cook had arrived and, in any case, would not have had time to shop."

"Should have told her Mrs. Pickery arrived yesterday and doesn't like this nonsense."

"Thank you," Brett said then added, "And Piper thanks you also."

"Can I order up a couple of baths?"

"Yes, and send Molly up to help Piper with her dress. Can't say that I should do that."

"Understand," Bobby said, "If you did, it might be another hour or more before she meets her mum."

"Of course that's what I was thinking too. I'll have my bath after

Piper. It will take her longer to dress and get everything else ready for this momentous event." Brett rose then, pushing back the covers and walking to the table holding the tray.

He poured two cups of coffee and settled a pastry on each plate before walking to the bed. "He's gone. You can come out now," Brett whispered, lifting up the sheet with one hand while balancing their meals with the other.

She poked her head out, sitting up again, but keeping the covers pulled over her breasts in case they had another unexpected visitor. Her stomach growled as she reached for the cup of coffee. "This time just saying it was nice of her to think to send food. But I'm sure Molly and Mrs. Pickery would have figured out something even though they didn't really have time to shop yesterday."

"You just don't want Charlotte to be a nice caring person."

"I don't. You are perfectly right about that. If she is such a paragon of virtue, I will have to like her and invite her to our home. She will want to visit of course when the babe is born then she will want to stay and give her motherly advice about bringing up a child. I don't want any of that."

"Would that be so bad?" Brett asked with a chuckle. "It could be worse. She might not want anything to do with the child. How would you feel if the tiny babe grew up without a grandmother?"

"That might be better. She will probably pinch the baby's cheeks. A grandfather would have been better," she said, wishing the words had remained behind her teeth.

"How would you know anything about pinching cheeks?" Brett was leaning against the headboard laughing, and she wanted to punch him.

"Molly told me," she told him indignantly, hands on her hips while the sheet slipped to her waist. "She said that's what grandmother's do to babies. They pinch their cheeks. For the life of me, I can't figure that out. Why would anyone do such a thing?"

"You should lay down grandmother rules and tell her no cheek pinching allowed." He stared at her breasts.

Piper wanted him to keep staring and make love to her again. "Yes, I should do that, Brett. I will do that. Grandmother rules, that is just the thing."

She set her breakfast on the table, ducking back under the covers when the door opened again. Servants filed in with hot water for her bath. And she wondered at how Brett found all the servants. Perhaps Drake or Charlotte helped him. It had been two days, most of which they'd spent in bed together doing delightful things. Well, one of the days was delightful. She didn't remember much of the first day because she slept it away.

"You should make Charlotte happy and call her mother or mum. Just once," Brett said, rising from the bed. "I'm going to look for a proper dress for you while you take your bath. Don't want you to be underdressed when you meet the formidable woman you call mother."

"I'm not calling her mother. Ever."

"Don't make statements you know may not be true in another year." Brett slipped on a pair of britches before striding from the room.

Once the door closed behind him, she walked to the bath and settled into the hot water. "This is bliss," she murmured, "and I will never ever again take a bath for granted." She soaked for a few minutes, letting her mind wander to Brett and the way he touched her, loved her.

He told her he was foolish for her. She supposed falling for and marrying a guttersnipe from St. Giles was foolish.

As was a guttersnipe marrying aristocracy. Not only was she foolish for him but she loved him. She didn't know when that happened but somehow he wormed his way into her heart. It would certainly be nice if he loved her too.

One could always hope.

When he stepped inside the room, he surprised her. "You should be about finished. I set your things on the bed and Molly will be here in about five minutes." He held out a large bath sheet for her.

"Do I have to?" she asked, even while she stood, water sluicing down her body. He helped her from the tub wrapping the towel around her.

"You should go in the other room." His voice turned husky with desire. "The sight of you is testing all my powers of control."

The control she held over his body was amazing, but the sight of his naked body did the same to her. "You're right, of course." She left, shutting the door behind her.

Molly was in the room. "Piper."

"Yes, I suppose this meeting cannot be put off a moment longer." She sighed heavily, looking at the dress Brett had picked out.

"You chose a beautiful dress," Molly said, holding it up and inspecting it.

"Brett's doing. I have no idea what gown is worn when. I'd be the laughing stock if left to my own devices."

"I suppose he chose all the underthings too," Molly said, a twinkle in her eyes.

"Yes." The dressing process always took longer than she expected. When she lived in the parish, dressing was accomplished in a matter of minutes, but now that she was a baroness, she had so many layers to put on it was a wonder Brett ever got them off her.

He was adept at undressing a lady though. The unexpected thought sent a wave of jealousy through her, which she tamped down reminding herself he had a life before her, as well as mistresses.

Dressed and with her hair, swept into a beautiful chignon, tendrils falling delicately around her face and a tiny bit of makeup, she was ready to meet Charlotte. Brett dressed in the bathing room and now sat on a chair in the bedroom, watching Molly put the finishing touches on her.

"Lovely, very lovely," he stood, offering her his arm. "One would never guess you grew up in St. Giles and not the Leighton townhouse."

"You think so?" she queried, her voice shaking.

He wrapped an arm around her then bending close, she felt his breath whisper across her cheek. "Charlotte will be proud of you, her daughter, and before we go down there, I want you to know I love you."

Her heart seemed to stop for a moment at his unexpected words then she turned in his arms, touching his face with the palm of her hand. "Brett, I love you too. Always have, I think. It's why I let you catch me."

"Oh, let me catch you?" he laughed, one eyebrow slanting upward. "I'm glad you return the love. I've known since I watched Avery race after you, and I knew he would catch you and take you from me. I wanted to tell you now because you should hear me say the words first and not at the same time I tell Charlotte.”

“You’re going to tell her, my mother?” She didn’t understand.

“Only if she asks, but I’m sure some of our conversation will revolve around whether or not I’m good enough for you and if I love you. She will expect that from me and for her daughter.”

“Really?” She felt stunned any of what he told her would be included in their conversation. “Why is it any of her business?”

“Because she is your mother, like the fact or not. Now, take a deep breath and we will go from here.”

Together they walked down the steps and to the impending meeting.

Charlotte sat in the parlor of Brett’s townhouse, tapping her cane on the floor and eating one of the lemon bars she brought with her.

Brett poured her brandy then accepted a lemon bar, with a wide smile.

Piper sat down, her hands folded neatly in her lap. She was silent for a long time, having no possible idea what to say. Then she looked at her mother, really looked.

Charlotte was sitting, hands folded in her lap, watching her. It became apparent to Piper that the woman was as anxious about the meeting as she was. For some reason that gave her strength as well as courage.

“Charlotte, may I call you that? Don’t know what else to say.”

“Of course,” she hesitated for the longest time. “Piper. Just as you probably can’t find it in your heart to address me as mother, I’m sure your given name, Portia, seems just as foreign to you.”

Piper was nodding her head, realizing she wanted to learn more about this woman. “I grew up in St. Giles, as I’m sure Drake has told you. I was not...” she moistened her lips. “I was a guttersnipe, not really someone who would be presentable to you. There is nothing about the aristocracy and the way they live I know. Brett has to teach me everything. I didn’t even know how to read, but now I can just a tiny bit.”

“Your life wasn’t easy and I’m sorry for that. You should have had the best money can buy, a season. I can blame my brother in law for that.”

"Scarface is not altogether horrible. Until recently he treated me well, made sure I had food and clothing that I was protected."

"You give the man too much credit, my dear. He was only protecting his investment. If he really had your best interest at heart, he would have never kidnapped you. Revenge was his motive. He hated my husband, loathed him." She tapped her cane on the floor. "Perchance you would like to know about the rest of your family. Your brother and your cousins maybe."

Molly brought a tray of food into the room. "Some, I'm afraid that...well, all of this is so overwhelming. Less than a year ago I had no family except the band of thieves I lived with."

"Let's just begin with your brother who is older than you. His name is Richard Oakes Crandall. His friends call him Roc." Charlotte smiled then and it seemed to transform her face.

"A brother." Piper mulled that over and it sounded nice. "A real brother, I like that. Billy and Bobby always treated me like I was a sister, but of course it wasn't real."

"They have taken good care of you but for now." She looked up at Brett who'd remained silent while they talked. "I'd like to know if this man takes good care of you. Gives you everything you need."

Piper smiled at her husband. "He has always done that. I love him, you see, and was so lucky that he found me and took me into his home. Lucky too that Rogue picked his pocket."

Charlotte stared at Brett as if she expected something from him, and Piper realized this must have been what Brett anticipated. "I love Piper very much, with all my heart in fact. While I was infatuated at first, one might call it lust, I do believe love was the inevitable outcome."

"He thought I was a boy," Piper said, staring at her feet. "Tried to give me a bath but I protested so much he asked Mrs. Pickery."

"Stunned is the word that comes to mind," Brett said. "Startled she, he, wouldn't care if a woman saw him naked but protested me."

Charlotte chuckled at the further description of the incident, "You were a scrapper then, pulled a knife on him, but I'm assuming it wasn't long after that the two of you decided to wed."

She looked to Brett for help. "Drake suggested marriage as a way to keep her safe from Scarface."

"You were willing to marry my daughter just to keep her safe." She waved her hand in the air. "Pshaw, a man like you doesn't do anything he doesn't want to do. You wanted her too much to let her go."

"You're right, of course, but until that moment I hadn't thought of it that way."

"But you'd thought of bedding her or of course making her your mistress." The Duchess leaned forward, clearly chastising him.

Brett flushed slightly. "I won't deny it. That is in part why Drake made the suggestion. He interrupted what would have most likely ended up that way, Piper in my bed, my mistress. I never gave marriage a thought before that. It was obvious we wanted each other."

"Good then, I'm glad you took his suggestion. Now, you look tired, Portia. Perhaps another day I will tell you all about the rest of your cousins and their husbands." She rose then, "The two of you will come to dinner tomorrow night."

Piper stiffened at the use of her birth name as well as the assumption they would do her bidding, "That wasn't a question."

"No, it was not. I expect the two of you as well as Ella and Drake to be at my home by six o'clock sharp tomorrow evening. Ella is the only cousin who is close by. The rest live too far away. You will also have to wait to meet your brother. He is in some country doing something that Drake possibly knows about but I do not."

"Of course, and you can tell me a bit more about my cousins." She had become resigned to the dinner. Even if she protested, Brett would find a way to convince her she needed to be there.

Charlotte turned to Brett, the sweetness returning, "Will you help an old woman out the door and to her carriage?"

When Brett returned, Piper was standing by the window, watching the carriage pull away. "My mother, she is sweet."

"And formidable." Brett pulled Piper into his arms. "Formidable and sweet just like her daughter. I love you, Piper, Portia MacLachlan, and I'm foolish for you, always will be."

"I will always love you just as Charlotte must have loved my father."

"Will you always be foolish for me?" he queried.

"Always foolish for Brett."

"Then I will always be foolish for Piper."

Epilogue

Brett and Piper sat on a grassy knoll near his home in Scotland watching their son play with a ball, pushing it down a hill and squealing with delight when Rogue retrieved it. He was a year old today and he was just beginning to walk. The day was sunny, the sky blue and the air had a crisp feeling about it.

"Ach, lass, are you happy?" His hand settled on her belly, hoping another child would be growing there soon.

She was wrapped in his arms, her eyes closed and he could feel her breathing, slow and steady. He wanted Molly to retrieve the little one so he could make love to his wife.

"I know what you're asking even though the question is subtle. I am happy, but I'm not ready to go through childbirth yet again. We should enjoy our son, watch him grow and all the new things he will learn. We want to remember these days, not clutter them with another child so soon."

"We don't have to wait to do all those things." He kissed her behind the ear, delighting in the shivers of passion he still so easily elicited. His fingers finding their way up her skirt.

"Well, I do. You understand how this one child has disrupted our lives. I am just now getting to sleep through the night and you want to end that."

"My people will question my manly prowess." He laughed as he bit down gently on her ear.

"Of course they won't. They wouldn't dare, besides many families don't have children one right after the other. Men don't want their wives worn out to the extent they don't want to make love."

He sighed heavily, reminded of the fact childbirth was dangerous to women. He'd already made plans not to have too many children. "You're right, of course. I would rather have you beneath me than pushing away from me, although it takes all the control I can muster not to empty myself inside you."

"And I admire you for that. In another year..."

He groaned and heard her laughter. "It will be trying to do that, lass. What if I lose my head and forget to withdraw?"

"I have faith in you, Brett." She patted him on the leg.

The little boy latched on to his father, and Brett tossed him into the air to the boy's delighted squeals.

"See, if we had a newborn, you would be called on to do other things. Like diapering the babe after I have fed her. You would miss all this playtime." She was surprised he overlooked her reference to the next child as a girl.

"I do enjoy playing with him."

"Of course you do. Now no more talk of additional children, at least not yet."

"I love you, Piper." And with the little boy in his arms, he kissed the woman he'd been foolish for, brushing hair from her eyes. "I'm foolish for Piper," he whispered.

Coming April, 2020
from
Rogue Phoenix Press
by
Christine Young

My Sweet Broc
Bad Boys Book One

Chapter One

Scotland 1823

Bad Boy whatcha gonna do when he comes for you?

Broc Wallace leaned on the saddle horn, watching the lady fly across the open field on her horse. Her hair coming loose from the pins previously holding it and streaming out behind her, his heart caught in his throat. Afraid for her safety, he set his black stallion after the woman. Hooves pounding on the ground, he raced after her, praying he could reach her before she fell off.

Gaining ground and finally coming abreast with her horse, he reached out and holding on to the reins brought the mare to an abrupt stop. The horse reared and the lady slid from the back of her horse, a satchel of papers and pencils flying into the air then spreading along the ground in wild disarray.

"Bloody hell!" she cried out. "What do you think you are doing?" She sat on her arse, staring at him as if he was a fool. Her aqua eyes blazed, simmering with anger or perhaps passion.

He slid off his horse, reaching her in a quick stride, ready to examine her for broken bones, "Are you alright, miss?"

"Yes, but no help from you." She pushed hair from her face, grimacing slightly as she tried to move. "I've lost my glasses." She started crawling on hands and knees, seeming to search with her hands. "And my papers, they're everywhere."

Feet braced apart, his hands on his hips, "I rescued you," he said indignantly yet somehow he couldn't stop looking at her shapely rear as she searched the ground.

"If that's a rescue then I wouldn't like to see what would happen when you wanted to completely incapacitate someone. I'm perfectly capable of riding a horse without incident." She continued to search the ground, mumbling words he couldn't make out, her rear sticking higher into the air as she bent closer to the earth.

"What did you say you were looking for?" He got down on his hands and knees, now eyelevel with her. He needed to help her find whatever it was she lost.

She glared at him, her cheek smudged with dirt, "My glasses. I lost my glasses and without them I don't see too well."

He chuckled despite his best efforts. She was incorrigible and at the same time possessed a sweetness about her he couldn't deny. He found himself drawn to her. "Is this what you're looking for?" He held up what appeared to be a pair of glasses. "Do you have a second pair? These don't look to useable."

She snatched them from him and sat back. "Thank you and yes I do." Her voice was curt. "Now tell me why you thought I needed rescuing. Do you just assume that a woman galloping on a horse is out of her element?" But she didn't seem to pay attention to him. She began to pick up the other debris and stuff the things into the satchel she'd been carrying. When everything was picked up and in their proper place, she grabbed the reins of her horse and walked toward the river.

Broc caught up with her, his hands stuffed in his pockets. "You didn't need rescuing? It certainly appeared your horse was racing uncontrolled."

"You saw wrong." She puffed a breath of air, moving a strand of hair that lay across her face. "For your information I'm a very good

horsewoman. I've never ever needed a man or anyone else to save me."
At the river she found a grassy spot. After spreading a blanket on the
ground, she pulled out the papers she had recently packed away.

"You could have been hurt racing that way." He continued
unwilling to accept the fact he might have been wrong about what he saw.

She hummed softly, sketching the scene in front of her, and
effectively overlooking him. The drawing developed as he watched
intently, captivated by everything about her.

At a loss for anything to say, he continued to watch. Relaxing and
stretching out on the blanket she spread for herself, he leaned on one
elbow. The natural sounds of the river and the meadow encompassed the
little scene.

"What's your name?" she asked, suddenly breaking the silence
and setting her pencil on the paper. She gazed at him then with those aqua
blue eyes that captivated him, reminding him of the Mediterranean Sea at
it's bluest. He wanted to see inside her soul.

"You tell me yours and I'll tell you mine." He wasn't sure why he
challenged her, but he needed to see her reaction. She looked somehow
familiar, but he couldn't place where he'd seen her before.

She shrugged her delicately slim shoulders. "Bliss." She shot him
a quick smile before her attention focused on the sketch again. Pencil in
hand she appeared not to have a care in the world. Yet somehow he knew
that wasn't true about her.

"Bliss? Bliss what?" He pressed her for an answer, wanting to
reach out and smooth the escaped strands of hair from her face. He needed
to feel its texture and see if it was as silken as it looked.

"Just Bliss," she said, her voice soft and it seemed that was all she
meant to say.

"I see." Two could play this game. "Broc. Just Broc," he told her,
reaching for a piece of grass to stick between his teeth. Despite his best
efforts to appear relaxed, his body tensed. His reaction to this lady was
unusual and put him at unease.

"Nice name." Bliss continued to draw, seeming to pretend he
wasn't sitting so close to her he could reach out and touch her.

"What are you going to do with the sketches?" He wanted to
thumb through them, all of them but didn't think she'd go that far to give

her approval of the invasion of her privacy.

"I turn them to paintings, oil or water color then I sell them in town." She set the pencil down. "I earn my living that way.

"Don't stop on my account, and why would a young lady such as yourself have to pay their own way in this world? Surely there is a man..." He started to reach out and touch her but caught himself, quickly withdrawing his hand.

"I'm done and you're making me nervous." She turned to stare at him. "Don't want anything to do with men. At least not the ones my..."

"Sorry." He couldn't believe he apologized for watching her. "The ones your..." he cocked an eyebrow. "Care to enlighten me."

She laughed softly, "No, you're not sorry and no, I don't have any intention of telling you what I almost said. You've probably never been sorry for anything in your adult life."

He liked the way her voice sounded when she laughed and she was right. He couldn't think of a single time he apologized to someone and really meant the words. "In my defense, until now, I've never had anything to apologize for."

"So, you believe you're always right."

"I didn't say that." Unable to resist any longer he picked up a strand of her hair, rubbing it between his fingers. "So soft, is the rest of you this soft?"

"Didn't you?" she queried. "You didn't say the words but you talked around it enough for any intelligent person to come to the conclusion."

It seemed she ignored his second question. "I was raised to be confident," he answered. "What about you? Do you apologize if you know you're wrong?"

She cleared her throat, "Never wrong, just like you."

"Are you through sketching?" he asked her, picking up the pad that was sitting on her lap. "May I?"

She nodded a few times, "Nothing too unusual about the sketches. That's just what they are, simple drawings I mean to put on a canvas. That's where they come alive."

His breath caught when he ran across a sketch of him, riding on his horse. "You know who I am?"

Several times she was shaking her head as if she meant to say no. But, "Of you, I've seen you riding across this meadow before. And yes, I know who you are and who doesn't know who you are?"

"You did these from memory?" He was impressed with her ability but was even more curious about who she really was. And there were more. She'd watched him chopping wood, half naked. The thought sent a wave of hot and very potent desire through him. He wanted to investigate further with her. Too soon, though, it was way too soon for her to understand what he craved from her.

"I'm good," she told him, grinning as she said the words almost as if she meant to challenge him.

"You should never say things that aren't true." He closed the pad.

She started to protest his words he was sure but he didn't mean to give her a chance. "Hush." He placed a finger on her lips, a bit presumptive, he knew, but once again he couldn't seem to help himself, his blood suddenly pumping double time.

"You, my sweet Bliss, are very good, amazing even, particularly if you can sketch these from memory."

"I've watched you cutting wood, too, over by the stables. Indeed, one day I..." she moistened her lips but stopped short of telling him what she was thinking.

"You watched me and I had no idea that was what you were doing." He wasn't sure where to go with this new knowledge. He would have to think about it for a while.

"Would you like to walk along the riverbank and discuss this a bit further? I need to stretch my legs." He stood holding a hand out to help her up. Her hand in his was a simple and non-intrusive step to her seduction, because he did want her in his arms and craved her in his bed.

She accepted the help, letting him enclose her small hand in his larger one, "A walk would be nice. I'm a bit restless."

Broc didn't want to let go of her hand, at least not until she made it clear she didn't like this tiny advance. He was inexplicably drawn to her and hoped she wasn't some debutant who would seek a commitment. He liked his freedom and didn't mean to lose it anytime soon.

"Bliss," he paused, "where do you live?" he asked, trying for a bit more information from her. The thought of a debutante seeking him out sent a wave of precaution through his head. But what would some random debutante be doing riding hell bent across a meadow on MacTavish land?

"Why?" Her answer was curt.

"Just curious. It seems you know more about me than I do you. It's only fair, don't you think?"

"No, fairness has nothing to do with any of this. I barely know you," she said. "I'm not going to give you my address. A lady needs an air of intrigue about her."

"You know me well enough to watch me half naked chopping wood," he told her, thinking he'd like to see her naked. Her dress hid her curves fairly well, but he could still tell quite a lot about her body. "I'm sure you know exactly where I live."

"And you weren't a wee bit bashful either. I also saw a beautiful woman ride to the stables. I saw you kiss her. When you were half naked. So," she paused gazing at him, her eyes simmering, "I'm sure you don't care if I saw your chest and rippling muscles." With that said she looked away as if she didn't want him to see her reaction. He was sure he saw more than she intended.

"Jealous?" Good lord but that was at least two months ago. His mistress paid him an unusual visit and he sent her away with the order to never come to his home again.

"Of course not," she protested to quickly.

"The blush rising on your cheeks tells me you're not speaking the truth. I think you should apologize or let me kiss you. Perhaps we should make a bet. Every time you lie you have to kiss me."

"No, I wouldn't like to make a bet like that with you. I've been told you're a very bad man where it comes to women."

"Who told you that?" He could only think of a few people who would say that about him, and it would be in jest or to warn a debutant away from him.

"Just heard it. Don't remember where. Probably one day when I was in town to sell my paintings." She smushed her lips together, squinting her eyebrows as if she was thinking.

"Something doesn't ring true."

"Don't know why you say that?"

"Back to my question, are you jealous? Should we find out if you like my kisses?" He grinned at her hesitancy, but the way her tongue swept across her lips told him she was thinking about telling him yes, or at least about a kiss.

"Probably not a good idea." She backed away from him but she didn't take her hand from his. "A kiss. No something like that could lead to other things."

"Other things? What do you know about other things?"

"Nothing really."

He decided a bit more persuasion might be appropriate here. He traced gentle circles on her wrist with his thumb and he watched her eyes cross for a second. "Probably not, but what if kissing you is a very good idea? What then? You'd miss something you would enjoy."

"Again, I barely know you. It's not proper to kiss a man when you've only known him for a few minutes."

"Proper!" he roared. "You are the least proper woman I've ever met. And we've known each other over an hour now, not a few minutes."

She pulled her hand from his. "I..." She walked away from him hurriedly, not really paying attention. She stumbled but righted herself quickly.

In any case, he wasn't sure how well she could see without her glasses and perhaps that was why she quit drawing with only one sketch completed.

"Bliss..."

She stopped and turned. "Perhaps I'm not proper, maybe I don't want to be. But it doesn't change the fact that you hurt my feelings when you made that statement."

"That had not been my intention. I'm glad you're being honest with me, at least about that. I like honesty in a woman. Don't like to be blindsided."

"So you say." She started walking again.

A few rapid strides and he was beside her once more, walking step for step with her, wondering how far she meant to go. The horses were still tethered a ways back and the sky was darkening. He didn't like the idea of a rainstorm catching them out in the open.

"We should go back." He set his hand on her shoulder, turning her slightly.

She stared at him then followed the direction of his gaze. "I suppose you're right. It could rain."

They reached the horses before any rain started, but a brilliant crack of lightning brightened the sky. Quickly, he set her on her horse. "My drawings." She reached out seemingly intent on dismounting.

"I'll get them. Head for the stables at my place. We might make it that far before the storm hits. Would rather not get a drenching." Yet if they were soaked through to the skin, he could think of some delightful possibilities, all included being naked with her.

She had turned her horse seeming to head in the opposite direction then she nodded to him. He swept the items into his arms before mounting. Following her they raced the storm.

The tempest raged behind them. The little mare she rode seemed to be a good sound horse. She kept the animal under control despite the noise and the lightening. He realized she was right. She was a damn good horsewoman, and this afternoon she had not needed saving.

He had no regrets.

Inside the stables, she slid from the horse, rubbing her down with a cloth she found. Seconds later hail pounded the top of the barn while wind howled around the eaves. Darkness seemed to enshroud the inside of the barn.

"It seems we just beat the storm." She told him, rubbing her arms and looking a bit forlorn. "I would have never made it home."

"You're chilled." He wrapped her in the blanket she'd spread on the grass earlier then he sifted through her sketchpad. "Everything seems to be in order."

"I'm glad we had some place dry to go, but I'm not sure about getting home if this rain keeps up. I don't like to ride in the dark by myself."

"Are you asking me to accompany you home," he asked, grinning, understanding he might just learn more about her than she'd been willing to tell him earlier this afternoon.

She bristled, her back stiffening. "I'll have to think about it. I didn't mean to say anything to you. I'm perfectly capable of doing things I don't like if the situation demands it."

"Makes sense to me. It's settled then. A woman shouldn't be out by herself in the dark. I would be remiss if I let you go by yourself."

"Would you?" she asked, "Be remiss? I think you just want to learn what I didn't want to tell you."

"I can't visit you and watch you paint when you're not looking if I don't know where your home is." He chuckled at her look of chagrin.

She found a bale of hay and sat down, keeping the blanket wrapped tightly around her and shivering uncontrollably. She didn't say anything but he heard a heavy sigh. For a few seconds she fiddled with the edge of the blanket.

"Why?" He sat down beside her, stilling her fingers by taking them into one hand and wrapping an arm around her.

"Why what?" She kept her face turned from him.

"Why indeed. What is it that you need to keep so secretive? The more you try to evade my questions it seems the more I want to know what you hide." She was secretive yet it seemed to him, she liked him, seemed to feel at ease with him, perhaps even wanted to divulge more about herself.

"It's just that I like my privacy. You're a man and you don't have certain things to worry about. I don't want to seem overeager or jealous or whatever men think about women. I'm not chasing you and have no intention of doing anything of the sort."

He touched his lips to the back of her hand, wondering what it would be like to explore her mouth and if she would let him discover untold secrets. But she thought of him as a bad man. He didn't believe her story about hearing it on the streets, so where did those words come from?

"What is it you have to worry about?" he asked, turning her hand over and kissing her palm, his tongue making gentle forays across the tender flesh.

She shivered from his caress. "Well, right now I have to worry about a man seducing me, she told him but she didn't take her hand from his.

"Is that what I'm doing?" he grinned shamelessly. "Seducing you?" He brushed his lips on her neck.

"Perhaps. Not really sure what a seduction entails."

"I believe it's to lead astray."

"Then you couldn't be seducing me," she said, her voice a thin whisper.

"Perhaps you're enticing me to engage in a relationship with you."

"Me enticing you?"

She let her head fall back, giving him better access to her neck. "I'm still not sure what it means."

"Some more of this." He brushed her hair from the back of her neck then kissed her gently, delighted by the tiny noise she made. "And more of this." He explored her ear with his teeth and tongue.

Her breath caught in the back of her throat. "Should my heart race?" she asked and her voice broke on the words.

"If I'm doing it right." He pulled the blanket from her shoulders before turning her and drawing her into his arms. What he craved and what he was going to do right now didn't match even though she seemed more than willing. If he took his time with her, she would be his.

"Does this make you a bad man or does it take more than this?" Her breaths seemed to come sporadically while she spoke.

He paused a moment, wondering at her words once more. "No, just a man who's wants to learn more about a very special lady."

"I suppose seducing and enticing someone requires more than just a kiss on the back of the neck." She touched his lips with a finger before running the tip across his mouth. "How much more?"

He groaned, wondering at her innocence. "You presume right and as to how much, that's a discussion for another day." The relationship was one he needed to pursue longer than one night. The way her body responded to the slightest touch gave him reason to smile, but he wanted this connection with her to last longer than a few enjoyable hours.

"What are you going to do now?" Her eyes were wide pools of liquid passion.

"After I kiss you, I'm going to see you home." He wanted to undo all the buttons on her dress and... Bloody hell, but he needed to make love to her but tonight he wasn't going to be a bad man he was going to be a very good one.

"You're going to kiss me?" she asked, her voice whispered across him.

"Nothing to be afraid of. I promise you'll like it and beg for more," he told her, running the back of his hand along her cheek. "Have you ever been kissed before?"

"Arrogant man."

"Confident," he told her, his hands on both sides of her face. "That's it, get ready for me, let me see your tongue run along your lips, just like that." He wanted to know if any man had ever kissed her but realized if she told him yes... Good god, but he felt jealousy rise to the forefront of his mind.

"My...me..." Her hands rested on his chest, her fingers winding into the fabric of his shirt.

"See, I am good. You can't even talk you want me so much." His lips molded on hers, his tongue searching for entrance. His body ached with a thrumming desire to be inside her. Soon he told himself but not too soon.

For a second he pulled away from her. Bliss' eyes were closed, her fingers digging into his shoulders. He kissed her again, encompassing her mouth within his, probing inside with his tongue and playing with her then pulling away.

"Did you like my kiss?"

"Am I seduced?"

~ * ~

"Not even close, little minx. When I seduce you, you won't have to ask. You'll know."

His roar of laughter startled her, the kiss making her head spin and her heart beat crazily out of control. She punched him in the chest, "Why are you laughing at me?"

"Hopefully, with you. I'm laughing with you."

"I'm not laughing." She turned from him, her back stiff, feeling a wave of inadequacy and innocence sweep through her. She needed to get away from him and his potent charm then sift through all that happened this afternoon. "The rain has stopped. I need to get home."

"You don't want to stay and let me coax another kiss from your sweet lips?" he chuckled, refastening some buttons that had inadvertently come undone on her dress.

She couldn't recall when he unfastened her dress, or had she?

"No."

She had to get home or her brother would be out searching for her, but she couldn't tell Broc about her brother or that she was a MacTavish. Broc and her brother were best friends and she knew personally neither one would ever marry, at least not until they found a need for an heir and that didn't appear to by any time soon, at least not for her brother.

"Since I'm seeing you home you could stay a bit longer. We could explore some other avenues of your seduction or you could seduce me."

"I have to get home, my..." She almost said her father. Her father was dead as was her mother. Flynt, her brother, was charged with taking care of her and her sisters and of finding them a husband.

"And where is home?" he asked, still seeming to probe for answers when she didn't want to give any.

She inhaled long and deep searching for the courage to continue this lie, this necessary lie. "The whereabouts of my home is none of your business, but if you must know, I rent a small cottage nearby." She didn't want to bring up the name MacTavish or lead him to the estate where she grew up. If she did, he'd never see her again.

"You do?" he questioned. "How?"

"Painting money. Both my parents have passed on." The tears filling her eyes were not a lie. They were very real. "I have to live somewhere and I have to earn an income. So..."

"I see." But the expression on his face told her he wasn't believing a word she said.

"You can take me to the cottage," she told him, placing her hand on his. When he left her there, she would ride the rest of the way home by herself. It wasn't far and she'd done so several times at night when time slipped by and she realized too late it was dark outside.

Truly, she didn't think Flynt would miss her tonight. He rarely checked in on her or her sisters. He was just too busy with his affairs. Before she left to sketch this afternoon, he'd told her he was heading into Glasgow for a night of carousing. He didn't say the word carousing but that was what she told herself he was doing. He was going there to be a bad man or bad boy as he and his friends called themselves. The only difference this time was that Broc wasn't with him. He was with her being bad. Well not really so bad, probably not what he anticipated when he kissed her.

"I would like to see where you live and to make sure you're safely inside before I leave for home." He brought her horse to her and helped her up then mounted his stallion.

The tempest that passed through the area left a trail of broken branches and debris on the ground. The ride was slow in the dark of the night. Despite her fear at Broc seeing where she lived, Bliss was happy to have him by her side and even more pleased to see the tiny cottage in front of them.

"Is this it?" he asked, pointing to the home, she called her studio. "You even have a small barn." He turned his horse in that direction.

"You're not staying," she told him, eyeing him critically. "Told you, you could take me here not follow me into the house."

"No, of course not." He grinned at her, "But a gentleman would never leave a lady to groom her horse and he would never leave without checking inside to make sure no one was inside the home."

She caught the retort in the back of her throat. "Another something I'm quite capable of, grooming my horse." He caught her reins, stopping her mare.

"Then come with me and I'll watch before I accompany you inside the house and make sure everything is safe." It seemed he wasn't going to get caught up in the game she was trying hard to play just to keep her emotions from showing.

"I'm not going to change your mind, am I?" she sighed, resigned now to letting him do just about anything he wanted. He would have an argument for everything just to get his way.

"Nope." He dismounted, leading the horses inside the stable. He reached up to help her down.

Shaking her head several times, she allowed him to help, "Something else I can do by myself. Could get off a horse before I was five." She had to admit to herself, she liked the feel of his hands on her waist and the unsolicited attention he lavished on her. She'd never been treated so well.

"I wouldn't be a gentleman if I left you to your own devices. Now you spoke of taking care of your horse." He stood back his arms crossed. "I'm going to water and feed mine too."

He allowed her to do as she asked and when they finished with the horses, he held out an arm to escort her.

At the door he stopped, "It's not locked?"

She looked at him surprised, "I never lock the door."

"Something we need to discuss," he told her, a sudden darkness covering his face, his brows drawn together.

"Whatever are you talking about now?" This time she was truly baffled with his comment.

"An unlocked door? You're far too trusting." He stepped aside so she could enter the room. "What if someone let themselves in while you were gone?"

"Perhaps," she agreed with him, but she didn't mean to tell him he was right. If she actually lived here, she would keep it locked. As it was there was nothing here to steal except her painting supplies. Besides the door didn't have a lock, so what could he expect?

Following her, he stepped inside. He paused for a moment, searching the room, seeming to take in the absence of everything that would make it livable. Then, running a finger along a shelf, he looked at her, a wide grin on his face as if he found something amusing.

"Not much of a housekeeper, are you?"

She stiffened, wishing she had protested his entry into what she was pretending to be her home. "Never said I was." She set the satchel carrying her sketches on a table. Her discomfort grew with each second. He would see through her ruse, figure out who she was and leave.

She would never see him again.

"I see supplies but no paintings." He investigated the living room before making his way to kitchen.

"I was in town yesterday with all of them. Sold them all so I could pay my bills." She called after him.

She stayed put, listening to the cupboard doors as one by one he opened and closed them. His footsteps on the kitchen floor thundered in her ears. Inhaling a long deep breath, she paused, hands clasped in front of her, waiting for his assessment.

Broc stepped out of the kitchen a bottle of brandy and two crystal glasses in hand, "Not a bite to eat and nothing to cook with but you've got something to imbibe on a cold night, or hot one. Care to have a brandy with me."

"What does that matter?" Why she asked that question, she had no idea. She didn't want to hear his evaluation.

He shrugged broad masculine shoulders, "One has to eat. Would you like a drink?"

She didn't answer, instead she fidgeted with the satchel and the sketches within. Before she could say no, he had poured her a drink and was handing it to her. He sat down in an overstuffed chair, dust flying. He coughed then sneezed, brushing imaginary or perhaps real dust particles from his jacket.

"I'm going to send over a housecleaner tomorrow." He sipped the drink staring at her. "Could clean and tidy up this room before the morning passes."

"No." she bristled. "No, you're not."

He smiled and sipped, looking more relaxed than anyone should. She knew her no meant nothing to him. He would do as he pleased when he pleased. "I wouldn't have it any other way."

"I won't let a housecleaner inside." She protested adamantly, her hands fisted at her side. "You can't take over my life. We barely know each other."

"Won't be much trouble with an unlocked door." Nonchalantly, he rose from the chair, once again walking around the room, picking up things and tracing more lines on the furniture.

"A lock will be on tomorrow. I promise." Exhausted, she sat down, the glass of brandy in her hand a tempting diversion from this complication she brought home with her and could not get rid of. Well, she didn't want him to come into the cottage for this very reason.

"Not by the morning."

She wanted to throw the glass at him even while she wanted him to kiss her again. The lies of omission seemed to grow too rapidly for her to explain anything away. Not that she should have to clarify anything to him. If he'd just do what she expected of him, everything would be fine right now and she'd be on her way home.

"Drink your brandy. At least it will be something in your stomach and it will help you relax. Your shoulders are rigid and that can't be comfortable." His voice sounded harsh for a moment. Then he grinned, showing perfect white teeth. "I could give you a massage."

She wished he would go home. She did sip the brandy though and it pooled in her stomach like a brick. "Don't you think you should leave?"

"Too many questions," he told her, stepping through another door into the smaller bedroom as if he owned the cottage.

Bliss didn't know why her heart raced and her hands shook. At this moment Broc was nothing to her. Just a kiss in the stables, just someone she'd like to spend time with. Having heard enough of her brother's stories, she understood this man would never have a relationship with her. And yet...

"I'm not giving you any answers." She turned away as he walked into the second bedroom.

"Ah a bed, so you sleep." He set his brandy on a side table and plopped on the bed crossing his legs that were stretched out in front of him. "Care to join me?"

Bloody eyes, but she'd like to know what he was thinking. "No."

"I could easily convince you otherwise."

"Let's move on to the discussion about your departure." She couldn't help herself. She walked into the bedroom, needing to see him and his expressions to help her understand what might be in his head.

"Not leaving until I have answers and I know you'll be safe at least until morning." He patted the bed beside him, his grin still broad.

She inhaled several short rapid breaths of air, her body quivering and unable to think of anything to say. "I'll be safe." Stupid man, as soon as he left, she meant to ride to Deepwood, the MacTavish estate. It didn't seem he meant to depart anytime soon.

"Join me." He patted the bed again. "While the bed is clean, which does surprise me given the condition of the rest of your home, it's not comfortable. Too many lumps."

"It wasn't meant for your comfort." Yet she walked to the other side of the bed and sat down next to him with her back against the headboard.

"You shouldn't have a bed unless it's comfortable to everyone who is going to sleep in it." He placed her hand in his, bringing it to his lips for a quick kiss.

"Broc, no." She tugged it back, afraid of what might come later if she allowed him to have his way.

He shrugged. You liked your hand in mine only an hour ago. You also liked the kiss. Me thinks you protest too much, lass."

She turned to face him, her legs curled around her. "What are you really doing here?"

"I've been more upfront with you than you've been with me. You're not telling me something and I'd like the truth. In fact, I don't believe anything you've told me today is true."

She gritted her teeth together, frustrated and confused. "Those are truths I'm not comfortable in giving you. Can't you just forget about what I haven't told you? We'll probably never see each other again, and..."

"We will see each other," gazing at her, "again and again, until we tire of each other."

"You won't give up and neither will I." She liked the part of seeing him again and the promise the words held but not the part of until they tired of each other.

"All the evidence, except this bed, point to the fact you don't live here. I'm suspecting that as soon as I leave, you're going to hightail it home, wherever that is."

She felt the color drain from her face and after she looked away, he touched her chin with a finger, effectively turning her so she had to look at him.

"I'm not going to another home because I don't have one." She persisted in her story, intending to beat him at this game he was playing of truth and lies. He was waiting for her to slip up which she wasn't going to do. The dratted man couldn't take no for an answer or an answer to a question either for that matter.

"You're very beautiful but there's a haunting look in your eyes. You don't lie easily. In fact, I think you have very little experience in subterfuge." He stopped for a moment, gazing into her eyes. "There is something so familiar about you, but I can't figure it out. I will though."

"I don't know what that could be." She rose then walking from the room and to the front door, "It's time you left." Hands clasped in front of her, she stood beside the door.

"We are at an impasse then. I'll just make myself comfortable. It would be nice if you had some food in the cupboard. My stomach is rumbling." He shirked out of his waistcoat before loosening his cravat.

"What are you doing?" She was inside the bedroom again, watching as he pulled off his Hessians.

"Getting comfortable as I said I intended." He crossed his feet again as he settled back on the bed.

"You can't do that."

"Bliss, really, pacing will do you know good while the truth will exonerate you and I'll leave for my home. Although as the hour grows later, I believe I would prefer to remain here. I don't relish a cross country ride in the darkness of the night."

Bliss walked back to the sitting room and poured herself more brandy. Talking to him would do no good. She pulled a pillow from another couch and found a blanket back in the main bedroom.

"What are you doing?" he asked her his voice deep and gruff. "You can't sleep out there on a chair." The command in his voice was evident.

"I'm not going to bed with you," she told him, angry with him, angry with herself and the situation she got herself into. Thinking if she could turn back time, she would have made different decisions.

"But you're bedding down out here." He hovered above her. "I'd never keep a lady from her bed."

Sometime in the last few seconds he'd removed his shirt and his pants were unfastened. She inhaled a swift deep breath of air. "You're naked."

"You've seen me without a shirt."

"Not this close," she told him, her voice a squeak. Reaching out to touch him then realizing what she was doing she pulled her hand back as if she burned it.

He was grinning, clearly enjoying her impulsive actions. "You can touch me any time you like."

"No."

"Don't trust yourself? Afraid I might find a way to get you on your very own bed and have my wicked way with you? I won't, you know. Not unless you tell me how much you want me."

She pulled the blanket over her then punching the pillow, she tried to get comfortable. Before she could close her eyes, she was in his arms and she found herself on the bed with him beside her, closer than she'd ever been with a man, a very nearly naked man.

"Bliss, truly I'm not trying to give you a bad time." He brushed hair from her face, his lips so close she could almost feel them against hers.

"Don't kiss me," she told him, her voice quivering. "Don't." The palm of her hand rested against his chest, pushing him away. "Please don't."

"Why, Bliss? You didn't mind my kiss before." He persisted, his breath ruffling across her face.

"No, you're right. I liked your kiss but not now. Not when you're on a bed with me and it doesn't seem you're going anywhere." She trembled, wishing for one thing but her mind telling her something else entirely.

"Tonight at least I'm staying with you."

"If you go home, nothing will happen to me. I promise." Her fingers dug into his shoulder and she pushed against him but this time it wasn't to push him away.

"I'm going to make sure nothing happens. I wouldn't be able to sleep at night if anything happened to you because I was careless." He kissed her cheek, the line of her jaw then.

"No, Broc. I'm not your whore."

"Never." But he pulled away as if she slapped him. "I realize I've overstepped some bounds. But I've never in the few short hours I've known you have I thought of you as a whore."

"I won't be your mistress either."

"No, I don't suppose you will. I have a mistress."

~ * ~

Flynt sat back in his chair. A barmaid brought him and his companion, Cam, a second pint.

"Where's Broc?" she asked.

"Must be with his mistress," Flynt said, having wondered that same question several times in the last two hours. It wasn't like his best friend to miss this one night out every week. The five of them had a pact.

This night was sacred to their friendship and their dedication to stay single. No simpering, music playing and ball-dancing debutantes for them.

"Nope, not there," Donel said. "Rode by the house on my way here and his horse wasn't tied up at the hitching post."

"Where the blazes do you think he is?" Flynt asked. He was leaning back, watching the barmaids as they plied their wares. No one here bedded any of these women. Didn't want to take the risk of pox.

"Told me he was going for a ride. Was looking for something he'd seen another day," Cam said.

"Sounds like a riddle to me," Flynt added with a frown. "But something niggled in the back of his head. Something his sister Bliss had said but for the life of him, he couldn't think of it.

"When are you going to present your sister? Isn't it time for her to have a season?" Donal asked. "You've got to do your duty by your sisters or they're going to be living in your home until they're old and gray.

"Stuck on the shelf, so to speak," Cam added.

Flynt ran his fingers through his hair, knowing he left it in a disheveled mess. "She doesn't want a season."

"Then she's going to stay a spinster," Leslie asked. "Don't know her well but I doubt if she's meant to be a spinster."

"My oldest sister doesn't care about any of that. I've presented several men to her. In fact, there's one coming to call on her in two days. She doesn't like any of them." Flynt knew exactly why she didn't like them, but bloody hell she needed someone who would stay true to her. Not someone like him or his friends, acknowledged bad boys.

"And who pray tell have you sent her?" Leslie asked, laughing hard. "Not one of those bookish men who sit and read all day. Those types are really too boring for any of your sisters and they would never succeed in making them happy. You are going to have to go beyond what you want and think about what your sister and later on sisters will want."

Flynt rambled off a list of the eligible suitors he sent her way. "She says she could never go to bed with any of them."

"Why is that?"

"It seems there have been a few evenings we've not been discreet in our carousing. She's seen more than one of us without our shirts on and as she says, she's not going to settle for anything less in a man."

"You have power over her. Tell her who she has to wed and be done with at least one of your sisters," Cam said.

"Then you'll have three left to find husbands for."

"I can't do that to her." He was shaking his head, feeling the need to see Bliss happy. He had to do that for her. It was just that someone like him, a known rake would not make her happy in the long run.

"Your heart is too soft."

"Perhaps, but put yourself in her place and you will soften too. She doesn't care about a title or money she cares about the man. I've got to say, I respect that sentiment too much to gainsay her or force her into a marriage where she'll be miserable the rest of her life. Not really sure what I'm going to do." Flynt gulped down the last of his drink.

"You could always let her find a man on her own," Cam suggested, grinning.

"That could be a complete disaster. She's an innocent in the ways of men. What if she fell in love with a complete cad, someone like us who would break her heart?" Donal asked.

"Men like us are who your sisters are attracted to." Leslie said, sipping the brew he just ordered and refusing to let his emotions get the better of him. "Never bargained on having to find husbands for three sisters."

"Who's left?"

"All of them and I've not accomplished anything with my oldest sibling. Chelsea, Daryl and little Lacie are all in need of husbands."

"You've got some time with Lacie and Daryl, though," Leslie pointed out.

"A respite, just what I need but I doubt if they'll be any easier. Mother and Father raised them to have a mind and think for themselves. They know what they want, and I'm sure they won't settle either."

"Focus back on the oldest. What does she enjoy?"

"Music," Flynt began, "and painting."

"Problem solved. Find someone who appreciates the arts."

"The men she would find suitable appreciate the art of seduction above all else," Flynt said, tossing back the Guinness and motioning for another one then making a mental note to stop at his mistress' home tonight.

Other Books by Christine Young
Available at Rogue Phoenix Press

Taylor's Destiny

She traveled to another time and place to changing destiny...

Enjoying a day of sailing, Taylor Maxwell never expected after a suffering a concussion she would wake up in another century. A resilient independent woman in the twenty-first century, the blond beauty is ill prepared for life in the 1800s. Her first sight of the naval captain who rescues her makes her heart stop, giving her hope for her future.

His life is transformed by a woman who appears from nowhere...

Born to a life of ease, Reid Stewart defies the dictates of those born to aristocracy and chooses a life of adventure in the navy and as a spy for the crown. When he discovers a nearly naked woman on the bow of small sailing ship, his heart warms. His love for Taylor and his need to protect her from a man who pursues her might cost him his life as well as hers.

Caitlin's Duke

She played a fiddle in an Irish pub....

Caitlin O'Shea Is the most beautiful woman Roc Leighton has ever seen. With her blue violet eyes and long black hair she captivates him. In turn he mesmerizes Caitlin. Caught in the power of his gaze as he watches her, she is wise enough to know he desires her but will never give his heart to her. Caitlin has vowed to never be any man's mistress.

And fell in love with an English Lord...

Roc knows the first time he watches her play the fiddle and dance around the pub, she will be his next mistress. Despite her protest, he will find a way to convince her that her place is with him. While Caitlin's determination to keep her vows, fate takes a cruel turn and she is forced to seek refuge with Roc.

Catching Meara
Book One in the McKenna Clan Series

Meara Thorton was a feisty, world-class computer hacker—cornered by the FBI and shockingly given the chance to be their newly acquired technical analyst. Brilliant and intuitive, yet aching with the loss of everyone she has cared about, her restless heart led her to discover a love she fought and a world she didn't know could possibly exist.

Sweet Sexy Sadie
Book Two in the McKenna Clan Series

From the first time Sadie's eyes met those of Brody McKenna in the hot Sierra Madre Mountains, theirs was a potent attraction—not gentle, slow, and easy, but hot, hard, and all-consuming. The daughter of a dysfunctional family, Sadie had dreams no man could wrench from her with hot sex and an all-consuming passion. She'd challenge this alpha male with all the strength she possessed. But her red hair, fiery temperament, and indomitable spirit obsessed Brody...and he knew he had to find a way to show her he was more than he appeared and convince her to make a life with him.

Sweet Misbehavin'
Book Three in the McKenna Clan Series

Cast adrift after fleeing the home of Jokul, the ice demon, Atantsi, a firestarter, grew to womanhood as she moved through time to keep the demon from finding her. Though stubborn and courageous, she was ill prepared to use powers she had not been taught. Her first sight of the intoxicating Carr McKenna left her breathless, and her second encounter gave her hope for a future she never thought she had.

A playboy, a second son and a shifter, a man who thought his life would be carefree, Carr McKenna was shocked to discover the woman he'd paid as an escort is a firestarter who is running for her life. He is the leader of all the McKennas around the world and that he has multiple powers. His passion for Margo and the need to defend her might cost him his life as well as hers.

Sweet Talkin' Sugar
Book Four in the McKenna Clan Series

Lyonesse McKenna, was dreaming or was she? From the instant Lyn saw Deacon McClain across a black jack table in a crowed Las Vegas casino the unmistakable attraction sent Lyn's senses flying into overdrive. Her family of shapeshifters believed in soul mates. She'd always been skeptical yet she couldn't help but question the way her heart sped when he looked at her.

When Deacon appeared in Las Vegas he knew his first job was to save Lyn from a Sea Demon, but the next order of business was to convince her he would someday mean more to her than she'd ever expected. But her stubborn nature and unbendable spirit consumed Deacon...and he had to chase away all the demons real and imagined in order to win her heart.

Sweet Surrender
Book Five in the McKenna Clan Series

Ripped from her family at the top of Infinity Cliff, Kimi McKenna finds herself thrust somewhere into the future. Dark elements threaten to destroy the earth unless Kimi can work together with the white witch to stop the destruction. Confused by her mate's role in the conspiracy, she refuses to acknowledge the connection. But amidst raging fire and attacks on the people she is coming to hold dear, she allows Maska O'keefe into her heart.

Maska O'keefe has loved the beautiful shapeshifter for years. Unable to save her life years ago, he vows to watch over her as he is given a second chance to convince her that even though he is a witch and not a shifter, they are indeed soul mates. Kimi's divided loyalties between her family and the cause she is now a part of will determine their relationship. Only the part she plays as the messiah can bring this to a conclusion in the final battle.

Dakota's Bride
The first book in the Lakota/Pinkerton Series

When Emma St. John received her brother's letter imploring her to escape her stepfather's vengeful scheme and to trust Dakota Barringer with her life, she was willing to chance it. But the handsome, brooding riverboat owner Emma found in Natchez a danger of another kind. For Emma soon found herself surrendering to an unrelenting desire.
Raised by the Sioux when his parents were killed, Dakota had been betrayed once before by a white woman. He wasn't about to trust another, especially one claiming that her stepfather, a powerful U.S. senator, had framed her as a murderess. But he couldn't let Emma's intoxicating effect on him. Now Dakota would risk his very life to protect the innocent beauty who had seduced him with her tender love.

My Angel
The second book in the Lakota/Pinkerton Series

A BEAUTY IN BUCKSKINS
When her father decided to send her to a finishing school back East, Angela Chamberlain refused to be confined to stuffy drawing rooms. Instead, the daring spitfire who could shoot like a man and ride like the wind longed for a life of adventure and romance—and she knew exactly who could give it to her. Devil Blackmoor was a hired gun with a dangerous reputation. But Angela was willing to go to the ends of the earth to capture the handsome devil's heart.

A DEVIL IN DISGUISE
He'd come to America looking for excitement, but Devil Blackmoor got more than he bargained for when he encountered a beautiful rebel who answered his kisses with a wild innocence that touched his very soul. Yet standing between them were more obstacles than either ever dreamed. For Devil had strapped on a gun for the wrong man. And that made Angela his enemy. Now he'll have to choose between his duty and the woman he loves more than life.

The Locket
The third book in the Lakota/Pinkerton Series

The year is 1894. Seeking revenge for crimes against his family, Misha Petrovich follows a path that leads straight to Ariel Cameron's boarding house in Mist Harbor, Oregon. A family heirloom in Ariel's possession leads Misha to believe she is guilty. The locket has been handed down to the oldest girl in the Petrovich family for generations. Ariel is innocent of wrong doing, but her father is not. Misha is torn by his feelings for Ariel and his need for restitution against her father. Knowing that the relationship between them is fragile, Misha does everything in his power to protect Ariel's father. His efforts are to no avail when her father is shot. Ariel comes to realize Misha's steadfast courage and determination to protect her and her father despite what has happened to his family. Ariel's love and devotion heals Misha's heart.

The Talisman
The fourth book in the Lakota/Pinkerton Series

Running from a marriage that lasted one night, Dr. Moriah McKeown discovers the land she has settled on is coveted by determined and lawless men. Yet the proud young woman who once vowed never to abandon her home has second thoughts when her adopted children are threatened. Her only recourse is to enlist the aid of a dark, dangerous gun for hire.
Haunted by the past and a betrayal he will never forgive, Ian Civanovich uses his fast gun and his reckless courage to forget the faithlessness of a woman in his past. He will trust no female—nor will he rest until the threat hovering over Moriah McKeown is put to rest.

Forever His
The fifth book in the Lakota/Pinkerton Series

Struggling to come to terms with the part she played in Jacob St. John's death, Etta Barringer resigns from Pinkerton Agency and seeks peace and solace in a Rocky Mountain Cabin.
Jacob has vowed to discover the reason Etta has betrayed him, sold him out to his enemy and left him for dead.
Isolated in their cabin, they discover their love for each other and learn to trust. But the trust is shattered when Jacob learns she is married to his sworn enemy; the man who left him in the desert to die.

Allura's Secret
Twelve Dancing Princesses Book One

Allura McClellan is horrified by her father's decision to take out an ad in the Times awarding her to the man strong enough and smart enough to win her hand and uncover her secrets. She's an intelligent young woman who takes great delight in the freedom allotted to her by her father. She's well aware that marriage would effectively curtail the adventures she's shared with her sisters and cousins.

Hunter Gray is nothing like the other men who've arrived to vie for Allura's hand in marriage and everything that goes along with it. However, he is the first to refuse to concede defeat and pursue her despite her attempts to disguise her true appearance. It's her temperament that is of more concern to him than her looks. Hunter has worked all his life with the hope of someday owning his own land. Now that it looks like there's a very real possibility that everything he's ever wanted is within reach nothing is going to deter him – including Miss Allura's disagreeable disposition.

Amorica's Wager
Twelve Dancing Princesses Book Two

Amorica Hepburn was sent to London to find a husband. Finding a man was the last item on her agenda. With her two cousins, Amorica wagers she can dissuade her suitor before the others. Despite her efforts she discovers a chemistry that cannot be denied. Suddenly she is the arrogant man's wife, pledged to a marriage neither desire. But swept off to his ancestral home above the Dover cliffs and into his strong embrace, Amorica is soon possessed by a raging passion for the husband she had vowed to despise…

Damian Andrews couldn't afford to trust the emerald-eyed spitfire who happened upon his secret. Amorica's hatred of all men of his kind only inflames the war that rages between them. Still, he can not control the intense desire his stubborn bride inspires, or make her surrender to his will until he has conquered the headstrong beauty on the battlefield of love…

Ravyn's Marriage of Inconvenience
Twelve Dancing Princesses Book Three

A REGAL BEAUTY
When the duchess decides to wed her to a wastrel and a fop, Ravyn Grahm takes matters into her own hands and declares her engagement to another man. Instead of fessing up and telling her great aunt what she has done, she goes through with the pretense. Aric Lakeland is the bastard son of an earl and has a dangerous reputation. But Ravyn is willing to do most anything to keep the duchess from discovering the lie.

A DEVIL-MAY-CARE SMUGGLER
He'd bought land in America, looking to put down roots and end his life of adventure, but Aric Lakeland got more than he bargained for when he encountered a beautiful heiress who made a promise she didn't want to keep. But the promise could not be undone and standing between them were more obstacles than either ever dreamed. Aric had made plans to spend the rest of his life in America and that was at odds with Ravyn's plan of living in England and running her father's estate. Now, he'll have to choose between his dreams and the woman he loves more than life.

Christel's Sunrise
Twelve Dancing Princesses Book Four

He Made Her An Offer...

Life has thrown Christel McClellan some experiences that could have devastated a less determined woman. Beautiful, self-assured and fiercely independent, she is trying to forget the loss of her stillborn child. But is the child alive?

She Couldn't Deny...

Life is carefree for Ryder MacLaren who loves to see what is on the other side of the sunrise. Laird of Clan MacLaren, he is wealthy, handsome and happily unencumbered...until stunning Christel McClellan enters his life. When he hears her story, he believes the child she thought dead has been sold to a wealthy buyer.

Storm's Passion
Twelve Dancing Princesses Book Five

SHE MADE A PROPOSAL...

Life strikes Storm Graham a shattering blow when she learns her father has bartered her to a man she detests. Storm is beautiful, self–assured and fiercely independent, and refuses to be a pawn in her father's schemes, yet she can find no way out of this bargain made in hell. Going on the offensive she asks the wealthiest man on the eastern coast of England to marry her, never believing she might fall in love.

HE TRIED TO REFUSE...

For Hadden Johnston life has provided everything he ever wanted, including a sanctuary for homeless children. He is wealthy, handsome and happily unencumbered...until stunning Storm Graham marches into his life and proposes a marriage of convenience. Yet this type of marriage to a woman who inflames his senses is far from acceptable. If he's going to be tied down, he will move heaven and earth to have this woman warming his bed.

Gotta Have Fayth
Twelve Dancing Princesses Book Six

A regal beauty with raven hair and piercing blue eyes, Fayth Graham is unwilling to parade herself in front of the wealthy Lords of England during the season. Seeking a means to dissuade any man wishing to wed her, she seeks a way to ruin herself for marriage. When she unexpectedly meets a man with sparkling gray eyes and an infectious grin, she decides this is the man who will keep her from agreeing to obey.

He returned from six months at sea, looking for a few nights of pleasure with a willing lass, but Jarret Kinsley got more than he bargained for when he met a beautiful debutant who responded to his kisses with a wild innocence that touched his heart. Yet the obstacles looming between them might rip them apart. Both had vowed never to marry, so when consequences of their dalliances got in the way, Jarret would have to choose between the life he's always desired and the woman he loves more than life.

Ella's Pleasure
Twelve Dancing Princesses Book Seven

A WHISPER OF PLEASURE

Ella Hepburn was an auburn haired debutant from the harsh Scottish coastline—a wild innocent to be seduced and tamed. A spirited beauty, she captivated Drake Montgomerie's jaded heart—while succumbing to the smoldering desire she felt for her unyielding suitor.

A WHISPER OF DANGER

In Drake Montgomerie's glittering world of money and privilege, young Ella discovered passion and desire could overcome everything she'd been taught to resist—entangling Drake, the heir apparent, in a lethal coil of aristocratic family intrigue. But grave peril would only nurse the sparks of a love that knew no limits and a magnificent ecstasy that would not be denied.

Eveleen's Seduction
Twelve Dancing Princesses Book Eight

A WHISPER OF SEDUCTION

A brutal attack on Eveleen Hepburn's cherished island off the Scottish coastline leaves her shattered and bewildered. Learning a man she once trusted can kill as easily as he can breathe even though the deed saves her life, creates questions that need answers. An innocent beauty, she enchants Logan Maxwell's cynical heart—giving in to the raging passion she feels for her mysterious suitor.

A WHISPER OF INTRIGUE

In Logan's Maxwell's world of espionage and privilege, young Eveleen discovers truths about herself she never expected, and a need for passion and love can overcome all her fears if she learns to accept certain truths. She finds herself entangled in a lethal battle for land that was once owned by French nobility, taken from them during the revolution and sold to Maxwell. But grave peril would unleash the flames of love that simmers, creating a magical union that cannot be refuted.

Tavia's Deception
Twelve Dancing Princesses Book Nine

WHISPERS OF DECEPTION

When her father decides to send her to London for her season, Tavia Hepburn resolves to see the world instead. The raven haired beauty decides to disguise herself as a lad and find employment on a ship bound for Barcelona as a cabin boy. But she never bargains on finding passion and love to a red haired sea captain who rescues her from certain death.

WHISPERS OF MURDER

For James Macmurra, the world is black and white until he meets a young debutante, who turns his world upside down. He's unable to deny Tavia's intoxicating effect on him. In a match tense with obstacles, unwillingness to divulge secrets, and unforeseen peril, irresistible desire and passion grows into undeniable love. James would risk his life to shelter and protect the innocent debutante who seduces him with her sweet love.

Larena's Fascination
Twelve Dancing Princesses Book Ten

WHISPERS OF FASCINATION

Fiery, free spirited Larena Graham never wanted to marry a duke. She is thrilled to be in love with the fourth son of an aristocrat, Gavin Broon. But when it seems Gavin ignores her, she set her sights on politics and bettering human life. Unsuspecting intrigue and a plot against her, she continues her dangerous plans despite Gavin's wishes.

WHISPERS OF TRUST

Gavin has every intention of properly courting the beautiful Larena until he must leave the city in order to put his affairs in order. Returning to London, he finds the woman he means to make his own is embroiled in political protests that could lead to a prison ship. Larena must learn to trust the handsome Scotsman whose most pressing mission is to protect her and keep her from harm.

Tira's Eeucation
Twelve Dancing Princesses Book Eleven

WHISPERS OF EDUCATION

Learning how to build ships is Tira Hepburn's only dream until she meets Jamie Lundin and her world is turned upside down. With her raven black hair and vivid green eyes, she tempts Jamie and pushes him to defy his vows. She never bargains on finding an irrevocable love and a passion to a man who cannot fulfill her dreams despite his burning desire for her.

WHISPERS OF A BARGAIN

Arrogant and self-assured Jamie is brought up short when Tira captures his heart. All his carefully made plans are put to the test when he decides to teach her the art of ship building if she will spend a week with him alone on his ship. He is unable to deny Tira's intoxicating effect on him. When Tira leaves him behind unwilling to live with him without the benefit of marriage, he races after her. Jamie will risk everything to shelter and protect the innocent debutante who seduces him with her sweet love.

Tira's Eeucation
Twelve Dancing Princesses Book Twelve
Whispers of Love

Aidan McLellan has loved since she first set eyes on him as a young girl. Spontaneous, wild and eager to grow up, Aidan haunts his waking thoughts day and night, insinuating herself into his life. With her fiery red hair and sparkling sapphire eyes, she seizes Blade's heart even while he tries to resist the innocent child until she becomes a woman.

Whispers of Courage

Blade has waited what seems a lifetime to claim the woman who captures his heart as a little girl. Claiming his inheritance before his younger brother takes what is rightfully his, Blade must convince Aidan of his sincerity after years of avoidance and wed her before his father dies so he can return home, securing his rightful place. Everything is put to the test when his life as well as Aidan's is threatened by the man who once called him brother.

Twelve Days to Love

When Archer Steele shows up at Calanthe Durand's failing plantation with an alligator over his shoulder, Cali thinks she's never seen a more handsome man. During the war she had to defend herself and her servants from both union and confederate soldiers. Independent and self-sufficient, she vows to never marry.

But Archer Steele has different ideas. The first time Archer sees Cali in town, he feels an instant attraction. He decides he will do everything and anything to convince the beautiful Miss Durand he is worthy of her love. During the weeks leading up to Christmas, he gives her twelve gifts in hopes she will fall in love with him. Yet they are faced with challenges they must overcome before Cali can commit to a marriage.

Door to Heaven

Jessica Lawrence is the stepdaughter of a woman born in the twentieth century transported back in time to the year 1868. An acclaimed suffragette, she raises Jessica to believe in the equality of women. Jess Law believes everything she was taught, and when the time is right she becomes a private investigator. Courageous and impetuous, Jess finds danger in her quest to save all women from white slavery. Her passionate mission results in a wedding to Roc Newman, a man she knows can steal her heart...

Roc can't trust the sapphire-eyed spitfire who invades his home in search of secret papers and knocks him flat with her karate moves. Jessica's refusal to obey his wishes serves to inflame the war between them. Still, he cannot control the intense desire his reluctant bride inspires, or make her surrender her independence, until he has conquered the headstrong beauty on the battlefield of love...

Rebel Heart

HER REBEL SPIRIT DEFIED HIS OUTSIDERS SOUL...⌐SEP⌐She was velvet and silk, eyes the color of a summer storm and amber hair. Victoria DeMontville, because of a promise and a codicil to her father's will, was forced to marry one man to protect her from another. She hated Cameron Savage with a fierce passion. But to hold on to her genetic research and find a cure for the deadly Signe virus, she must pretend to love the enemy at her door, come with weapons of fire to melt her icy heart...

HIS OUTSIDERS TOUCH IGNITED RAGING PASSIONS...He wore a mask, disguised as the Phantom, a true legend come to life. Even as war and debate over new genetic research engulfed them all, he would find his greatest adversary in the beauty who'd branded him an outsider and barbarian, the woman he was born to possess, his soul mate.

Safari Moon

Solo St. John, a wildlife photographer, is preparing for a trip to Alaska. Suddenly, Solo finds women of all sorts invading his privacy, his home and his office, all cooing nonsense words and blatantly throwing themselves at him. Solo doesn't know why, and he has no idea how to rid himself of the persistent women. He finally decides to beg a favor of his best buddy Nyssa Harrington.

In love with Solo for the past ten years and knowing he doesn't return her feelings Nyssa doesn't want to talk to Solo. She knows if she accepts his phone call, she will not be able to resist the temptation to hope again.

Straight to Heaven

Running from demons, Alexandra McMurdie stumbles into Forbidden Ground where up is down and elements of nature are contested. Though a strong independent woman in the twenty-first century' she is unprepared for life in the 1800s. Her first site of the formidable James Lawrence makes her heart skip a beat, giving her cause to reconsider her desperate need to find a way home.
Born with a silver spoon, James' life was torn apart during the War

Between the States. Moving west he vows to put the life he once knew in the past. When he discovers a half-frozen woman near Gold Hill, his heart begins to thaw. His love for Alexandra and his need to keep her from a man who has pursued her through time might cost him his life as well as hers.

A Valentine's Anthology

The Lending Library-a fantasy by Christie L. Kraemer

Faeries try to fit into the human world when the forest where they make their home is destroyed by a mysterious enemy.

Chasing Rainbows-a contemporary romance by Genene Valleau

An eccentric aunt, an inventive uncle, a mother who wears poodle skirts, and a brother who wears pearls provide a hilarious backdrop for the courtship of a young woman who yearns for a "normal" family.

The Gift-an historical romance by Christine Young

A man and a woman on opposite sides of the Civil War get a second chance at love after one final battle returns soldiers to their war-torn homes to rebuild their lives.

A St. Patrick's Day Tale
by
Christine Young, C. L. Kraemer, Genene Valleau

Tumble through time…

…to Ireland in 1817, when tensions are high between Protestants and Catholics and faey people guide the fate of villagers. A lovely Catholic lass stumbles upon the weakly ritual fisticuffing between Irish lads. She falls into the lap of a handsome young Protestant. Family ties, grudges, and two conniving faeries threaten their budding love. But the faeries outsmart themselves when they hijack a time machine that has mysteriously appeared in their forest and are whisked to…

…Eugene, Oregon in the 20th century, amid a property feud between the local faeries and night elves. The conniving faeries from Olde Ireland try to stir up more mischief. However, a warrior gnome convinces the magic folk to control their own destiny, and forces the intruding faeries to take refuge in the time machine again, spinning their way toward…

…A modern day castle in western Oregon. An eccentric inventor is determined to reclaim his wayward time machine and save his beloved wife from her latest misadventure. If only they can travel safely past the black hole…

a May Day Anthology
by
Christine Young, C. L. Kraemer, Rosemary Indra, Genene Valleau

Highland Miracle — Christine Young

HURTLED THROUGH TIME, Sean Michael Sterling, landed in the midst of a May Day celebration he didn't understand, assuming the role of Laird Sterling.
ILLIGITAMATE CHILD OF NOBILITY, Reagan Douglas searches for a way out of her half brother's house.

Defying the Odds — C.L. Kraemer

The night elves on the hill aren't happy without their magic. They concoct a plan to punish those who were involved in the act that rendered them almost human. Meanwhile, Uther, the rogue night elf, has returned to woo the Librarian to be his eternal mate.

Love in Bloom — Rosemary Indra

When childhood friends reunite it takes two fairies and a matchmaking daughter to help them admit their true love for each other.

No More Poodle Skirts — Genie Gabriel

After drifting for years in the innocent age of the 1950s, a woman struggles to join today's world by finding a career and a new love, with some help from her zany family.

Once Upon a Christmas Moon
by
Christine Young, C. L. Kraemer, Genene Valleau

TWELVE DAYS TO LOVE

When Archer Steele shows up at Calanthe Durand's failing plantation with an alligator over his shoulder, Cali thinks she's never seen a more handsome man. During the war she had to defend herself and her servants from both union and confederate soldiers. Independent and self-sufficient, she vows to never marry. But Archer Steele has different ideas. The first time Archer sees Cali in town, he feels an instant attraction. He decides he will do everything and anything to convince the beautiful Miss Durand he is worthy of her love. During the weeks leading up to Christmas, he gives her twelve gifts in hopes she will fall in love with him.

BOOTS AND BLADES

An ancient evil from the old country has arrived in the high desert of Oregon. Gnome children are vanishing then re-appearing, showing various stages of traumatization. Tiamoon, warrior gnome, will put her skills to use alongside Killian, a handsome warrior, also in need of a cause.

CHRISTMAS PAWSIBILITIES

With their world destroyed and their space ship malfunctioning, the dogizens of Planet Canid have little choice but to crash land on Earth. They face tortuous experiments at the hands of the Geeks in Green...or they can trust an eccentric inventor and his zany family to deliver the Canine Queen's puppies and help them celebrate new lives.

www.ingramcontent.com/pod-product-compliance
Lightning Source LLC
Chambersburg PA
CBHW061938170626
46813CB00006B/2446